Pitch

The Hollow Trilogy: Book Two

Brent Kruscke

The Hollow Trilogy: Pitch

ISBN: 978-0-692-08785-5

This is a work of fiction. Names, characters, places and incidents are the product of the author's imagination or are used fictitiously. Any resemblance to any person living or dead is purely coincidental.

Printed in the United States of America
3rd printing January 2022

For my brother,
For always facing the monsters with me.
Whether they were Liches in a digital graveyard,
or Blood Suckers in our very own back yard,
I could only face them because I
knew you had my back.

Thank you.

Pitch

Chapter 1

Spent twigs and dried leaves crunched underfoot like bones, as the kid ran for his life. Worries brought on by absolute fear hummed like a nest of wasps in the kid's head. Thoughts were frequent flashes of instinct.

Left foot. Right now. Don't step on tha... Oh, God. That was clo... It's right behind me, I... No, it's gone. It... What was that?

He didn't dare look to see. If he took his eyes off the path in front of him for even a second, he knew he would fall. The trees were not his friends. They weren't even neutral onlookers. They were fighting for the other side, opposing forces surrounding him and closing in on all fronts.

But I will fight on.

And fight on he did, running at a breakneck pace. Leaves brushed his clothes. Branches grabbed at him like beggars reaching for the last bit of change, change they wouldn't use for booze or drugs. No, no. They had given all that up now, and you could trust them.

Pitch

The kid knew better. Even at his young age and with the minimal amount of world traveling he'd done, he knew better. As soon as he trusted them, he'd be a goner. Taken for all he was worth. He might not be worth much, but he liked what he had. He wasn't going to give in to these monsters.

They weren't monsters. Not really. Not compared to what chased him. What gained on him?

No! You're okay. You just need to keep running.

Even as he told himself this, he knew he couldn't. The air he sucked in with every wheezing breath never seemed to reach his lungs. His arms were flailing, his feet threatened to give out with every step, and his eyes began to blur from tears of pain. That was how the kid ran, and ran, and ran.

After a few more yards, the kid felt himself slowing. It wasn't fractional like his earlier decreases. His hands kept dropping to his knees as he hopped over large, fallen debris, holding him up. When he would land, his top half would waver, feeling heavier than usual. He'd catch himself by putting a hand on a nearby tree and then straighten and be off again. The top half of his body leaned forward controlled by his mind, wanting to get away, but his lower half protested, only trying to stay beneath the teetering top.

For a second, he thought he was going to fall. Just as he had come to terms with the fact that he was slowing, the kid had taken his mind off the forest floor and paid the price. His ankle caught underneath a root, and he flew forward.

Not like this, the kid thought as he threw his arms out to catch himself. To his surprise, he was able to wrap his left arm around a tree and save himself from the deadly descent. With only a moment's hesitation, the kid freed his ankle and began running again at full speed.

He couldn't keep up the pace, however. Not for the mile back to town. Not for the three hundred yards to the water. Not for ten more feet. He had only one option. Stop, and fight.

The kid rounded a tree and spun on his swelling ankle. From the belt loops behind his back, he withdrew a knife. The dastardly point thrust forward, intended for the advancing beast. The fine steel cut through the night air with the cruelty of death itself.

There was nothing there.

The kid began to back up, taking it step by careful step. He turned left to the sight of trees and moonlight. To his right, he found trees and shadows. The night air seemed to grow colder. The light waned, and the forest became even darker, making shadows into the black abyss of obsidian. But, still, nothing came for him.

Warm air billowed from his nostrils as his breath heaved. He tried to stay quiet, tried to listen. There was no noise. He couldn't even hear the waves crashing against the coast from here. The forest was as still as a coffin. Then…

SNAP.

The noise sent a shock down the kid's spine, making him straighten stiff as a board. It had come from behind him. More silence followed and then a soft humming followed by a series of quick clicks.

The kid inhaled one short breath.

The beast rushed forward.

The kid turned to face it, raising the knife. It was closer to him than he anticipated. He brought the knife down as quickly as he could. The beast brushed it aside with ease, flinging the kid's arm back and up into the air, almost popping the shoulder right out of the socket. The kid's only defense spun out into the darkness, moonlight glinting off the blade one more time before disappearing forever.

The kid tried to howl in pain, but the thing was already upon him. Huge eyes filled with hunger and anger stared down accusingly. Pincers were snapping in preparation as the thing went in for the kill.

Pitch

The kid had lost, and no one would be around to hear his screams if he had time to scream. The only thing that would hear him would be the creature, and it wanted to hear that sound, craved it even.

He had one final moment to think of her before the jaws snapped shut, slicing his face in two.

"Isn't this great?"

Nicholas Wake leaned forward with his elbows on his knees. He leaned so far forward that the smallest amount of misplaced weight would send him face first into the rounded glass screen of the television and to a most certain busted lip.

Poor Bobby Darian had it much worse, though. He was getting consumed by a humanoid bug monster and the kid, Nicholas, was eating it up, metaphorically speaking.

Dusk was in his usual half laying, half sitting pose, his head resting on one bent arm and a leg stretched on the coffee table. For the last hour of his life, Dusk had been trying his best not to fall asleep watching some half thought-out horror film. The kid had assured him this one was one of the better pictures featured during the television block moronically titled *Darkness Falls*. So far, Dusk wasn't impressed.

"So, this is what you do on your nights off? Watch grown men dress up in rubber costumes and pretend to molest other men?"

Dusk swung his head over at the kid hoping he would catch his jest, but he was mistaken. The sheer wonderment in the kid's eyes told him the kid hadn't heard a word of it.

"Oh, oh. This is a good part," the kid said, pointing at the screen. As if Dusk hadn't known where to look.

The creature on screen was halfway through his kill when another character just happened to come upon the scene. He was the hero of this picture. Dusk thought his name was John or Don or something like that. It was always easy to spot the heroes in these things. Combed back hair, strong jaw, jutting chest. Gentleman. The perfect Prince Charming mixed with the all-American dad.

Dusk looked down at his ratty clothes. He shifted his face, feeling the week-old stubble scratch at his cheeks. One arm reached up, and fingers ran through his mop of a hairstyle.

Ha, heroes, he thought.

"Oh, man. Isn't this great?" the kid said, not turning away from the screen.

"Yeah, great," Dusk answered, sinking deeper into his chair.

"What? You don't like it?"

"No, it's not that, kid." Actually, it was, but he didn't want to hurt the kid's feelings. "It's just after you fight real monsters, almost die more times than you can count, and save a small town from certain destruction, foam costumes and exaggerated arm movements just don't cut it."

They both chuckled and continued watching the movie. Dusk sat up straighter, adjusting his arm. It was a little stiff, so he began to make a tight fist, then release and tighten again, to loosen it up. It had only just healed from the savage break it had sustained a few months ago. He sure didn't want to press his luck and end up in a sling again.

After a sudden twist of fate in the movie, the television made a quick cut from the film to an obvious soundstage graveyard, where a man with thinning hair and a humped back stood as if not noticing the cameras.

He stirred as if awoken from a trance. The man affectionately known as Graveyard Jerry acted as if he could see them sitting in the luxurious sitting room of Winter's Hall in small Pointe's Hollow, Michigan. This was, of course, crazy, but Dusk's entire life had been made up of crazy, so he went along with the game.

"My, my. What an awful bit of trouble our heroes have gotten into this time. Who is friend? Who is foe? And will anyone survive?" Graveyard Jerry rose up high on his toes and held himself there for a dramatic second. Then, with the speed of an auctioneer, as if rushed for time, he finished with, "Find out right after these important words from our sponsors."

"Oh, I can't wait," Dusk said, sarcasm dripping as thick as the fake blood of the film. The kid shot him a look.

"What?" Dusk said, shrugging.

The kid just shook his head.

Dusk pushed on, not wanting to be forced to sit through commercials in silence, "So, what got you into these movies anyway?"

"What do you mean?"

"I mean, why horror movies? Did your Pops use to watch them with you?"

The mention of either of his parents set the kid on edge. Dusk had said it without even thinking.

Maybe these movies really can rot your brain.

He must be losing it if he had brought up the kid's parents so casually. The kid's parents had died in a car crash when the kid was young. Dusk didn't know all the details, and he never asked the kid about it. Anyone could see he wasn't ready to talk about them. Maybe he never would be. Either way, Dusk knew he had made a mistake, but he also knew bringing up the mistake would be worse. So, he sat and waited.

"Ah, no," the kid got out. "He was more of a western guy. Never got into monsters."

"Westerns!" Dusk almost jumped straight up at the word. It was his way out of the parental discussion topic. "Now, those are movies. Nameless gunslingers rolling in from somewhere no one's ever heard of. American steel strapped to their hips and scowls permanently cemented on their faces."

Dusk finished his monologue with his own scowl and a pair of finger guns. The kid looked over at him. His eyes looked like they held so many more years of experience than his sixteen years. There was strength and intelligence, but there was also fear and, most of all, sadness. Dusk wanted to help the kid fill whatever hollowness plagued him but didn't know how.

"Well," Dusk continued, "it sounds like your father was my kind of man."

"Yeah." The kid's voice was soft and heavy as if it was being weighed down by everything the kid had been through in his short life.

Dusk shifted his legs to the floor and stood up. "Well, it's getting late. You should probably get going. We don't want your aunt worrying about you."

The kid just kept staring at the television. The movie had started up again while they talked, and it had already sucked him back in.

"Hey."

The kid didn't move.

Dusk whistled. The kid's head twitched as if to turn, but still, his eyes were glued to the mayhem on screen.

"Hey, kid!" Dusk said, kicking at the kid's chair.

The kid jumped and looked up at the man.

Dusk raised his hands out wide. "I'm kicking your ass out. The least you could do is listen."

The kid smiled. "Oh, sorry."

He jumped up from his chair and started for the hall. Dusk followed him and found him bundling up in the main foyer. The foyer, which only months ago sat vacant and covered with dust, held small tables, a coat rack, and an ornate love seat. The whole house had gone through a serious makeover. Last November, Dusk had just been a ghost in the small town of Pointe's Hollow. A ghoul, withering away in his large castle of a tomb.

Now, he was a local. A townie, if you would. Even though his house sat a few miles outside of the one-street town the locals referred to as The Hollow, he had been adopted as a sworn native. With this induction, he had to make changes. He could no longer let the house around him decay and rot. So, he had fixed it up. Filled it with things people would expect a man of his financial status to have. Of course, his financial status was only his because of the interest from neglected accounts and a life insurance policy of his own personal angel.

The kid now sat on one of the new and, to Dusk, useless flourishes as he tied up his boots. A lightly padded, wooden bench that Argyle assured Dusk was designed specifically to adorn the entryway of a stately manner such as his. Dusk thought it looked like a few hunks of wood nailed together with a beat-to-hell pillow on it, but what did he know. Once the kid was done lacing his shoes, he donned a cap and wrapped himself in a coat.

"So, will you be back tomorrow?" Dusk asked.

"No," the kid said, aligning his zippers. "I've got school and should probably spend a night or two at home for Aunt Sherri's sake."

"Ah."

The kid's aunt had come down pretty hard on him when he had disappeared during the storm of the century last November. Of course, if she had any idea what he really had been caught up in, she probably would never let him leave the house again.

"She's only tough because she loves you."

"Yeah, yeah. I know."

The front door to Winter's Hall opened up to the outside world. The house was living up to its name. Thick, white snow blanketed the front yard and surrounding trees. It was late, but the white snow made the night seem brighter. It was an eerie kind of light, but in Dusk's experience, anything was better than darkness.

"So, I guess I'll see ya when I see ya," Dusk said, putting one hand on the door, preparing to shut it after the kid departed.

"Yeah." The kid started to leave but then stopped. He looked out into the trees. Dusk followed his gaze, assuming the kid had seen something, a deer maybe. This was northern Michigan after all, where deer seemed to outnumber humans two-to-one.

"I think you were right," the kid finally said.

"About what?"

"I think you and my dad would have gotten along."

The kid looked up to Dusk. The statement caught Dusk off guard. He opened his mouth to say something but wasn't sure what would be right.

"It's a shame you guys never got to meet," the kid continued, turning back to the trees.

"Yeah," Dusk said. "A shame."

They stood there like that for a minute or two, just looking off into the woods. After a while, the kid did leave. Before he did, he wiped his eyes, trying to hide his tears from Dusk. Dusk pretended not to see, for the kid's benefit and his own.

Chapter 2

The usual clatter of the cafeteria seemed to be turned up to a whole new level today. Kids yelled back and forth at each other trying to be heard over the others. Laughter would break out at a moment's notice, making the kids talk louder to be heard. All the while, the slapping of lunch trays set the base for the extravagant ensemble booming around Nicholas.

His thumb and forefinger were pressed tightly around the bridge of his nose. His glasses rested on his knuckles and bobbed as he massaged the pain in his eyes.

"You alright?"

Nicholas let his glasses drop, falling low on his nose. He looked over at the kid across from him. William Carrol, Will to those who were close to him, sat with a mouthful of lunch lady special looking at him. He was a tall, fit kid who had a face like a rock star. Yes, Will was the need and want of almost every girl at Pointe's Hollow, and he was also Nicholas's best friend.

Will had come to Pointe's Hollow to live with his grandparents, Betty and Howard Carrol. He moved here right in the middle of Christmas break. Once school started back up again, he was in the world of high school in a town where new people were always noticed and pushed to the top of the gossip column.

One day after the break, Nicholas had been sitting alone at lunch, reading a book. This was how he usually spent most of his lunches. Emily, his girlfriend, had lunch at a different hour of the day, so Nicholas mostly just kept to himself in the wild world of the cafeteria.

"How is that?"

The voice had startled Nicholas. No one ever talked to him during lunch. Well, sometimes, but it was usually to ask him to move down a seat so a group could all sit together.

"Ah, I'm sorry. What?"

"I said, how is that? You liking it?" Will was pointing at the book in Nicholas's hands.

Nicholas looked at the cover of the book as if he hadn't realized he was reading it. It was *I Am Legend*, an apocalyptic vampire story by Richard Matheson.

"Yeah," Nicholas said, unsure of himself, "this is actually like my third time reading it."

"Really? Groovy. Is this seat taken?"

He pointed to the seat directly across from Nicholas. Nicholas shook his head and raised a hand, offering the seat. Just as Will had taken his seat, Maryann Dunkel had walked over and tapped him on the shoulder.

"Hey, new kid. You wanna come sit with us? We saved you a seat."

Will and Nicholas both followed Maryann's gaze toward a table filled with a group of giggling girls and take-themselves-way-too-serious guys. In the brutal jungle that was high school, these people were considered the crème of the crop.

Will took one look over at the other table and then looked to Maryann, "No, I'm good here."

Maryann was so taken aback by the quick shut down that she stood there for a whole thirty seconds before she returned to her own table. A table which now held the shocked and insulted faces of the school royalty.

"Sheesh, what a weird chick," Will had said once she finally walked away. "I'm Will, by the way." He extended a hand.

"Nicholas," Nicholas answered. They shook hands. A couple of girls walked by Will and Nicholas, eyeing the new kid. Nicholas began to feel like he was sitting next to a pile of hamburger meat in a lion's cage.

Will, however, didn't notice. It was like he didn't know how attractive he was or, better yet, didn't care.

"May I see it?"

Nicholas looked down at the copy of *I Am Legend* and handed it over without complaint. Will took the book, flipped to the back cover, read a few lines, and then fanned the pages.

"Have you read it?" Nicholas asked.

"Me? Naw. I'm not the best reader. Of fiction at least. I usually prefer non-fiction stuff, easier for me to get my head around. But I love scary shit." He slid the book back to Nicholas's side of the table. "Hey, you ever watch a program called *Darkness Falls*?"

That was the beginning of a beautiful friendship.

"Yeah, I'm alright," Nicholas said, fixing his glasses on his face. "I just didn't sleep that well last night."

Will nodded. He had shoveled in another mouthful of what the school lunch program passed for spaghetti. When he tried to speak, noodles and marinara sauce hindered his progress. He chomped down a few more times and swallowed the heap in one go.

He must have an iron stomach, Nicholas thought. He had tried the lunch program a few times, but in the end, decided brown bagging it was best for all parties involved.

"I see," Will finally said. "You talk with Em?"

Nicholas shook his head. Emily and Nicholas had been dating for almost three months now. Well, dating may be a strong word. It was hard to date a girl whose father saw you holding a bloody tomahawk near the dead body of your former teacher. Of course, Emily didn't know anything about that. Still, though, Nicholas found their time together had to be done on the run. Nicholas wouldn't go over to Emily's house for the threat of Sheriff Gordon seeing him there, and Aunt Sherri wasn't the best at keeping things to herself, so Nicholas's house was also out. Instead, they spent time together walking around the small town, hand in hand, just enjoying being near each other. Other times, Will would come with them, and the three of them bummed around town like the Three Musketeers, if the musketeers mostly enjoyed eating burgers at Shores and tossing rocks into the tide of the lake.

Seeing Emily within the halls of Pointe's Hollow High wasn't any easier. They had separate lunch hours and only one class together this semester. The only chance they had time to really talk was in the brief lapses between classes and the time it took for Mr. Sorento to start the next lecture. Five-minute conversations and impromptu palavers, a relationship did not make. Unless, of course, you were Romeo and Juliet, and we all know how that turned out.

"Well, you know what they say. Distance makes the heart grow fonder."

Nicholas rolled his eyes. He looked down at his sandwich – ham, pickles, and mustard - and decided he wasn't hungry. After he wrapped up the remnants of his half-eaten lunch in the crinkled, brown bag it had come in, Nicholas deposited the heap in one of the five trash cans spaced throughout the cafeteria.

Once he made it back to the table, he and Will discussed last night's edition of *Darkness Falls* until the bell rang, signaling them back to class. As Nicholas made his way down the hall toward his next class, he spied Emily making her way to lunch. She blew him a kiss, and he motioned the act of catching it. Then, she was gone.

"Ah, young love," Will gushed.

Nicholas pushed him a little, and they both laughed.

Nicholas found his seat in his next class. His movements felt sluggish. When he sat, he felt his body sway, wanting to topple over. Nicholas had to rub his face clear of sleep to gain some sort of posture, but even that began to wane into a slouch.

History classes at Pointe's Hollow High School were taught by a young teacher by the name of David Fidel. At least until Nicholas discovered Mr. Fidel to be a werewolf, and Dusk shot him out of a second story window. The beginning of a night that had played out in a crescendo of terrible events, ending with a resounding bang.

Now, history classes had Mr. Brown, a man even more boring than his name suggested. He was short; was mostly bald, holding on to the short, cropped circle of fuzz on the back and sides of his head; had a different sweater vest for every day of the week; and had a voice that would put a spastic child to sleep after a buffet of candy and soda.

"Alright, class. Settle down. Now, I know you have gone over the French and Indian war in past classes, but I think the text for this class goes into a side of the war your other books seem to miss. So, if you would please open to page two hundred and sixty-seven, we can begin with the reading."

Nicholas could feel his eyes growing heavy already. It was strange. A few months ago, all the late nights of almost dying and seeing unheard-of horrors had plagued his energy levels, but not like this. Nicholas guessed that when you're trying to stay alive with monsters on your tail, being tired falls by the wayside.

That's what I need. Another series of killings.

The thought was so dark and sad that Nicholas physically shook his head to get rid of it. The last thing The Hollow needed was another string of grueling murders. The town was enjoying its respite from the macabre. The snow had come a week after the killings had concluded and had not gone away since. It was like the white blanket that covered the town had also cleansed it of past horrors. Like a cool, protecting coat, covering up past scars that needed to heal, the snow soothed the town.

In fact, the last few weeks had been so quiet that Dusk had joked with Nicholas about maybe picking up stakes and moving to a new town. The idea of Dusk leaving alarmed Nicholas, but he was reassured that would not happen, mostly due to Dusk's laziness. Nicholas also suspected that as much as Dusk didn't want to show it, he cared about The Hollow. It had been the last place he and his love Angela had been together. The flip side of that coin, however, was it was also the place where she had died.

The secret truth neither he nor Dusk would talk about, that no one would talk about, was that no one was allowed to leave. Not until everything that was happening in The Hollow was done at least. Nicholas could tell that everything wasn't over. They just seemed to be in the eye of the storm. A false sense of security until everything really started, and that wouldn't begin until he was found.

The man in shadows.

This ghost of a man was the cause of all of this. Nicholas and Dusk had heard of this phantom from the mouth of a dead man. Ever since then, no matter what the two of them had defeated, there was a lingering panic and fear of the true darkness still waiting in the wings or in the shadows, as it were.

Nicholas reached up to pinch the bridge of his nose again. Mr. Brown was reading aloud from the book now. The only thing more boring than reading about history you're already familiar with was listening to Mr. Brown read it. Nicholas knew if he didn't do something, he would be found at the end of the period face down in a puddle of his drool.

So, he did what he always did when he needed a break — he pulled out a blank piece of paper and began to draw. Most times, Nicholas began drawing before he knew what the final image was going to be. He'd start just by drawing lines. Some straight and then a couple curved. They were all different lengths and thicknesses. Then, he'd start to see the image come to life on the page.

The picture coming to life in front of him was a small battle sequence. In the history textbook that he had pushed to the front, right corner of his desk to make room for his drawing paper there was a picture of the French and Indian war. A British soldier was in the foreground wielding a sword with his free arm on an Indian. Behind each of them, clusters of fighters on either side stood with their representatives.

Nicholas had used this picture for his drawing, and in place of British soldiers, he drew vampires. In place of Indians, he drew werewolves. It was a fun doodle. It took him the rest of the class to finish it. In the end, he was surprised how much it looked like the picture in his textbook. Once you removed the fangs and fur that was.

Out in the hall, Nicholas saw Emily waiting by his locker. The sight of her standing there made him smile. He may still be tired, and he had only five minutes with her until he was in the next class, but just seeing her made him feel better.

He thought back to six months ago. He had been a quiet loner with his nose firmly planted in one book or another. He had no friends, and definitely no girlfriend. Then, Dusk had come into his life and with him the monsters. Nicholas was glad everything that had happened last November had happened, because it got him to here, but he was also glad it was all over. Even if it was just the momentary calm he was reveling in, he was happy with it and hoped it would go on a lot longer.

Unfortunately, Nicholas didn't know what was about to come, how close it was, and how much of it was his fault.

The ship rocked with the even current underneath it. It had been a quiet night, and the swells rolled in with a smooth rhythm. Ropes swayed with the motion, creating a whispering song in the night air. The soft whoosh of the ship calmed Randy Packers.

He had been a fisherman for over thirty years now, and the tepid commotion of a swaying ship always put him at ease. There had been nights when he had begged for an easy time of it. Nights where storms had raged, nets snapped, and all hell broke loose with them. This wasn't one of those nights. This was the kind of night most fishermen dreamed about. The only thing that could have made it better was some moonlight.

The night was black, darker than black even. The night was so dark it almost seemed solid. In the past, the old lighthouse had shone brightly over the waters off the coast of The Hollow, but last year a storm had knocked the old tower right over. The temporary light that had been constructed in its place was a weak replacement. The small ship Randy and his crewmates, Alan Hooper, Sean Nye, and Colin Mortensen, were in had a few spotlights on it, so they could see what they were doing, but the night still collapsed in around them.

Randy had been working with Alan and Sean for almost seven years. Colin was the new guy and at least fifteen years younger than the other three. The guys called him 'boy' and made him do the grunt work. To the kid's credit, he never complained. Besides the occasional sigh, Colin was agreeable to everything Randy and the guys threw at him.

Randy looked over his right shoulder to see how Colin was doing. He was on the deck wrapping ropes and cleaning up for the night. Randy smiled. He turned back, finding Sean and Alan doing the exact opposite of the boy: nothing.

"Hey, why don't you two go over there and help the boy?" Randy said, waving over his shoulder.

Alan and Sean both looked over at the boy. "Why don't you?" Sean finally said.

"'Cause, idiot. I'm driving the boat. Boat don't go nowhere without a driver. No driver, no going. No going, no getting home."

It had been a long day of fishing, and they were all ready to be home. They had probably stayed out later than they should and had come out earlier in the season than most would, but Randy had had a feeling. The water almost called to him, beckoning him out to see what it had to offer him. He had listened, and it had been worth it. They were sailing home with a mighty fine catch that would put them leaps and bounds ahead of schedule once the weather broke and fishing was in full swing. Plus, with the weather on their side, the trip was something Randy would never pass up. The only thing that made it short of a perfect outing was the cold. The cold made the guys move slowly, especially the ones getting up there in age. Randy would be the first to admit it; he was getting old. It was only a matter of time before he'd be hanging up his fishing game for good.

Randy stretched his neck to either side, feeling the weary bones creak and crack. He wanted his oversized armchair, a cold drink, and some old movie on the TV.

Maybe a Charlie Chaplin picture.

Randy always liked Chaplin's character of The Tramp. Made him think of his old man laughing so hard that he slapped his knee. There was this one time his old man had laughed at Chaplin's antics so hard that he slipped out of his chair and fell to his oversized ass with a crash. What made it all the funnier was that Leonard Packers was not a small man. At a husky three hundred and fifteen pounds, when he hit the floor, it was felt through the whole house. Randy remembered his mother had come running into in the room asking about an earthquake. It only made Leonard laugh harder and Randy right along with him.

Randy was deep in his Chaplin memories when Colin screamed. Randy turned to see what the boy was making all the racket for when the boat shook, creating a clatter of metal, and then stopped. It was like it had run aground, but that was impossible. They were still on the west side of the island that had housed the deceased lighthouse and its inferior substitute. The lake was easily a hundred feet deep, probably more.

The spotlights positioned around the boat shifted, and things that were bright a few moments ago became dark while new sights were brought to life by the light.

"You hit something?" Sean yelled. "Felt like you hit something."

"I didn't hit nothing, and if you don't shut it, I'll be hitting you, and believe me, you'll be feeling it."

Randy turned off the engine, and the world grew silent. He turned back toward Colin and saw only darkness. The light that had been on the kid had shifted down. The only part of him that was visible was his feet.

"Colin, what the hell were you...," but Randy couldn't finish. There was something wrong with Colin's feet. They weren't standing on the deck. The toes of his boots grazed the wood, but his ankles were bent awkwardly as his legs swung as if suspended. If that wasn't weird enough, Randy began to hear a sound.

"What's going on?" Sean yelled. He had made his way toward Randy but had yet to notice Colin.

"Sean, get a light on Colin."

"What for?"

"Now, god damnit!"

19

Randy heard the fear in his voice. Something was wrong. He had no idea what it was, but Colin didn't look right. And there was that sound.

Sean, apparently, had heard the fear as well, because he hustled over to the spotlight and began to move it up Colin's body. As soon as Sean touched the light, Colin's body jerked like flicking an agitated animal's tail. The motion was accompanied by a ripping sound.

As the light went up, Colin's body dropped. Movement flashed behind him as something seemed to move into the sky behind the boy with a whap, whap, whap. Randy saw the movement but immediately forgot about it. Colin's body had fallen but didn't lay flat on the deck. It sat there propped up by folded knees, head tilted to one side. Where his torso had been, a large, jagged hole of gore gleamed in the light.

"My God," Randy whispered as he felt his last meal try to make a return trip up to his mouth. Sean was yelling a string of obscenities behind him.

Colin's body began to jerk and twitch out of control as, to Randy's horror, his arms reached up to the hole in his chest. Colin's head remained slack to the side, but his hands slowly raised up and began to trace the outer rim of the hole. Fingers, worked tough from the ropes, felt the ragged circumference and then slipped into the wound as if looking for something.

The ship shook again as if hitting ground. Colin's body flopped to the side in a wet crunch, and Randy had to catch himself. His well-weathered sea legs suddenly went weak and bowed.

We're not even moving, Randy thought, trying to make sense of everything.

Now, it was Alan's turn to scream. Randy turned but was only able to catch a glimpse of Alan's legs being thrown skyward, his screams growing fainter as he went upward. The screams grew louder again as gravity pulled him back to earth and then ended with a splash.

"Man overboard!" Sean yelled at the top of his lungs, years of experience kicking in. Like an ex-cop whose hand drops to his hip before realizing he handed his gun and badge in a long time ago.

Splashes erupted all around them. It sounded as if rocks were falling from the sky. Randy looked around and into the abyss around his boat. Head on a swivel, arms outstretched in defense, Randy Packers readied for the worst. Too bad for Randy, his imagination could not comprehend what was about to befall his little tug.

"OH, GOD! RANDY!"

Sean's screams cut through the splashes like a bullet. Randy looked over and saw Sean grappling with something around his waist. It looked like a set of slimy inner tubes. These tubes were too tight for Sean, however, and seemed to be getting tighter by the second.

They squeezed around Sean. He pushed and beat on the tubes, but they never let up. Randy saw Sean's ribs give way with a pop. Blood exploded from Sean's mouth, and his screams turned to gurgles. His teeth ground together in a grimace as his hand slipped on the sheen of the topmost tube, and he fell forward, sending more blood from his mouth to spatter across the deck.

Water whipped Randy in the face then, sending him to his knees. Once he got his bearings again and wiped the wet hair from his face, he looked back toward Sean. He was gone. All that remained was a yellow boot, in a dark red puddle.

Randy's mind was muddled, and his legs were like wet noodles, but, somehow, he kept his feet. He became aware that some of the commotion had stopped. His ship teetered back and forth, but the splashing had stopped. Randy had hopes of it all being over, but then he felt the first droplet.

Small tears of water plopped on his slicker. He looked up and saw only the night sky. That wasn't exactly true. He saw the night sky to the right and the left. But in the middle, he didn't see anything. Not even stars.

A droplet hit his nose, and he blinked. The middle darkness shifted and swayed. Randy had a moment of perfect clarity, and then the black mass fell upon him. It crushed the fisherman. The top of Randy Packers's head met the soles of his feet in an explosive fraction of a second.

The boat underneath Randy suffered a similar fate. The deck cracked straight through, and water began to fill the hull. Fish that had been captured earlier in the day were returned to the sea. They didn't make it far, however. The creature that had ravaged the small vessel ate them as they sank.

As bits and pieces of Randy Packers's ship and crew floated hither and thither in the cold waters of Lake Michigan, the beast fed upon its bounty, reveling in the carnage of the night's escapades.

Chapter 3

Nicholas was much more refreshed today than he had been the day before. He had finally given in to his body at the early hour of nine-thirty last night and fallen into a deep sleep. Sleep of the dead some would say.

Even when the rude clatter of the alarm went off the next morning, Nicholas slept on until the third repetition. After that, he had stretched, stopped the bleating of the clock, and was awake in a matter of blinks. After the trudge of the previous day, today he felt alive. His blood pumped at a rapid beat, and he felt more in the moment than he had for a long time.

Nicholas paid attention in class, joked with Will during lunch, and had even picked Emily up in a swinging hug when they first saw each other. Her red hair fanned out behind her, and she giggled like the young girl she was. It made Nicholas smile. It even made Will, who was privy to the whole thing, smile.

Once Nicholas had returned Emily to the ground, he kissed her. Usually, that would be the moment Will would break in and make a scene about the two's affection.

"Ah, ladies and gentlemen, may I have your attention, please. We have Nicholas Wake and Emily Gordon here doing the tongue tango. I'd give them a nine for effort, but I think the technique is a little lackluster."

Not today, however. No, today Will just politely averted his eyes until they were finished.

"Well, you look perkier today," Will said after Nicholas and Emily had disengaged.

"You know what? I feel perkier," Nicholas answered, still smiling.

"Sorry, Nicky. I was actually talking to Emily here."

Emily and Will laughed. Nicholas frowned for a moment, and then he, too, laughed. It was the beginning of a good day that turned into a great one.

The final bell of the day rang, freeing all the captives of Pointe's Hollow High into the world. They skittered outward like spiders whose hiding place has been discovered. The metaphorical cover had been lifted, and they all rushed before they could be squashed by the school system and its tyrannical rule. Of course, they'd all return, but that was their future selves' problem, not their now selves' problem.

Today was made even better because it was one of the few times Nicholas and Emily were going to get to spend time with each other outside of school. Usually, Will would accompany them on their after-school adventures. Neither of them minded this, but on the occasions when Will was busy, it felt especially nice to just walk around The Hollow with nothing better to do than just be with each other, hand in hand. Even in the bitter cold that their small part of the world was currently cascaded in. With Emily beside him, Nicholas could always find a bit of warmth to fight off the sting of freeze.

Will waved his goodbyes. He was heading home to help his grandfather, Howard, whom Will affectionately called Papa, with some projects around the house. Then, the two of them would join Will's grandmother, Nana, in a selection of board games. When Will had first told Nicholas about these nights, he had tried to pass them off as things he did to make his grandparents happy, not actual events he enjoyed. Nicholas, however, thought the plan sounded wonderful, which allowed Will to open up about them. In fact, Nicholas thought the plan was beyond wonderful. If he were telling the truth, he would have told Will he was jealous. They both had lost their parents at a young age, but Will still had a parental dynamic. Aunt Sherri was one of the best people Nicholas knew, but she wasn't exactly like a mother, nor was there a father figure in the house. It was a hollow spot Nicholas had always been aware of but pushed to the back of his mind where all the other bad stuff stewed in a boiling pot.

Once Will had departed, Emily pulled in close to Nicholas with a slight shiver, lacing her fingers in his and grabbing his bicep with her other hand. Her head fell onto his shoulder without a second thought, and Nicholas turned, kissing the top of her head. The smell of her and her shampoo intoxicated him, and he held his face against her head for a moment to take it in. Then, they, too, were off, walking to nowhere in particular.

"I can't believe you wanted to walk in this."

Emily removed a cap from her coat pocket and pulled it down low over her ears. It covered most of her fire-colored hair, but small tendrils still blew out behind her in the February wind. Nicholas smiled at her, and she smiled back.

"What? Do you enjoy freezing your ass off?" Emily continued with a tone almost as bitter as the cold.

Nicholas shook his head, laughing. "No, not particularly. I just had a good day."

"Oh, you did, did you?"

"Did and am," Nicholas concurred, reaching for and placing Emily's gloved hand onto his arm. He also gave the one still wrapped in his hand a squeeze.

She smiled and looked away from him and toward the direction in which they were walking.

"Your aunt still giving you a hard time?"

They had talked back and forth about the recent strain in Nicholas and his aunt's relationship. Nicholas brushed it off as nothing, but Emily could tell that it was bothering him.

Nicholas sighed, "No, not really. I think she still worries, but she also knows I can take care of myself. What about your dad?"

Emily laughed. "He's a different story altogether. He worries as if there's still a serial killer on the loose and doesn't think I can take care of myself at all. All the while, I'm the one taking care of him most of the time."

Nicholas nodded. He had heard her say things like this before but never really knew how to answer. His aunt was tough when she needed to be, but she always used the phrase, "I know I'm not your mother." This made Nicholas sad. It just reaffirmed that he had no mother, no father. A feeling Nicholas knew Emily could sympathize with on one level but could never fully understand.

"I know he cares about me; he's my father, after all. But I just wish he'd treat me a little bit more like an adult than just a helpless child."

Nicholas was nodding, but he had drifted off into his thoughts. Emily squeezed his hand, bringing him back.

"Hi," she said, "I thought I lost you there for a second. Do my family troubles bore you?"

"No, not at all." Nicholas could feel his face redden at being caught daydreaming. Emily tilted her head and gave him a look he was getting familiar with. It was the 'I know you're lying to please me' look.

"Where do you go?" she finally asked.

"What?"

"Where do you go, when you go all dreamy like?"

"Aren't I always dreamy?" Nicholas said, an unaccustomed smirk breaking across his face.

"You know what I mean," she said, giving him a solid pat on the arm.

"I don't know," Nicholas said, speaking the truth. His mind wandered; it always had and probably always would. It was why he drew and wrote. It helped him stay in the moment.

"Uh, huh, sure," she finally said. "I'll get it out of you eventually, Nicholas Wake. Just you wait."

"I have no doubt you will," Nicholas said, smiling but unsure what that would mean for them. He had secrets, just like everyone, but his secrets could get someone killed.

"Okay, okay," she said, looking up into the sky. "I get it. And I know I've said this all before. So, let's talk about something else."

"Okay," Nicholas said, feeling like another, happier topic would be a better conversation anyway.

"What about you?"

"What about me?"

"You. Your life." Emily said this as if it explained everything.

Nicholas just looked at her, confused. "You know my life."

Emily looked exasperated. "I know your life since we started dating. I know most of your life in Pointe's Hollow. What about before? What about your parents?"

Nicholas's smiled dropped a little. *Geez, first Dusk, now Emily. What's the obsession with my parents?* The thought made him think back to the days when he was a loner. Didn't talk to anyone or go out with anyone. He just read his books, watched his shows, and kept his own tragedies to himself. Had it been so bad back then?

"If you don't want to talk about them, I get it." She had been watching him as she waited for a response. "It took me a long time to talk about my mom. But once I did, it really helped."

Nicholas had a moment of fierce anger. The anger he felt at anyone who ever told him that talking would make him feel better. He had heard it all before, and he hated it. The moment quickly passed though, because this was Emily. Not some adult trying to control a grieving child whose world had ended; she was the girl he loved.

"They died in a car crash when I was young," Nicholas said before realizing he was saying it. Emily already knew this, but she nodded and listened all the same. "After that, I moved in with my aunt and have been there ever since."

It wasn't groundbreaking. No waterfall of emotions, but it had felt good to finally say it to someone. Nicholas felt a small bit of weight that had been pressing down on him for a long time break and fall away.

Realizing he wasn't going any farther without some prodding, Emily picked up the conversation. "Your aunt, is she your father's sister?"

"No, my mother's."

"Oh, I just assumed, because you guys have the same last name."

"Yeah, we do. My dad took my mom's last name."

"Really?" The strong woman inside Emily awoke and flared with excitement. "Why?"

Nicholas took a moment, and then said, "When he was alive, my dad just told me he hadn't liked his family's name very much and thought Wake was a better fit. Once they were gone, my aunt explained that my dad's dad had been a drunk. Angry and abusive."

Saying this out loud was easier than Nicholas thought it would be. It was easier than hearing it from his aunt. Most likely, it was because he was telling it to Emily. The girl had a way of getting things out of Nicholas he hadn't even known were there. He guessed that was the way it was supposed to be.

"Apparently, my dad's side of the family had a long line of abusive relationships. My father, being an only child, took it upon himself to end that streak. The first step was to kill the family name. I think he saw it as an act to kill the darkness in the family, even if it was nothing more than a name."

Nicholas looked at Emily. Just the sight of her made him smile.

"Plus, he used to say that Wake would look better on a dust jacket if he ever got around to writing his book."

Emily smiled now, too, and they both shared a soft laugh. "Do you know what the name was?"

Nicholas thought for a moment. He didn't.

"No, I don't."

"Your aunt never told you?"

Nicholas shook his head. He was pretty sure she hadn't. *Why was that?*

"I'm sure I could look it up somewhere."

Emily took a step closer, releasing his hand and hugging his arm instead. Leaning her head on his shoulder, she said, "I guess you will."

They walked like that for another few minutes. Neither one of them was talking, but they were feeling closer than ever. It was nice, and Nicholas would have been content to walk on forever, but suddenly a voice came from across the street.

"Emily!"

The two turned, both feeling the sensation of being awakened from a lovely dream.

Mrs. Dresser, a woman with no job who took it upon herself to take on all the town's projects, waved and began walking across the street. The Hollow had very few events throughout the year. A farmer's market every other weekend throughout the summer, a small fair during early fall, and a pitiful excuse for a Christmas parade was about all the town could lay claim to. Behind all of those was Mrs. Dresser.

"I am so happy I caught you, Emily," Mrs. Dresser said as she got within range to start the conversation. "Oh, and hello Nicholas. How's your aunt?"

"She's fine," Nicholas said. Not ever being good at these conversations, he stuck with the theory that less was more.

"That's good; that's good, dear. Anyway, I wanted to ask you, Emily, if you would be interested in volunteering for this summer's big project?"

"What project is that?" Emily asked. She sounded polite, the perfect example of the sheriff's daughter, but Nicholas could tell she felt trapped. He gave a little squeeze of her hand, and she returned it in kind.

"Well, just last week, we officially hit our goal to rebuild the church. We're trying to collect volunteer names now, so we can be ready to break ground as soon as the ground is breakable."

Nicholas stiffened at the mention of the church. The church had been destroyed four months ago by a fire, a fire Nicholas himself had helped set. He hadn't had anything against the church, nor did you find him sitting in a pew every Sunday. It had been a necessity to cover up the carnage of the crimes of his former teacher and a madman.

"That's wonderful news," Emily said, sounding excited.

"It is, isn't it?" Mrs. Dresser's excitement dwarfed Emily's, and Nicholas had to fight back a laugh. "So, can I count you in?"

As the sheriff's daughter, Emily got pulled into a lot of town events. Most of the time, she didn't mind doing her part for the town. But she had admitted to Nicholas that sometimes she felt like she was always being pulled in fifty different directions just because of who her father was.

"Of course, I'd love to help."

And another tug takes her, Nicholas thought.

"Wonderful!" Then, Mrs. Dresser turned to Nicholas. "And what about you? We could use strong men like you."

Nicholas was taken aback. He hadn't expected to be pulled into this and didn't have an answer ready. He felt Emily squeeze his hand and from the corner of his eye, he thought he saw a ghost of a smirk come over her lips.

"Ah, yeah," Nicholas finally said, seeing no other way out.

"Excellent!" Mrs. Dresser said, patting her gloved hands together in a small, excited clap.

All of a sudden, Nicholas realized there was a fourth in their tight circle. A man had followed Mrs. Dresser across the street. He had stopped a few paces behind her, and Nicholas had failed to notice him until that moment. It was as if he had been hiding in Mrs. Dresser's shadow and only now came into the light, which was absurd considering he stood at least a whole foot taller than the woman. That, along with the immediate conclusion that this man was a stranger, set Nicholas on edge.

The man had long, black hair tied in a ponytail at his neck. Glasses rested on his nose, which hung above a well-kempt goatee. While Nicholas stood taller than Mrs. Dresser, the man dwarfed both of them in his shadow. At first assessment, it made Nicholas feel small and insignificant. If the man wanted, he could be a terrifying presence, but Nicholas sensed a wave of calm coming from him.

"Oh, where are my manners," Mrs. Dresser said, following Nicholas's eyes to the man. "Nicholas, Emily, I would like to introduce you to Father Adrian. He's going to be the one running the place once we get it finished."

"It's a pleasure to meet both of you." Father Adrian offered his hand to shake. Emily shook it first, followed by Nicholas.

"Wait a minute," he said, raising a finger to his lips. "You don't look much like an Emily," he said, pointing at Nicholas. "And you are far too pretty to be a Nicholas."

Emily and Mrs. Dresser laughed. Even Nicholas chuckled. The guy seemed nice. Nicholas wanted to like him, but something stopped him from falling for the guy. Something about the man just didn't fit right. He was too nice, or maybe too friendly. In the end, however, Nicholas knew the real reason he didn't want to like Father Adrian had nothing to do with how nice he was or how friendly he seemed. It was because of the plain fact that he wasn't Father Christopher. It was in poor taste to dislike a man for not being another, but Nicholas couldn't help it.

"I think it's great you two are volunteering to help out," Father Adrian continued. "I heard about everything that happened. Terrible thing."

"It really was," Mrs. Dresser said, putting a hand on Emily's shoulder as if she needed comforting.

"Well, it's always good to know there are good people out there willing to rebuild after even the most monstrous of circumstances."

Father Adrian smiled, and Emily and Mrs. Dresser smiled back. "I'm actually just showing Father Adrian around town. You know, getting him accustomed to the hustle and bustle of our little town."

The three looked around the deserted main strip of The Hollow. If it had been an old western like the ones that Dusk was fond of, they would have seen a tumbleweed bounce across the street.

"So much to see; so little time," Mrs. Dresser said, unperturbed by the silent state of the street. "Give my best to your father, Emily, and your aunt as well, Nicholas."

They both said they would and then exchanged goodbyes. Father Adrian reiterated it was a pleasure to meet them both and then made a point to say they would see each other again. Then, they were gone, and Nicholas and Emily were alone again.

No one would have noticed it. No one in the entirety of The Hollow or maybe even the world would have noticed it. Except Nicholas did.

"… most monstrous of circumstances."

That is what Father Adrian had said. These could be just words, but Nicholas didn't think so. Father Christopher had known about the monsters. He had known about the thin spot, The Other, and so much more than even he and Dusk knew. Did Father Adrian know, too?

It almost made sense. They were both men of the cloth. Did all men in their profession know? Nicholas never thought about asking Dusk how Father Christopher had known. He didn't even know if Dusk knew. Father Christopher had been the one to tell Dusk everything. Maybe the church was a secret army of soldiers gridlocked in a battle with another world.

Does that mean Father Adrian can read my mind?

Nicholas looked over his shoulder toward the direction Father Adrian and Mrs. Dresser had headed. He saw nothing. They had either disappeared into one of the buildings along the street, possibly Berk's to get a cup of coffee or warm donut, or turned down a side street to see more of the town.

Either way, Nicholas knew it was something he couldn't deal with at that exact second. He decided to file it away for later and ask Dusk about it as soon as he got the chance. Of course, that didn't mean Nicholas wouldn't keep an eye out for Father Adrian as he and Emily walked around town. Most likely, the word choice had meant nothing. Or if it was on purpose, Father Adrian was possibly signaling for Nicholas to know he was a friend. Father Christopher had been on their side, after all; it only made sense Father Adrian would be as well.

Nicholas knew this was the most likely scenario besides him reading too much into the situation, but his experiences had taught him to be cautious and suspicious first; ask questions second; and then, and only then, make friends.

Snow crunched underfoot as Sheriff Gordon walked the shoreline. It was a strange sensation to walk over a beach covered in snow. He had been a Michigander his whole life, so snow was not a foreign concept. But no matter where you live, when you think beach, you think of sand, sun, and fun. Today, however, Sheriff Gordon walked along the shore thinking of hot coffee and his recliner tucked away in his living room back home.

He wore a flannel-lined sheriff's coat, along with thick, leather gloves. Although not in keeping with the season, he still sported his large, brimmed hat and sunglasses. The hat was just a staple to make sure everyone knew he was in charge. The sunglasses were for practicality sake, as well as status-affirming. Whether the skies were grey and overcast or blue as far as the eye could see, the white of the snow always shone brightly, causing the sheriff's eyes to protest in pain by the end of the day.

The beach had The Hollow's police force out in droves today. Deputy Donald was walking the shore with his head down scanning left to right, head swinging as if he was watching the world's smallest tennis match. Chris Redding, another officer, was further down, also doing the tennis head bop. The two appeared to have the situation under control. Sheriff Gordon could tell he wasn't needed. He had taught his people well, but he showed up here anyway. He had to. He was the sheriff, after all. It was his duty.

Striding forward with purpose, the sheriff walked up to The Hollow's coroner, Steven Steely, who was down on his hands and knees inspecting something. As he approached, Sheriff Gordon spoke up.

"What's the good word, Steely?"

Steely looked up from whatever had grabbed his attention and smiled his queer, little smile that set Sheriff Gordon's teeth on edge.

"Well, I'm not sure, Sheriff. But I definitely think something is afoot."

Sheriff Gordon sighed heavily and adjusted his belt under a sizable, but respectable gut. "Steely, I'm not sure I've ever told you this before, but you are one hard man to understand. Which is not a good thing for a coroner to be, especially when I have to work with them."

"I'm sorry, Sheriff. Sometimes, things are just slow-pitched to you, and you have to swing."

Sheriff Gordon looked down, his glasses reflecting Steely's blood-chilling grin right back at him.

Sighing again, Sheriff Gordon pressed on. "What the hell are you talking about? And just give it to me straight for the love of God."

It had been a long day, and the sheriff was ready to be home. The sooner he was done with this, the better.

"I mean exactly what I say," Steely said, throwing a thumb over his shoulder. "We have a foot."

Sheriff Gordon followed the thumb. On the shore, still getting hit by the occasional swell of the surf, was a yellow boot. The sole was trimmed in thick, black rubber. The sight was so shocking against the white of the beach. It looked like it had been put there on purpose, as if it was the centerpiece of a photographer's contrast piece.

Even more in contrast with the surrounding world was the red flesh that stood out from the top of the boot. Within the crimson mess, white as the snow, sat a snapped bone.

Pitch

His mustache felt hard and brittle as Sheriff Gordon rubbed a hand over his mouth. He hunkered down to get a better look at the boot, and now he was regretting the choice.

"So, we thinking boating accident?"

Steely's smile finally dropped. "I'm not sure. A little early to be out on the water, don't ya' think?"

"May be," Sheriff Gordon began, "but sometimes these guys can't wait."

"True, true. Still, hard to tell if it was a boating accident with just a foot. It looks like it was snapped off, not cut. So, if it was a boating accident, my money would be on rocks and undertow more than propeller."

Sheriff Gordon nodded.

Just a boating accident. Nothing more.

It sounded good to him. He did not want another catastrophe like they had had before. No, sir. He would keep an open mind; he was the sheriff, after all. He had to follow evidence when some came about, wherever it would lead, but this wouldn't lead anywhere.

Because this is just a boating accident.

"Any boats reported missing or not tied up this morning?"

"I don't know. I deal with the dead things. Living people creep me out."

For a moment, Sheriff Gordon thought he was going to laugh. An actual laugh. In the end, though, he settled for a large, tooth-filled smile.

"I swear, Steely. I will never understand you."

"Noted Sheriff. My mother used to say the same thing."

"Well, once you get what you need here, make sure you bag that thing and get it back to the station. I want to know who that foot belongs to by tonight, you hear me?"

"Loud and clear," Steely said, raising his hand in a mock salute.

"How about we leave the military out of this one, huh? What do you say?"

"Aye-aye, Captain."

Shaking his head, Sheriff Gordon stood up and stretched. He felt his old body complain about the unusual exertion of effort. Not for the first time or the last, he thought he was getting too old for this job.

"Let me know if there's anything else," he said as he turned around to leave.

Sheriff Gordon guessed he was about fifteen steps away from his car. Fifteen more steps, and he would've been in his car and unable to hear his deputy's yell. As luck would have it, he was able to hear the yell and, in turn, hear what was being yelled.

"We got another body part over here!"

Turning around was the last thing Sheriff Gordon wanted to do. But turn around he did.

"Is it another foot?" Steely shouted down the beach. Sheriff Gordon had returned to his side, and from the corner of his mouth, Steely said, "One more, and we have a full set."

This comment neither entertained nor annoyed the sheriff. It seemed to flow in one ear and then out the other. He just kept walking, and Steely eventually followed.

It was not another foot. It was an arm. After some quick investigations, Steely confirmed this, too, looked to have been ripped off of its owner.

Still an accident, Sheriff Gordon thought.

"Hey, guys! You better come look at this!" Chris's shout came from further down the beach. They looked down to Chris, who was standing with an arm over his nose and mouth.

"Arm or leg?" Steely shouted.

"Neither," Chris shouted back, his arm leaving his face just long enough for him to get the words out. Once he finished, his arm returned to cover his face.

Pitch

The group of three walked over prepared for anything. Deputy Donald gagged when they got within ten feet of the finding. Sheriff Gordon held his composure, but it made his face curl in revolt. Steely was the only one to move right up next to it and lower himself above it.

The body was torn almost past recognition. One leg was missing at the knee, the other's thigh was pulverized into oblivion. The calf attached by fabric and paper-thin strings of flesh. The right arm ended in a bone protrusion around the wrist area, while the left had three separate bone breaks protruding from the sponge-like tissue. The worst was the chest. A hole the size of a softball sat vacant in the body's left breast. Rib bones bent upward toward the sky like a twisted jungle gym for the certifiably insane.

Steely reached forward and stuck two gloved fingers into the hole. They circled the rim, feeling around inside. Another gag from Donald made Chris turn away.

"He has both his arms," Sheriff Gordon said. He didn't know he was going to say it until it had already left his lips.

"Yup," Steely said. His usual uplifting demeanor nowhere to be found. "Which means we have at least two victims."

That stopped Sheriff Gordon for a second. He looked up from the body and stared out over the water.

Still could be a boating accident, he thought, pleading. But deep down, as much as he didn't want to admit it, he knew it wasn't.

Chapter 4

The ball flew through the air. Up toward the ceiling, and then it would peak, rotate, and fall back to Nicholas's palm, landing with a plop. He'd squeeze the rubber or roll it between his fingers before sending it back up.

He found himself doing this more and more. The life of a teenager in a small town had come back hard. It hit him like a blow thrown from a blind spot. Before meeting Dusk, Nicholas had been content with his life. He didn't mind that his day-to-day was more rinse and repeat than adventure. Now, however, he felt bored. Worse than that, he felt useless. He felt like if he were to die right then and there, no one would ever know he existed in time. His presence was so fleeting; it was like he wasn't there at all.

The ball fell into his hand harder than he had anticipated. It bounced off and slipped between his closing fingers. Leaving him behind, the ball pattered across the floor, decreasing its height until it just rolled to a stop at the foot of Nicholas's desk chair.

Pitch

He sighed and lifted himself from his back to sit on the edge of the bed. Debating about collecting the ball, Nicholas decided to leave it and walked to sit at his desk instead. Paper, pencils, and other discarded utensils littered the desk. In the middle sat the ancient typewriter. The debris lay around the machine as if it were siege destruction surrounding a castle. Strong and noble, the typewriter's battlements stood unperturbed by the chaos around it.

Next to the typewriter, amongst the mess, stood a pile of three hundred typed pages. It had started as a journal but quickly became a sort of novel. A novel that, if it ever were to be published, would be cataloged in the fiction section even though the content was anything but.

In three hundred pages, Nicholas had recounted his adventures with Dusk. It wasn't designed to be read by outside parties. Ideas, events, and emotions swirled in and out of order. He had written down everything as it came to him. If he wanted to, he could go through the pages and organize everything into chronological or narrative order so someone else could read them, but he didn't need to. The writing of it had been just for him and so could the reading. At least, for now.

The roller of the typewriter held a fresh sheet of paper, ready for Nicholas to write something new. This was turning out to be harder than Nicholas had anticipated. After three hundred pages, some would think writing would be easy.

It was not.

Nicholas had had to think of the words for his story with Dusk, but the story was real. It was easy to write down what had happened. To make up a story from nothing was something Nicholas was beginning to associate with Russian roulette. Five times out of six, that gun wasn't going to fire. It would fall on an empty cylinder with a confidence-crushing click. But one hammer pull would eventually strike a live round. In Nicholas's case, he would get an idea when this happened, not a quick flash of light and fire.

Unfortunately, that idea hadn't come yet. So, the paper sat blank.

Or was it?

As Nicholas inspected it further, he noticed a small dot of ink low on the page. So low in fact, it disappeared behind the mechanics of the typewriter. Nicholas rolled the paper forward to see how severe the damage was. It wasn't bad, but that was because it wasn't a smudge at all. It was a letter.

Did I type that by accident?

It could happen. The mess on his desk was a testament to his carelessness.

But then what? Accidently roll the paper back and hide it from myself?

That was less likely. The 'P' gave no answers. It just sat there, a dark stain on a field of white. Not only did it stand there in opposition, but it seemed to have a friend. A phantom 'P' stained the white behind it. On his typewriter, something had caused the 'P' key to double tap. The second hit was lighter and off-center causing the second 'P' to be faint. It was a ghost of its more prominent counterpart, making it look like the true 'P' had a shadow.

Deciding he would never know, and it wasn't worth fretting over, he pulled the paper free and crumpled it into a tight ball. Spinning in his chair, he turned to see his trash can. He had moved it across the room for this very reason.

Straightening himself to the goal, he tossed the balled 'P'. The paper flew straight but fell short.

Everything seems off, Nicholas thought, troubled. Then, the more rational part of his mind said, *As if you make that every day.*

Leaving the paper for later, Nicholas turned back to the desk. He retrieved a clean sheet from his pile and reloaded the rollers. The typewriter was cocked and ready for his next shot.

His fingers cracked as he prepared himself to pull the figurative trigger. After a few moments of lying to himself, Nicholas finally admitted he still wasn't ready. If he was telling the truth, he knew he wasn't ready the moment he sat down.

Nicholas let out a long, slow breath. A muffled ring came from below. Spinning in his chair again, he gazed at the collapsed ladder on the trap door leading to the lower portion of the house. There was a second ring. It was followed by the sounds of shuffling as Aunt Sherri put down whatever she had been fiddling with and went to answer the phone. The third ring was cut off, and Nicholas held his breath to hear.

His aunt politely addressed the caller. There was a moment, and then the real, bubbly Aunt Sherri exploded forth. The two exchanged a murmur of rumblings. There was a beat of silence, and then Nicholas heard what he was waiting for.

"Nicholas!"

Almost jumping out of his chair, Nicholas rushed to lower the ladder. As soon as his legs hit the carpeted hallway floor, Nicholas shouted in return, "Yeah?"

"It's Emily."

"Hey," Nicholas said, a little out of breath. The only phone in the house hung on the wall separating the kitchen from the living room. Its spiraling mess of a cord hung limp until Nicholas wrenched it straight to sit at the dining room table. Once she had handed it over, Aunt Sherri had exited to the living room to finish folding the laundry she had been working on. Small, neat piles sat like landmines all over the floor.

"Hey, yourself," Emily answered.

Nicholas smiled. He always did when he talked to Emily. No matter how much they talked or how many times they hung out around The Hollow together, she always made him smile.

"I didn't expect you to call," Nicholas said.

"I hope it's okay that I did." Her voice sounded so hurt, it broke Nicholas's smile in an instant.

"No, I didn't mean it like that. I'm glad you called. Just surprised that's all." Emily and Nicholas usually had to plan calls ahead of time with the threat of her father always looming over them.

"Yeah, well my dad is gonna have an all-nighter down at the station. This whole bodies-washing-up-on-shore thing has everyone a little spooked down there."

"Yeah, I bet."

The response was reflexive. Not until after a good moment of silence did it register to Nicholas what she had just said. He exploded forth, "Wait, what?"

"You haven't heard?"

She sounded surprised. Nicholas began to shake his head but realized that she, of course, couldn't see him. Instead, he said, "No. I haven't heard a thing."

"Well, I'm not really supposed to talk about it. My dad always goes on and on about ongoing investigation this and too many people knowing is bad that."

Nicholas was nodding along like one does when they hope the speaker will just get on with what they are saying. This time, he was glad Emily couldn't see him.

"But," Emily continued, "considering most everybody in town already knows, I'll let you in." She said this in her 'I have a secret' tone. "Apparently, three bodies washed up on shore."

"Three bodies? Was it a boating accident?"

"I'm not sure. That's what they're calling it, but I don't know."

Nicholas furrowed his brow, "What do you mean?"

"Well," Emily's voice grew soft. "My dad has been a cop my entire life, and even with that, I could count the number of times he was truly upset by a case. This hasn't gotten that bad yet, but it's close. Plus, the way they found the bodies is just too similar to a few months ago."

Emily took a second. When she finally spoke, Nicholas had to strain to hear her. "They were in pieces. Broken apart as if... well, I don't know what."

As if something had ripped them apart.

Nicholas could almost hear her say it. The receiver whined in his tightening grip.

It's happening again.

He needed to let Dusk know. Who knows what was out there or when it would kill again? In his experience, as limited as it was, it wouldn't take long before blood began spilling all over town.

"...et disconnected?"

"What?"

"Oh, I thought I lost you."

"Sorry, I was just thinking, I guess." Nicholas didn't want to say what he was thinking about. Luckily, Emily didn't need him to. She had a knack for knowing exactly what Nicholas was thinking even when he said nothing at all.

"Creepy, isn't it?"

"Yeah." It was all Nicholas could think to say. His mind was still in darker places.

"So, I was just calling to see if you wanted to hang out after school tomorrow. It's Friday, and with my dad busy with the case, I thought it'd be fun. We could grab a bite at Shores?"

Nicholas's head was already a million miles away. Things were clicking, and old gears had begun to turn anew.

"No, I can't," he finally said.

"Oh," Emily sounded surprised, and a little hurt. This time Nicholas was too distracted to notice.

"Yeah, I'm sorry. I have to go up to Winter's Hall tomorrow night."

"Really? I didn't think you worked Fridays."

Work?

As Nicholas thought about what he was going to tell Dusk, he had forgotten what he had told Emily. When Dusk became a part of The Hollow's community, in the limited capacity that he was, he and Nicholas came up with a plan to explain why Nicholas was spending so much time at Winter's Hall. As far as anyone in town was concerned, Dusk hired Nicholas to help around the house with small chores and yard work. This had become a cover for them to continue their protection of the town if the need ever arose again and a favorite joke of Dusk's to bring up to hassle Nicholas.

"Oh, yeah, well," Nicholas was fumbling. He hoped it wasn't too obvious. "He's got a big project in mind that he asked for my help with."

"Wow. Didn't he just have the whole place renovated a few months ago when he moved in?"

"Yeah, but you know how these rich guys are."

Nicholas could feel how thin the lie was on his tongue. He hated lying to Emily, but what could he do? Tell her the truth?

Actually, Emily, the project he has in mind is to hunt and capture or kill the thing that mutilated the bodies that washed up on shore. Suspects could be, but not limited to, zombies, werewolves, killer sharks, and the Loch Ness Monster.

Yeah, that'd go over well.

"I guess when you can afford anything, it's hard to settle on one thing."

"I guess so," Emily agreed, but something in her voice told Nicholas she wasn't one hundred percent sold.

"Well, I'm gonna have to go. My aunt needs to use the phone."

"Oh, okay. See you at school tomorrow then?"

"I'll be there."

"Alright. 'Night then."

"'Night."

Nicholas hung up the phone and let out a tight breath. He took a moment to think everything through. Bodies were washing up on shore in pieces. Emily's dad was working late on the case, which made it less likely this was just an accident. It not being an accident most likely meant murder, and murder involving dismembered limbs usually pointed to deranged psychopaths or monsters. Nicholas had dealt with both already, and he knew the next thing he needed to do.

He punched in the number for Winter's Hall. The phone rang twice, and Nicholas was greeted with Argyle's proper yet defiant voice.

"Hello, Winter's Hall. Argyle speaking."

"Hey, Argyle," Nicholas said. "Is Dusk there?"

"Mr. Dusk is at home, yes."

Of course, he is, Nicholas thought. *Where else would he be?* Nicholas waited a moment. There was only silence.

"Hello?" Nicholas finally asked.

"Hello," Argyle answered.

"Argyle?"

"Yes, sir."

"Where's Dusk?"

"At home, sir."

"Are you getting him?"

"Do you need to speak with Mr. Dusk?"

Nicholas sighed. "Yes, I do. Could you get him for me, Argyle?"

"Right away, sir."

The line went quiet again, and Nicholas shook his head. *Prissy old man,* he thought. There was a rustling; then, Dusk came on, voice thick as if he had been sleeping.

"Yeah?"

"Dusk? It's Nicholas."

"Who else would it be?"

"Right." He readjusted his grip on the phone. "I think we have a problem."

"Yeah, you calling me at all hours of the night."

Nicholas checked the clock on the kitchen stove. "It's eight o'clock."

There was a brief beat of silence as Dusk thought this over. Then, realizing nothing would sound right, he said, "What's the problem, kid?"

"Dead bodies."

"Pretty typical."

"Washed up on shore."

"Different but not unheard of."

"In pieces."

"That may be something to worry about. They thinking boating accident?"

"Most are but...," Nicholas wasn't sure what to say.

"Sheriff Gordon isn't convinced," Dusk said when Nicholas didn't continue.

"Yeah, at least that's what Emily says."

"She would know." Dusk sighed, and then continued, "If he's sensing something, then there is something really wrong."

"What do we do?" The question was out of his mouth before he could stop it. It wasn't a bad question. It just made him sound like a scared little kid, something he didn't want to sound like.

"First things first," Dusk said, finally sounding awake. "We need to figure out what we're dealing with."

"So, we need to see the bodies?" Nicholas said, following the script they had laid out in previous months.

"Yup. Best way to know what's out there killing is to see what it's killed."

"Great," Nicholas said, falling against the door frame.

"How about you meet me down at the library?"

"The library?"

"Yeah. That's where your aunt is going to think you are anyway, right? Wouldn't make sense for you to come here and work this late."

"Again, it's only eight o'clock."

"The library it is then," Dusk said, ignoring Nicholas's comment.

"Yeah, I guess so."

"Alright then. I'll see you there in about an hour."

Then, he was gone. Dusk wasn't one for fond farewells, over the phone or otherwise.

Nicholas hung up his receiver. He looked around, vibrating with anticipation. He wasn't scared; he was excited. He had grown bored of the normal. He was ready for excitement, adventure. He was ready for the hunt.

"Aunt Sherri. I'm going to the library."

Nicholas knocked on the front door of the library, his cold knuckles taking the knocks harder than they normally would. He had already looked in the office and seen that Mr. Lloyd wasn't behind his desk as he normally would be. That meant he was either in the bathroom or within the rows of books somewhere in the main room of the library. After a few moments, and two rounds of knocking, the door was opened, but not by Mr. Lloyd.

"Hello. I'm sorry, but we're closed."

A girl with dark, curly hair tied back with a multi-colored bandana stood in the open gap of the door. She looked pretty, but her turtleneck sweater and extra-long skirt made her seem plain. She wore glasses that were too big for her face. The sight of them so far down her nose made Nicholas push his own up.

"Ah, yeah. I know."

She looked Nicholas up and down.

"Um, is Mr. Lloyd here?"

She opened the door a little wider, as a hand went to her hip.

"Yes, he is. But we're closed."

She was trying to sound firm, and she was on guard, unsure if Nicholas posed a threat. New to The Hollow, which Nicholas assumed she was, she was unsure if she was in danger or just misunderstanding the locals.

"I know you are, but Mr. Lloyd knows me. I'm Nicholas."

She thought for a second and then held up a finger. "Hold on one second, please."

Then, she shut the door, leaving Nicholas out in the cold.

Nicholas swayed on the balls of his feet. He looked around, not knowing what else to do. He thought about knocking again just as Mr. Lloyd opened the door.

"Nicholas, my boy. How are you?"

"I'm good. How are you? You have security now?"

Mr. Lloyd looked confused for a moment, but then he understood. "Oh, you mean Michelle? No, no. Nothing like that. She's just here to help out a bit. Like an assistant more than security."

"Assistant?" Nicholas asked, surprised.

Mr. Lloyd chuckled. "I am ashamed to admit it, but my age is getting to me. I must have relied on your help around here more than I realized. And with Linda taking on librarian duties at the school, I just decided to get a little bit of extra help."

Nicholas smiled and then thought that over. He couldn't remember the last time he had stayed late at the library. He had just gotten so busy with Will, Emily, Dusk, and writing. After everything Mr. Lloyd had done, Nicholas had just left him to pick it all back up alone.

Don't I feel like an ass?

Nicholas almost considered telling Mr. Lloyd about his writing. Mr. Lloyd had always shown an interest in Nicholas, and he was sure to like the notion that Nicholas had typed three hundred pages worth of an adventure Mr. Lloyd himself had had a hand in. Then, Nicholas remembered what a mess that writing was in and decided against it.

"Hey," Mr. Lloyd said, catching Nicholas's look. "No worries. She's great, really. Not as good as you, but we're getting there."

They both smiled.

"Well, come in. I'm sure you didn't come all the way down here at this time to stand outside."

Once inside, Nicholas found a chair and sat down. Mr. Lloyd took one across from him, shifting a pile of books out of the way.

"You know, for a small town, we have a lot of history." He motioned to the pile of books. "These are just about the evolution of fishing the lake. So, what brings you here?"

Nicholas gave the books a quick glance, and then said, "I'm actually just meeting Dusk here."

Mr. Lloyd's face darkened. He turned to check on Michelle. She was in the back, replacing books, well out of earshot.

"What happened?" Mr. Lloyd said, turning back.

"We don't know yet." Nicholas looked down at his hands. Mr. Lloyd was serious and concerned. Had Nicholas been excited not an hour ago about the prospects of all this?

Sure, monster hunting had a flashy title, but the actual act was dark and macabre.

"Some bodies washed up on shore," Nicholas continued.

"I heard about that," Mr. Lloyd cut in. "People are saying it was a boating accident."

Nicholas shrugged, "Maybe it is."

"But he doesn't think so."

It wasn't a question, but Nicholas answered anyway, "No, and neither does the sheriff."

"Really? Are you working with him, too?"

"No," Nicholas answered with a start. "Emily told me."

"Ah, I see." Mr. Lloyd's eyes twinkled in the amber light of the desk lamp. He smirked.

Nicholas felt his cheeks grow warm. He looked down again. Once he cooled, he looked back toward Mr. Lloyd.

Mr. Lloyd wasn't looking back. He was looking out the closest window.

"It's happening again, isn't it?"

Nicholas didn't answer this time. He had thought the same thing.

There was a knock on the library's main door. Nicholas and Mr. Lloyd turned at the sound. From where they sat, they could see Michelle move the books she was placing in their correct spots back on a cart and start toward the door.

Mr. Lloyd raised a hand, "Ah, Michelle."

Michelle stopped and looked back toward them.

"Better let Nicholas get that."

Michelle looked confused. Her head tilted like a dog's would when given a command it didn't understand.

Mr. Lloyd smiled and sent a wink toward Nicholas. Nicholas smiled in return, half picturing Michelle questioning Dusk like she had done to him, and got up to answer the door.

Chapter 5

"We just have to be careful, that's all I'm saying."

This was the third time Nicholas had said this in one variation or another. Dusk was already shaking his head and waving his hand dismissively. It was worthless to argue. Nicholas knew this even before he started. Dusk was going to do whatever Dusk wanted to do, however he wanted to do it.

"I'm sure we will be fine. It's late. He's had to have left by now."

Nicholas shook his head. He had told Dusk everything already. If he had wanted to heed Nicholas's advice and be careful, he could have.

About a hundred yards behind The Hollow's police station was a thick line of trees. Dusk and Nicholas stood just on the outside of those towering sentinels, obscured in shadow. They looked across the expanse, scouring the scene.

"I don't see anything," Dusk said.

Neither did Nicholas. He looked, trying to spot even the slightest hint of a certain police cruiser. The only car in the lot, however, belonged to the man they had come to see.

"That's strange. Emily said he was going to be here late."

"I guess he already called it late."

Nicholas nodded, but he wasn't sure. Emily knew her father and knew him well. They had been taking care of each other most of their lives, and Nicholas would bet she did most of the looking after.

They walked toward the station. They stayed vigilant. Well, Nicholas did. Dusk walked toward the home of dead bodies and police officers with swinging arms and a pep in his step. Dusk wasn't worried, so why was Nicholas?

Should I list the reasons chronologically or alphabetically?

It was true. There were many reasons for Nicholas to be concerned. But there was only one thought that worried him at that moment.

If the sheriff isn't here, and he isn't at home, then where is he?"

This was one of the absolute last places he wanted to be. There were worse. His past allowed him to imagine worse, but this was bad.

Sheriff Gordon knocked on the large, ornate door. His knuckles hit with all the authority his position granted him. Even though he didn't want to be there, he had a job to do.

He waited. A slim man came to the door. Sheriff Gordon had heard about the man but had not met him in person. He immediately made the sheriff straighten.

"Hello, Sheriff. How may we assist the Pointe's Hollow Police Department?"

"Hello. Argyle, is it? I don't believe we've had the pleasure."

On the porch of Winter's Hall, Sheriff Gordon extended his hand to Richard Dusk's butler.

"That's correct, Sheriff." Argyle also extended his hand. The shake was cold and crisp.

When they finished, Sheriff Gordon put his hands to his belt, while Argyle placed his behind his back.

"I was wondering if the owner of the house was home. I have a few questions for him."

He was employing a friendly tactic he usually used on the more well-off crowd. This man may be a butler, but if Sheriff Gordon pushed hard, this man would push back. That would get him nowhere.

"Unfortunately, Mr. Dusk stepped out."

"Really?" Sheriff Gordon mocked surprise. "It's a bit late. You know where he went?"

"He did not say."

"You didn't ask?"

"Not proper for a man in my position to ask such questions. Even if he is curious by nature like I tend to be."

"I see." Sheriff Gordon shifted his weight, so the palm of his hand rested on his service revolver. Not a threat; the situation didn't call for threats. It was just a friendly reminder that it was there, and he was the authority here.

Sheriff Gordon hadn't wanted to come here. He put it off all day. It probably was going to be a waste of a trip. The tragedy from earlier in the day could still be just a boating accident. A severe boating accident, but an accident all the same.

The investigation, personal more than official, had pushed Sheriff Gordon here. He wanted to call it a boating accident just like everyone else was. There was just one thing holding him back. His gut. After years of relying on his gut, it was a hard thing to overcome.

Still unsure if he believed what he had encountered the last time he had been around this house, Sheriff Gordon had been fighting the truth of that night for months. Discounting other people's stories of terrible things was easy. It was much more difficult to shake it when you had seen the terror with your own eyes. Either way, it didn't matter. Whether he believed it or not, Sheriff Gordon had decided to ask some questions of the guy who always seemed to be around when the bad things were happening.

"Does he go out late often?"

"Not often," Argyle said.

"But sometimes," Sheriff Gordon said. His tone was light, but his ears were sharp, listening for a chink in the armor.

"People go out, Sheriff. I thought it would be more suspicious if a man were to stay in all the time."

"Never said it was suspicious."

"That's true. You didn't." Argyle straightened up even more. "Is there anything else, Sheriff?"

The way this guy said 'sheriff' made Sheriff Gordon's blood boil. It was polite, yet degrading.

It appears the butler follows the path of the master. Right onto my person of interest list.

"No, I guess not. If he's not here, that is?"

"I'm sorry Mr. Dusk was not here to help you, Sheriff. If you'd like, I can tell him to give you a call when he gets back."

Help me? The thought revolted Sheriff Gordon. Richard Dusk was not a helper. He was suspect number one on anything out of the ordinary in The Hollow. Especially when bodies turned up dismembered.

If the sheriff was open to giving up information, which he never was, he would have explained to Argyle that he not only had questions for Dusk but would have slipped in hidden threats as well. He planned to bring his round of questioning around to a point where he could put his suspicions in Richard

Dusk's lap and watch how the man reacted. This was something he couldn't do over the phone.

"No, I'm sure I'll see him around. Small town."

"Alright, then. If that's all."

Sheriff Gordon took a moment and sized up Argyle. "Yup, that's all for now."

Argyle bowed his head. "Alright, then. Good night, Sheriff."

"'Night." Sheriff Gordon threw Argyle a friendly wave. He turned around and walked back to his cruiser. The encounter hadn't gone according to plan, but he wasn't discouraged. Ever since the night he had seen Mr. Fidel fall from the window into the same yard he now walked through, Sheriff Gordon knew something bigger was going on in his small town than he or maybe anyone had realized.

Definitely something going on. And this Richard Dusk character is at the middle of it.

Call it police intuition or jumping to conclusions, the sheriff didn't care. He knew he was right. He might not know exactly what was going on, but he knew he would find out. Questioning Richard Dusk just seemed like the best way to move forward. Slipping accusations and threats into his questioning seemed to be the best chance he had to get something from this guy. But tonight, it seemed, wasn't the night he was going to get that chance.

If only I knew where that son of a bitch was.

Dusk and Nicholas walked through the dark police station. They passed the frosted glass door with a certain name stenciled on its surface. They passed a small side table with an ancient coffee pot on it. Beside that sat a pile of filters, a half-empty bag of dark roast, and a tower of foam cups. Some stir sticks and sugar packets populated a small assortment rack. Once they cleared these sightings and the maze of cubicles, they descended the cold staircase to the bowels of the station where there are no secrets.

Dusk went in first. Nicholas was fine following. Dusk was the real detective here, not him. Actually, neither of them were real detectives, but Dusk carried a gun, so Nicholas considered him to be close enough.

"Dusk! And Nicholas! I knew you would be coming. I just knew it." Steven Steely, The Hollow's friendly neighborhood coroner, was almost jumping out of his skin with excitement. "I have everything ready."

Nicholas walked right into it, "Everything's ready for what?"

"The show, of course!" Steely said, raising his hands up into the air. "Now that both of our contestants are here, we can begin." He stepped to the side, revealing three gurneys with lumps under white sheets.

"You, contestant number one, you look like a strapping man, not young," Steely slapped Dusk's shoulder, "but who still is these days, am I right? Now, you go ahead and pick, would you like to see behind Curtain Number One, Two, or…"

"Steely."

Steely stopped his announcer voice.

"Just show us what you've got. It's late."

"Ah, right. Not a game show kind of man, I see."

"No, he's more of a western guy," Nicholas said, smiling. Dusk gave him a sideways glance.

"That I can see," Steely said, pointing a finger up and down Dusk. Dusk shifted his glance to Steely and put a little steel into the look.

"Alright, alright. Onward and forward to the breach, as they say."

Steely walked back to the sheets, taking up position by the far-left gurney. Nicholas looked to Dusk. Dusk just shook his head in exasperation, and they both walked toward the bodies.

Calling the things under the sheets 'bodies' was putting it a little strong. One sheet seemed to be covering a body, or at least something resembling a body. The other two sheets rose and declined like a snow-covered terrain. Most of the sheet lay flat against the metal top of the gurney; small lumps broke up the monotony, like children's toys left out after playtime.

"Three victims. At least that's what all the pieces we found add up to."

That wasn't the most comforting of opening statements.

"Randy Packers, Sean Nye, and Colin Mortensen. Alan Hooper was also supposed to be out with them, but we haven't found any sign of him yet. Probably never will."

"So, four victims?" Dusk asked, eyes serious.

"Not officially, but," Steely paused and, uncharacteristically, grew melancholy. "Yeah, four victims."

"Fingerprints ID the victims?"

"I sent the paperwork out on the fingers we have. It'll be a few days before we get the results back, but we're pretty sure it's them. Not as many ships out on the water these days, and families reported they didn't come home last night."

"We sure it wasn't a boating accident?"

"Pretty darn," Steely replied, dropping back to a more casual tone.

"The bodies were beat up pretty bad?" Nicholas said.

"You could say that."

"And what would you say?" Dusk interjected.

"I'd say they were torn apart." He reached down and pulled the sheet back.

Nicholas had seen dead bodies before. More than his fair share if truth be told, but the pieces under the sheet still shocked him.

A foot rose up into a chunky red ankle. Above that lay a deteriorated arm. A few fingers lay on the gurney where a hand should be, but the fingers just laid alone, detached from each other. They looked like little worms on the sidewalk after a rainstorm. There was also a foot near the bottom of the gurney; a piece that, by its positioning on the table, was most of a thigh; and above the fingers sat possibly an elbow. Other hunks of flesh littered the surface, but they could have been from anything. Nicholas lacked the knowledge and the stomach to place them.

"As I said, torn apart." Steely looked at the mess, shaking his head as if to say, *This is the best I could do.*

"You weren't kidding," Nicholas squeaked out.

Dusk leaned in, trying to take in every inch of the mess, paying special attention to the foot. Once he had spent enough time there, he moved to the bit of elbow.

"Do we know if the ship ran aground? Maybe on some rocks or a sandbar?"

Steely was already shaking his head. "Maybe, but the tide wasn't particularly low, and these were seasoned sailors. Besides Colin, who was just a kid, they had fifty plus years out on that water between them. Plus, with a crash, I would expect to find more chunks of the ship ashore."

"But there are pieces?"

"Yeah, but they're fragments." Steely held up his fingers in a rough estimate of size. "As if the boat was pulverized more than hit something."

Dusk nodded and began to rub his chin as he pondered the bits in front of him. "Any ideas about what could have torn them apart?"

"That's the weird thing. It's not clean enough to be a cut, but it doesn't show the normal signs of teeth."

"Teeth?"

"Well, I don't know," Steely said, throwing up his arms. "Don't most of your guys' cases involves teeth of some sort?"

"Some," Nicholas said shrugging. "Not all."

"But you don't think this one was teeth?" Dusk said, pulling the conversation back to business. It was funny how he could switch gears. One moment he was cracking wise and smiling; the next he was stone serious.

"No, not teeth. If I had to put a name to it, I'd say beak."

"Beak?" This time it was Dusk's turn to be incredulous. "Are you telling me a bird ate this guy?"

"I'm not saying that. There was also a lot of tearing as if something rather large pulled them apart."

"You're saying something with a beak, that was big enough to pull a human body apart, got to a boat in the middle of the lake, ripped up some guys, and then chewed on them for a bit until it decided to demolish the boat into splinters?"

"I'm not telling you that, the bodies are telling you that, Dusk."

Dusk decided to chew that over for a second. Nicholas thought the idea was ludicrous. *What kind of bird was gonna eat a person? On a boat? In Michigan?* Nicholas had no answer. If it was sixty-five million years ago, he would maybe say pterodactyl. *Could there be a pterodactyl in The Hollow?* Nicholas didn't even want to say it out loud, afraid it sounded just as ridiculous as he thought it did, or worse.

"You have anything else?" Dusk said as if he had no hope for good news.

"Well," Steely turned to face the other gurney. "Curtain number two here is just more of the same."

Apparently, Game Show Host Steely was back. Now, however, Nicholas wasn't finding it that much fun.

60

"Curtain number three, on the other hand, has something interesting."

"More interesting than beak evidence?"

"You can be the judge of that."

Steely walked past curtain number two. Nicholas and Dusk followed him as he pulled back curtain number three.

On the gurney lay a battered body. Some limbs were missing, and some were hanging on by threads of stuff Nicholas didn't want Steely to explain to him. It was hard to tell which was harder to look at - the bits from the first two gurneys or this.

Dusk leaned down close to the body and investigated as he had done with the pieces on the first gurney. He took his time, inspecting wounds and looking over every inch for clues.

"Well, it's a bigger piece, I'll give you that, but I'm not sure if we'll get anything more out of this guy than we would from the others."

"True, but there is something different about this body." Steely stepped forward. He reached out, pointing at the corpse's chest. "You see that? That is a weird one."

Dusk looked at it, and his brow furrowed. Nicholas decided he should get a closer look. He stepped toward the wound and leaned over, much like Dusk. There was a hole in the man's chest about the size of a softball. Bone poked up through the torn flesh. It was jagged and cracked. Looking through the wreckage, Nicholas could see the space inside was empty. Whatever had been in there appeared to have vacated the premises. He could see all the way to the back of the body where the ribs curved back and attached to the spine.

"Looks like he got impaled by something. Maybe a rock or a part of the ship?"

"At first, I thought the same thing," Steely said, looking up at Nicholas. "But as I went through my inspection, I saw some strange things. You see the costal cartilage of the third, fourth, and fifth rib."

"Steely, hold up. You've already lost me. Keep it simple."

Steely looked startled. "Oh, right. I'm sorry, Dusk. Um, the ribs here and here have broken away from the sternum or breastbone here. On top of that, the ribs show signs of outward strain. As if something burst out of the chest." Steely laced his fingers together and then broke them apart outward. One minute they were together, and then pop, they were apart.

The visual image Steely demonstrated made Nicholas gag a little. He had seen people shot and even one guy torn apart, but what Steely was talking about was something on an entirely different level.

"Are you saying something killed him from the inside out?"

Steely started to speak, paused, and then spoke, "Not exactly." Steely put his fingers back together. "The bones also show that something forced itself between them before they were broken forward."

"So, he was stabbed," Nicholas said, almost relieved. It had been a strange few months to make Nicholas feel comfortable with the idea of someone being stabbed, but it was comforting compared to the alternative.

"Yes, again, but also no. Again. Whatever happened to him was much more savage than just a run of the mill stabbing."

"Then, what do you think happened?"

Steely looked at both Nicholas and Dusk in turn. "I think something reached into his chest and pulled something out. In this case, his heart."

Nicholas's relief was short lived. *Something ripped out his heart?* He looked back down at the body. After a moment, he looked from the body to Dusk. Dusk never looked away from the body. He was rubbing his chin in contemplation.

The last time they had been in this situation, Dusk had worked a miracle. He had used some mysterious green liquid to make the corpse of Earl Hutchins wake from the dead and talk. The memory of that breathy voice still gave Nicholas chills.

"Man… in… shadows."

He had pointed Nicholas and Dusk toward his own killer. They were, unfortunately, unable to find the so-called 'man in shadows', but it had opened their investigation and given them a starting point.

This time, none of the bodies had a head. It was very hard to get the dead to talk. It was impossible if they didn't even have a mouth to talk with.

"So," Dusk said, pulling Nicholas out of his trip to the past. "If we weren't us and you didn't know what you know, how would you explain all of this?"

Steely exhaled in a quick burst. "If I had to make an official report, which I guess I'm going to have to do eventually, I'd label it a boating accident. The late hour mixed with the rough waters and weather caused even the experienced sailors to lose control of the boat, and they were all killed in the crash."

Dusk was nodding, but was still looking at the body.

"The extreme condition of the bodies would have to be left up to interpretation of the severity of the crash, which must have been at high speeds, and against strong obstacles given the facts and the evidence we can perceive from the bodies."

Dusk stopped nodding, and said, "And this wound here, on the chest?"

Steely shrugged, revealing that he was going to be reaching to press on. "It could have been an oddly-shaped rock or debris from the ship that slipped in between the ribs, pierced the heart deep enough and severe enough to rip it from the arteries, and then pulled out in the exact right way to cause the striations on the ribs and remove the heart."

Nicholas was nodding along but only out of habit. It sounded like a fabrication, even to Nicholas who had very limited police experience. But the town would buy it, because they didn't want it to be anything more. For everyone outside of town, they'd just accept it, because they knew nothing of what it could really be. There was only one person Nicholas thought would question it. Not because he wanted to; in fact, he would want to believe it, but he wouldn't. The sheriff would see through it and ask questions, not a doubt in Nicholas's mind about that.

"Okay," Dusk also didn't sound convinced, but he also knew it was the best Steely could do under the circumstances.

"Now, what do you really think?"

"Well, in my professional opinion," Steely began, adjusting his glasses on his face. "I'd say we are all very lucky that it isn't swimming season."

Chapter 6

After their meeting with Steely and his twisted game show curtains, Nicholas and Dusk discussed the case. They realized there wasn't much to discuss. So far, all they had was a boating accident that most likely wasn't an accident, puzzle pieces of three dead bodies, and something lurking out in the water or flying over it.

"So, what do we do next with all of this?" Nicholas asked, excited by the thrill of the chase and hope for vanquishing evil, but also worried about where it would lead.

"Well, in the good old days, I would have talked with Father Christopher about all this. He was the brains behind this operation."

The name alone made Nicholas's heart ache. He had known Father Christopher for only a short time, but his death had hit Nicholas hard. It was difficult not to blame himself for the priest's untimely death. Adding on the fact that they found his limbs in a church filled with blood and had faced off against a burnt marshmallow version of him at the lighthouse made everything cut deeper.

Wait a second, Nicholas thought, an idea coming on so strong it almost knocked him over. He had forgotten to tell Dusk about Father Adrian. Maybe there was somewhere to go for help after all. He explained the encounter he and Emily had had with the priest just a few days ago.

"And what's your point?" Dusk said, not connecting the dots.

"Monstrous. He said monstrous."

"Yes, and it was."

"Yeah! That is my point. It was monstrous!"

"Alright, now you've completely lost me."

Nicholas sighed, "Don't you think it's strange he used that word. He used the exact word to describe a case involving real monsters. I think he was tipping me off that he knew."

"Then, why didn't he just come out and say it?"

"Because Emily was there. She doesn't know anything. I haven't told her anything about what's going on."

Dusk thought for a moment. "But how would he know that you know about the monsters?"

This didn't trip Nicholas up in the slightest. "Father Christopher had, well, you know. The sight. Maybe this guy does, too."

"Just because he put father before his name?"

Nicholas shrugged, "Maybe it's a gift from God."

Nicholas himself couldn't speak one way or the other about what God could do, would do, or if he even existed, but it seemed like a good enough explanation given the circumstances. Nicholas wasn't even sure if he had answers to those questions for himself, let alone for a world where monsters prowled.

Dusk took a moment to ponder. Just when Nicholas thought he was going to stay silent, he said, "If he did have the sight, and knew you knew about monsters, but wanted to keep Emily in the dark, then why didn't he ask to speak with you privately. Even if it had been awkward, it would have been important given what has happened. There's no reason for this whole cloak and dagger routine of his."

Nicholas took a breath in, and then stopped. He hadn't considered that.

"Because," Nicholas started, but didn't know where to go with it.

"I think you heard what you wanted to hear and drew your own conclusion based on what you wanted, not what it really meant. Priests are religious, remember, even the normal ones. Everything evil is either a devil or a monster. It was probably just coincidence that he used the word 'monstrous'."

Nicholas wanted to argue, to fight for his side, but he had no ammo. Dusk could be right. Nicholas had quickly jumped on that word. Besides, so Father Adrian said a word. That didn't mean he was a fighter of monsters like Father Christopher. It was just a word.

But it was more than that, he thought. *There was just something about him.* What that something was Nicholas couldn't be sure. It was just a feeling. A feeling of familiarity? Maybe. Or maybe it was a feeling of foreboding. Either way, it wasn't worth worrying about right now. They had bigger issues.

"So, what then?"

"Well," Dusk said, sighing and looking off toward the coast. "Are you ready for another boat ride?"

Nicholas followed Dusk's gaze. He took a moment, and then he offered a weak smile.

"Sure," he said, rubbing the back of his neck with his hand. "I mean, the last time we went out there, everything went so well."

Pitch

A Friday morning can be a beautiful thing. To most, it means the weekend is close. The monotony of their jobs is about to be put on hold for a whole forty-eight hours. They were about to be free to enjoy what they loved in life, instead of what they had to do to live.

Sheriff Gordon was not one of these lucky ones. Sheriff Gordon rarely had a day off. As the sheriff of a small town, he was never off duty, never away from the job, and never free for the weekend, especially when dead bodies were washing up on shore on Thursday.

His Friday morning had been an early one, and it followed a late night. A late night that held no answers, only more questions. Questions that needed to be solved or more people were going to die.

Randy Packers, Sean Nye, and Colin Mortensen were cold and shelved at the morgue. Alan Hooper was presumed lost at sea. None of them had been relatively close to the sheriff, but he had known of all of them. Now, in the daylight, Sheriff Gordon was hoping the answers to their deaths would come to him. He had stated in public that it looked like a boating accident, but he knew it was much more than that.

The daylight, however, had failed him. He had been staring at the page of notes he and his officers had compiled for almost an hour. Even combined with Steely's analysis of the bodies, he had come up with exactly what he had the night before.

Nothing.

Sheriff Gordon began to rub his mustache in frustration. For months now, he had been slowly concluding something was going on in his town he could not control. Not because he was unwilling, but because he didn't have all the information he needed. Someone did, but so far they weren't sharing.

I just need to get them in a room. Then, I'd have answers.

There was a knock on the sheriff's door.

"Come on in," Sheriff Gordon said with a half sigh.

"Hey, Sheriff," Deputy Donald Huckle stepped through the opening door. "I have those crime scene photos for you."

"Oh, yes. Thank you, Donald. Just throw them over there." Sheriff Gordon pointed to the front corner of his desk closest to the door. It was the only bare spot left.

Deputy Huckle walked forward, dropped the file with the pictures, and turned to leave.

"Donald," Sheriff Gordon said, stopping him dead. He wasn't sure exactly where he was going, but a plan was forming.

"Yeah, Sheriff?"

"How long have you worked here?"

"Oh, um," Donald reached up, lifting his hat and scratching his head with the same hand. "That's a tough one. Six, seven years by my count."

Sheriff Gordon smiled; by God, he liked the kid. "That's what I got to." He sat back in his chair, dropping his sheriff demeanor for a more relaxed stature. "And of that time, how many times have I asked you for a favor?"

Donald took a moment and then laughed, "None, Sheriff. I work for you. I don't do favors; I take orders."

Sheriff Gordon chuckled, too. "Well, I think I'm about to ask for one." His voice took on a more serious tone, but he kept his body posture light, so Donald felt he was a friend more than a boss.

"Alright, whatcha need?"

"You know about the guy that moved into Winter's Hall?"

"That Richard fella?" Donald shrugged. "I know of him, not much about him. No one in town really does. I think he's one of those quiet, rich types, you know. The type who owns some big hotshot company in New York or some other city and runs it from behind a group of guys who spend more money in a day than we'll ever see in our lives."

Sheriff Gordon nodded. Donald was a talker. A true small-town resident who loved to share what he thought he knew about other residents. Sheriff Gordon would usually cut him short, but he was going to ask a lot out of the kid, so he let him talk.

"Or maybe he just doesn't like people. As I said, no one really knows him, Sheriff."

"I see. Well, how would you feel about learning about him?"

Donald's face scrunched in confusion. "What do you mean?"

"I mean," Sheriff Gordon leaned forward. "How would you feel about shadowing this guy for awhile. On the clock, but off the record."

There was a long silence at that moment. Sheriff Gordon never faltered. He kept staring at Donald, with a little knowing smile.

"You think," Donald began, wary about what he was going to say. "You think this Richard guy has something to do with Randy and Sean and them?"

Not as slow as people think, Sheriff Gordon thought, his smile growing.

"I'm not saying that. All I'm saying is he's new to town, and I don't want bodies piling up on us like last November."

At the mention of the last horrific murders that happened in The Hollow, Donald shivered. He shifted in the doorway. He looked down at his feet and seemed to be taking it all in.

"What do you want me to do?"

There we go, Sheriff Gordon thought.

"Nothing crazy. Just spend a few hours a day and take a drive out there on Coast Line. If you happen to go out by

Winter's Hall, drive and park for a bit while you're out. I wouldn't complain."

Donald was nodding. "And if I happen to see him wandering around The Hollow and happen to see where he goes and what he does, that would be okay as well."

The kid's a natural.

"Exactly. Now, if you feel uncomfortable with any of this at any time you... ."

"Sheriff," Donald's call stopped the sheriff short. "I can handle this." Donald looked stern. It didn't fit him perfectly, but it fit well enough, and for a moment, all the kid was out of his eyes. He was in full cop mode.

"Thank you, Deputy. That will be all."

"Sheriff," Donald said with a curt nod as he started to leave again.

"Oh, and Donald?"

Donald turned back, this time with an eyebrow raised.

"I know you can do this. Wouldn't have asked you to if I didn't think you could."

Donald's eyes took a quick shine. *Oh, God. Don't go crying on me, kid. We have such a good thing going.*

Donald took in a deep breath, and then let it out. "Thank you, Sheriff."

Sheriff Gordon nodded and waved him out. Once he was gone, Sheriff Gordon leaned back in his chair and began to twiddle his thumbs. He hadn't lied. He did believe in Donald, but he was also worried about him. Richard Dusk may not have killed these sailors, but the sheriff knew he was involved somehow. Anyone who was involved in those atrocities and recently taking refuge in The Hollow was going to be carrying around some dangerous baggage. Anyone who got in the way of that baggage was apt to get hurt.

In the minutes that followed, Sheriff Gordon debated telling Donald to forget the whole thing. Then, he would think of how proud and determined Donald had looked and decided to stay seated. Most likely, Donald would come back empty handed. Sheriff Gordon had tried to look into Richard Dusk himself and had come up with nothing.

He'll be fine, Sheriff Gordon thought. *If you want to worry about someone, worry about everyone else in town that doesn't carry a gun.*

His eyes dropped to the file of crime scene photos Donald had brought to him. Did he have the strength to look at those right now? Did it matter if he did?

He decided if he didn't have the strength, a good cup of coffee would help him find it. He pushed himself up from his desk and left his office. The pictures and files of death covering his desk would wait. For a moment, at least.

Who is this man? The thought came to Dusk in a repulsed tone. *It can't be me, can it?*
Of course, it was. There was his mess of black hair tainted with grey. He could see his eyes with heavy bags sagging below them. With those eyes, he saw his scars. Especially the new one on the inside of his left arm.

But then what is this?

He grabbed the small collection of fat that had gathered around his mid-section. *I don't remember this being here.* To be fair, it hadn't been there before. To be even fairer, it was minuscule in comparison to most people. To Dusk, however, it felt like the loss of his strength, the loss of his power, and the final sign that he was getting old.

He let go of his stomach and then ran a hand through his hair. His breath hissed out like a deflating balloon. He grabbed his shirt, which he had laid across the basin before getting in the shower. It fell over his shoulders and still hung off his body like dead skin.

As he left the bathroom, he yawned. A wide-mouth yawn comparable to a lion's roar.

"Late night, Mr. Dusk?"

Wiping the sleep from his eyes, Dusk noticed Argyle standing in the doorway to his room.

"You could say that," Dusk replied.

It was strange to have someone in Winter's Hall all the time with him now. For years it had been him and just him. Now, every time he turned around Argyle was there. The most surprising thing about it was Dusk liked it. Argyle had been an accidental addition to the crew. While looking for companies to do renovations on the house, Dusk had run across an ad in the newspaper. The ad was simple and plain. What caught Dusk's eye was one line, 'Discretion is our specialty'. He had called later that afternoon and had Argyle hired by the end of the week.

"And it's probably gonna be another late one tonight. We're going fishing."

"Fishing, sir?"

"Yup, gonna catch us something big."

"Make sure to keep warm. I'll pack you something to eat."

No questions. Perfect.

"Oh, and I'd keep an eye out for the sheriff if I were you."

Dusk was caught off guard, "The sheriff?"

"Yes, sir. He paid a visit last night and was inquiring for you."

"What did you tell him?"

"That you had gone out for the evening, and I didn't know where you had gone."

Dusk nodded. It was true. Dusk hadn't bothered to mention where he was going. Not because he didn't trust Argyle, but because he hadn't even considered it.

"I guess I'll have to keep an eye out then."

"Very good, sir."

"Argyle, I've told you before you don't have to call me sir. It's Dusk. Just Dusk." But Argyle was already leaving the room.

As he left, he called over his shoulder, "Of course, sir."

Dusk shook his head. After a moment, his hand came up to his chin as he pondered what was happening. *Why would the sheriff come looking for me now?*

Most likely because he had bodies showing up on his shore, and Dusk was the new guy in town, at least to the sheriff's knowledge. The sheriff was a simple man but not a stupid man. The kid had told him he thought the sheriff knew it was not a boating accident.

Dusk wondered why the sheriff had never come to talk to him after the night he had seen Mr. Fidel fall from the library window.

'Cause he doesn't believe.

Sheriff Gordon was a smart man, but he was also a rational man. Unfortunately for them all, they were in an irrational world. The sheriff would no doubt have trouble believing in the existence of monsters. In his line of work, he saw the worst of people. He didn't need monsters to be evil. He saw humanity's evil.

So, why look for me now? He couldn't possibly still consider me a suspect in this?

As soon as he thought this, he knew that the sheriff could think that and most likely should in his position. That wasn't going to help Dusk do what he needed to do, and in the long run, it wasn't going to help the sheriff catch the killer.

The sheriff was a real concern and something he would have to deal with, but for now, he had to be more concentrated on tonight. He gathered his gun belt from the bed, his jacket from the closet, and his boots from beside the door. After he collected his things, he left the bedroom to get the rest of the things he would need, even though he had no idea what he would face.

Chapter 7

The school day was over before Nicholas could even consider how he was going to survive it. Half was because it had been a late night, and Nicholas had felt the effects all day. It seemed his return to full energy was stopped in its tracks by a single night with Dusk. The other half was because he was thinking about the hunt to come. His limbs vibrated with excitement as they quivered with nerves.

It was like the first night that he had gone out with Dusk. This time he knew more about what to expect. It was less nerves and more excitement, but the intensity of the emotions was still there.

After school, Nicholas rode home to quickly make a sandwich and tell his aunt he'd be working at Winter's Hall until late. Aunt Sherri wasn't happy about the late part but relented because it was work. If she only knew what the work entailed. Their relationship had been strained recently. She was trying to be the fun-loving aunt she always had been but at the same time be the responsible adult. The late night when

Nicholas had saved the town from a savage monster with Dusk had terrified her more than he realized.

At first, it was the usual worry and relief of seeing him okay. Then, it had turned into more questions than normal. After that, she had started commenting on things. The kind of comments that suggest alternatives to what Nicholas wanted to do. A sly adult way of telling kids they know better and the kids should listen.

Most of the time, Nicholas ignored her. He didn't blame her, but it bothered him that after all this time, now she was trying to be the adult. Nicholas was fine with the way their relationship had been for years, but now it was complicated. After so much time enjoying easy, complicated was the worst thing to deal with.

Once clear of the house, Nicholas peddled up the cold streets, warm breath puffing from his mouth like the exhaust of a train. He had bundled up extra warm for the night, so as he peddled, the sweat immediately began to run down his limbs. By the time he reached Winter's Hall, he was drenched.

Argyle opened the door mere moments after his gloved knocks.

"Ah, Mr. Wake. Mr. Dusk is expecting you. Are you ready for your fishing trip?"

Nicholas thought the question was strange, but he guessed a situation such as this called for nothing less.

"I guess so," he said with a sheepish smile.

Not long after being let in, Dusk entered the room where Nicholas had decided to have a seat and wait for him.

"Alright, you ready for all this again?"

Nicholas jumped up from his seat, saying, "Can't wait."

"Eager? That's an interesting response."

"What?"

"Nothing," Dusk said with a shrug. "You just make it sound like we're getting the old band back together, not that we're going out onto a lake with something that took out an entire fishing boat and a crew of four seasoned sailors."

Nicholas thought about it for a moment. "You don't think you still know how to play?" he said, smiling a wicked grin.

Dusk gave him a look, and for a moment, Nicholas thought Dusk took it the wrong way. There was a pang of sadness in his eyes. It took Nicholas aback, but just as his fun was going to falter, Dusk smiled as well.

"I can still rock with the best of them, kid. Don't you ever forget it."

Nicholas's smile grew even bigger. He stepped aside, raising an arm toward the front door. "Age before beauty."

The docks were dark, and the water was as still as a pane of glass when they arrived at the coast. Dusk looked around more often than he usually did. Nicholas asked him if everything was okay.

"Yeah, just being cautious."

The statement was completely reasonable, but something in Dusk's tone made Nicholas wonder if he was holding something back, as if he expected to be followed. He had half a mind to ask who he was looking for but decided Dusk wouldn't tell him even if he did suspect someone out there in the shadows.

"What are we going to take out?" Nicholas said, ignoring Dusk's suspicion.

"Well," Dusk said as he looked up and down the length of the dock. "After the last time we decided to take to the sea, I thought there might come a time where we might have to go out again. So, I procured a boat for just such an occasion."

"That's good," Nicholas said, picturing a boat Dusk could buy with all the money he had.

"There she is."

Dusk pointed to a vessel four bays down, and Nicholas's face fell. The boat Dusk had decided to get was not much more than the dingy they had taken to the island last November. It was about twenty feet long, broken up by two seats that reached from one side of the boat to the other. Two hooked oar wells sat on the edge of the boat. In the middle was a small contraption where one could install a sail.

"I know she don't look like much, but neither did you when you first showed up, so give her a chance."

Dusk looked down at Nicholas, smiling. Nicholas did not smile back. "Let's just get this over with."

As Nicholas walked toward their dingy, he could hear Dusk snickering behind him. *He better watch it, or I'll push his old ass into the water and leave him.*

The water was like ice. As they paddled, small droplets splashed up into the boat hitting Nicholas and Dusk in the face. They both emitted small puffs of breath, and soon Nicholas was sweating again. Nicholas had to give Dusk some credit; the boat did move smoothly. It cut through the surface as if the water wasn't even there. Besides the small creaks of the wooden oars and the musical plip plop of water, they coasted out into the lake like silent spirits.

Before long, they passed the island that used to house the Pointe's Hollow lighthouse. Nicholas thought he saw the spot where they had pushed their other boat ashore not so many months ago. Before he could be sure, they were past the area and going around the island's crest.

Once they were clear of the island, they continued to paddle out a way. It was almost pitch black out here in the night. The only light was a small makeshift light flashing in place of the lighthouse that had met a destructive end. It wasn't nearly as tall as the original tower; however, the height of the cliff made the light useable. The cold weather mixed with the consuming blackness of the night made its spark seem weak and hollow.

"Alright, this should be good." Dusk pulled in his paddle and motioned for Nicholas to do the same.

Nicholas could feel the silence weigh down on top of them. He looked back the way they had come. The small light cast a glow over the water and coastline of the island. It would click off, and light phantoms would dance in Nicholas's vision. Then, the light would be back, bringing everything into focus. Behind that, the coast of The Hollow was invisible.

They were completely alone.

The light continued to blink on and off. Nicholas had a sudden thought that the light was a heartbeat. As if the island was alive, and the light pumped it full of blood. Nicholas began feeling his heartbeat. It was low, but as darkness surrounded him, the heartbeat quickened.

Dusk shifted around in his seat and pulled something from behind him.

"What's that?"

Dusk placed a small box in the middle of the boat. Nicholas saw it, but it took two rounds of the light flashing to fully realize what it was.

"A cooler?"

Dusk nodded, "Yup, best way to keep the bait fresh."

He popped the top off the cooler, and Nicholas caught the smell of meat and blood. His stomach was thankful that he couldn't make out what was in the cooler in the dark. He reached behind himself and found that his knife was there. It had been a long time since he had needed to carry it. He was glad he had remembered it and hoped he would not need it.

Dusk reached into the cooler and began to pull out chunks. One by one, he dropped the chunks overboard. They sat and waited for a moment. After nothing happened, Dusk said, "Paddle around a bit. We'll try to spread it out."

Nicholas took an oar in each hand and began to paddle.

"Keep it slow. Try to disturb as little as possible."

"Why? You think I'll scare the monster away?"

"No, but if it is some giant bird, and it's gonna dive bomb us, I wanna be able to hear it coming. And keep the flashlight off until the last possible moment."

This was one of the many reasons Nicholas was happy he wasn't out here alone. He would have never thought about that. Like a normal person, Nicholas relied on his eyes too much. Being a true hunter of things that go bump in the night, Dusk used every sense he had. Nicholas even thought he had a sixth sense that allowed him to know what was hunting him and what would be the best way to kill it.

For an hour, the two of them continued like that. Nicholas paddling through the water with consistent strokes as Dusk dumped whatever he had brought along to entice the beast. Back and forth they went. No matter how much Dusk threw over, nothing happened.

Dusk picked up the cooler and dumped what remained into the drink and sighed. "I don't remember it being this hard." He dropped the cooler back in the boat and closed it. "Who knew it'd be this difficult to try to get attacked by a monster. We may have to start waving that flashlight around."

Nicholas lifted the paddles out of the water, and they both sat, coasting in silence. There was a small splash about fifty feet away. Nicholas and Dusk both turned toward the noise. Then, there was silence.

In the light flash, Nicholas saw water rippling. The world went dark again. The light came back, and there was nothing. Nicholas felt a shiver ripple over his skin.

PLIP. PLOP.

The light shone and cast a shadow across Dusk's face. Nicholas at first thought he had imagined it. It seemed to float in the air.

PLIP. PLOP.

Then, he realized it was rising from the water. It was long, curved, and water dripped from it, flicking Nicholas's nerves to attention. He raised the flashlight with caution, worried that if he went too fast, he would be found.

PLIP. PLOP.

Nicholas clicked the flashlight on. It bloomed to life in a yellowish glow. Dusk's head shot back as the beam hit him in the face.

"What are you doing!?"

Nicholas had a moment to think of how cold the water was, and then he was tossed into the air.

The force of the strike caught Nicholas by surprise. He had seen it coming, but even with that foresight, he was unprepared for the ferocity of the attack. His arms and legs flailed like a child as he flew. The water slapped him in the face like a truck. It was even colder than he had thought it would be.

Trying to gain a footing and figure out which way was up after being thrown from a boat is hard enough. In the dark, as his appendages went numb, Nicholas found it impossible. The light came on, giving Nicholas a sense of direction. As the light blinked out, he oriented himself, so he was facing the surface, and waited for confirmation.

When the light came back, it brought horror to life. In the water between Nicholas and the boat was a dark mass of circling tentacles and a bulbous body.

Nicholas's lungs burned for air, but between him and the surface was a floating, writhing giant octopus.

Dusk had sensed the monstrosity as the kid noticed the thing behind him. His honed reflexes were what allowed him to keep his seat in the boat. Even with those on his side, his fingertips were the only things that saved him from the deep cold.

The small boat rocked as if it was in a hurricane after the first blow landed. He had seen the kid hit the water, and he felt the need to dive in after him, but he had to worry about the beast first, or they both would die.

The rocking settled as Dusk assessed the situation. He had only a fraction of a second, and then four tentacles broke the surface. They writhed in the air as if being freed for the first time in centuries. They bent and wriggled with the tenacity of a cornered beast. Then, they settled and seemed to curl, pointing their tips at the small boat.

Raising his foot to the side of the boat for balance, Dusk released his revolver from its slumber and took aim. If the literary-keen kid could have seen him, he would have described him as a gothic Ahab, facing down his very own Moby Dick.

BANG!

Fire burst forth from the mouth of the barrel. Lead flew on mark, smacking into the beast's slimy appendage. The reaction was immediate. The tentacles curled as if the thing was drying out in the sun. Then, they whipped forward. They all missed the boat, but the force of the blows sent water in all directions, causing havoc for the small vessel.

Dusk tried to keep his feet, but the waves were too strong. As he fell, his back hit the bottom of the boat, and his left arm smacked the side. His wound had healed, but the beating brought the pain back in a raging flame. Teeth gritted, Dusk swallowed a scream. The bone didn't break again, but that didn't stop the vibrating discomfort from rebounding up and down the infernal thing like an electric shock.

Once on his feet again, Dusk looked for the next attack. The tentacles were back in their demonic dance, circling the boat, positioning for the strike. His shot had created a reaction but didn't cause any real damage.

The light from the island flashed again, revealing the mass sitting just below the surface. As the light began to fade, Dusk aimed down into the water and fired.

BANG!

BANG!

BANG!

The three shots rang out in the silence of the night, but there was no reaction from the beast. Either he had missed, or the bullets were too weak to do any harm.

Dusk holstered his weapon and decided on another tactic. The tomahawk flashed in the light as the bulb ignited again.

As if the beast could sense Dusk rearming himself, it swung at him. He ducked, dodging the blow by mere inches. The tomahawk swung in reflex, missing the passing appendage but swinging through the air with deadly intent. The movement took him off balance, and the beast used the advantage. Its strike wasn't perfect, but it was hard enough to send him to the other end of the boat.

Air was forced from Dusk's lungs as he hit the lip of the boat with his chest. The blade was a great weapon but left him defenseless on his other side. He put his hands down to help him to his feet. His fingers wrapped around the shaft of an oar.

Perfect.

He stood for a third time, a tomahawk's bite in one hand and the blunt force of an oar in another. The thing was quick, though. It sent in its next attack. Dusk ducked to the left and smacked the fleeting appendage with the back side of the oar. It created a cracking sound that would have floored a grown man. Spinning on his heels, Dusk swung a full baseball bat swing behind his next blow. The blow was so hard that the oar cracked against the tough flesh of the tentacle.

There was no way he could hear the thing's screams from below the water, but Dusk imagined them. It writhed with wild thrashing, causing more unstable water. Growing a good set of sea legs out of immediate necessity, Dusk kept his feet, balancing on the bouncing boat like a surfer.

Even after his moment of triumph, Dusk found no respite. The beast attacked again. This time, Dusk could only duck, so duck he did. Water droplets dripped onto the back of his neck sending gooseflesh rippling through him as the thing sailed over. There was a tug at his arm that held the oar, but his fingers held fast and retained his grip.

He stood back up, ready to take the fight to the next level when the load in his left arm lifted. With a pang of disappointment, he turned to see that the oar that sat in his grasp was now only a fragment of the original length. Its top half had been carried away by the swinging tentacle.

The hits keep com…

As if from nowhere, Dusk was hit squarely in the back by the next tentacle. Falling forward, Dusk caught himself with a hand that landed on the plank that served as one of the seats of the boat. His right hand still held the tomahawk, the blade shining mere inches from his face.

Anger began to boil up and fuel his limbs. He didn't like that this beast seemed to be getting the better of him. No matter how out of practice he was, this thing would not land another blow.

A flash of light came with the next onslaught from the beast. Dusk stared as he saw it coming the entire way.

"Aw, come on!" Dusk screamed as he raised the tomahawk ready to counter. One giant suction cup on the underside of the tentacle became enveloped in his internal reticle. It fell within striking distance, and Dusk took his shot.

THUNK!

The blow hit, biting into the soft flesh of the creature as if it was piercing soggy wood. Dusk gritted his teeth in a fiendish grin of triumph.

Pitch

The short-lived victory was ripped from Dusk as he felt his feet being lifted from the wooden floor of the boat.

Son of a bitch, Dusk thought, teeth clenching harder. Reflexes took hold, and Dusk kept his grip solid on the handle of the tomahawk. The strength of the monster's wounded appendage was still abundant, becoming evident when it lifted Dusk from the minimal safety of his boat into the open sky.

Before he knew what was happening, Dusk was more than thirty feet in the air. A broken oar hung in one hand while his lifeline, in the form of a tomahawk wedged in the flailing leg of the massive creature, sat in the other. Below him, the thing swung at the boat with one of the other tentacles, still thinking Dusk was there.

The thing got a good strike, coming straight down on the small boat with a heavy blow. With gravity helping its attack, the beast shattered the vessel into two splintered halves.

Well, this is a bit of trouble you've gotten yourself into here, Dusk.

Looking down, he saw the kid break the surface, sucking in fresh air. Dusk wasn't sure how long he had been under, but he knew it had been longer than just a casual dive. The light from the island faded, and the kid disappeared into the thick, inky blackness of the night.

Dusk wasn't the only one that was in trouble. He had one tentacle covered, true, but that left seven other tentacles at the thing's disposal. Seven against one; the kid's chances didn't look good.

Air rushed into Nicholas's hungry lungs. Once they were filled, he exhaled and tried to inhale again but caught a mouth full of lake water. Coughing, he tried to clear for another breath, but the water was churning from the fight, making it difficult to breathe.

Through squinted eyes, Nicholas made out a dark silhouette floating on the surface in front of the night sky.

The boat, he thought.

His arms waved in large circles as he swam for the sanctuary of the boat. Reaching safety, he pulled himself up with one thing on his mind: air. He needed to catch his breath. He crawled on top of the floating surface and rolled onto his back. Beautiful, fresh air flooded the sting in his lungs.

As Nicholas's thoughts became less murky, he opened his eyes. Light flashed, and he saw an obscene sight. Above him, tentacles danced around like ritual participants. Hanging from one of them, a man swung as if he was Tarzan on a vine.

Dusk? What are you doing up there?

Mind still foggy but clearing, Nicholas began to piece things together. Before the whole picture was revealed, however, Nicholas felt water high on his thighs.

"Whoa," Nicholas said, crawling backward from the cold water.

The boat, his safety, was sinking. While he spent his time underwater, things had gotten out of hand up here.

I'm gone for five minutes, he thought as he clambered up to the highest part of the sinking ship. It granted him only moments of safety until it was swallowed by the choppy lake.

Back in the water, Nicholas trudged through the wetness. He worried he'd be blindsided by a wave and be choking on water again when the lake floor rose up to him.

But that doesn't ha...

Before he could even finish the thought, Nicholas's kicking legs were met with a solid disturbance. Soon, his legs were picked up, and then Nicholas himself was lifted clear of the surf.

The large, bulbous head of the giant octopus crowned the churning water with Nicholas straddling it. The slick surface gave him little purchase, but he was able to hang on. As the thing's face broke the surface, a screech resembling squealing tires and a garbage disposal thrashed the night air. It took all Nicholas had to hold onto the creature and not cover his ears. In the light flash, Nicholas saw a beak perched in the thing's deformed head.

For the first time, Nicholas saw this thing as not just a huge octopus but something more resembling a creature of legend. A thing mythology had talked about for a millennium. Nicholas found himself sitting on what he now thought of as a Kraken.

After an uncountable amount of time, the sounds stopped. Nicholas was able to think again. He brought his knees to his chest and rose up onto them, riding the beast.

What now? What do I do now?

Nicholas fought to think, but the combination of his soaked clothes, the flashing light, and the creature writhing kept him from thinking clearly. He slid on the monster's body. Readjusting to catch himself, Nicholas felt his knife at his waist.

He reached his hand around and grabbed the knife handle. Pulling the blade free, Nicholas raised his hand to take a stab. The blade cut through the gooey flesh, digging in up to the hilt. The cross guard bounced on the thing as if it was on springs.

The monster shivered and then recoiled. It screamed, wailing like a banshee. It began to move backward in the water as if it could swim away from the blade. Just as he was going to lose his balance on the thing's head, Nicholas flopped down flat against it and grabbed the knife with his other hand. His grip was weak because of his numbing fingers, but it was enough for him to hold his position.

Once it realized it couldn't get away from the pain, the terror thrashed a few of its tentacles down into the water, one striking its head in its fury. The blow fell next to Nicholas, splashing him with small bits of water. The tentacle rolled across the thing's own head trying to find the source of its pain. Finally, it found Nicholas, grabbing hold of his ankle with a rabid grip.

This can't be good.

The beast threw Nicholas to the sky. There was a momentary pause as Nicholas held tight to the knife, and then there was a plop as the blade came free. Nicholas flew upward faster than he previously thought possible. The light flashed as he flew. A blur of water droplets fanned out around him as if he was in a snow globe and a child had shaken it to make the flakes dance. Nicholas felt like he was not only in the snow globe, but he was the trinket itself, being tossed about without a care. The situation was escalated by the thought that it would end much worse than just a soothing snowfall.

Much, much worse.

Yanking the handle, Dusk tried with all his strength to get the tomahawk free. The tentacle was somehow pinching the blade. Muscle spasms or the internal workings of the beast's appendage grasped the weapon, not letting go.

"Goddamn you," Dusk growled into the night.

A screech from below broke Dusk's concentration. He looked down to find the kid holding on for dear life to a spent blade.

Stupid kid, Dusk thought, but he also admired the kid for fighting like he was. It sparked a fire under his ass. He began pulling again. Try as he might, however, the blade was solidly stuck.

Even if you get it out, then what?

He was right. If the blade were to pop free, he'd fall to the water, smacking it with the great force of gravity, turning the water into solid ground. That much of a drop could kill a man.

Or...

A plan began to form in his mind faster than he could articulate. The beast below had stopped its movement and had decided to splash at the water. Dusk took the broken oar in his hand and tossed it up, flipping the pointed end around.

The shoulder supporting the arm holding him up had started at a dull burn but was now escalating to unbearable. He lifted himself even as the joint protested and put his feet against the tentacle, relieving some of the strain on his body.

Below, Dusk noticed the beast had ensnared the kid in another tentacle. He was holstered high, and soon, the two of them would be sharing the same airspace, completely at the monster's whim.

Not this time.

Dusk took the broken oar and stabbed at the tentacle right where his tomahawk's blade had skewered it. Wrenching it back and forth, Dusk tried to free the blade. He repeated the process, stabbing a new spot and wrenching at the wound. The force of the blows was draining Dusk's strength faster than he would have liked, but the fourth attempt caused space, and the blade ripped free. The wound, which now hung open to the night, spilled dark, blue blood from the creature. The gore poured over Dusk as he was cast from the creature.

He found himself in a free fall, coat rippling in the wind. Rolling in midair, Dusk extended his arms and legs to steady himself as his stomach was buffeted by air.

The kid flew by in the opposite direction, heading skyward. In his right hand, Dusk wielded the tomahawk, stained blue but free. In the other hand, he held the thing's undoing, the oar whose broken end was fractured into a macabre point. The blood from the monster had caused his grip to be slick and not as strong as he would have liked, but it was all he had. To counter the uneasy grip, Dusk brought both his hands together above his head with the splintered oar pointed downward. Clothes and hair whipped in the wind as his speed increased. A scream ripped from his mouth.

The light flashed just in time for the creature to see him. For the briefest of moments, Dusk wondered if the thing was smart enough to realize what was happening, but then he made contact. His body hit the squishy mass of the octopus. He felt a shock go through his own body as crunching wrecked inside the creature's. Two feet of the wooden weapon sunk into the beast without resistance. The remaining foot was more difficult, but it, too, sunk in. That final amount of oar broke some interior barrier and hit vitals. Blue blood oozed out of the contact point.

There was a pause when the creature sank back into the water with the force of the blow. Then, it wailed with a scream caused by the obscene pain. The beaked face sunk into the water, and its screeching transformed into bubbling water. As it sank deeper, all sound fell silent.

Dusk rode his kill all the way down until he felt his body dip below the waves. Knowing the job was done, he let go of the oar and kicked off toward the surface. The liquid around him became a mixture of water and blood.

When Dusk met air, he just waded in the water, watching the show around him. The tentacles that still rose above the lake followed the body down, and then they curled, rolling in on themselves. They floated off-center, drifting away angelically in contrast to the monster to which they were connected. It felt like the world had slipped into a space of slower time.

SPLASH!

Dusk looked to his left where the commotion had come from. Water rippled, settled, and then the kid's head popped up. He coughed up a bit of the lake, turned in circles looking at the almost-gone tentacles, and then finally his eyes landed on Dusk.

They both waded in the water. The light from the small island flashed, and they just looked at each other, both surveying how the other came out of the battle. They looked like they came out alright, everything considered.

"Well," Dusk said, spitting water out of his mouth as he dipped a little too deep. "I guess that could have gone worse."

"Besides us dying, how could it be worse?"

Dusk thought for a moment. "You could be missing a limb. Think how hard it would be to swim with one arm."

The kid rolled his eyes. Dusk couldn't see it in the dark, but he knew the kid well enough to know what the slight shift in his head meant. The kid finished his disapproving gesture and made for the island. Dusk blew the access water from his upper lip and followed. Below them, the monster sank into the dark abyss.

Chapter 8

Thick steam rolled off the hot burger like fog rolling off the lake on a cool morning. Spatters of fat popped along the griddle's surface as the meat cooked from a pale pink to a dark grey. It smelled like something the gods would have eaten on Mount Olympus. The smell alone electrified Nicholas and brought him up from his exhausted state.

He reached down and grasped his massive meal with both hands. As he brought it to his mouth, the smell grew, and he closed his eyes in preparation of taking a bite. Juices oozed out of the corners of his mouth as he tasted the burger. It was even better than the smell the cooking burgers let on. The bite was a bit larger than normal. It took Nicholas a moment to get through, but once he did, he let out a reflexive groan of enjoyment.

Nicholas opened his eyes to find a quizzical Emily and Will staring at him. He wiped an arm across his mouth, and said, "What?"

"Nothing," Will said. "It's just…," Will waved his hand as if trying to find the right words.

"Like you haven't eaten for a month instead of hours," Emily finished for him.

Nicholas shrugged, "It was just a long night."

After the Kraken-like creature sank to the bottom of the lake, Nicholas and Dusk swam back to the lighthouse island. They got to the opposite shore, commandeered a boat and rowed back to The Hollow. It was a long night before they got to the house, made even longer after a soaking wet boat ride in Michigan in February.

"Mr. Dusk work you hard?"

The question threw Nicholas off for a second. First, because he could never get used to anyone calling Dusk 'Mister'. Second, because he had forgotten he had told Emily he was going to be working late at Winter's Hall. That made it two nights in a row he had pushed off hanging out with Emily to be with Dusk. Not because he didn't want to hang out with her, but because he and Dusk had had bigger fish to fry. As it turned out, literally.

"Naw, wasn't too bad. He's a good guy," Nicholas said, trying to play it off. "Just late, that's all."

"Man, that house gives me the creeps," Will forced this bit out through a mouthful of food. "I don't know how you deal with being there. Especially at night."

You should have seen it a few months ago, Nicholas thought, fighting back a smile.

"Well, if you're gonna stay in The Hollow long, you're gonna have to grow some thicker skin." Emily emphasized her statement with a bite of a French fry.

Will paused his chewing, looking a little shocked. He chomped through what he had remaining in his mouth, and said, "Yeah. What's up with that? You guys have a hard time keeping people alive as I hear it."

Emily waved him off, "Please, we have one or two isolated events, and we become Murdertown USA. Every town has their thing."

"And murder is Pointe's Hollow's?"

Will's use of the actual name of the town only made it more evident he wasn't a local. Emily and Nicholas looked at each other and smiled as if they had an inside joke. Will motioned as if to say, *What, no comment?*

Emily shrugged, unable to contradict him. Due to recent events and everything her house had to deal with on a daily basis, death just seemed to be a common occurrence.

Nicholas felt a churning in his stomach as he thought about all the murders, of which he had witnessed a few too many. "Could we talk about something a little happier?"

"Aww, poor Nicholas," Emily cooed.

"Yeah, I thought you loved this kind of thing," Will added.

"I do. In books and movies. It's different when you witness it firsthand."

The words were out of his mouth before he could think about what he was saying. He dipped a fry in ketchup, and when he looked back up, chewing, Emily and Will were looking at him again, interested.

"You saw one firsthand?" Will asked, intrigue playing across his face with a splash of excitement.

Emily looked at Nicholas, concerned.

"I, ah, no. No, I haven't. You know what I mean," Nicholas said, trying to back track. "I mean a girl from our class died a few months ago. It's not like we are just watching faces pop up on the news. We know these people."

Will nodded, dropping his head in a slight apology for making light of it all. Emily, on the other hand, didn't seem one hundred percent convinced. She was too smart for her own good sometimes. Far smarter than Nicholas. One of the many reasons Nicholas knew she was too good for him.

"Well, you guys are lucky I'm here then," Will said, putting a bit of bravado in his voice.

"Is that so?" Nicholas said, trying to get the new conversation to catch so Emily would stop giving him the look she was.

"Yeah. I'm here to save the day."

"Uh, huh," Nicholas continued. "What do you think, Emily?"

Emily gave Nicholas one last moment of her look and then turned to Will. In response, Will sat up straighter in his seat to look more heroic. He pulled it off quite well with his natural charm.

Raising her arm, Emily stuck her thumb out to the side over the spread of food between all of them. She held it for a moment of consideration and then turned it so her thumb pointed down, rejecting Will.

Nicholas and Emily shared a laugh. Will took on a look of false hurt.

"I get no respect," he said. "No respect at all."

The trio finished their food and walked outside into Michigan's cold winter air. A breeze washed over them, carrying a bite of the lake sitting just to the west. Emily walked close by Nicholas, and he tossed his arm around her. She didn't pull away, but moved in closer, tucking her own arm around his waist. Will brought up the rear, moaning.

"Ah, man. I ate way too much."

"I warned you. Mike's burgers aren't anything to take lightly."

"And you weren't joking. I was going to go with the chicken, but all they had was on the bone."

"Is there a problem with that?"

"No, it's just I don't eat chicken on the bone."

Nicholas craned his neck back, not wanting to let go of Emily, but wanting to give Will a look. "Are you serious?"

"Yeah," Will said as if it was no big deal. "What's wrong with that?"

"What's wrong with that? What's right with it?"

Will raised his hands in a defensive gesture. "I am just a firm believer in if it goes on the plate, it should be able to go in my stomach."

Nicholas finally let go of Emily to turn completely around to face Will. "It's chicken. Of course, it's edible."

"The chicken, yes, but the bone, no."

"The bone is the method for delivery. You're not upset by the fact you can't eat your fork once you're done with it, are you?"

"Now you're just getting ridiculous."

Nicholas scoffed. "I'm the one being ridiculous?"

"If it walks like a duck," Will said, shrugging.

"Em, please back me up here."

"I don't know," Emily said, a smile tugging the corners of her mouth. "You both bring up excellent points. I may be converted, though. Will's argument makes sense."

"Yes! Score another for the bone haters of the world."

The two shared a high five, and Nicholas was left shaking his head. "Guess you can't argue with crazy."

Emily came back to Nicholas, hugging him around the middle. "No, you can't. But don't worry, we still love you." She perked up and kissed him. Soft and sweet and smiling when she broke away.

How could you argue with that, Nicholas thought, a smile of his own warming his cold face.

"Hold on!" Emily said, putting a hand on Nicholas to stop his walk.

"What is it?" Nicholas asked, feeling himself tense up in preparation for a fight.

She grabbed Will and pulled him close to her and Nicholas. The three jostled a bit and then found their footing. As if from nowhere, Emily produced her Polaroid camera.

"Come on, get in close, I wanna make sure we all fit."

Nicholas smiled. Emily had done this more times than he could count since they started dating. It was as if she was afraid she would miss something or forget it if it wasn't immortalized in film. The wall that housed one picture of the raven she had given him the previous fall had been populated with tons of pictures of the two of them in past weeks.

"Make sure you get my good side," Will said, pretending to mess with his hair.

"To get that, you might have to step out," Emily countered.

Nicholas laughed.

Emily never gave a count down. She would just announce 'cheese' and then snap. This time Nicholas had barely calmed his laughter before she snapped the picture.

The square card of film popped out of the underside of the camera, and the three watched as the black surface slowly faded into a still life of the scene before its lens.

Nicholas had been laughing in the picture. He was smiling, but his eyes were too squinted, and his teeth were parted in uncontrolled mirth. Emily was dead center with her arms extending toward the edge of the frame as if holding them all in place. Will had decided that his 'good side' was his face contorted, resembling Quasimodo from *The Hunchback of Notre Dame*.

"A definite keeper," Emily said with a matter-of-fact tone.

Nicholas was nodding, although he would have said any photo with her was a keeper.

"I do have to say that handsome devil on the right definitely makes the picture," Will said, pointing at himself. "But we should have probably chosen a better background."

Nicholas looked at the photo again, and realizing where they were, turned to the real world. They had ended up in front of the vacant lot. The makeshift dump in the middle of downtown Pointe's Hollow, which broke up the picturesque line-up of buildings. Nicholas had to agree with Will. It wasn't the prettiest sight. Luckily for them, the thick snow covered most of the trash, leaving only a large stump, the dishwasher, and the rickety fence visible, with each having varying amounts of snow cover.

"I think it's fitting."

"Well, I guess that says what she really thinks of us, huh, Nicholas?" Will said, patting him on the shoulder.

"No," Emily said, laughing. "I didn't mean it like that. It's just. We've all had bad things happen to us."

Nicholas's mind went through a lot, but it always ended up back with the death of his parents. Just as he was sure it did for Will and with Emily and her mom. They had all lost a lot. Maybe that's why they were so close after so little time together.

"But all that is behind us. Just like that lot is behind us. You don't see what's in front of us, and that's where the good is."

They took a moment to take that in. It was strange, but Emily had a way of drawing meaning out of everything. She always dug deep and sucked the marrow out of every situation.

"Yeah," Will said. "But in reality, the street is in front of us and, in turn, traffic. I don't know about you two, but my Nana would much rather I stay out of the way of traffic."

And then there's Will. Everything is a joke.

The three laughed. The sound got lost on another cold gust coming from the lake. The tall pines of the surrounding forest waved in a hypnotic arc even greater with the weight of the snow clutching their branches.

"Come on," Emily said, starting again at a brisk pace. Will and Nicholas took a moment to share a look. Will shrugged and jogged to catch up with her. Nicholas looked back at the lot. Maybe the worst was behind him. Maybe it was behind all of them.

Pitch

Nicholas inhaled the cold air and chased after his friends, not knowing how wrong he was and how much bad was still to come.

After spending the whole day getting into trouble - well, as much as three kids can in a town the size of The Hollow - Nicholas decided to visit Dusk before calling it a night. Technically, he had work scheduled that night at Winter's Hall, so his aunt wouldn't expect him home anyway.

His puffs of breath disappeared behind him at his heightened pace. He pedaled fast, weaving in and out of the tire grooves through the snow on the road. It had been a good day, a really good day. The night before he had fought off a creature of myth, and today he had spent the day with his trusty sidekick and princess. Figuratively speaking, of course, but it still felt great.

A hill appeared in front of him, and he smiled at the challenge. His heart quickened as he pedaled even faster. The gears in the old Schwinn seemed to sing with exertion. Before he knew it, he had crested the hill and was gliding down the other side, sliding in the snow drifts. He stood, leveling the pedals and using gravity to propel him even faster. Wind whipped his hair, and he seemed to forget the cold around him. Life was good.

The gravel of the Winter's Hall's drive felt solid in the frozen ground, but the snow created a crunching noise he was accustomed to. His bike was rolling beside him as he reached Winter's Hall in what he considered record time. His chest heaved from the ride.

After placing his bike near the front steps, Nicholas reached the door, taking those same steps two at a time. He knocked, expecting to be greeted by Argyle's stern yet polite demeanor Instead, the man of the house himself answered the door.

Dusk opened the door but had his eyes on something in his hands instead of Nicholas. He held a piece of paper. There seemed to be something written on the page, but Nicholas could not read it from where he stood.

"Hey," Nicholas said, breath finally regained.

Dusk said nothing, just let go of the door and stroked the rough surface of his chin, encapsulated by the paper.

"What's that?" Nicholas said, adding a little volume to his voice.

"Huh," Dusk said, finally looking up. "Oh, good. You're here. I have something." He held up the paper. "Come in."

He turned and walked into the familiar study that branched off to the left of the great hall.

After shutting the door and kicking his shoes off, Nicholas followed Dusk. There was a fire in the fireplace and a handful of empty Coke bottles on the coffee table.

"Take a look."

Nicholas had barely entered the room when Dusk was shoving the paper at him. Closing the gap between them, Nicholas took the paper, flipping it in his hand so it was the right way up. It felt familiar, but he shook the notion away. He had been right; there was something written on it, but only a few words.

there are many shadows, in between the trees
-P

Poetic, Nicholas thought, a sour tone invading his own mind. The words meant nothing to him, but the note had upset Dusk, so he reread the message.

Even on the second reading, nothing stood out. But on the third pass, Nicholas's breath caught. It wasn't what the paper said, but who had signed it.

P.

That was all. That one character. It had a ghost image on the paper behind the letter itself. Almost like a shadow of the true letter. It sat there faded and haunting. Just like all the others did on the three hundred pages from Nicholas's own typewriter. His father's typewriter.

Nicholas's fingers rubbed the paper they held as his hands tensed. *That is way too familiar.* After rolling and piling three hundred pages, Nicholas knew the feel of the paper stock he used. This was the same.

But how could that be?

"You see it, too," Dusk said, startling Nicholas back to reality.

"Yeah," he said, voice a whisper. *How would Dusk know how the typewriter's P worked, or what paper I use?*

"I think it's from him."

Now, fully confused, Nicholas said, "Him who?"

"Him. The him. The man in shadows."

Nicholas's head was spinning in circles trying to make sense of that jump in logic. "The man in shadows?"

"Yeah. He practically brags about it. Shadows in the woods." Dusk put an emphasis on 'shadows' and 'woods'. "Who else could it be?"

Nicholas had a thought but didn't dare say. He just nodded in agreement. He was trying to be sure this was from his typewriter. The paper being the same could be dismissed. Surely, many people used that kind of paper. It was a common brand and cheap, which made it a big seller. But how could he dispute the similarities in the forming of the 'P'.

He couldn't.

"If it's from him, then what's with the P?" Nicholas asked, hoping to calm his mind.

"That," Dusk said, stroking his chin again. "Is the troubling part. He could be signing it. Giving us a clue to who he really is."

Nicholas still nodded, but again, thought something else. *Maybe it's for me. Just me.* For a few more moments, he was unable to tear his eyes away from the 'P'.

"Why would he do that?" he finally said.

Dusk thought for a moment. "I'm not sure. But I think this is an invitation to meet. I think he wants it on his terms, so he's baiting us with the first letter of his name."

"Maybe," Nicholas said.

Dusk looked Nicholas over. "You see something else?"

Nicholas met Dusk's eyes. *I should tell him. Maybe he could help figure out what is going on. If anything, he should know what he is walking into.*

"No, it's nothing." Cold steel slipped into Nicholas's veins as he set the paper down on the coffee table and turned back to Dusk. "What's our next step?"

Dusk nodded. "Right. Well, I don't think he gives us a whole lot of options. I hate going in blind, but I think we have to go meet him."

"You think he wants a truce or something?" Nicholas asked, hoping beyond hope that it could be true.

"Yeah, I'm sure that's it," Dusk said, chuckling. Nicholas smiled in surprise. "In fact," Dusk continued, "I'm sure he'll bring ice cream and maybe a new puppy as a peace offering. Now, I'm sure you have some idea for names, but I'm thinking something strong like Hercules or...."

"Alright, I get it. Enough. You could just say no, you know."

"I know," Dusk said with a wink.

Nicholas shook his head. The feeling of his good day was back. He loved his friends, and he considered Dusk to be his best friend. A strange friend, but a friend nonetheless.

Then, why don't you tell him about the P?

This thought ate away at Nicholas with a ravenous hunger. When he tried to come up with the answer, he was able to find one. He just knew he couldn't, not until he knew what was going on. Some deep part of Nicholas feared what all this meant, and he wanted to know the truth before he shared anything.

They went to the front door of Winter's Hall and opened it, letting in a harsh gust of winter air. Dusk was shifting his coat onto his shoulders while Nicholas walked out onto the porch. Covering the entire surroundings of the house were woods. The forest surrounding The Hollow was probably three times the actual size of the town. Their search area was massive.

"Where do we even start?"

Dusk exhaled, joining Nicholas on the porch. "That is a great question. You take the tree to the right; I'll go left. Once we meet around the other side, I'm sure we will have found something."

Nicholas shot Dusk a look. He knew he was joking, but he couldn't help thinking about his Saturday cartoons, especially Scooby-Doo. There was a part in every episode where they split up, and it never ended well. Usually, one of the pairs ended up being chased by the monster and would lead said monster to the rest of the group. It was all fun in a cartoon, but out here, in the dark, it was a different story.

"I don't think splitting up is the best plan."

Dusk blew warm air into his hands. "I'm sure you're right." He blew a few more times and then rubbed his hands together. "Let's head that way." Dusk pointed to the right of the house, toward the coast.

"Why that way?" Nicholas asked.

Shrugging, Dusk said, "It's as good a way as any. Besides, this seems like one of those situations where they're more apt to find us than we will find them."

Nicholas agreed. The two of them stepped off the porch having no idea what they were about to walk into.

Chapter 9

It's never ending.

This thought had come to Nicholas many times over the hours of walking through the trees. For the first hour, Nicholas had put up his guard, tensing his muscles at every thick patch of shadows clinging to the trees and bushes around him. Every time, however, nothing jumped out. No hand reached from the darkness clutching at them. No monster pounced, thrashing, to rip them apart limb from limb. They hadn't found a thing.

After the second, third, and even fourth hour, Nicholas became annoyed. *Why would the man in shadows write a note like that, then just not show up?*

If he was the one who wrote it.

Nicholas couldn't help but think that maybe this had nothing to do with the man in shadows. Or if it did, he wasn't the one who wrote the letter. He was just the puppeteer pulling the strings. The train of thought just raised more questions than it answered, however.

Nicholas stopped on a small hill. He put his hands on his hips and took a moment to catch his breath. He whipped an arm under his dripping nose as he looked around, trying to see anything between the thick trees. His glasses shifted down, and he had to push them back into place. All he saw were trees and snow. To the left and to the right: trees and snow.

Dusk was a fair distance away surveying his own area. They had stayed close in the beginning hours, but as the morning grew closer and closer, they got more relaxed with their caution.

Nicholas called out to Dusk, "Anything?"

Dusk gave the surroundings one more glance and then shook his head.

Perfect, Nicholas thought. *A wild goose chase running around the woods all night.* Nicholas wiped his nose again and then blew warm breath into his frigid fingers. Maybe it was the man in shadows's idea to kill them slowly with the common cold. It was working. Nicholas lost the feeling in his toes an hour ago. His face hurt with every brush of air, and he felt a cold, wet sweat all over.

Nicholas began searching once again. Frustrated that their night had come up with nothing, he wanted to find something, anything that would point to why someone made them come out here. But no matter how hard he looked, he found nothing.

More and more time passed, and yet their search continued to yield no results. Eventually, night drifted away and the first signs of morning began to break free. The pure white of the surrounding snow emphasized the small amount of light coming from the morning's sunrise. It still sat nestled below the horizon, but its rays reached around the earth welcoming the new day. Nicholas rubbed his eyes while letting loose a large yawn. He had already found himself beyond tired at school, and now, after a night out, he was going to be barely more than a walking corpse.

Better than a non-walking corpse.

Nicholas stopped his search and turned to tell Dusk they should call it a night or morning, as it were. It hurt to admit they had been fooled by a piece of paper. They both felt like they should be better than that, but as it turned out, maybe they weren't. When Nicholas caught Dusk's roaming eyes with his own, he saw the same conclusion he had reached.

That's when what they had been waiting for, what they had been dreading, happened. A scream cut through the morning stillness like a knife, freezing them both in place. They both looked off to the west. Nicholas looked back to Dusk to see what they should do, but Dusk was already off. Snow kicked up in lofty pinwheels as he flew, sprinting toward the coast.

It's another attack. Maybe a werewolf or something worse.

The thought whispered through his mind and then he, too, was off. He had to thrash through the thick snow to keep up with Dusk's pace. The cold inches around them hindered their progress, but they fought through the added weight and distraction like the heroes they were.

A second scream crackled through the air. It wasn't a scream of pain, at least not yet. It was a scream of utter terror. Whoever was screaming was horrified beyond belief.

Dusk picked up the pace, batting branches aside, sending snow up in fans of ivory. Nicholas didn't think he could go any faster, but he tried. His feet lifted heavier and heavier every time more snow compacted into the treads of his shoes.

Nicholas saw a break in the trees ahead. They seemed to have come to the end of the forest, and if they didn't slow, they were going to end up in the lake. In contradiction to the danger enclosing, Dusk never slowed. The two of them broke through the edge of trees and skidded to a stop at a cliff's edge. Below, the cold air pushed the even colder water into swells of white foam. They were on the southern edge of the coast line. Here, a small land outcrop curved back in so when they looked out over water, they faced east into the rising sun.

What do we do now? Where are they?

He looked over the edge of the cliff in case someone had fallen off. He couldn't see anybody, but he didn't dare get too close.

"Dusk?"

The two whirled around. The sight was so surprising, Nicholas thought he was imagining it. Not until Dusk spoke did he realize it was real.

"Dear God," Dusk whispered.

In front of them was Clara, the vampire who had given them advice when the first bodies started showing up in The Hollow. Her arms were raised and tied together with a rough rope. The other end of the rope wrapped around a thick, low hanging branch. Her feet dangled off the ground, a hair's breath from supporting her weight. On top of all of that, she was naked.

Nicholas just blinked. He had never seen a live, naked woman before. Now, he stood ten feet away from a naked vampire. His stomach seemed to squeeze in on itself. His head began to whirl. He felt warmth, desire, and logic warring for control. It wasn't just biology fueling his emotions. Clara had her own type of influence. He had felt it when they had first met. It was just a calming then. Now, it was a million times stronger. With her fear putting it into overdrive, the power added in the feeling of emotional dependence and sexual desire. It made his mind fuzzy and created feelings that were false but so enjoyable.

The sun broke the horizon at that moment, sending a single line of light sailing across the surface. The orange glow kissed Clara's suspended toes. Sparks ignited, popping into existence from her very skin. The world was filled with the sound of eggs and bacon sizzling in a hot pan. This all would have been enough to break most people, but it wasn't everything. Clara began to scream again. Not in fear this time, but in pain. Pure, true, and shameless pain. Her neck muscles tensed, and her veins protruded like snakes slithering under her skin.

As she screamed, her mouth opened. Before, she had two fangs, the arrangement Nicholas had seen countless times in old films. Now, her mouth was that of a shark. Two rows of razors populated her mouth. Her skin turned from her ebony beauty to the grey of dead flesh as she transformed into an actual monster. Ears extended into points, face fell gaunt, eyes filled with blood, and yet she still hung there, hauntingly beautiful.

"Come on!" Dusk shouted as he sprang forward.

The shout startled Nicholas. He felt Clara's powers fall away as she lost control of everything in her pain. After a moment of shaking his head clear, Nicholas followed. They reached her in a few strides. Once they got close, Nicholas could smell a mixture of sulfur and burning wood. It didn't dawn on him until later that he wasn't smelling the tree burn, but Clara.

"Here," Dusk said, shrugging off his coat and thrusting it into Nicholas's hands. The coat was heavier than Nicholas expected, so it took him a moment to get a handle on it. He eventually did, but he didn't know what Dusk wanted him to do with it.

"For her, damn you. Cover her before she loses a foot."

After a startled jump, Nicholas understood the plan. He shook out the coat and held it up, blocking the sun from her the best he could. Meanwhile, Dusk was rummaging through the coat pockets. He found what he was looking for and removed it from the folds. In his haste, he jostled the coat enough to allow a bit of sun to touch Clara. It brushed the top of her foot and intensified her screaming.

Dusk ignored the screams and swung the tomahawk he had retrieved from his coat at the rope binding Clara. The first swing did very little. The rope's girth was much larger than most, so no matter how sharp the blade was it was going to be a task to break through. It laid there unaffected as Dusk swung again and again. A few swings in, Nicholas could spy snapping strands, causing the rope to fray. After another swing, Dusk had delivered enough damage for Clara's weight to become a factor. She lowered to the point where her toes touched the ground. They were too damaged to support her, however. The cracked skin curled in the snow, causing small tendrils of steam to rise.

The final strands of rope broke away, and Clara fell forward, free from her torture. She fell right into Dusk. He caught her, but awkwardly, still holding the tomahawk. Nicholas tried to keep the scene covered the best he could, but parts of Clara became glazed in sunlight, creating new burns, fresh pops, and even more sizzling.

"Give that to me," Dusk said, waving the hand with the tomahawk. "And take this thing, will ya?"

Nicholas handed over the coat and in return armed himself with the weapon, not sure of what was going to happen next. Nicholas stood as Dusk wrapped Clara in the shaded safety of his coat.

The struggle had become too much for Clara. Nicholas wasn't sure when it happened, but now that Dusk was supporting Clara, he could see she had fallen unconscious. She hung, heavy with dead weight, like a doll filled with cement. As if she was a child, Dusk put an arm behind her knees and scooped her up. Cradling her as such, Dusk took a moment to adjust his hold and then kicked up snow as he ran back toward The Hollow.

They ran through the woods. Nicholas didn't know how Dusk could know where he was going, but he had trusted him with his life on multiple occasions, so trusting him with directions was easy. It was as if Dusk was constantly being pulled toward Winter's Hall. From no matter where in the world, if you gave him enough time, Dusk would make it back without a single look at a map.

It's like he's super human.

This referenced the fact that he couldn't get lost and that his pace had not slowed. Whether he was running by himself or carrying an unconscious body, Dusk somehow reached speeds Nicholas would have thought nearly impossible in the heavy snow.

Is he even real? Nicholas thought again as he heaved and tried to keep up with Dusk.

As they ran, the sun began to fill the woods with light. The thick collection of trees blocked a lot of it, but the thick snow reflected its beams back up at them in a million different directions. Nicholas could see Dusk trying his hardest to keep Clara covered, but with the expedited wrap job and rough road, things were missed. The coat fell away in places, and the sun struck like a hungry snake. It dove, sinking its own brand of burning venom into blistering skin.

Suddenly, they were out of the woods. Their feet plowed through a final layer of thick snow and padded onto the compact frost of a road. Nicholas looked down the road trying to gauge how far they were from Winter's Hall or town or anything besides trees. He had but a moment and then the sound of a car skidding to a stop and a car horn broke his concentration. The car came to a Michigan winter stop a few yards from the three of them, sliding on the road with the grace of a practiced hand.

Nicholas's chest heaved from the exertion of the run. In his hand, he still held Dusk's tomahawk. Dusk stood holding a dying, naked girl whose body still smoked from the burns. Whoever was in the car could not be persuaded they didn't see what was right in front of them.

Well, this isn't gonna be good.

Sheriff Gordon sipped from his coffee cup. It was almost gone and what was left had gone from hot to lukewarm. It didn't bother him. A hot cup of coffee on a cold day was the best thing for a good wake up call, but he was already awake and had been for awhile now. He was waiting, like a hunter waiting for the deer to wander into range.

The back door to the station opened, and Sheriff Gordon heard someone stomp the excess snow from their shoes. Only one person showed up at this hour. Sheriff Gordon himself normally showed up about an hour later than it was right now. He arrived this morning at an unaccustomed hour to have a talk with someone. That very someone was making his way into the station as Sheriff Gordon took another sip of his coffee.

"Good morning, Steely," Sheriff Gordon said as the thin coroner rounded the corner into the main room of the station just outside the small bullpen of desks. Steely's head was down since he was not expecting anyone else to be here. Sheriff Gordon had made sure that Steely assumed that all the way in by parking his car in the front lot instead of the back where Steely parked his car. He had startled the coroner with his call, causing Steely to halt abruptly.

"Oh, Sheriff. You about gave me a heart attack. I must have missed your car in the lot." Steely pulled his hat off his head. The hat was a foolish thing, a size too large with flop down ears and heavy fur lining. "What are you doing here so early? Did we have another body come in?"

Sheriff Gordon was put off by the hope he heard in Steely's voice about the possibility of another dead body, but after a moment of consideration, he concluded the coroner had always been like that. Sheriff Gordon knew he didn't want people to be dead, but dead bodies were his life as strange as that sounded. They interested and excited him, which is what made him so good at his job.

"No, no. I just wanted to come in to get working on the bodies we already have. Have you got anything new to report on those?"

Steely removed his gloves one finger at a time. "Nothing that wasn't in the report. There wasn't much with those bodies. A lot on the surface level, you could see that for yourself, but for any more, they were clean. Figuratively speaking."

"I understand," Sheriff Gordon said as he took another drink of coffee, killing the cup. He placed the empty mug on a nearby desk and said, "They still pointing to boating accident?"

Steely exhaled, "Could have been a boat accident, yeah."

"But you don't think so?"

"Neither do you, Sheriff."

Sheriff Gordon put his hands on his hips. He looked hard at Steely and then softened. "Well, if you find anything that could help prove us both right, you be sure to let me know. No matter how small."

"Of course, Sheriff. As soon as the dead decide to speak, I'll be sure to pass on their message."

Steely smiled. Sheriff Gordon smiled back, with less gusto.

"I usually prefer my information to come from the living, but I'll take anything I can get right now."

"I'll take another look over everything, and if something jumps out, I'll be sure to holler."

"Good, good," Sheriff Gordon said and started to turn, a sign the conversation was over. Steely thought as much, for he continued to make his way to the cold, sterile walls of his office.

"Oh, Steely, before you go, I wanted to get your opinion on something."

Steely stopped and turned to the sheriff once again. He didn't say anything, just raised his eyebrows, waiting for Sheriff Gordon to speak.

"Mr. Dusk, the new guy that moved into Winter's Hall on the ridge."

Somehow, Steely seemed to turn whiter than usual. His clean sheet appearance dropped all the way down to ghostly.

"Wh-what about him?" he said, swallowing hard in the middle of the first word.

Wonder what's making him so nervous, Sheriff Gordon thought, not really wondering at all. He hid his coy smile from the coroner, almost challenging the man to question him.

"Nothing, just wanted your opinion on the man."

Steely licked his lips. "Not sure I really have one. Never m-met the man myself."

Why do they always lie?

"Is that so? I have. He's a hard man to read."

"I could see that."

Sheriff Gordon raised his eyebrow as if to ask how Steely could come to that conclusion without having met the man. Steely caught the look, and the meaning. He started to backtrack.

"Y-you know. A… A guy like that, buying a big ole house, alone, in the middle of the woods. Gotta have some sort of issues."

Sheriff Gordon thought it was funny, in an ironic sort of way, for Steely to question someone else's life choices while he was the guy who chose a life surrounded by dead bodies. What made the irony empty, however, was that the statement wasn't true. It was just a cover and a poor one at that.

"Yeah, but those rich types are always like that. I'm more interested in the man himself. You haven't heard anything?"

Steely was shaking his head even before the sheriff had finished asking. "Nope, sorry, Sheriff. Of course, I don't see many people. Well, live ones that is. I'm also not the gossip type."

Steely smiled at this joke. Sheriff Gordon did as well, just to keep the conversation cordial.

"Of course not. As sheriff, I don't have that luxury. You never know what bit of information could be the one that breaks the case or who that information will come from. People love their secrets. It's my job to get those secrets out, one way or another."

The accusation hung thick in the air. Sheriff Gordon let that happen on purpose. He wanted to make sure Steely got it.

He did, loud and clear.

"Yeah, well I better get downstairs and see if I can get something going for you."

Apparently, he needs a day or two to come around.

Sheriff Gordon nodded as he said, "Of course; don't let me keep you. And if you find anything or hear anything?"

"You'll be the first to know," Steely said with a quick smile.

Sheriff Gordon gave a smile of his own and thought, *Liar.*

After Steely retreated to the morgue, Sheriff Gordon moved back, leaning on the door frame to his office, and contemplated the engagement. He was sure his message had been received. Now, he had to see what Steely was going to do with it. The coroner hadn't dropped to his knees and confessed to knowing the man as soon as he was confronted with the sheriff's words. Sheriff Gordon hadn't thought he would. It was hard for Sheriff Gordon to figure out how long they had known each other, but it seemed like it would take more to break Steely than just a single shakedown.

Although he had seen Dusk and the Wake boy leaving the station at an hour when only the coroner had been present, he didn't think the coroner was an accomplice on anything illegal. He was too weak and would give in too easily to be up to anything too foul. Especially when he spent most of his days one floor below the entire Pointe's Hollow police force. Sheriff Gordon could read people, and he read Steely like a book. He was a strange, little man, obsessed with dead things but harmless.

Richard Dusk is the real danger here. Steely is just the first step to get to him.

The station's front door opened, shaking Sheriff Gordon from his inner investigation. He heard it open from where he stood in the door frame of his office. It was Donald's turn to pound his feet upon entry, this time on the well-worn rug by the front door, instead of the one by the back as Steely had done. He looked thinner than usual, and the pep that usually spiced his step was gone. Noticing the sheriff watching him, Donald gave a quick wave.

"Howdy, Sheriff, what brings you in so early?" His voice was low and clotted with phlegm. The sentence was accented by a sniff.

"Just wanted to get an early start. You feeling alright?"

Donald fell in the chair nestled behind his desk. "Oh, yeah, Sheriff. Just seems like my nose wants to run right off my face." He pulled a tissue from the box on his desk. "I did as you asked," mid-sentence, he stopped and blew his nose. "I kept an eye on Mr. Dusk last night."

Sheriff Gordon perked up on that, "And?"

"Well, he and Nicholas, Sherri Wake's nephew you know, met up late and walked off into the woods together."

"Into the woods? Where were they going?"

"Not sure. Don't think they were, either. I followed for about an hour, and they just seemed to be walking to walk. No real place to go."

Sheriff Gordon thought for a moment. "Something must have brought them out there at that hour. It was a cold one last night. Were they looking for something?"

"That's the best I could figure. They seemed to be kinda tense at first as if they knew I was following or something, but eventually they got wrapped up into whatever they were looking for. Unfortunately, I lost them before they found it, if they found it." Sniffle, sniffle. "Took me all night to find my way back. Wouldn't surprise me if they're still out there walking in circles."

Sheriff Gordon was wondering the same thing. Maybe he'd take a drive out to see what he could see.

Donald blew his nose again.

"How about you go home and get some rest, Donald. You look like hell."

Donald sniffed and wiped dripping snot from his nose. "Naw, I'll be alright. I'm a quick healer. Had perfect attendance in school. Ain't gonna start missing now."

Sheriff Gordon smiled, a true, honest smile. "Alright, well I'm gonna take a turn out there. How about I bring you back a coffee from Berk's?"

"I can make a pot here, Sheriff. I don't want to bother you."

"No, you deserve something better than that swill after last night. I'll get you some of the good stuff. Help you with that cold."

Donald smiled, sniffled, and then said, "That'd be great, Sheriff."

"Alright then," Sheriff Gordon said, collecting his keys and coat. "You rest up, now. You did good."

"Yeah?"

Sheriff Gordon patted his deputy on the shoulder as he walked by, "Oh, yeah. You take some time to recoup here. Keep an eye on the place, and I'll be right back." Sheriff Gordon could feel himself vibrate with anticipation. He was getting close; he could feel it.

As he put his hand on the door, Donald called out after him, "Hey, Sheriff?"

The sheriff didn't speak, just turned and looked at him in response. Donald was already leaning back in his chair, kicking a foot up on his desk. He blew his nose again, creating a noise that resembled a drowning elephant.

"Grab some extra sugar packets. I think I'm gonna need the extra energy."

Sheriff Gordon smiled once again.

"You got it, Deputy."

Sheriff Gordon let the door shut behind him. The cold air seemed to cut right through his big patrol jacket. Warm breaths came out in puffs, and he felt his skin prickle in gooseflesh. But he felt alive as well.

We will all need energy for what's about to come.

"Nicholas?"

The sound of his own name made him tighten even more. The movement reaffirmed that he was still clutching Dusk's tomahawk. Not the first time he'd been caught with it. *At least this time it was blood free.*

"Is that you?"

The driver of the car stepped out as he opened the door in a single movement. He stood, leaning on the roof of the car behind the open door.

"Will?" Nicholas said, surprised.

"Yeah," Will said, confused. He was looking between Nicholas and Dusk. "What's going on?"

"You know him?" Dusk asked out of the corner of his mouth.

"Will? Yeah, he's a friend of mine from school."

"Do you trust him?"

Nicholas hesitated for a moment. Will was a great friend, one of his best friends. But did Nicholas trust him with all of this?

"Yeah, I trust him."

"Good," Dusk said as he started walking toward the car. "Hey, Will, is it? We need a ride."

"I, uh, but, ah," Will mumbled as Dusk reached for the door handle to let himself into the back seat of the car. He had to juggle Clara's body, so it took some time, but eventually he got it. When he pulled, however, the door didn't release.

"Ah, kid, do you mind?"

Will looked to Nicholas. Nicholas just shrugged, and said, "Please?"

That was all Will needed to hear. Apparently, he trusted Nicholas as well. "Alright," Will said, unlocking the doors.

Once everyone was inside, Will threw the car in gear and began driving.

"What's that smell?" he said after a moment of being in the tight enclosure of the car.

"It's her; she's been on fire recently," Dusk said, with an even tone as if he had done this before. Not for the first time, Nicholas wondered if he had.

"What!" Will exclaimed. "We have to get her to a hospital!"

"No, to Winter's Hall."

"What?"

"Big house, on top of the hill."

"No, I know what it is. I meant, why are we going there?"

"Because if we don't, she dies."

"Whoa," Will said, turning to look at Dusk. "If someone's hurt, we need to get to the hospital."

"They can't help her."

"What? Why not?"

Dusk looked to Nicholas as if to ask him if he was sure about Will.

Nicholas answered by saying, "Because she's a vampire."

Chapter 10

Back and forth, Will paced, like an expecting father in a cartoon. All that was missing was the chugging cigar smoke and the ever-growing groove in the floor created by the repeated impact of his worried feet.

CRUNCH.

Nicholas turned to look at Dusk as he munched his way through a mouthful of barbeque chips. Dusk's head followed Will pacing across the room and then back again. He chuckled to himself and looked at Nicholas to join in. Nicholas gave him a look and turned back to Will.

"Will, are you alright?"

Will continued to pace, "Alright? Yeah, I'm alright. Just currently having my entire concept of reality blown to smithereens."

From left to right and then right to left, Will continued to pace. He was trying to chase down the answers to all of his questions right there in that room. Once he'd get close, the answers darted around him and went back the other way. Just as Nicholas thought he would have to stand up and physically stop him, Will stopped all on his own.

"So, this is real?"

Nicholas sighed, hesitated for a moment, and then said, "Yes, this is real."

"And it, or she," Will pointed upward as he spoke. The finger was in the general direction of the other room where Dusk and Nicholas had put Clara to rest and, hopefully, recover enough to tell them who had done that to her. "She is a vampire. Like a, like for real."

"Yes."

"And she was burned by sunlight?"

"Well, that is usually what happens to vampires," Dusk said, between mouthfuls of his salty snack. He tossed another handful in and followed up with, "You ever cook a hotdog for too long over a campfire? Just think of that, but instead of you having a crunchier lunch than expected, they burst into flames and agonizing pain."

Nicholas shot Dusk another look, and Dusk shrugged in return. Instead of looking back to Will, he became preoccupied with which chips would be in his next heap. This was when Nicholas finally stood up.

"Will, I know this is crazy, and at first it didn't make any sense to me either, but I swear I'm not lying to you. This is real. Clara is a vampire." Nicholas sighed again, "And that's not all."

Will swallowed hard. "You mean there's more vampires?"

"For starters," Dusk chimed in, low and nonchalant.

"There's more than just vampires, Will."

Nicholas let this sink in for a moment. Will didn't respond. He was looking at Nicholas, trying to see if the joke was going to end. Once he realized there was no joke and Nicholas was, in fact, telling him the truth, his eyes drifted a little bit. They all waited there for a minute, Will thinking, Nicholas worrying, and Dusk eating.

Finally, Will came back. "So, what are you two in all of this? I mean, Nicholas, you're not a vampire or a monster or something are you?"

Dusk snorted at this. This time Nicholas wasn't able to hold back his smile, either.

"No, I'm not a monster." The words sent a shiver down Nicholas's spine and made his smile run cold. He couldn't have said why, but he felt like he was lying.

Will sighed and grabbed his chest. "Oh, thank God. So, what then?"

"Well," Nicholas said, looking at Dusk. Dusk nodded as if to say, *We've come this far, go on.*

"We're more like monster hunters."

Will looked from Nicholas to Dusk and then back again. "Really?"

"Pretty much," Nicholas said through a sheepish smile.

There was a moment when Nicholas wasn't sure what was going to happen. Then, Will exploded, "This is so groovy!"

"Ah, what?" Nicholas said, awestruck at the response.

"This is awesome! Monster hunters, oh man, I don't believe it! How many monsters have you guys killed? How long has this been going on? Can I be a monster hunter? Is there like an initiation or something? I want to join."

"He's an excitable one, isn't he?" Dusk said, putting aside his chip bag.

"Will," Nicholas said, not sure how to explain. "It's more complicated than... what I mean to say is..."

"People die."

Dusk's words cut through the room. As he stood up from the couch, his light demeanor from before seemed to fall away as the hunter came forward. Will seemed to deflate a little.

"Yeah, we try to stop that as much as possible, but it still happens. No matter what we do. People die."

Dusk looked down on Will. Will, who usually would stand face to face with Dusk, shrank within himself. His face burned from embarrassment, and he crossed his arms.

"You could die."

Nicholas stepped forward, but Dusk put out a hand to stop him. "Are you willing to take that risk?"

Will raised his head a little, "I think so."

"You're going to have to do better than think if you wanna hunt monsters."

Will lowered his head again, took one breath in, and then raised his head even higher than before. "Yes, I can."

Nicholas felt something was off in Dusk's tone. Nicholas had been on the other side of his scolding before, and this wasn't how it usually felt. It could have been because Nicholas was on the outside of this one, but he didn't think so.

Dusk leaned in close, "Are you sure?"

Face tightening, fists clenching, Will said, "Yes."

Suddenly, Dusk snapped back up and clapped his hands together. "Perfect. Initiation is complete. You are now officially a monster hunter of The Hollow Guild. Please raise the first two fingers on your right hand, cover your heart with the left hand, and repeat the sacred oath."

Will shuffled his arms a little bit to follow the commands. Once in position, he waited for further commands.

Dusk burst out laughing. "Kid, we don't have an oath."

Will looked to Nicholas, confused. Nicholas sighed and shook his head. After a few seconds of confusion, Will's hands dropped to his sides, and he scowled, "Hardy har har, very funny."

Falling, Dusk regained his casual position on the couch, trying to calm his laughter.

Nicholas didn't laugh. Although funny, Dusk's joke had made real points, points that couldn't be ignored but needed to be considered. There were risks. How many times had Nicholas almost died a few months back? Could have been tens of times or hundreds.

Countless, Nicholas thought.

"Will," Nicholas said. Will looked at Nicholas. "Jokes aside, it can be dangerous."

Seeing if he was being put on again, Will looked at Nicholas for a moment and then to Dusk. Dusk rubbed his rough face and looked away.

Turning back to Nicholas, Will said, "I understand."

"Okay," Nicholas said, followed by a soft smile. Will returned the smile.

"So, what now?" Will said, rubbing his hands together. "Do we need to kill that thing?"

"No!" Nicholas said with a start. Will was pointing toward Clara's room again.

"Okay," Will said, turning his pointing hand into a flat gesture, every finger separated in a fan. He teetered it back and forth as he said, "Is she like a good vampire?"

"No such thing," Dusk said. "She and I have an arrangement."

"Okay, got it. No killing her, but why save her?"

Nicholas had been wondering this, too. Obviously, he didn't want anyone to die. But Clara was still a monster. Dusk already had said that if she stepped out of line, he would put her down, so why save her?

"She was in that position because of me," Dusk said, not looking at the two of them. Will looked to Nicholas for further explanation, but he only shrugged.

Turning back to the two of them, Dusk said, "She was hung up there because of us, Nicholas. She was a message."

Nicholas began to connect all the dots now. All the gears were set in motion, and things started to click into place. Will showing up like he did had thrown Nicholas off, but even then, he should have still seen it for what it was.

"A message?" Will said, in on some of the details but still naïve to the bigger picture. "A message from who?"

Dusk leaned forward, interlacing his fingers, "The man in shadows."

Snow blanketed all of the world. Ice crust covered the topmost layer, making it crunch underfoot instead of just give way. The morning light was so brilliant, it turned the winter into a land of diamonds. Small beams of light danced and played about the trees, making a wonderland of a bleak landscape.

CLICK.

Emily lowered her camera and took in the sight with her bare eyes. The sight was stunning. Looking through her camera, Emily was able to disconnect herself from being in the world. But without the camera in the way, she was immersed. Breathing in, she felt the cold air fill her lungs, and she felt alive.

That same breath came out in a warm cloud. A chill rolled in on the wind, and Emily raised her shoulders in defense. She had decided to come out this morning on a whim. A typical weekend would find her taking her morning slow. Having the house all to herself, she would spend a long time in pajamas, adopting a slower pace getting around than she usually put forth. After spending a sufficient amount of time lazing about, she would take some time doing house chores and doing any homework she hadn't finished throughout the week.

This morning, however, was nothing like a typical weekend morning. Emily's eyes shot open, and she almost jumped out of bed when she woke. There had been a dream, she was almost sure of it, but as soon as she had gotten her bearings, it was gone. Then, she heard the wind blow outside her window. As if the snow was whispering to her, she heard the outside beckon on that wind.

She answered.

First, she walked around downtown, waving to the other early birds and catching the smells from Berk's, trying to decide if she wanted a donut. Deciding she might grab one on the way back home, Emily continued on her way. She didn't know where she was going, but she was going to keep going until she found out.

She started snapping pictures here and there of things that caught her eye, but nothing particularly eye catching. She thought they would end up in a box in her closet, not being frame worthy. Then, she had found this place.

On the west side of town, she got on Genoa Road and was met with the wall of trees marking the beginning of the forest. Emily took a picture of the sight. Not a lot. She wasn't the type of photographer to snap a million pictures and figure out the best one to frame once they spit out of her camera. She took one, and that was the picture.

She had taken one of the forest in all its glory, and then she had taken in a breath. The picture spit out, and it looked good. Not as good as it did in real life, but it looked good. Sometimes, photographs could encapsulate the whole vision of the world and add to it. Sometimes, nothing could beat the real thing.

The frame of life she had decided to capture was a patch of trees perfectly silent in the thick, snowy morning. In the middle of the picture, digging through the trees, were two sets of footprints. They broke the perfection of the blanket that covered the ground, but they only added to the brilliance of the scene.

After a few moments of staring at the picture in hand, Emily caught something she hadn't noticed before. Deep in the woods, beside a tree almost obscured by the focal length of the lens, was a dark shape that seemed out of place. It appeared to hang in the air beside the tree. But the shape was almost human like. There was maybe a head and a shoulder. Possibly, it wasn't hanging there, but someone was leaning out from behind a tree. Someone, watching Emily.

WOOP, WOOP.

The short siren blasts made Emily jump so much that the picture almost slipped from her fingers to the cold ground. She kept hold, spinning to see what had startled her. Her dad's police jeep was crunching snow under tires as he slowly approached.

As he pulled up beside her, Emily wondered if she was going to be conversing with Sheriff Gordon or her dad. When he was in uniform, it could go either way. When he sat below the red and blue sirens, he mostly leaned one way. This time, however, Emily was relieved to hear her dad say, "Hello, Emily. What brings you out of bed so early this morning?"

"Hey, Dad. Just going for a walk. Taking pictures."

"You and that camera," he said, shaking his head with a chuckle.

Emily smiled in return, "What about you? What brings you out here so early?"

Her father shrugged as he scanned the surroundings. "Just having a look around. Never know what you might find if you look."

Emily nodded, but she had an itch in the back of her mind that there was something else that brought him out here. He wasn't the kind of guy who did things without reason. She had but a moment to try to figure out the truth of the matter, and then he was talking again.

"Plus, it helps the town keep calm, seeing the sheriff around. Dangerous times. It's important we keep everyone calm."

"Yeah," Emily agreed.

She had felt the town's unease for the past few days. Ever since the dead bodies were found on shore, everyone had been on edge. A few months ago, the town had been struck hard by what Mr. Fidel had done. It was known by everyone that Mr. Fidel had gone on a murderous rampage killing residents and who knows how many missing travelers. There were many rumors about that time, but this was considered fact. A fact Emily had a hard time swallowing. She could believe Mr. Fidel had done what they said. She had been a sheriff's daughter long enough to know evil was everywhere, especially in the most unlikely of places. There was just a feeling there was more to the story.

"By the way," her father was saying, looking around conspiratorially, "you see anything suspicious out here this morning, miss?" He smiled.

Emily laughed, "No, officer. Everything is right as rain," she thought for a moment, "or I guess as snow."

Her father's smile grew even larger. "Good, good. That's what I like to hear." He looked out through the windshield again. If Emily had been looking, she would have seen the change, but she wasn't. Everything was going so pleasantly, she didn't expect it.

"What about the Wake boy? You see him this morning?" Sheriff Gordon said.

Emily's smile faltered. He had been doing this more and more. When she had told him she was dating Nicholas, she thought his heart was going to give out right then and there. That had been a long night and a very unpleasant conversation. In the end, Emily had won. She usually did, but it didn't make the battles any easier.

"No, I haven't, Dad, and I've told you before that I won't be your spy around town. I have my life to live."

Sheriff Gordon turned back to her. "I know, I know." He took a moment. Emily thought he might be realizing he overstepped and an apology was on the rise. She was mistaken.

"Just be careful around him, Emily. He's dangerous."

A flush ran across her chest, up her neck, and into her cheeks. The redness was fueled by the anger of hearing this same warning over and over again.

Nicholas? Dangerous?

There was just no way. She had gotten to know him even better over the past few months. They had talked, they had kissed, and they had laid next to each other, falling asleep watching some of his black and white horror movies. On one heated night, there had even been exploratory touching both had found quite pleasant.

No matter what her father said, Nicholas was the furthest thing from dangerous she could think of. Especially given the other options at Pointe's Hollow High. Most fathers would be overjoyed with their daughter picking a boy like Nicholas to date. He didn't wear leather. He didn't drive a motorcycle; he didn't drive at all. He had no piercings or tattoos. His biggest scare was his strange obsession with horror movies, which Emily admired.

But her father believed he was dangerous. After months of hearing this, Emily had grown annoyed. Every time her father brought it up now, it pushed her to immediate anger.

"Dad," her tone poisoned with ferocity.

Sheriff Gordon held firm, looking at her through his big sunglasses.

"Just promise me you'll be careful."

Emily rolled her eyes. No matter how many times she promised, it did nothing to calm him. "I promise, Dad. But you have nothing to worry about. Nicholas is a good guy, like I've told you a thousand times."

Sheriff Gordon nodded, but he was looking off again. It was as if he could see something she couldn't.

More like knows something I don't.

She had thought this before. The strange thing was it wasn't just with her father she thought this, but with Nicholas as well.

Maybe there is something going on here.

"Well," her father's voice said, breaking her thought process. "You make sure to get back home soon. Don't want you walking outside of downtown alone. Get your pictures, then get inside and warm up, alright? I don't want you catching a cold."

As if it reminded her she was outside, Emily shivered at that. "Yeah, I'll be heading back soon."

"Okay, I'll see you at home later."

"Bye, Dad."

He gave a small two-finger salute and drove away from her. She watched him go, wondering what he and Nicholas knew. She wasn't a stupid girl, but somehow, she was missing something, and she had a feeling she had been missing it for quite awhile.

She tucked the picture she still held into a pocket of her coat among a collection of others. Her father's conversation and the following thoughts had distracted her. She completely forgot about the dark shape in the picture and once again missed something that was right in front of her.

"Okay, let's go through this again," Will said, rubbing the back of his neck. He had stopped his pacing, but he still stood while Nicholas and Dusk sat on the couch.

They had been talking for hours. They had checked on Clara earlier, but she was still out cold. Getting what they wanted out of her would have to wait. The three had returned to the living room and continued their conversation. This had turned into Will asking questions while Nicholas and Dusk took turns trying to answer.

"So, all these monsters are from another world," Will asked for the third or fourth time. Nicholas had lost count in the repetitive nature of the conversation.

"Yup," Dusk said.

"But we don't know where or how they get through?"

"Yes," Nicholas said, taking his turn to answer.

"And there's this so-called man in shadows who's behind it all."

"So, we believe," Dusk said as Nicholas followed with, "Yes, he is."

"But again, we don't know who he is, where he came from, or if he's even a he?"

"Well, he's gotta be a man." Nicholas said. "Why would he have 'man' in his title if he was actually a she?"

"Subterfuge?"

"Identity crisis?"

Nicholas shook his head at the two of them. Somehow, he had become the voice of reason within the group. To his right was a seasoned monster hunter, scarred physically and emotionally by life, and still Nicholas was the most mature one.

"Either way," Will said, trying to pull them back on track. "That's all you guys know?"

Nicholas looked over to Dusk. Dusk just shrugged.

"Yeah, when you put it that way, it doesn't sound so good."

"Yeah, well, it could be better," Will agreed. "How long have you guys been going at this?"

"Only a few months," Nicholas said. He said it quickly as if he had to apologize for his ignorance.

They both looked at Dusk as he shrugged again.

"Let's just say, up to a few months ago, I wasn't very motivated."

"Okay, but now you are?"

Dusk looked to Will. Once again, he shrugged and then smiled.

"That's the closest you're going to get to a yes from him," Nicholas said, giving a shrug of his own in apology.

"Alright," Will said, clapping his hands together. "So, I think the first order of business should be research."

"Research?"

"Yeah. That's how all the cop shows work."

"Cop shows?" Dusk said, derision clinging to the words like an accent.

"Oh, yeah, like Steve McGarrett on Hawaii Five-O. He and his partner always get the case in the beginning of the episode, then they do their research. They put the screws to some low life, ask the hard questions. Then, by the end of the episode," Will's voice took on a new tone, and Nicholas was left to assume he was doing his best impression of the Steve McGarrett character. "Book 'em Danno."

Dusk turned to Nicholas with a look that simply asked, *Is this guy serious?* Nicholas thought he was but still had no idea what he was talking about. Filling his TV time with monster movies, Nicholas had never watched a 'cop show'.

Will finally concluded that neither of them had any idea what he was getting at, so he made another point. "There's gotta be someone or something somewhere that knows about all of this."

"That's a no go," Dusk said. "The only other person who knew more than us in this town is, unfortunately, no longer with us."

Nicholas's mood fell somber as he thought of Father Christopher. Dusk's lost mentor, whose death Nicholas still felt responsible for. He was sure Dusk shared the feeling.

Thinking about the fallen priest made Nicholas think about the new priest in town.

Father Adrian could know something.

"Books!" Will almost shouted the word. "There has gotta be something written about all this somewhere."

It was so obvious, Nicholas slapped himself in the forehead. He had spent so much time in the library it was infuriating he hadn't come to this conclusion on his own. For God's sake, he had almost died there fighting a shadow.

On top of all that, Mr. Lloyd was actually someone they could ask for help. He was one of the few people in town who knew what was going on. He had actually been aware of everything before Nicholas. Maybe he had even done research of his own. They had stored up enough bad luck they were due for some good. Maybe this was it.

"We could go to the library," Nicholas finally said. "They're sure to have something there."

Dusk laughed. Both Nicholas and Will thought he was going to shut down their plan. The hurt expression must have been clear on their faces, because Dusk took one look at them both and laughed again.

"What? You think it's a waste of time?" Nicholas said, a bit of venom in his words.

"Not at all," Dusk said between fits of mirth. "It's just… ."

"Just what," Nicholas said, cutting him off.

Dusk's laughing slowed, and he made a show of wiping a tear from one of his eyes.

"It's just," he continued again, "leave it to you to find a way to work being in the library into monster hunting."

Chapter 11

Mentally cursing, Nicholas stirred in bed. He had never and would never understand how you could wake up more tired than you were when you went to bed. Staying out late with Dusk, fighting monsters, had made Nicholas familiar with the feeling of getting home and just falling into bed. The act of being asleep before his head hit the pillow was not foreign to him.

Recently, however, he had awoken unrefreshed. He would sleep nine or even ten hours and somehow be as tired as if he hadn't slept all night. The phenomenon was infuriating. No matter how hard he tried, he couldn't seem to get a good night's sleep.

His alarm on the bedside table buzzed again, rattling a spoon in a bowl he had never taken back downstairs after finishing the cereal inside. Nicholas grunted in anger. He lifted his body and crawled like a slug to reach the clock before it could sound again.

After talking with Will and Dusk yesterday, they had decided they should get up early and get started at the library.

Well, Will and Nicholas would get up early and start at the library. Dusk would wait at home until, as he put it, "They needed him to shoot something." Reading was not in his repertoire of skills.

Nicholas had set his alarm, and now he clicked it off, regretting he even owned the damned thing. Nicholas thought about rolling over and forgetting about the whole arrangement. Getting a few more hours of sleep sounded pleasant and like something he desperately needed. But he knew he couldn't.

Nicholas sat up in bed and rubbed his face, trying to cast off the web of slumber that clung to his skin. He needed to have his wits about him today if they were to find what they were looking for.

To notice what we're looking for when we find it more like it, Nicholas thought.

Even though Will and he both agreed the library would be a good place to start looking for answers, they were unsure of exactly in what form the answers would come or if they would recognize them if they found anything. So, to be ready, Nicholas needed to be quick as a whip as Mr. Lloyd sometimes told him he was. Right now, he felt as quick as solidifying concrete.

His rubbing was supported with a wide yawn. The effort of waking up while still in bed had become too much, so Nicholas twisted out of bed, resorting to the idea that a shower might be the best thing for him.

His feet reached the ground, and he pushed downward as he stood. Body in complete defiance, Nicholas made his way to gather some clothes for the shower. So tired, he didn't even notice the piece of paper forgotten on the ground, marked with a 'P'.

When Nicholas arrived at the library, he realized he had gotten there just as the doors unlocked. After he pushed through, he found Mr. Lloyd taking off his coat and wool cap.

"Good morning," he said, waving at the old librarian.

"Ah, Nicholas. Decided to get an early start as well?"

Nicholas gave a half yawn at that, and said, "Yeah. Just waiting for a friend, and then we'll get to work."

"Oh, well…," Mr. Lloyd started, but he was cut off by another voice.

"Nicholas! You're here. Perfect."

Will walked up to stand behind him. He put an arm on Nicholas's shoulder in a friendly slap. Apparently, he had gotten much better sleep than Nicholas.

"Yeah, and so are you."

"Yeah, your friend here beat even me here this morning," Mr. Lloyd said. "A tough task to do."

"Just excited to get started," Will said, smacking his hands together.

"I see, you two have a school project coming up?"

Nicholas shook his head, "No. We've come to try to learn about the town. We want to know everything we can about The Hollow, so, hopefully, we can figure out how to beat the man in shadows."

Mr. Lloyd froze for a moment as his eyes shifted toward Will, wary. Nicholas nodded as if to say go on, and then said, "He knows about everything. It's okay."

"Ah, I see," Mr. Lloyd said, but instead of being relieved, he sounded even more concerned.

"Yup," Will interjected. "I found out everything last night, after saving a vampire." He sounded so proud as if he had saved her all by himself.

"Saving a vampire?" Mr. Lloyd said, befuddled. "I'm not entirely sure, but don't you usually do the opposite of that, Nicholas?"

Nicholas started to speak, but Will jumped in again. Maybe Nicholas was slow with sleep, or Will was more excited than he realized.

"Yeah, usually, but ah, she was a good vampire."

"A good vampire? My, this is getting interesting."

Mr. Lloyd smiled, a small twinkle nestled in the corner of his eye behind his glasses. Will looked to Nicholas to explain further, but Nicholas had nothing left to say on Clara. When Dusk said she was to be saved, he didn't question it. But away from Dusk, he did wonder. A question that would be better not to discuss here.

"We need everything you have on Pointe's Hollow. We need to get reading and figure out what the man in shadows is all about."

Mr. Lloyd nodded, "So, you're finally tired of going at this blind, huh? Decided to do some research instead of going out half-cocked like a common acquaintance of ours prefers."

Nicholas smiled, a little embarrassed. As of late, he and Dusk had heard the warnings of danger and run in headlong.

Mr. Lloyd saw the embarrassment and just moved on. "Well, you're in luck. We have much on our small town here."

"Really?" Will said. "How much is much?"

Mr. Lloyd smiled, and the spark in his eye shone bright and knowing.

Black letters swam before Nicholas's eyes. Some came into focus, sharp and unyielding. Others flew by in a blur with fuzzy edges and a murky consistency. If someone had told him to account for everything he had read in the past hours, Nicholas would have considered it a success if he could recount around thirty percent. That's how the day was going.

The book he had been holding in front of his face fell to the wood table unceremoniously as he reached up to his eyes. Fingers slid under glasses and pressed on tired eyes. Lids rolled under the solid yet cautious pressure of his fingertips. He felt a yawn, and he let it roll long and loud. It was strange how different it felt to be sitting here reading books about the town opposed to reading the fictional stories he had spent most of his life reading.

Looking over the piles of books that had accumulated, Nicholas saw Will. Surprising to Nicholas, Will had thrived on their research venture. It had been Will's idea to come to the library to research, but it still took Nicholas by surprise to see his friend fall into this role so naturally. He had two books opened on the table in front of him. One was perched up by three larger volumes, so he could reference it at a glance, while the second was open to a map of The Hollow from two hundred years ago. When he had first found the map, Nicholas and Will had looked at it hoping they would get lucky and spot something. That had been three hours ago.

Along with those, Will still held another book in his hands. He was reading, completely unaware Nicholas was looking at him and maybe not even aware he was still in the library. Every so often, Will would slowly raise an arm and reach across the sea of history written out in front of him, pick a chip from the open bag between them, and deposit it in his mouth with precision. The chip would crunch and crumble with every methodical stroke of his jaw.

When this is more entertaining than reading, you know you're in trouble, Nicholas thought, looking down at the books in front of him. He was trying to decide which would be the next book he would try when Will leaned forward with a loud sigh.

"Wow," Will said with a smile. "This is a crazy town. Lots of crazy things happen around here."

Nicholas jumped at the opportunity for conversation, so he wouldn't have to go back into the books. "Yeah? I mean, it's always just been The Hollow to me. A small town in the middle of nowhere, I'm sure there are a ton of towns like this, with crazy stuff happening, in Michigan alone, let alone the rest of the country."

"Oh, yeah, I'm sure." Will closed the book he was reading, placed it on a pile, and continued, "But the list for this place ranges all up and down the crazy spectrum. And apparently deaths or missing people, not just a recent thing, my man. Everything you read about has got an undertone of death. It's like all the bad luck in the world ends up here."

"Cheery," Nicholas said with a half-smile.

"My bad. I don't mean to put it down. This is my home now, too. It's just fascinating."

Wish I thought it was as fascinating as you do.

"Yeah, totally. So, you find anything to help us find the Other or who the man in shadows is?"

Will started and then stopped short, "Ah, well, no. Not exactly. But anything we can learn about the town has got to be helpful, right?"

"Hopefully," Nicholas said.

He looked back down to the books in front of him. He was riding on the hope that Will's unrelenting devouring of the material would have found something, because he was coming up blank. Well, not completely blank, but what he found didn't make him more confident in their chances.

For the first little while at the library, Nicholas would jump between books at a rapid pace. Between shipping notes, fishing history, and nature wildlife stories, Nicholas felt he could have filled an entire room with useless pages.

Useless to us, anyway.

After an hour, he had come across a book that held his interest for a little while. It went into a brief history of multiple Native American tribes that called Michigan home. Chippewa, Potawatomi, and Ottawa Indians were the names that first jumped to Nicholas's head. He had never been one for Native American history. He could remember doing a report in the third grade, but that was the extent of his knowledge in that area of his homeland's history. Every student was given a tribe and one or two books about the tribe to use to deliver a report. Thinking back on it now, Nicholas couldn't even be sure which tribe he had been given.

As he got into the book, small things came back to him, but overall, he was venturing into a world in which he had no personal investment. It was enthralling to read about all the tribes, how treaties were settled slowly, and sometimes not so slowly, between them and the Europeans, moving into their territories and their way of life. He was content with reading about anything and everything the book wanted to share with him. But then it took a turn that grabbed him.

The book had a few sections dedicated to talking about multiple tribes describing a dark area of Michigan. The book didn't go into specifics about whether all the tribes were talking about the same area, but on every page, it described this area as being in the north and on the coastline of Lake Michigan. Most people wouldn't have noticed the similarities. It was one of those illusions that if you weren't looking for it, you wouldn't see it. But Nicholas was looking for it.

The dark area was a spot of land that would not, or in some cases, could not be settled. It was prime land, with access to fresh water and food resources, and many tried to call it home. Most would fall on hard times. Fishing nets would come in empty. Crops would die or be eaten by wildlife. Or in the worst cases, disease would ravage entire villages. In a few cases, some settlements just disappeared. It called to mind the stories of the Roanoke Colony Nicholas had learned about in school. These weren't big enough cases to be taught in classes, but the story was the same. One day there would be families building their lives with all the hope in the world, and then the next day, everything would be gone. As if they had never been.

After years of these occurrences, it seemed everyone had learned to avoid this dark area. It laid dormant, waiting for the next chance to cause devastation to people who didn't know what they were walking into.

As treaties were signed and land passed hands, that next chance came. Nicholas had to assume what happened from there, because the book didn't get into it, but it was easy to fill in the holes. Eventually, people did resettle here. Shipping lanes were charted, businesses were built, families were cultivated, and now Pointe's Hollow sat upon the once-dark area. The area a few knew as a thin spot between worlds.

As if he needed any further proof of his hypothesis, Mr. Lloyd walked past and with a single peek over his shoulder, said, "That one was actually written by a Pointe's Hollow native. Back in the twenties, I believe. Before my time, I'm afraid, but I have read that name in records, and after a bit of research, I confirmed that man was definitely a Hollower. Hollowian?" Mr. Lloyd rubbed his chin for a moment, "Well, he was from here, however you want to call it."

That was the final nail in the coffin. It didn't help them directly in what they should do next, where the Other was, or who the man in shadows was, but it showed this wasn't a new thing. This place had been evil for a long time, far longer than Nicholas had first realized. It seemed, to him at least, the evil here predated people here. It had always been here, maybe always would be. The man in shadows may not be the end all or be all of evil, but just a pillar holding up the actual evil in the Other, which spilled into this town.

If this was true, Nicholas still saw the man in shadows as his evil. A pillar may just stand as one part, but it is designed to hold up the whole structure. If he, Will, and Dusk knocked that pillar down, the rest could fall.

That's the hope.

Nicholas let out a long breath. Looking over the plethora of books in front of him made him feel tired all over again. He contemplated picking up the book covering Native American culture again but thought it would be a waste of time. No matter how interesting it was, he had pulled everything he could out of there.

He picked up a different book. Choosing a smaller one, hoping the task would seem less daunting holding a thinner book. Fate, however, had a sense of humor and decided to make Nicholas the butt of the joke. Once the book was in hand, he was greeted with some of the smallest print he had ever seen. The pages were jammed from margin to margin with the rough-edged type. Paragraphs spanned a whole page at times, and to top it all off, the whole thing seemed to be broken down by years instead of topics, which meant he would have to go through the whole thing with a keen eye to make sure he didn't miss something.

Sighing, he flipped through the pages, loosening the book up. Then, he dropped the back half, opening to the first page. Nicholas dug in. It took only five minutes for him to feel his head begin to droop with sleep.

This is gonna be a long day, Nicholas thought.

Dean Morgan cursed himself under his breath. "You stupid, son of a bitch."

He had closed the store yesterday and had to get up early to be there to open today. It was a task he normally didn't mind doing. The store closed at seven during the week, so he was home no later than eight, which gave him more than enough time to get rested for the next day.

He had greeted Curtis, the very round store manager, with a friendly hello. Curtis was thirty years older than Dean, white hairs freckling his goatee, but somehow, they had become admirable friends. They never got together outside of work, but they were able to pass the day chatting with relative ease. They somehow always seemed to fall on topics in which they shared common opinions and found out they shared similar interests. Dean was a good worker and Curtis, a fair boss. This allowed both of them to have easy days together, something everyone wanted at work.

None of this was why he cursed himself now as he stood in the doorway to the warehouse of the store. Dean had come back here prepared to start counts for the cleaning equipment order when he saw the two large trash bags leaning up against the wall. They were full of cleaning rags, expired food, and other odds and ends. This he knew without a second glance, because he had filled them himself. In his rush to get home last night, it appeared he had forgotten to take them out.

Usually, it wouldn't have been that big of a deal. He'd just take them out, toss, and then get on with work. This morning, however, was different. There was snow out on the ground, and the air coming in from the lake could freeze a man down to his boots, the exact things Dean had just switched out for his work shoes. Now, he would have to get all bundled up again to go outside and take the trash out and then unbundle himself again to do the counts. An annoying waste of time he dreaded. Again, he cursed himself and his neglect as he went to put his boots back on.

The wind pushed back against the glass door of the store as Dean shuffled himself and the two bags of trash out. The back door would be more appropriate for trash disposal during business hours but being early in the morning, Dean decided on the front door. There was a small alley next to the store where the wind would be less harsh in comparison to the open space of the back lot. Plus, this protective path cut the length of the walk between the store and dumpster by half.

After a few steps, Dean turned into the small alley, and the cold fell away in an instant, and his extremities began to feel warmer. He shook himself, trying to dispel the final bit of cold from his skin. The bags whined as they rubbed against each other and the walls of the surrounding buildings. As he moved toward the back of the store, he noticed a shape, low and near the end of the alley.

Confused but unconcerned, he kept going. It appeared someone else had been using his alley to dispose of trash.

However, this someone didn't make it all the way before depositing their piles of trash. For a third time this morning, Dean cursed under his breath, but for the first time, it wasn't directed at him.

Lazy assholes.

As he approached, Dean prepared to add this load onto his own. The time came to collect, and that's when he noticed it wasn't trash after all. It was a man.

"Whoa, hey man, you alright?"

The man stayed quiet. He sat on the ground crunched into a ball. Dean had seen some sailors crashing out on the docks after a night of drinking but never in his alley and never when it was this cold. It occurred to Dean that if this guy had been out here all night, he could be hypothermic, if not already dead.

"Seriously man, you okay? You're kind of freaking me out."

The man remained quiet.

Dean put the trash bags down to the side. Crouching, he reached out with one hand. "Come on, man."

Dean grabbed the man's shoulder and shook him. The body swayed with the motion, but there was no resistance. Dean, beginning to fear the worst, shook harder.

The motion became too much for the body, and it seemed to peel itself free from the wall. It rolled forward, causing the man to fall face first into the dark slush of the alley.

"Ah, shit," Dean said. He had accepted the man was dead, but he wasn't going to leave him face down in an alley.

He grabbed the man's side, had to call him a man, not just a body, or he'd be too freaked to touch him, and pulled him over. The movement made Dean slide in the slush, but the man rolled to face upward all the same.

Dean gasped as soon as he got a look at the body. For now, there was no fighting the notion this was just a body. Rivulets of blood, long frozen from the cold night, stained his cheeks and mouth. The maroon lines traced from his eyes and nostrils down over his chin, disappearing below his shirt collar. The mouth hung open as if it was still trying to scream for help. Hands frozen from cold or rigor mortis sat raised on either side of the body. All in all, the body still looked like it was fighting what had happened to it; a fight that it had lost due to the evidence of a large puncture encapsulating half of the man's chest.

Dean stood, frozen in his own right. It was the most morbid thing the man had ever seen, and yet he couldn't look away. Suddenly, movement caught his eye. It looked as if the body was breathing. Soft heaves lifted and lowered a small section of the chest, and Dean's breath caught. For a moment, it seemed the person who was actually alive in the ally wasn't breathing, and the dead one was.

Running through what he could do to help a man that should be dead, but somehow was still breathing, Dean came up with nothing more than running out of the alley yelling for a doctor.

It didn't matter that he couldn't do anything to help. It didn't matter that there would be no one to hear his ridiculous cry, because, as it turned out, the man was not breathing. The man was, in fact, dead as dead could be. The soft movement coming from the body turned out to be a rat. A rat who had dug into the body to save itself from the frigid night. A rat who now popped its head free of the innards of the body to breath the day's air through the large cavity that had turned the man into just a body.

That's when Dean felt his stomach lurch, and he turned to release a stream of vomit all over the wall beside him. Once his stomach had rejected everything it felt like it could no longer possess, he stumbled in the slush back toward the front of the building.

As he burst back into the store, he called for Curtis to call the police. Curtis poked his head out of the small office, asking if he had heard the boy right, and once again, Dean told him to call the police.

"There's a dead body in the alley, and it's got rats in it," Dean said, wiping the spittle and vomit from his lips.

After a few more minutes of conversation, Curtis called the police, and they both went outside to see the body. Curtis was curious, but Dean was worried he wouldn't be able to hold down whatever was left in his stomach. When they returned to the body, it laid exactly as Dean had left it: back down, soaking in the wet slush of the alley, a steaming streak of vomit on the wall beside it. The rat, however, was gone.

Chapter 12

After a few more hours of reading about aspects of a small town that most would find boring, Will and Nicholas called it a day. Nicholas found it hard to remember which parts he had and hadn't read whenever he took a moment to look up at the clock, which he did more and more frequently as the day went on. Even Will, who had thrived at the research, found the day tiring and conceded that a break might do them both some good.

The only downside to the whole ordeal was they had agreed to check in with Dusk after their reading. They were going to have to go to Winter's Hall empty-handed.

"You don't think he'll be upset, do you?"

"I'm sure he won't be surprised."

"Good. I just feel like he's the kind of guy you don't want to make mad."

"You have that right. He's only been mad at me one time, and I ended up with a tomahawk against my neck."

Will gave an audible gulp, which made Nicholas laugh.

The two rode in Will's grandparents' car and got to Winter's Hall faster than Nicholas did when he rode his bike. Adding Will to the team was already working out for the better.

Once inside, they had the usual back and forth with Argyle, said their hellos with Dusk, and explained what they had found.

"So, in conclusion, you guys found nothing?"

"Well," Will began. "Not nothing, just not exactly what we needed... per se... ." He looked to Nicholas for help.

Nicholas, who had been with Dusk long enough, told it the way Dusk would see it, "Yeah, we got nothing."

Dusk nodded. They all took a moment of silence for that to sink in. It wasn't a long moment, however. Will seemed determined to make the best out of this. Somehow, he had become in charge of the moral of the group, and he was working in earnest to keep it high.

"Look, yeah, maybe we found nothing today. But I did learn some things that I think will help me understand the thing we need to know when we find the thing we need to know... . Whenever we find out what the thing we need to know, ah, is."

Dusk took a moment to run through that and make sure it checked out. "Okay," he finally said, half invested.

"And there are still a ton of books in that library we haven't even touched yet. Right, Nicholas?"

The thought of sitting and reading all the books in that library like the ones he had today made Nicholas's head hurt. No matter how it made him feel, however, he couldn't argue with Will's statement, so he said, "He's right, Dusk. The answer to all of this could still be in there."

"Yeah, it could!" Will said, more enthusiastically than he needed to.

Dusk again took a moment. He seemed to be processing everything they had told him. When Nicholas had mentioned the book about the Native Americans and their dark land, he had nodded as if that made perfect sense to him. It made Nicholas wonder how much of what they had said Dusk already knew.

"Well, you guys keep at that, but in the meantime, I'm gonna try to get some answers from our eyewitness."

"Clara woke up?" Nicholas asked.

"Yup, about an hour ago. She's still pretty skittish, but I need to try to get what I can out of her. Make sure whatever this is isn't worse than we think it is."

"Can there be a worse?" Will asked.

"In my experience, anytime someone asks that that is exactly what we get."

The door creaked open as the three of them entered. The room was so dark that Nicholas had to fight the urge to put his arms out in front of him to make sure he didn't hit something. Dusk moved smoothly in the darkness, but for the kids' sake, struck a match and lit the wick of a small candle that sat on the bedside table.

The room was bright for a moment, and then there was a warm, orange light illuminating everything. It made the room feel small. Darkness left the room endless, but the flickering light from the safe part of the room made the space feel confined to the dimensions of a closet.

Or a coffin.

On the bed, Clara laid under a thick layer of blankets. Ragged breaths wheezed out of her mouth as her chest rose and fell in an uneven rhythm. Nicholas, for the first time, didn't see Clara as a vampire, but as something that once was human. A once-was human that seemed to be dying in front of them.

"Are you sure she's going to be alright? She doesn't look good," Will said, looking to Dusk.

"It won't be like a spa vacation, but after a few days here, she should be good as new."

"How do you know?"

Dusk took a moment, and then said, "This isn't the first time she's been here."

It took Nicholas by surprise. He wanted to press Dusk with more questions, but the way he had said that made Nicholas feel like the discussion would go no further.

Dusk moved closer to the bed. As he neared, Clara stirred under the heavy covers.

"Dusk," she whispered. Her usual velvet tone was muted and frail.

"Yeah, it's me, Clara."

"And the boy?" she said, her nostril giving the slightest twitch. "And another."

"Yeah, the kid's here, and he brought a friend. We used his car to get you back here."

Clara seemed to think about this for a moment, but when she talked, it became evident she was thinking about something else.

"The new one smells delicious."

Nicholas heard Will gulp. He imagined Will's heart beginning to pump faster, the blood in his veins flowing at top speed. Then, he again thought about a Saturday cartoon where a character would put a fan by a freshly baked pie and the scent would flow toward another, enticing them with its rich odor. He could almost see the vapor lines floating toward Clara.

Dusk reached down to his left and pulled a small cooler from under the bed. With a soft pop, he lifted the lid and pulled out a rectangular bag. For a moment, Nicholas couldn't place it. Then, he realized what it was: blood.

The small bag shifted shape in Dusk's hand as he handled it. He pulled a knife from his pocket or belt, in the darkness Nicholas couldn't be sure, and cut into the bag. As the blade pierced the thin material, Clara's chest rose. She inhaled, and her mouth opened wider in response, but she lay still. Nicholas wondered what she looked like under the covers but then decided he didn't want to know.

The red liquid oozed from the bag as Dusk squeezed the blood into Clara's mouth. It looked like Dusk was topping off a burger with the small packets of ketchup at fast food joints. That thought also made it easier to watch Clara lick and swallow huge gobs of the stuff as if it was air flowing into a drowning man's lungs. Thinking someone would just drink ketchup did make his stomach flop a little, but it was better than seeing it for what it truly was.

Once the packet had been drained, Dusk dropped it in the cooler, tossed the top closed, and kicked it back under the bed. Clara spent another minute or so licking at the small drips that fell on her lips and cheeks as she ate. Then, she settled back into her previous position, lying still as the grave. Her breath had grown softer, however, and her chest didn't heave so much.

"Clara," Dusk said, making sure she didn't just go back to sleep.

"Yes, Dusk?" a small hint of her velvet tone returning to her voice.

"I need to ask about what happened to you."

Her brow furrowed, but she didn't say no.

"Do you know who or what attacked you?"

Clara remained quiet for a long moment. Nicholas looked over at Will, who just shrugged. Dusk was running the show; they were here to watch. As Dusk seemed to prepare to ask again, Clara finally spoke up.

"Yes. A vampire."

"A vampire?" Dusk said, not bothering to hide the surprise in his tone. "Like you?"

"No," Clara said. She swallowed, and then continued, "Not like me. This one has gone mad. Blood-starved for too long. He's wild, deranged."

Her voice was weak, but her words flowed through the dark room like melody. As if she was singing a slow song that only they should hear.

Pitch

"You mean like a rabid dog?" Will said, making Dusk and Nicholas turn to look at him. "My Papa, Howard, said he had had a dog when he was younger. It got bit by something when it was out and about. After a few days, it came down with rabies. Had to be put down in the end. Said the dog acted crazy as if it was a wild animal."

"Yes," Clara said. "It is as the tasty friend says."

Will seemed to shrink back again. Nicholas thought he'd be less likely to jump into the conversation again.

Dusk took control again, "And this thing is what tied you to the tree?"

Clara's chest sped up just a little at the memory. "No, not him. It was the shadow."

The flame on the small candle flickered. It waved from side to side as if a breeze had picked up in the room, but there was none. It had grown warm in the small room, almost stale with stillness. Nicholas could feel the sweat begin to pop up on his brow, and the rusty smell of blood was still in the air. The candle acted like the very weight of her words shifted the air in the room.

"The shadow?" Dusk asked, confirming what he heard.

"Yes, dark. Tall. Half there, half not."

"So, what? The shadow and this rabid vampire were working together?"

Clara shook her head. The movement was slow, but it still got the point across. "Beast chased me. Didn't realize, I had no blood to give. Once I thought I lost it, the shadow grabbed me. When that thing caught up with us, the man sent it away."

"The man?" Nicholas said, not being able to contain himself. "What man?"

"The man who came out of the shadow."

Nicholas couldn't believe what he was hearing. This was him, the man in shadows. And he was here, and he had rabid vampires under his control.

154

Dusk was right. This is worse than we thought.

"But how? How could he control the vampire?" Will said, previous fear forgotten.

"Don't know. Doesn't make sense. The thing should have killed him. But it didn't."

"Clara, what did the man look like?" Dusk said, picking up the thread.

Again, Clara slowly shook her head. Then, she finally opened her eyes and looked at the three of them. The area surrounding her irises was dark maroon. She looked like a demon straight from hell, but when she spoke, she sounded like an angel.

"Like the darkness. He was not there and there at the same time. But different from the shadow. He wasn't the reflection of nothing, but everything."

The description was what Nicholas had feared it would be. Ever since he heard Earl utter the three words from beyond the grave, Nicholas had thought about the Man in Shadows.

"Man. In. Shadows."

The whispery voice of a dead man slithered through Nicholas's mind like a snake gliding through sand.

He tried to consider what the man could possibly be like, and in his worst imaginings, he pictured what Clara was describing.

"Anything else you can remember about this man, Clara? Any bit of information could help. You sense anything else from him?"

Clara stared at him with her sinister eyes. The usual sensual controlling look was absent. Now, they held pain and fear, but they still held Nicholas's eyes all the same.

She finally spoke, and it wasn't good.

"Evil."

Pages shifted back and forth under Sheriff Gordon's watchful gaze. Words swam in front of his eyes, blurred by repetition. He had looked through this folder more times than he could count. Time and time again, he would bend the front page to the back of the pile until the entire stack was folded over. Then, he would let the lot roll back to start and go through it again.

Behind the folder in hand was a pile of other folders. Most of these folders contained closed case files. They described the series of murders that swept through his small town. A well-regarded teacher named Daniel Fidel had killed three of the sheriff's town folk and an unknown number of tourists and passers through.

The files on the desk, in addition to the file in his hand, painted a picture Sheriff Gordon didn't like. What made the whole matter worse was no matter who the file said was at fault for the events, Sheriff Gordon knew one person was involved, and he was still out there.

Richard Dusk.

As he thought the name, Sheriff Gordon got to the end of the folder again. The pages fluttered back closed, and then he threw the folder down onto the rest of the pile. Everyone else was ready to accept that these weren't linked. The Fidel murders were closed and ready to be put behind the town. The bodies found at the beach were believed to be a boating accident, and again, everyone was ready to move on. Sheriff Gordon, however, couldn't let it go. He had been doing this for too long to let this all go with what he knew.

Plus, there had been the body found this morning. A local named Theodore Henderson was found with a hole in his chest down in an alley in the middle of Harbor Street. A hole that connected too many dots to a body retrieved from the so-called boating accident. The similarities were too close to be a coincidence. A word he didn't believe in; no true cop did.

After an extended exhale, Sheriff Gordon decided he was done looking at files. It was time for action. Grabbing his coat, Sheriff Gordon moved to his office door.

"I haven't met him yet, but I heard some ladies talk about him down at the salon. What do you make of him?"

The voice cut across the small desks, stopping Sheriff Gordon halfway through closing the door to his office. He looked up and saw Sheila looking up at a visitor leaning on the tall, front counter of the station.

"He seemed nice, but I only talked with him for a minute," Emily said, her forehead furrowing as she did.

Sheriff Gordon's sour mood fell away from him like a heavy snow drift from a low branch. Emily had always and probably would always have that effect on him. Seeing her and Sheila talking reminded him of when his wife had died. Sheila had been there for the both of them like no one else. Even though she was technically his employee, she had been thought of as family for a long time. She had been a rock for Emily and kept him sane through a time of madness.

"Oh, hey, Dad," Emily said, waving at Sheriff Gordon.

Sheila turned, her eyebrows raised. "Well, look who finally decided to come out of his cave." Leaning back toward Emily, she continued, "You sure you wanna eat with a troll like him? He's been in a mood."

Emily scrunched up her face in mock consideration. "Yeah, I think I can turn him around. I have that effect on men."

"I remember the days when I had that effect," Sheila said as if she could mentally go back to that time if she just thought about it hard enough.

"Please stop encouraging her, Sheila," Sheriff Gordon cut in, moving toward them and tossing his coat over his shoulders. "I have a hard enough battle without you pushing her out into the world."

"Pish posh, Sheriff. Girl like her gotta use what she's got in a world like this one."

"And we all know I got it," Emily said, flipping her hair off her shoulder.

Sheila laughed as Emily giggled at her joke. The two were at least forty years apart in age, but at the moment, they could have passed for gossiping classmates.

"Alright, alright. Enough. You two know it's unfair teaming up on an old man."

The mirth subsided between the two of them, and Emily said, "Sorry, Dad." The apology was appreciated but hindered by the smile still plastered across her face.

"Yeah, uh, huh," he said, unconvinced. "So, what brings you here today on your day off?"

"I'm here to take you to lunch," Emily said, smiling and pushing off the front counter she was leaning on. After a small pause, she added, "Your treat, of course."

"If it's my treat, then how are you taking me out to lunch? Sounds like I'm taking you."

"Well, if I didn't come here and get you, you would have probably eaten some crap from the vending machine in the break room or skipped it altogether."

"My vote would have been on the latter with the way today has been going," Sheila said.

Emily raised an arm and pointed at Sheila with an open palm as if to say, 'See'. Sheriff Gordon gave Sheila a look that was shot down with a simple shrug.

"Alright, alright. To Shores then?"

Emily stepped forward and grabbed her dad by the arm. "To Shores."

The two walked arm in arm. As they reached the front door, Emily shouted over her shoulder, "Bye, Sheila. I'll catch you later."

"You two have fun."

"Call over to Shores if you need me, Sheila. Anything comes up, you let me know," Sheriff Gordon said as Emily pulled on his arm.

"Have fun!" Sheila reiterated as the door closed behind them.

Sheriff Gordon had to raise a hand to hold his hat on his head as the wind tried to rip it off. Emily's hair spun in a whirlwind of snowflakes next to him. It took a moment for both of them to make sure they had their footing, and then they were running across the parking lot. Emily laughed and screamed as she slipped in the snow, staying up only because of her firm hold on her father's arm.

With every laugh, a strong smile widened underneath the sheriff's mustache. The files on his desk, the murders in his town, and the name that had been haunting him were left behind. All but the faintest of notions of all three forgotten, for now.

Mr. Lloyd rubbed his eyes and the bridge of his nose, the small, half-circle lenses bouncing up and down on his fingers. He had stayed late at the library every night for the last month. It felt like he never left this place. Last night he had been here until eleven, and tonight he was still here at, he looked over at the clock. The longer hand pointed upward, while the shorter one shot out perpendicular to its brother.

Nine o'clock? When had that happened?

The library had closed three hours ago. Most nights he was wrapped up and out by six-thirty. Mr. Lloyd leaned back in his chair and adjusted his glasses. There was still work laid out across his desk and probably always would be. Not all was the fault of the library, Mr. Lloyd conceded.

Pitch

Without talking with Nicholas or Will about his plans, Mr. Lloyd had taken it upon himself to help them with their research. Mr. Lloyd knew Nicholas was a voracious reader and could get through books with ease, and even Will seemed to have a knack for the research, but he knew books. Books had become his life after his family had died, and Mr. Lloyd wanted to help any way he could.

The book he had in front of him was making it difficult, however. His old eyes weren't half as good as they once were, and he had trouble making out the small type on the pages. The late hour didn't help his eyes nor his mind in its attempt to retain the information he was reading. He decided there would always be time tomorrow. He pushed his chair back and stood up from his desk, stretching.

Suddenly, from outside his office, he heard the sounds of pounding followed by a succession of clicks.

Mr. Lloyd froze his arms in mid-stretch. Quiet followed the clicking. Still, the librarian stood, waiting.

THUD. Click… Click…Click…

Ice filled Mr. Lloyd's veins. Images put Mr. Lloyd back to a few months ago. He saw the dark shades of shadows. The threat of darkness and the foreboding of death. Leaning down, Mr. Lloyd retrieved something he had hidden in his desk for a situation just like this. The dark, cold steel of a pistol glinted in the desk lamp. His grip felt weird on the weapon. He had never fired one before and wasn't sure if he ever wanted to, but if he needed to, he knew he could. Another memory came to him, and he reached down again, grabbing a flashlight from the same desk drawer.

Click… Click… Click…

The doorway of his office slipped past him as he slowly made his way into the main room of the library. It was dark out here away from the desk lamp, but Mr. Lloyd kept the flashlight dark. He wouldn't light it until he knew what he was dealing with.

160

Click… Click… Click…

It was coming from the front door. Someone was trying to get in. Someone, or something.

Mr. Lloyd kept inching forward. He felt his arm raising in instinct. The small gun pointed at the heavy front door of the library. He felt something try to come up from his stomach, and he swallowed it down.

Click… Click… Clunk…

The lock finally gave way. The tumblers had been raised, and the deadbolt slid out of the way. Now, whatever was on the other side had nothing between it and Mr. Lloyd besides the door that was swinging wide as he watched.

With a click of his own, Mr. Lloyd flashed the light on what he hoped would be the intruder's face. Intending to blind the thing before it had a chance to attack. And as the door finished its swing, Mr. Lloyd felt his finger twitch on the trigger, almost firing the moment it opened.

Luckily, he didn't. For Michelle stood in the doorway, a hand in front of her face blocking the beam from Mr. Lloyd's flashlight.

"Michelle?" he said, realizing he had been holding his breath. He exhaled, feeling his rapid heart rate begin to slow.

"Mr. Lloyd? Is that you?" She was squinting, trying to see him but not being able to see past the light shining in her eyes.

He realized he was still pointing the light at her face. Mr. Lloyd lowered the flashlight, followed by the gun a second later. He didn't want to frighten Michelle, and he also didn't want to explain why a small-town librarian needed a gun at the office.

"Yes, it's me. What are you doing back here?"

Michelle stomped her feet on the ground, knocking snow on the rug. "I'm sorry, I thought you'd be home by now. I stopped by the store to pick up a few things, spent some time in town, and then got all the way to my house and realized I had forgotten my keys. I had to walk all the way back here if I planned on sleeping in my bed tonight instead of in the snow. Luckily, I knew you kept this key under a rock outside, but I guess it didn't really matter considering you're still here. What are you still doing here? I didn't mean to scare you."

Mr. Lloyd couldn't help but chuckle a little, still catching his breath. "Me scared? No, it's quite alright. Do you know where you left them?"

Before she responded, Mr. Lloyd heard the jingle of keys in the darkness. "Yup, they're right here on the front counter. I put them up there so I wouldn't forget them, and wouldn't you know it, that's exactly how I forgot them."

"Funny how things work that way," Mr. Lloyd said, smiling, his heart rate back to a normal pace.

"Yeah, alright. Goodnight, Mr. Lloyd. Better get going."

"Good night, Michelle."

Mr. Lloyd turned to go back into his office, and then stopped. "Michelle? Did you say you walked here?"

"Yeah, I don't have a car. I'm saving up for one. It's not a bad walk, probably would have gotten back here before too late if I hadn't dawdled around town for so long as I did. Luckily, it's so cold out I don't have to worry about the milk going bad sitting out on the porch."

Mr. Lloyd half smiled at that, but his mind was in darker places.

"How about you wait up a second, and I'll give you a ride home. It's late and not the best time to be walking alone."

Michelle didn't know about The Hollow's dark side. Mr. Lloyd had decided he shouldn't tell her everything. A lot of the town folk felt the darkness, but very few knew what was really out there, and with Michelle being from out of town, she was even more clueless than most. But everyone had heard about the bodies that washed up on shore. So, he wasn't surprised when she put up no argument.

"Yeah? Are you sure? That'd be great."

"Of course, I'm sure. Let me just finish up, and we'll get you home."

Michelle smiled, "Thanks, Mr. Lloyd. I really appreciate it."

Mr. Lloyd smiled back, "Really, it's no problem. I'd hate to have something happen to you on a walk home from here."

She nodded, and he turned back into the office. He put the flashlight away and then gave the gun a final once over. He ended up not having to use it, and he was grateful.

Not this time, he thought, dreading the time when he wouldn't be so lucky. He put the pistol away. It lay quiet, cold and unfired; for now.

Chapter 13

Nicholas's head was laying flat on his school desk as he tried to focus on the book in front of him. After reading all day with Will two days ago and again last night, they had decided to each take a few books home to work on in their own time. Nicholas grabbed two while Will shuffled six volumes in his arms.

Right now, Nicholas found himself in the middle, or if he was being honest, first third, of a book that turned out to be all about Fort Mackinac. So far, they never got as far south as The Hollow, so everything he had trudged through was more or less useless to him. Some of the battle stuff was interesting at first, but the way the book had been written had somehow even made these events boring.

The fight between awake and sleep was edging to the side of sleep when the back side of the book was pushed down toward him. As the back cover lowered across his vision, Nicholas was greeted with the shining face of Emily.

"Hey," she said, smiling. It was a smile saying she wanted something. Nicholas knew that smile, but he chose to ignore it for now.

"Hey, when'd you get here?"

"A few minutes ago."

"Ah, that's good." Nicholas yawned. "Running a little late this morning?"

"Are we a little tired this morning?"

"Touché."

They sat there for a moment just looking at each other. Nicholas could have sat there and looked at her until he fell asleep. However, as Nicholas had known, Emily wanted something.

"Hey, can you help me out?"

"Ah, I see."

"What?"

"Oh, nothing," he said with a sleepy smile. "What can I do for you?"

She gave him a look but still asked, "Can I just take a look at your math homework. I think I got everything done right, but there's a few problems I just wanted to double check."

Nicholas was all of the sudden very awake, "Aw, crap."

"What?"

"Nothing."

"You didn't do it, did you?"

"Do what?"

"The math homework. Don't you play stupid with me, Nicholas Wake."

"Did you just last name me?"

"Don't change the... ."

"Of course, I did the math homework."

"Oh, then can I see it?"

"No, you may not."

"And why is that?"

"Because I didn't do my math homework."

"I knew it," Emily said. She shook her head, disapproving the whole while. "After all my careful planning, I still somehow ended up dating the bad boy."

Nicholas gave a half chuckle. "Ha. Ha. Very funny."

"Why didn't you do it?"

"I was busy."

Emily looked back at the book in his hands. Seeing her look, Nicholas shifted the book so she couldn't see the cover, as if that would stop her from speaking up about it.

"You were busy, with that?"

Nicholas thought quickly, "This? No, this is just for fun."

"For fun?"

"Yeah, fun. Reading for pleasure, you know."

"Oh, I know. And I also know you're a complete book nerd... ."

"Hey, whoa," Nicholas interjected, playing hurt.

"And usually it is very cute," Emily continued unperturbed. "But this is a little outside your normal list of titles."

"Well, you know. I decided maybe I could find some real ghost stories."

"Oh, I see," Emily said, her smile shrinking. Nicholas considered she could be thinking about all the murders around town and tried to get her mind back on track.

"Yeah, and I totally forgot about the math homework."

"It's not the only thing you've forgotten recently."

Nicholas looked at Emily for a moment, head tilted. "Did I forget something... ." He trailed off, pointing between the two of them, worried he had forgotten an anniversary or a birthday or some sort of couples-specific date. He was new at the whole dating scene, and he didn't want to become just another guy who forgot things like that, but it was hard to know what was important to remember.

"No, you haven't forgotten anything between us, Nicholas. I mean your school work. This isn't the first time this has happened. I know you at least missed the last English paper, and you like to write."

"I like you more," Nicholas said, trying to put on his best boyish smile.

Emily shook her head back and forth. "What is going on with you?"

"Nothing," Nicholas said, sighing, letting the smile fall away.

Emily sat back, crossing her arms, shooting a look across the aisle of desks that would freeze a hot cup of coffee.

"Well," Nicholas thought about everything he was going through. All of a sudden, Nicholas felt even more tired. He thought about what he could tell Emily. Lies could continue to flow between them as they had, but it seemed to be pushing them apart. Nicholas didn't want that. He still thought the world of Emily, and it would kill him to lose her. But did that mean he could tell her the truth?

Nicholas sat there at his desk a few feet away from the girl of his dreams, preparing to tell her everything. He chewed on the inside of his cheek. Whether everything meant the truth or whatever lie he was concocting, Nicholas couldn't decide.

What the hell is the matter with him?

Emily's leg began to bounce, causing a soft squeak to emanate from her desk. This sometimes happened to her when she was about to take an exam or got called on when she wasn't a hundred percent sure she had the right answer. No exam was on the docket today, but here she sat bouncing away, waiting to see if her boyfriend would actually start telling her the truth.

"You see," Nicholas said. It was his second build up that led nowhere. The bouncing increased. If he didn't speak soon, Emily was sure her desk would fall to pieces beneath her.

This delay in speech was most likely because of one of two scenarios. He was either going to tell her the truth, which would finally release all the tension between the two of them, or he was building an even better lie to hide behind. He had been lying to her. She knew it, and she would have called him on it, possibly even broken up with him for it. There was something about the way he was lying, however, that led her to believe he didn't want to be doing it. Whether he was doing it because he thought it was for her own good or some other force stopping him, she didn't know. All she knew was that she just wanted it to stop.

"Things at Winter's Hall are just getting a little overwhelming."

Not a lie, Emily said, her inner lie detector on full alert.

"And Aunt Sherri is just," he paused, wiping his eyes trying to wake up. "Just annoying."

Emily thought about that. It could be the truth, but it didn't sound like Aunt Sherri, and it sounded even less like Nicholas to call her that.

"No, annoying isn't the right word. She is just always trying to be there, you know. Always wanting to check on me, thinking I'm in trouble or something."

"Crazy thought," Emily said, sarcasm layered thick.

"I'm fine," Nicholas said, sighing.

"Uh, huh." She had heard this before. So, it seemed they were going to go down the same road they always did.

Just as Emily was going to give up, Nicholas said, "Sometimes, I get in over my head. I can be honest. But I don't mean to worry her, or you."

Truth again.

Maybe he was finally giving her what she wanted. Emily smiled, warmth exuding from her as she tried to welcome him and his words.

He was shaking his head, "I'm not in trouble. Nothing is the matter with me. Everything is fine. I promise."

Truth, she thought again. Then, something made her go back on that thought. *It is truthful, in a way. But something is still wrong. Something that is trouble.*

But then Nicholas smiled. It was his smile. The same dimples in the cheeks. The same lift around his eyes that his smiles always caused. Everything was the same. But one thing was different. This smile was hiding something.

Just like him.

"Okay," she said, displaying her own smile. "Just as long as you know, I am here for you, and you can tell me anything."

"Of course," Nicholas said. He reached out his hand, offering it to her. She knew he was still holding back, and deep down it terrified her to consider what was so bad that he would still hide it from her, but she also knew he had shared more than he usually did. When she had first become interested in Nicholas, she knew he was a quiet kid. She should have foreseen this closed-off nature. Even though she wanted more, this small progress would work for now. She couldn't push too hard too fast. It would have to count as a win, a small one at least.

She smiled, reaching out and taking his hand in hers. Their fingers interlaced, and she squeezed his hand to symbolize she was right there. It made him smile again

"Alright, Emily, Nicholas. If it's alright with you, I'd like to begin class."

The voice made them both jump. As they had talked, the room had filled in around them. Mr. Sorento stood at the front of the class leaning forward with both hands on his desk. A small piece of chalk was pinched between the thumb and forefinger of his left hand.

Class had apparently started without them noticing. Now, Mr. Sorento had called them out to bring them back to the room. Sixteen pairs of eyes were upon them now, all wanting to see what had stopped class.

Emily and Nicholas realized at the same time that they were still holding hands. Letting go, they shifted away from each other in their seats. The class gave a collective chuckle, and they all turned back to Mr. Sorento.

"Thank you," he said with the weight of years of dealing with kids burdening down his words.

As the lecture began, Emily's warm, embarrassed face turned back to Nicholas, smiling. Nicholas was already looking at her. They shared a conspiratorial look and smile. Then, both began paying attention to Mr. Sorento.

Truth, she thought. *He told me the truth.*

She stole a glance over at Nicholas, who had stopped listening to Mr. Sorento and had gone back to reading the book he had been lost in when she had come into class. He was trying to hide that he was reading from Mr. Sorento, but she saw it clear as day.

Well, at least a part of the truth.

The wood of the door seemed as dark as night in the hallway. For what lay behind it, the appearance was only fitting. Night had not only brought darkness outside, but it had cast a shadow in here as well.

There are shadows everywhere if shadows are what you're looking for.

The thought steeled him as Dusk reached for the handle. The old brass scraped as he did, but, in the end, it clicked its release, and he entered.

The room was darker than the hallway. Dusk noticed the change, but he had grown accustomed to dark places. The years spent hunting had given him above-average senses. While most would have seen close to nothing, Dusk saw everything.

He could see the ornate bureau on the west wall, its carved frame mirror tilting just enough to catch the light from the window when the drapes were pulled. Now, however, they hung closed, letting no light in. Soft, rectangular outlines hung on the walls, as Dusk scanned the area. These he knew were paintings; however, he could not have told you what they were or if there was any significance to them. He had let Argyle decorate the entire house however he saw fit. This place was just a cover anyway, a way for Dusk to appear normal as he prowled the underside of The Hollow.

All of this was clear to him and his well-trained eyes. Those same eyes also allowed him to see the bed in the room. A bed that held a small-framed body covered up to the chin by thick blankets.

Flashes of memories struck him then. Memories, or nightmares, of a time when someone else had been under blankets fighting a fight she was destined to lose. He felt his knees try to go weak. She had laid there, in a bed just like this. A woman thin and frail, the husk of the former brilliant light she once was, but still beautiful to him.

Dusk stepped forward to move into the room or to keep himself from falling. He didn't bother figuring out which it was. It didn't matter in the whole mess of it all. He had more important things to see to.

Making it to the bed, he looked down at the body. The body belonged to a woman, or what once was. Now, she was called a monster, but to be fair, Dusk had also been called that from time to time.

Fingers brushed the hair off her forehead with unaccustomed softness. A moment of tenderness between two monsters.

Clara's eyes opened at the touch. The whites of the small orbs blinding in contrast to the infinitesimal black holes of her pupils and her ebony skin. The white had been crimson hours ago, but she was quick to heal. The eyes didn't pop open as if startled, nor did they flutter as if she was coming out of sleep. The movement was controlled, deliberate, and elegant. Everything she did was, unless the sun was out.

"Checking up on me, Dusk?" Her voice was as smooth and as tempting as silk.

"Just wondering if you were dead yet," Dusk said, with a soft smile. Dark levity was the only type the two could partake in.

Clara pouted, "Sorry to disappoint."

Dusk put his hands up, waving away the back and forth and getting to the point. "How are you feeling?"

"Better," she said, readjusting under the blankets.

Dusk nodded. He grabbed the bottom end of the covers and pulled them up to reveal Clara's feet.

When Dusk had dropped her onto the bed, shouting at the kid to get the drapes closed, the feet weren't recognizable as body parts. Fragmented, burnt shapes resembling the texture of raisins had dropped flakes of ash across the sheets as they hit. Now, they had regained their former structure, and the skin was returning to a normal texture and strength. As he inspected, Clara wiggled the stubs that had been, and would be again, her toes with the strength of an infant.

"You look better. Another day or so, and you'll be able to walk again." He set the blanket back in place, covering her healing extremities.

"Luckily, I'm a quick healer," Clara said with a hint of smugness. The smugness that women use that most men can't help but think is cute. Dusk wasn't a normal man, so he nodded and began to move away.

As he moved, he sensed Clara wanted to say something. But she remained quiet. He kept moving, but when he got to the door, he stopped, giving her one more chance. Her eyes were far better than his, so he knew she would see him hesitate, even if it was just for a moment. When she saw it, she couldn't keep quiet any longer.

"Dusk?"

He turned to look at her, two white circles in the dark. She was sitting up on the bed now.

"Why did you save me?" Her voice was no longer suave. It fumbled forming the words.

This time Dusk was the one who remained quiet. This was not the first time he had been asked this question. He himself had asked it multiple times but could never really come up with a clear answer. However, this time seemed to be a time when he would have to answer. Leaving the door, he moved back into the room. He didn't stop at the bedside. Old aches poked him as he bent his knees to sit near Clara's feet.

They sat there for a moment in silence. The darkness enveloped them, making them no longer just two people alone in a room but in a world all their own. Dusk reached into his jacket. The left, inside breast pocket had a smaller pocket within it. Its contents were secured by a small flap Dusk tucked inside itself, creating a makeshift seal. From this pocket, he pulled out a single object.

"You know what this it?" Dusk asked.

"A bullet," Clara said, unsure if that was the answer he was looking for.

It was, in fact, a bullet, but Dusk shook his head all the same, and said, "No, this is *the* bullet. The bullet I fired into my own head after I lost everything."

The bullet had been the only round in the revolver that night. No need for more when one was sure to do the trick. When he had placed the barrel to his head, this bullet had been in the firing chamber. The trigger had been pulled, popping a soft click followed by a loud bang of igniting gunpowder. When Dusk woke up sometime later, he had found this bullet on his chest and the empty gun in his hand, still warm to the touch.

"For a long time, I told myself I was holding on to it so I could take another shot when I was ready." Dusk moved the bullet in his fingers, trying to catch what little light there was in the room to see the bullet better, but no light was caught.

"But," he began, dropping the bullet into his hand and closing all his fingers around it, "as time went on, as it always unfortunately does, I realized I was maybe holding on to it for a different reason."

The room fell quiet as Dusk was lost in the swirling pools of thought. He didn't intend it, but the pause forced Clara to ask.

"What reasons?"

Dusk came back to the dark room. "To remind myself," he said, not fully knowing what he was going to say, "that no matter how bad things get, there may still be some good there, too. To remind myself to look for that good. I think people are like that. Not all people, but some." Dusk sighed, returning the bullet to his pocket.

Clara brought her knees to her chest, hugging them, and said, "I don't think there is any good left in me."

As she sat there cradling herself, Dusk, for the first time, wondered how old she had been when what happened to turn her into what she was now happened. Usually, she looked mature and worldly. Now, she looked small and childlike.

Dusk put a hand on her knee. They both seemed to be out of character tonight. "I saved you because I believe you are wrong."

Dusk gave her knee a solid pat and then stood to leave. He walked to the door and this time did not stop to give her a chance to say something. There was nothing left to say.

Grant Calvert sang in unison with the song on the radio, hand keeping time on the steering wheel.

The newly christened Patricia Calvert continued, picking up the lower half of her off-the-rack wedding dress and swaying it side to side with Grant's tapping.

She looked stunning in that dress, no matter where it had come from. To Grant, she always looked stunning. He himself was dressed in a blue suit coat probably a size too large for him with a white flower pinned to the collar. In his opinion, he looked sharp but looked like a circus sideshow act next to Patricia.

The two of them had gone to the courthouse earlier that same day and vowed to be each other's one and only, each other's for as long as they both shall live. The ceremony, if you could call what they had a ceremony, had been no more than fifteen minutes long and was at eleven o'clock in the morning. Now, it was almost nine o'clock at night, and the two were on their way up north for their honeymoon. They couldn't afford much, but they were going to make the most of what they could.

While he was tapping out the beat, Grant would forget about the gold ring on his left hand and would find himself hitting it against the steering wheel, reminding himself that this was real. He had grown up a simple man and had no real dreams besides to be a good husband to a beautiful woman. He had found this beautiful woman at the local roller rink only nine months ago. After the first week, Grant knew she was the one. The rest of the time was spent convincing her that Grant was the one. If anyone had asked her, she knew he was by the second date.

The next part of the song they sang in unison.

When Grant's eyes returned to the road, something broke the beams from the headlights and out of instinct, he slammed his foot down on the brake. Patricia braced herself with her arms outstretched to the glove box, and Grant held on to the steering wheel in a death grip. The car gave a violent shake as it hit something on the snowy road, sending the car into an angled slide.

After moments that felt like hours, the car came to a stop, and the couple was breathing heavily from shock. Elton John and Kiki Dee still sang on the radio, unfazed by the crash.

"Are you alright?" Grant said, coming back to the moment and looking over to his wife. Patricia was wide-eyed and stared out of the windshield. Her fingers had gone white as she gripped the dashboard.

"Patricia, babe. Are you okay? Are you hurt?"

"I'm…," she began but had to swallow to finish, "fine. Just scared is all."

A wave of relief came over Grant. He was okay, but that mattered far less than if Patricia was okay.

"Yeah," he said. "That came out of nowhere."

"It did," Patricia agreed. "What was it even? Did you get a good look?"

Grant looked out the windshield. The car had pivoted, so the headlights pointed off the left side of the road into the trees. The beams illuminated about twenty feet into the surrounding forest, and then the darkness became too great.

"No, not really." He gave another look around the car and then made the biggest mistake of his life. "I'm gonna get out of the car. Take a look and see if I can see what it was."

"What? Why?" Patricia sounded even more scared now than she had been before. "Whatever it was, it's probably dead now. We hit it pretty hard."

"Yeah," Grant said, undoing his seat belt. "Or it could be dying. I'm not gonna leave an animal to suffer. That's not the type of man you married, Sweetheart."

Patricia gave a weak smile at this.

"Besides, I have to get out and check the car. Make sure it's still drivable."

She nodded now, seeing the logic in his argument. "Well, just be careful, alright?"

He smiled, "Yes, dear."

He leaned over and kissed her on the cheek. He was pulling away when she grabbed his face and gave him the second-best kiss of his life, only falling short behind the one she had given him after the judge had pronounced them man and wife.

That could have been the moment when Grant realized his wife had known something was going to go wrong. The moment he could have decided to just keep driving until they hit town. But he hadn't, and they didn't.

The car door swung open, and the cold air rushed in. Grant tucked his head and was out of the car with the door shutting behind him before too much air could infect the interior of the car. Surprisingly, there was little to no wind. The world was silent, and it chilled him more than a cold breeze.

Shoving the foreboding atmosphere aside, he moved to the front of the car. The damage appeared to be minimal. The car should drive at least until the next town where they could stop for the night, and Grant could give the whole car a better look over in the morning.

Leaving the car behind, he looked off into the woods. He didn't want to admit it to Patricia, but he had gotten a good look at the thing they had hit. The problem was that, to Grant, whatever they had hit looked human. He didn't want to come across a dead body on the side of the road, and he really didn't want to come across a person dying on the side of the road.

But I can't leave if someone is hurt. How would I sleep at night?

Grant moved toward the trees. He was using the headlights to guide him, so he had to walk all the way across the road to check the side to see if anything was laying just past the side of the road. Slowly, he approached, prepared at any moment to see something horrifying. As the edge of the road crested, Grant steeled his bones and took the last few steps in a jog.

There was nothing.

Grant scoured the ground looking for signs of anything. There wasn't a body; there was no blood. No disturbances in the snow whatsoever. It was as if whatever they hit just disappeared. He looked up deeper into the woods thinking the thing could have been thrown high up into the air. Still, he found nothing.

Weird, he thought.

Then, there was movement. Off to the left, in the darkness. Without hesitating, Grant moved toward the darkness out of the glow of the headlights.

"Hello?" he said to the empty night. "Is someone there?"

There was no answer.

Grant was sure he had seen something, though.

Could have been anything, though. A chipmunk, squirrel. Possibly a coyote. You really want to go messing with that?

Grant decided he didn't and turned back to the car. As soon as he did, he stopped dead. The car hadn't moved, and the night was just as silent as ever, but somehow Grant hadn't heard it. For a moment, he was sure he had to be imagining it. His worst fear come to life, but then he blinked, and when it didn't disappear, he knew it was all real.

The man had Patricia in one arm. It was wrapped around her waist, holding her one arm down with his hand. Her other arm pushed and beat at the man's arm, but it was as if he couldn't feel it. The man's other hand was covering Patricia's mouth so she wouldn't scream. He was bare-chested as if it was a balmy seventy-eight degrees rather than the bitter thirty it had to be close to, if not lower. The sight was ripped right from Grant's nightmares.

"No, oh, no, no. Please God, no. Don't hurt her." Grant stumbled over every word, trying to say it all at once. He didn't have time to think about how they had gotten here. He just knew he had to plead for his wife's life. "Please don't hurt her, I'll do anything. Anything, I swear."

The man did something Grant wouldn't have expected in a thousand years. He growled at Grant. A deep, throaty growl like that of a bear. He made no move toward Grant, but the noise was enough of a threat for Grant to feel his knees grow weak.

"P-P-P-Please," Grant stammered.

The man bear, or whatever it was, turned to Patricia now, its head tilting in a menacing gesture.

"Don't you hurt her," Grant shouted as his anger overtook his fear.

He stepped forward with his right foot, planning to follow with his left, but it wouldn't move. His foot was being held in place by something. The entire scene had so entranced him that he hadn't noticed the growing pressure on his calf. He could feel the intensity grow as it immobilized him.

Looking down, ready to break away from whatever was holding him there, he saw only darkness. The night itself seemed to be holding him in place. Dark coils wrapped around his leg like a python bent on squeezing the life from him. He tried to pull against the black mass to no avail. Another whip of night coiled around his right arm. A third wired its way around his torso.

"Let go!" Grant shouted.

He pulled, yanked, and struggled against the bonds but made no progress.

"Patricia! I'm coming! I...," his shouting was cut off by a thick tendril of shadow wrapping itself around his mouth. He tried again to scream to his love, but nothing came out. Moving his mouth against the gag, he tried to bite at the force, but how does one bite darkness?

The man turned to Grant and roared at him, actually roared. Whatever this was, it was no man. It released Patricia's mouth and reached for Grant. Instantly, he could hear the sound of his wife crying.

"No, you cannot have him."

The voice, so smooth and in control, came from behind Grant. It came out of the darkness just as the things holding Grant in place had. Reflexes made Grant try to turn to see who had spoken to the beast that held his wife, but the thing around his mouth made it impossible.

The thing snorted and growled again in retort. It wasn't happy being told what to do.

"You get that one, and I get this one. It is what's fair."

The thing growled once again but seemed to fall content with the arrangement. It turned back to Patricia.

"Oh, Grant! Please help me!" she cried, moving her face away from the beast the best she could. The thing moved its head forward as if to kiss her, but Grant saw more fiendish plans in the thing's eyes.

Again, Grant fought against his bonds of darkness, but still, he could gain no ground. More wires seemed to come from the night behind him and coil themselves around him. Patricia stopped fighting and reached out toward Grant.

"I love you," she said, crying freely now. "I love you so much."

Grant began to cry. He strained even harder at the night, trying to break free, and for a moment, he thought he had. There was movement, but it was in the wrong direction. The night around him had begun to pull him back, away from Patricia.

No! he thought, going mad.

The thing was right next to Patricia now. It appeared to be sniffing at her. Then, almost too quickly to see, its head whipped back and dove in. A flash of large, white teeth cut the night air and into Patricia's neck.

There wasn't even time for her to scream. Her body jerked, and her open mouth grew slack. Red blood spilled from around the thing's mouth and down the front of her white wedding dress. The ivory gown darkened with bright crimson.

Grant fought with everything he had, and still, he was being pulled back. For every bit of effort he put forth to try to move forward, he was pulled further backward.

Patricia's reaching arm fell to her side. Grant was far away now, but he could still see her eyes drift from him. They fell to the left looking at nothing but the black surrounding them both, and then, finally, her lids fluttered shut.

Now, Grant's vision darkened. It started at the edges of his vision. Then, the darkness wormed around his sight like searching fingers. The headlight beams, once so bright and blinding in the night, dwindled down to nothing more than pinpricks.

As the last vision of light passed out of view, Grant Calvert succumbed to darkness. He didn't know what was happening, but he knew the moment he died. It wasn't when breath finally left him. It wasn't when his heart beat for the final time. It was when Patricia's eyes closed. Grant Calvert died from something everyone suffers from at one point or another. He died of a broken heart.

Chapter 14

The book slid across the table, bumping into a few others on its way to a stop. The other volumes jostled as they were hit but remained where they were. More and more of their brethren were being added to the growing pile in the middle of the table.

"No luck?" Will asked, looking up from his own book.

Nicholas laid his face down on the table and spoke into the old wood, "Nope." Rolling his head on the table, Nicholas looked at Will. "You?"

Will shrugged.

Nicholas snorted.

Will seemed to have no limits to his optimism. Negative words or even the notion of negativity never found its way out of his mouth. He would take every discovery of nothing as just a step in the right direction to find something. It helped Nicholas keep high hopes through all of this. But he still couldn't help laughing at it all.

Sitting up, Nicholas leaned back, his head hanging over the back of his chair. The thinly padded, wooden chair felt fine for reading if you limited yourself to an hour or so, but after that, it began to take its toll. Nicholas had learned the cruel punishment of these chairs many times over when he had read here late with Mr. Lloyd. Growing accustomed to the pain, he could usually last much longer without getting stiff. Apparently, the months spent chasing monsters had made him fall out of practice.

"I need to walk," he said, sliding up and lifting his head. "Gonna grab a drink or something. You need anything?"

Will shook his head. He had already dug himself back into the book in his lap. Nicholas left him sitting there and went on another search through the library.

He walked through the rows of books, skimming the titles on the spines as he went. If anything caught his eye that could help them, he would grab it. It was unlikely he would find anything, however. Mr. Lloyd had already helped them find all the titles they had in the library about Pointe's Hollow, legends, fairy tales, and Michigan in general.

Besides the small information they gained from the local history books about the development of the town, the growth of the shipping business, and the legends Native American tribes had for this area, none of the books had turned up helpful. Nicholas thought back to the stories of people disappearing in this area and how so many thought of this town as a dark place, a black hole amidst the stars. This called up a memory from a few months ago.

"There is something very wrong in Pointe's Hollow."

Those were the exact words Mr. Lloyd had said in this very building. Apparently, many of the books they were reading shared the same sentiment. None could say exactly what was going on here, but all agreed that this was not a good place.

Making it to the front of the library, Nicholas passed the front desk and went to the small offset hall where the bathrooms were. The wall between the two bathrooms housed a small drinking fountain.

The water came out of the fountain ice cold as he turned the handle. He didn't think he was particularly thirsty until he started drinking. The water felt so good, and he drank it greedily. After he had his fill, he stood and wiped his mouth, eyes still closed as he took a deep breath, preparing to go back to the table of books.

Once refreshed, he turned and ran into someone. Both parties stumbled back, trying to regain balance. Nicholas felt embarrassed, because he knew he had not been paying attention.

"I'm sorry," he stammered.

"Oh, that's quite alright. No harm done on my end. You okay?"

"Yeah, I'm...," but Nicholas trailed off. He recognized that voice. Looking up, he recognized the face as well. "Alright."

"Good, good," said Father Adrian.

He stood in a large, black coat, shoes leaving a wet spot on the carpet. He must have come in behind Nicholas while he was at the drinking fountain. It was weird; Nicholas could have sworn he would have heard the front door open, but somehow, he missed it.

Even better water than I thought.

"So, is this where all the cool kids hang out?" Father Adrian said, pointing over his shoulder at Will at the table.

"No, we're just working on something for school," Nicholas said with an odd smile.

"Ah, I see. That's good."

"Yeah," Nicholas said, unsure of where to take the conversation from there. He had a suspicion that Father Adrian knew something more about the evil in town than he was letting on, but how did he ask about it without giving away what he was doing.

"Were you looking for something?" Nicholas asked.

"Ah, no. Actually, I was just returning some books."

"Oh, okay."

Dead end there.

"How are you getting along with life in The Hollow?"

Father Adrian adjusted his coat. In others, it may have come off as an annoyed gesture, but with him, it seemed to show he was willing to stand and talk awhile.

"It's going alright. It's much livelier than I'm used to and for what I expected from a town this size."

Father Adrian smiled, and Nicholas followed suit. "Yeah," Nicholas said, almost taking the statement as a judgment on his character. As most small-town folk do, Nicholas took pride in his town. The way people viewed The Hollow translated into how people viewed locals from The Hollow. It was an impulse reaction Nicholas didn't hold much stock in, but still related to when the situation arose.

"But I am enjoying it here," Father Adrian added, still smiling.

"That's good," Nicholas said.

A pause of silence spread between the two of them. Nicholas lost his train of thought and what he was trying to accomplish here. As he stood there, silence growing more and more awkward, the thread of his questions got further and further away.

"Well, if that's all, I should be off," Father Adrian said.

Nicholas stood there trying to think of anything to ask to make Father Adrian stay, but he couldn't come up with anything. It was as if all of his plans fell away in shadow, and he was unable to find the light to use any of it.

"Of course," he finally said, stepping aside. "I didn't mean to hold you up."

"No problem at all. You have a good day, alright? Hope you two find what you're looking for."

"Thank you," Nicholas said, adding a short wave.

"Until we see each other again, Mr. Wake." Father Adrian gave a tip of a fictional hat and moved toward the door.

It wasn't until Father Adrian was out the door and out of sight that Nicholas realized that he had missed something.

'I hope you find what you're looking for' is what he had said.

Of course, the library was the place in town to find information whether it be for school work or stopping an evil madman from destroying the town with monsters.

But it was the way he had said it, Nicholas thought.

Just like before when he had used the word 'monstrous'. It wasn't exactly telling, but it was a strange choice of words, and it made Nicholas's spider sense tingle. Nicholas regretted not pushing Father Adrian harder for information. He thought back to the conversation and could think of a hundred different directions in which he could have taken the dialogue. Of course, that was now. In the moment, he had locked up.

Figures, he thought as he started walking back to the table where Will waited for him.

As he made his way, he passed the front desk. On the chest-high countertop sat the usual odds and ends, including a small shelving unit holding a selection of bookmarks Mr. Lloyd gave out with rentals. A new addition to the counter was a neatly stacked pile of books. With half a glance, Nicholas scanned the titles, making a mental list of the books. The list stopped him, because they all were familiar. Not because he had read them all in his many nights spent reading through classics and new fiction alike, but because he had been through most of them earlier in the week.

All the books on the counter were either about Pointe's Hollow, Michigan, or the surrounding Great Lakes. It was as if Father Adrian had copied Will and Nicholas's reading list from their first day of research and took them for himself to read.

Or he was also looking for something.

Nicholas paused a moment and then decided to thumb through the titles once again. He read through the titles on the spines and was stopped up short about halfway through the pile. The volume that stopped him didn't have the title printed on the spine, so Nicholas shifted the books, so he could see the front cover. Once the top of the pile was put aside, Nicholas was stumped again as the book's cover was blank as well.

Having a strange sense of discovery, Nicholas picked the book from the pile and inspected it. It was a hardcover book, standard sizing with, he would guess, about two hundred and fifty pages. For some reason, the book felt heavier than the size allotted.

Opening the book, Nicholas found only more questions. The first few pages weren't set up like an average book. There was no copyright page for starters. Three pages just sat blank where the information would be. There was a title page, and after that, the book began. The title page didn't even have an author's name listed anywhere on it as almost all the others in the library had, fiction or non. Nicholas jumped to the back of the book. He found the final page of narration and then flipped through another three blank pages to get to the back cover. Nothing about the author, not even something denoting the ending of the book. The words just ended.

Nicholas flipped back to the beginning of the book. Going through the blank pages, he ended on the title page once again. Staring down at the book, Nicholas once again felt the strong sense he had found something. He wanted to feel excited, but the title was so foreboding that it was a dark stain on the diamond in the rough this book appeared to be.

In three words, the black text warned and at the same time called to Nicholas.

The Hollow Trials

The night air wafted onto Elena's skin, making it prickle with gooseflesh. It was almost there to stand as a counter-example of what she was going to feel soon. The sky was bright with moonlight, but all the shadows still hung as dark as obsidian. There was the soft rustle of leaves on the wind. The harsh crash of waves rolled over and over down by the shore.

One thing seemed wrong about the night. The usual chatter of animals that catered the surrounding woods was absent. No animal calls could be heard in the darkness. Even insects seemed to have vacated the forest. The night was heavy with the complete absence of life. Instead, it was populated with the stench of death.

She opened her eyes and saw the world around her. Not the world within the trees and the one within the waves of the lake, but the immediate world around her. The small, stone-covered paths that spider-webbed through the streets of the small village. Small bursts of orange popped around on the trails, painting the small buildings in golden glows.

Within this light, Elena saw dark shadows standing and staring up at her. They were black figures with evil eyes. Her head rolled from side to side. From all over, they stood, staring through the night with their wretched eyes. Not only did they stare, but they shouted. Shouted vows of hatred, curses, and sometimes just noises as if they were beasts, howling at her. Or maybe Elena just couldn't make out the words.

She blinked slowly, but that didn't stop the tears. This is not what she wanted, not at all. She had done awful things.

Things she never expected to be forgiven for. Things she never thought could be forgiven. The reason had been for what she thought was love. Love makes everyone do crazy things. This time, love had broken her down, spread her thin, and in the end, taken everything from her.

A single tear rolled down her dirt-ridden face. The clean streak almost burned her skin. Elena felt like she could remember her former self through that tear. It made her eyes burn worse. The rough texture of wood scuffed at her tender skin, but the pain was nothing compared to the loss of self she had had to face in the recent days.

That is when she caught the eyes she was looking for. They hung in the night with even less life than most. Those eyes, his eyes, appeared to have no color, just dark dots in white pools. The same eyes that she had fallen into so many times, but now they had solidified into marble stones. He had grown so hard and alien to her that he no longer had a name.

She wanted to look away. She wanted to roll her head to the other side and never see those eyes again, but she couldn't. They held her attention as much as the ropes cutting into her wrists and ankles held her against the wood pillar. Struggling was no use. She couldn't get out if she tried. Maybe if she was what they thought she was, she could. But she wasn't. Just as all the others weren't. They were just as innocent as her, more innocent in fact, and now she could feel the weight of her role in their stories.

Her nostrils flared, the overly rich scent of burning leaves coming on her in waves. A man had approached as the other had held her gaze. He carried a burning torch above his head. The orange and yellow licked the air in defiance, carrying her death in its heat. The dry timber and leaves below her feet had caught without protest, the flames drinking at the willing fuel. Black smoke wafted up through the air and buffeted her unrelentingly. More tears fell as her eyes began to burn. Yet still, she didn't look away from him.

Pitch

When the first few tongues of fire kissed her feet and legs, he smiled. His smile, which she had once thought of as handsome, was one of demonic intent. He was black as the smoke, but those teeth were white as the foam atop the waves down at the lake. Though her vision was blurry, she could see those teeth in the night. They looked jagged as if he had the mouth of a wolf. She could imagine it snapping as it began to presume the taste of its next kill.

But the mouth didn't snap. No, but it did hang open. It hung open as the man laughed. A wicked, wild laugh that emitted no noise, at least none she could hear over the crackling of fire.

The smoke became too much for her at that point. She began to cough and finally broke eye contact. The heat below was beyond anything she could stand, but yet she didn't cry out. She wanted to be strong. She wanted to be more like the person she had been in a time that felt so long ago. Strong, independent, and beautiful.

Her eyes opened again to see if she could see him. To show him that she was strong, and she didn't need him or believe in him anymore. Finding him through the smoke proved too difficult. Instead, her eyes fell upon the tree. The tree that stood out from the rest by standing right in the middle of everything. It stood as the symbol of life in this otherwise dead town. That is what it was after all: a dead town. In her heart of hearts, she had always known it; everyone did. But they all ignored it. They let the darkness win time and time again.

Like tonight. They let him win.

Finally, Elena's strength gave out. As the flames grabbed her thighs and waved all the way up to her belly, she screamed. She screamed in pain for what the flames did to her skin and her soul. She cried in sadness for the small town who let darkness always win. And lastly, she cried in loss for what she thought had been.

Over time the flames rose higher and higher. The smell of her hair burning somehow set her screams even louder. She could feel the flames on her, in her at this point, but it still shocked her. It was beyond anything she could have imagined.

As the minutes ticked by, Elena burned alive. Eventually, her screams stopped, because her lungs had no air left with which to scream. Then, her heart itself, one that had been so full of love and joy, burned with true fire. Her eyes didn't look for him again. They stayed on the tree. Until Elena Beaumont was nothing more than a memory, she looked at the tree.

Nicholas slowly let the back cover of the book, along with the small collection of blank pages, fall shut. He had read it all, cover to cover, in one sitting. Something he had not done with a book for a very long time. The story had left him feeling drained, alone and hopeless. It was the darkest book he had ever read, and it was darker than anything he ever wanted to face.

Elena Beaumont was a girl who grew up in a small town who had been swept off her feet by a man known as Pitch. Pitch had come to town one day under circumstances that were never fully explained in the small novel but were, instead, tossed aside within a love story built for the ages. When Nicholas had been in this part of the book, he had thought he had known where the story was going. It was the same story told over and over again, but at about the halfway point in the book, everything changed.

That was when the trials had started. Trials dedicated to find and eradicate witches. A copy of the stories that had been told for years about similar trials held in Salem. Dark, bloody, and horrifying as they were, the stories had always felt far away to Nicholas, as if they happened on another planet and had no bearing on him or his life. This story had been different, because the small town felt like his own.

Not only felt like, it is my small town, Nicholas thought, still staring at the back cover of the book.

He was sure that it was, too. They never said Pointe's Hollow in the book, nor did the small town have a name, but it was The Hollow. There wasn't a doubt in his mind that it was. It had been described in a way that if you didn't live here and didn't know what he knew, you wouldn't think twice about it, but to Nicholas, it was so vivid it could not be ignored.

Along with the town being his town, the book had taken a sharp turn in its characters. Elena stayed the truest, but Pitch quickly changed into someone, or something, else. As the trials began, women were accused, but it was mostly out of fear and misunderstanding. Then, Pitch stepped in, but to Elena's horror, he did not aim to stop the trials but turn them up a notch. He began instructing the town folk on how to test for witchcraft. He explained he had been in a town five years prior that had fallen under the same circumstances and would help this town cleanse themselves. The town fell at his feet, listening to everything he said. Elena began to see darkness in Pitch then but ignored it. She had loved him after all.

As the book continued, women began to die at the trials. More than that, they were put to death, murdered. They would be hanged, weighed down with boulders in the lake, or like Elena herself, in the end, burned alive. Pitch had taken over the town, seen as a prophet here to hunt out and kill all witches. Through all of this, Elena looked on, blinded by love and unwilling to see the truth.

The turning point came when Elena's friend, Samantha, came to her and told her that Pitch had come to her house looking for her company. Elena couldn't and wouldn't believe what she was saying and threw her out in a fit of rage.

The next week, Samantha was put on trial and stoned to death for witchcraft. When Pitch found Elena crying over the whole ordeal, he had comforted her but told her that he had to have Samantha killed. She was upsetting Elena. Through this, Elena discovered that Pitch was picking the women he put on trial, not because they were witches or thought to be dealing in witchcraft, but because he wanted them dead. Horror paralyzed Elena when she realized what Pitch really was, a demon or maybe the devil himself.

She tried to get help from the town. To seek refuge with someone away from Pitch, with plans to leave and never come back. Sickened with grief about what Pitch was and the naive role she played in all of it, Elena told her friends what was happening, and unwelcome ears picked up the tale. While she was hiding out, word got back to Pitch about everything she was up to. The rest of the town folk found her early the next morning. Her case was expedited to that very day, and by night she found herself on an execution pyre.

And he watched her burn alive. Laughing.

Nicholas at first began reading the book because it had been a change of pace from the monotonous drivel he had been sifting through for days. As the story took off, however, he hadn't been able to put it down. Putting the gruesome details of the book aside, he felt like it meant more or had more answers than it first appeared. As he had concluded, the town was not just any town. It was his town. It was The Hollow, plain as day. But there was something else.

Pitch, Nicholas thought. *Not just Pitch, but the way Pitch was described.*

That had taken awhile for Nicholas to become aware of. It was subtle at first. His eyes were described as dark and mysterious, something for Elena to get lost in. But as he read further, everything about the man was dark. If you added everything in the book together, Pitch was almost described as the night itself. As if he wasn't a man at all, but darkness in the flesh. A man made up of darkness.

A man made up of shadows.

In the end, it only made sense for Elena to see him as the devil. That was what she thought of as the essence of evil. Nicholas had his own evil, his own devil, and somehow, some way, this Pitch seemed to be a perfect fit. The only problem was that he was fictional. A character in this book.

But The Hollow isn't fictional, Nicholas's brain countered.

Nicholas rubbed his eyes. He couldn't be considering what he was considering, could he? It was ridiculous, but somehow, Nicholas felt like it also held some truth. He didn't know how or what truth it was exactly. But there was something there.

"You have something?"

Will's words made Nicholas finally look away from the book. It was apparent Will had been watching him for some time. Books were no longer laid out in front of him. They had been closed or pushed far enough away where reading wasn't possible. He was staring at Nicholas now, a look of hope and concern on his face.

Nicholas was up and out of his seat without a word. He spanned the sitting area of the library in record time and was at the front desk in an instant. His speed was so great, he hit the desk with his chest, almost knocking the breath out of him.

"Mr. Lloyd?" He said this louder than he normally would in the library, but his blood was pumping now, and he couldn't keep his voice down.

Maybe hearing the urgency in Nicholas's voice, or just excited for someone to talk to, Mr. Lloyd was at the door of his office in a flash.

"Yes, Nicholas. Need help with something?"

"This book," Nicholas held the book over the front desk, offering it to Mr. Lloyd. "Is this book from the library?"

Mr. Lloyd's face took on a quizzical look. It wasn't a question he usually got asked, and it was even stranger coming from Nicholas who was quite familiar with the library's collection himself.

"Well, I don't know. Let's see."

Mr. Lloyd took the book and spun it around in his hands, looking at each cover and binding in turn. Then, he leafed through the front few pages of the book. After he got to the page that started the narration, he jumped to the very back of the book and inspected the inside cover.

"Nope, doesn't appear to be. No check-out envelope in the front. Of course, those could be ripped out, but that doesn't appear to be the case here. More importantly, there's no stamp on the back cover."

Mr. Lloyd held the book open for Nicholas's inspection. The back cover was clean, no stamp or even the slightest sign of ink. Nicholas had read enough of the library's titles to be familiar with the stamp they all held in the bottom, right-hand corner inside the back cover.

"I thought so." Nicholas chewed on his lip for a moment. As he did, Will walked up behind him. Ignoring him, Nicholas continued, "Are you familiar with the book at all? Or even heard of it?"

Mr. Lloyd turned the book back toward himself and flipped to the beginning again. Finding the right page, he read out loud, "The Hollow Trials." He then pouted his lips and tapped the title with a finger. "Nope, can't say that I have. Title is pretty telling, though."

Nicholas had thought the same thing. It was all too much to be a coincidence. Finally, all the pieces to the puzzle were being put out on the table; now, Nicholas just had to start putting them together.

Mr. Lloyd handed the book back to Nicholas, who took it and turned to Will.

Pitch

"Nicholas," Will said, excitement plain on his face. "You got something, don't you?"

"Yeah," Nicholas said, looking back down at the book. "I think I do."

Chapter 15

Dusk sat on the couch looking at the two kids in front of him. Somehow, they had all become partners in all of this, and most of the time, Dusk could see them as helpful participants. But there were other times when he saw them for what they were: kids. This time the kids had brought him a story. A story they seemed very excited about. It was a crazy story, and Dusk was still trying to wrap his head around it all.

"So, let me get this straight. Just to make sure I'm following," Dusk said, leaning forward on the couch. The two kids stood, too energetic to sit.

"This book," he continued, pointing at the book in the kid's hand, "is a story about a witch trial?"

"Witch trial*s*," the kid's friend, Will, interjected, inflecting the 's' on the end of the word.

"Right, witch trials. And it says these trials happened here, in Pointe's Hollow?"

"Not exactly," the kid said, but followed with, "but I'm sure that's what it means."

"That's what it means? Does the book tell the story in riddles?"

"No, but it's not always a hundred percent clear."

Dusk thought this over for a minute. "But you're sure?"

The kid nodded, and Dusk saw no moment of hesitation or doubt. So, he took it as truth.

"Okay, and this Pitch character. You think he's somehow associated with the man in shadows?"

Nicholas shifted on his feet, but then said in a strong tone. "No. I think he is the man in shadows."

First Dusk watched the kid to see if there was any flicker in his demeanor. When there wasn't, he looked to Will. Will nodded one curt nod, agreeing with his friend as he always did. Then, he looked back to the kid.

"How can that be?"

The kid's eyes looked away from Dusk for a minute. Will opened his mouth to say something, closed and then opened it again, slower. "Well, that part, um. We don't know that part yet."

"But I know someone who may know," the kid said.

Dusk's eyebrows raised, "You're still thinking the new priest is involved."

"Of course," the kid said. "If it wasn't obvious before, you can't deny it now. He dropped off the book. He's practically telling us he has the answers."

"But he didn't," Dusk said, holding up a finger. "He didn't tell us he had answers or give any. All he did was give us this book and more questions."

The kid wanted to argue. Dusk could see it in his eyes, but he didn't; he just looked down at the ground again.

He's sure. I don't know how or why, but the kid is sure of this.

"Well, I guess there wouldn't be any harm in talking to this Adrian guy."

The kid looked up from the floor, fire reignited in his eyes. Dusk gave him a smirk and a nod as if they were conspiring on some secret plan.

"Alright!" Will said, slapping his hands together. "Finally, something new. I'm tired of looking at the same old books."

Dusk looked over at him. "You know, if you needed a change of pace, you could always look in the library upstairs."

Will looked dumbstruck at him. "There's a library here?"

The three stood, scanning the library, looking at the walls of books. Dusk stayed by the door, while the kid and his friend walked further in to inspect the volumes.

"How did you not tell us about this place?" Will asked, still taking in the sight of the library.

"He knew it was here," Dusk said, pointing to the kid.

Will looked over at Dusk and then turned to the kid. Taking a book off the shelf and beginning to flip through it, the kid took a moment to realize they were both looking at him.

"What? Last time I was in this place, there was a werewolf trying to kill me. Last thing I was thinking about was the books."

"Werewolf?" Will exclaimed, believing without a doubt but still shocked by the news.

"Oh, yeah," Dusk said with a smile. "That was a fun night."

"Ha, fun," the kid said, looking back down at the book in his hands.

Will was scanning the titles on the binding of the books opposite the kid. Dusk rocked on his heels for a moment and then decided he was no longer needed.

"Look, I've got some things to see to, and then we'll go look for the priest, alright?"

The two kids didn't even mumble an acknowledgment.
Okay, good talk.
Dusk left the library without another word.

While the two kids worked upstairs, he collected things downstairs. He didn't know who this Adrian character was or what he was capable of, so he prepared for anything. Refilling his coat with bullets, he took a moment to make sure something was in a particular pocket. He had been through a lot, but it had never left him. It was there, just as it always was. Once he was sufficiently full of ammo, he took out his tomahawk and slid it into a loop on his belt.

He felt like he was ready to take on an entire army, strapped for pain, punishment, and murder.

Alright, Dusk thought, readjusting his coat. *Let's go to church.*

The evening felt colder than it really should have. The small group of do-gooders who walked into the woods should have taken that as a sign. The sun wasn't fully below the horizon, but it already felt like the dead of night.

When Dusk had returned to collect them, the two had a pile of books scattered across two tables. Apparently having fresh resources had rejuvenated their desire to find answers, and they dug in deep. Even when they left, Nicholas had helped Will carry two armfuls of books down to his car so Will could keep working on things when he got home.

Now, Nicholas and Dusk walked through the trees with the ease of practice. Will kept up with the help of his muscular physique, but his head would twitch and shiver at the sounds of the trees. Nicholas found the snaps and rustling not quite comforting, but familiar. A feeling Will didn't share, at least not yet.

They shared one thing, however; their bodies were humming with anticipation. After talking the book over and coordinating the plan, they agreed this was the best option. It seemed logical to Nicholas that Father Adrian was subtly trying to lead them in the right direction. Dusk, on the other hand, would scoff and say the time for subtlety was over. Either way, they were on their way to where the father was staying.

In preparation, Nicholas and Will had asked around town trying to find out where that was. As they prodded the town folk for information, it became evident no one knew anything about Father Adrian. Many of them commented about seeing him around town and how nice it was to have another priest in town, especially after what had happened, but no one knew where to find him. Or where he came from. It was as if he just blew into town as a savior from some other plane of existence.

And should it seem any other way?

Father Christopher had had some special sight. It hadn't been fully explained to Nicholas, but he was sure it was something not of this world. Just like everything else they were up against. So, it stood to reason that Father Adrian may be the same. The only information they could compile, however, was that Father Adrian mentioned staying close to the skeleton of the old church. The plan was to rebuild once the weather warmed, and, as it was relayed to them, he liked being near the spot of his future parish. Whether he meant he was living out there in some form of a mobile home or would just spend time there, no one was sure.

"We have followed thinner leads before," Dusk had said when Will and Nicholas had told him what little they had found. "Might as well see what we see."

Will was in instant agreement. He was still enveloped in the excitement of all of this. He would agree to anything. Will would have jumped headfirst into the very forefront of a fight without a second thought.

Had I been like this? Nicholas thought. As soon as the thought finished, he realized he had been exactly like that. He barely survived a fight with a werewolf, and the next day, he had gone in search of Dusk and demanded to be involved in all of this.

Nicholas wished they had more to go on, but he was the one who thought that the best course of action was to find Father Adrian. That's how they found themselves out here walking in the woods toward the place where he and Dusk had burned the old church to the ground to hide the evidence of the terror that befell the place.

Dusk led the way with Nicholas and Will only a step behind him. They trudged through the snow and over branches, excitement building with every step. Only one had even a notion of wariness about what was to come, but none were quite ready.

"This is it?" Will said, waving his arms in a shrug.

"Yeah," Nicholas said, looking at the scene.

"What's left of it," Dusk added, walking straight through the place where the church used to stand tall.

The three of them were meandering about the small site within a clearing in the thick woods. Nicholas remembered how the church had looked when they had come here. Once to meet Father Christopher, once to help him, and a final time to bury him. Now, the place was empty.

"Okay. What now?" Will said.

Nicholas glanced at Dusk while he looked around. Dusk looked from left to right and then back. He tilted his eyes up to the sky and finally dropped back to the two of them. "I have no idea."

Nicholas frowned and then looked around for himself. There wasn't much to look at. Then, he spotted a structure sitting within the trees. It was about thirty yards behind Will. Dusk followed Nicholas's eyes and saw it, too.

Will thought they were looking at him. "What?"

"What's that behind you? Can you make it out?"

Will turned and had a look for himself. "Looks like a building," Will concluded.

Dusk chuckled, "Astute deduction."

Nicholas pushed past, ignoring the joke, and went to see for himself. Within the trees, they found Will was right. It was a building; in fact, it was a mausoleum. And in keeping with that, they now walked among tombstones as well as trees.

Stones lay on either side of Nicholas, and there was a moment when his mind didn't go to them. There was a moment when he had forgotten who was here. But it was just a moment, and then his heart broke, and he felt his eyes burn.

To keep himself from crying, he coughed in the cold, and said, "I don't think he's here."

Will was nodding, "Unless he decided to get a cot and shack up in there." He pointed at the mausoleum.

It was a smooth stone structure that may have been white many years ago. Now, the only white on it was the settled snow. It sat under the blankets of cold, worn and weathered. Stains of brown and burgundy painted the outside in layers. Like rings in a tree, it showed the age of the building. It could have been there since the dawn of time according to the number of lines on its sides.

Nicholas's eyes wouldn't leave the building. He was trying not to look at the stones. If he happened upon a certain two, he might not be able to keep the tears back. He thought they would be leaving soon.

There was no sign of Father Adrian or anybody for that matter. Dusk didn't seem ready to leave, however.

Pitch

He moved toward the aged structure, and Nicholas thought he might want to be sure no one was inside. No one alive that was. But Dusk stopped short of the mausoleum and dropped to a knee. He put a hand on the snow and seemed to be feeling something. Nicholas moved forward, and he saw Dusk was touching the snow itself. It didn't crunch under his fingers as it did underfoot. The snow was packed and solid, almost ice.

"Has there been a funeral lately?"

Nicholas thought about it for a moment. "I believe Randy Packers was buried a few days ago."

"The snow is more recent. Nothing today or yesterday?"

Nicholas looked at Will, who just shrugged. "None I can think of. Why?"

"People have been here recently."

Nicholas looked around. The cemetery was deserted at the moment, but people visited their dead loved ones from time to time. Not all people were haunted by what lies beneath the dirt here like Nicholas. He was going to say just that when he saw the whole picture.

Dusk was kneeling above a series of footprints. But that wasn't what stopped Nicholas's words. It was the realization that the small collections of footprints in front of him spread out in all directions. They peppered the snow and seemed to be everywhere. Nicholas even turned and saw ones he had missed behind them.

"Looks like someone was really looking for something," Will said, noticing the footprints as well.

Dusk was shaking his head. He stood, rubbing his hand on his pants. "Not someone. There are different sizes."

Nicholas looked again but saw only a mess of impressions. He had been at this long enough to trust Dusk, though, so he asked, "How many?"

"Lots," Dusk said.

That would have been enough, but just then, a moan came from the west, making them all spin on the packed snow.

Chapter 16

White bodies like wraiths shambled from between the trees. The stark whiteness of their skin was outdone only by the snow at their feet. The last time anyone had seen these horrors, it had been dark and rainy. Now, their pale complexion almost shimmered in the sunlight, and the sight was even more haunting.

As Nicholas spotted one of them, he blinked, and then there were two. He blinked again, and four now pushed toward them. Again and again their ranks rose until the three would-be heroes faced a mob of no less than twenty hobbled, wrecked, but still walking corpses.

"Oh, no. Not again," Nicholas said, under his breath.

He must have said it louder than he anticipated because Will's head turned toward him. "Again? You mean you've seen these things before?"

"We've been acquainted with their likes before," Dusk said, hand moving toward the gun on his hip.

"Oh."

The first creature to appear, a tall, lanky thing who wore a flannel shirt with brown, stained pants, picked up the pace as it got closer, smelling a meal in front of it.

The three began to back up. Swallowing hard, Will said, "So, how'd it go last time?"

"Good," Dusk started. "Besides the kid going over the cliff and almost falling to his death, it was a decisive victory."

Will looked to Nicholas, hoping to hear Nicholas tell him Dusk was making another joke. Nicholas gave Will a sheepish look and shrugged. To Will's credit, he appeared to be holding up alright in the face of all this. Sure, his skin looked almost as white as the creatures descending upon him, and he had begun to sweat despite the cold wind, but other than that, he looked strong. At least, Nicholas hoped.

BANG!

The flannel shirt of the creature cascaded in green gore, as Dusk's bullet not only struck the thing's head but obliterated it. These things, no matter how horrifying, were still weak. Time fed upon their bones and flesh, making them soft and breakable. Also, the green sores ripping apart the flesh was evidence that the ooze pumping through their veins that gave them life, no matter how little it resembled true life, also ate away at them from the inside.

BANG!

Another one further back popped like a balloon. White body populated by green insides fell to the snow in a shower. Nicholas knew Dusk had only four more shots in the chambers, but he was taking out the closest ones first. He'd be able to reload with his practiced fingers before the things would reach them and still have plenty of clearance to keep them back. If they kept retreating and Dusk's aim held up, they would be fine.

As soon as Nicholas thought this, the situation became not fine.

Will screamed. The howl made Nicholas whip around. He saw all of them had been too preoccupied with the things in front of them. No one had checked behind them. Now, as they turned, the force doubled in count. And they were surrounded. And one had ahold of Will by the shoulder.

"Will!" Nicholas yelled, but his feet were cemented to the ground. He tried to tell them to move, but still, they just sat there like one of the gravestones around him.

The thing stood there staring at Will for a moment. Its head tilted to get a better angle on the boy's neck. It wore a blue suit jacket with a mashed white flower in the lapel. On a finger of its left hand, the hand that held Will, shone a gold ring. The whole scene was a strange spoof of a wedding picture. The groom standing behind the bride with a hand on her shoulder. The bride, warm and sweet, looking over her shoulder up at the groom. Both leaning in for a kiss.

Will yelled again. Nicholas saw him reach up and try to pry the thing's hand from his shoulder. His fingers tried to find purchase underneath the thing's grasp. His strong hands seemed to have trouble at first, and fear made his movements shaky. Finally, he grasped the fingers that held him, and he yanked up as he pivoted away from the mouth that was snapping at his neck.

He was freed, well almost freed. Three of the fingers on the thing's hand cracked, snapped, and then popped off into Will's hand. His arm flung up into the air, resistance disappearing as the fingers left their original owner. Will almost slipped but somehow remained standing. The thing's face was only inches from his neck, and the ring finger and thumb of the once-full hand held on strong. The thing went in for its death-ridden kiss.

BANG!

The bullet whizzed by Will's face so close Nicholas imagined he could have smelt the hot lead as it dove through the creature's face. Because of the angle, the thing had its head tilted, and the bullet broke right through the top of the skull and sprayed out of the thing's lower cheek. Not exploding like the ones before it, but more collapsing in on itself, the head condensed into an unrecognizable ball.

Even though it didn't explode, Will was still splashed with a large number of bits and pieces. The hit was so shocking, it forced him to shuffle back. The movement and weight of the dead thing made him slip in the snow.

As soon as Will hit the snow, Nicholas came free from his stupor. He rushed forward, falling to his knees by his friend's side.

"Will. Will! Are you okay?"

Will looked dazed. He turned and blinked at Nicholas, green flecks dripping from between his eyelashes.

"It... It... got in my mouth," Will said, dazed.

If Nicholas had been anywhere else, he would have laughed out loud, and even in the situation they found themselves in, he almost did. Somehow, he kept the laugh contained and just squeezed Will's shoulder. Dusk was next to them the next moment, not shrinking down to their level but speaking to them all the same.

"We have to go. They're getting too close."

"Where?" Nicholas said, looking around. Every path of escape he thought he saw was blocked by a white figure bent on eating them.

"There," Dusk said, pointing to the mausoleum in the center of the graveyard. For a moment, the two on the ground didn't move. It may have been shock that froze them, or something else. Nicholas thought it might have been childhood superstition. The fear of being in a house for dead things.

"Come on!" Dusk shouted at them, already moving toward the building. That shook the two of them, and they were on their feet. They chased after Dusk before he could yell again.

The snow was tough to run through. Nicholas tried to watch out for surprise attacks from the oncomers, but he had to keep looking down. The compacted snow below his feet had reformed to ice, and he was having trouble keeping his balance. Nicholas heard Will behind him and deduced he was having the same troubles. Dusk, of course, ran as if he had been born on ice.

Just as Nicholas thought he would lose his footing, they reached the door of the crypt. Without missing a step, Dusk lifted his leg and kicked in the door. It was a large, heavy, wood door, built to stand the effects of weather and time, but it had not been built to withstand Dusk. It swung open with a crunch of snapping wood. Dusk used his momentum to enter first and get ready to close the door behind them. Nicholas rushed in shortly after.

The sudden switch from the bright outside to the dark cement building blinded Nicholas, and he feared he had fallen into a black hole as if he tumbled past the edge of the world and was sent spinning into an abyss. The world began to come into focus as Nicholas heard the door shut behind him.

They were safe.

His eyes began to see shapes. Three coffins, one on each wall excluding the one holding the door. The finer details started to materialize within the shadows. He saw carvings on the walls. Names, dates, and even pictures. In the ceiling above them sat a sky of stars carved into the old stone. In the middle of these stars sat a circle image. It was half a crescent moon, and the other half was a sun. Something about this place pulled at Nicholas. It was a sense that he was being beckoned. He could almost see a ghostly white hand waving for him to come closer. A call from another world. A call he would no doubt answer one day, a call all men answered one day, but would be fine with ignoring for now.

"Dusk?" Nicholas asked, turning to see the man leaning up against the heavy door.

"Right here," Dusk said, with a little wave. "You alright?"

Nicholas nodded. Of course, he didn't know for how long he'd be alright, but for now, he was.

"Where's your friend?" Dusk asked, puzzled.

"He's right...," Nicholas turned to indicate Will was behind him, right where he had heard him not moments before, but Will was not there. Will was not anywhere. Nicholas turned to Dusk, who looked back at him. Pounding came from the other side of the door.

"Oh, shit."

Why didn't you ever play hockey?

This absurd thought somehow struck Will as his face was pressed against the cold, wet ice on the graveyard lawn.

Maybe if you had, today would have turned out a little different.

As the three had run for safety, Will had seen Nicholas fighting against the slippery ground. A fight Will found himself in the middle of. Not completely over the fight he had just barely survived, Will found his legs unsupportive and his footing unsure of itself. Plus, he kept wiping at his face trying to clear some of the mess that had covered him. Thin, green lines would form in his vision, linking bottom eyelid to top eyelid. He'd wipe and have a momentary respite from the gore, and then it would be back.

Dusk, a man Will both admired and feared a little, had kicked in the door to their haven. All Will had to do was reach it. Something, as it turns out, he couldn't do.

A few paces from the safe cement walls and his companions, Will made the biggest mistake anyone in his situation could make. He knew it was a mistake. He had seen the movies. He had read the books. Not as many as Nicholas, but he still knew. But even knowing he knew he was making a mistake, he made it anyway. He turned to look over his shoulder and check behind him.

As he did, the dominos fell. Whipping his head back over his shoulder sent the gore plaguing his face right into his eye. Green pooled, turning his vision into a jade filter of its former self. The shock of this made Will recoil his top half. The top half of his body's sudden jolt proved too much for his lower body's spotty footing, and Will fell. Not only did he hit the ground, causing him to lose his breath to the winter air, but as he hit, the momentum made him slide across the ground.

He slid between two gravestones and then right past the mausoleum front wall, coming to a stop around the right corner of the structure. This is where his face laid on the cold ground, and he contemplated his sport choices in his youth. If he had chosen hockey instead of the myriad of other sports, maybe he would have been more sure-footed on the ice and been inside the mausoleum instead of beside it.

Will grabbed the side of the building for balance and got to his feet. No matter what choices he had made, he was here now, and he was going to have to live with it, or not live at all.

Without wasting any time, he moved toward the front of the building, again hoping to still find the door open so he could sneak inside. The door was closed, however, and not only that, six of the dead things stood outside the door banging on it with heavy hits trying to get inside.

Okay, Plan B.

He didn't have a Plan B, not yet, but he thought that given the right motivation, he could come up with one pretty quickly. A moan came from behind him, and Will turned to see three more of the things coming toward the mausoleum.

They didn't have eyes for the door, however. They were looking straight at him.

That's enough motivation for me, Will thought as he turned and ran again.

He ran down the right wall and past the building, leaving it and the others behind. As he ran, he jumped from the packed, icy ground to the thicker snow, making running more taxing, but it held less chance of slipping, which Will accepted without complaint.

He was making good progress when something grabbed at his ankle. For a wild moment, his mind went to visions of hands popping up from graves. The dirt-covered appendage wrapped its icy hand around his ankle and pulled him down to the ground. Down and down he went, deep into the fire caves of hell.

Instead, he fell to the cold ground again, sending up a cloud of snow. Rolling around, he saw that it wasn't a hand at all that had stopped him. A small board protruded from the snow now. It had been painted white at some point, but a lot of that had flaked away. Will grabbed it and pulled it free from the snow. It was a picket from a small fence. It was about three feet in length and ended in a jagged point.

Will looked and saw he had landed right by a gravestone. 'Geoffrey Dean' was engraved in the smooth stone, followed by the years '1890-1953'.

Thanks a lot, Geoffrey, Will thought, scoffing at the stone as he stood up.

He was about to toss the picket away when the thing was on him. He held the board up horizontally, fending off the creature's reaching hands as it tried pulling him toward its hungry mouth. Getting angry at this whole situation, Will pushed back. He pushed once, twice, and on the third push, he gave it all he had. The thing stumbled awkwardly and gave Will some room.

Without thinking, Will raised the board and, pulling from a sport he had played, swung the picket as if it were a bat and the bases were loaded with two outs. The board shook as it made contact with the thing, and Will tightened his grip. There was a moment of resistance, and then it gave way, and Will half demolished, half sliced the thing's head into a spurt of green confetti.

It crumpled to the ground as Will stood over it, breath heaving. He looked down at the board in his hand. Now, the white-flecked paint job was splattered with green. After a moment, he looked back down at the gravestone, "Thanks, Geoffrey."

A boisterous yell escaped him as he rushed forward, wielding the board high above his head, ready to take on the world.

The pounding on the door was deafening in the confines of the small mausoleum. Dusk's back pressed against the door. After a few moments, he spread his arms wide, grabbing the frame for leverage.

"Any more ideas?" Nicholas said.

Dusk grunted at the strain of holding the door, "I'm open to suggestions."

Nicholas looked around. There was nothing but stone all around him. In a back corner, there was a stone pillar. On top of that, there was a small pot of long-dead flowers. Nicholas moved to the corner and swatted the vase aside. Ignoring the sound of ceramic breaking against cement, Nicholas started to pick up the pillar. It was heavy, and age had made it stick to the ground. With a heave, Nicholas freed it from the floor and picked it up.

"When I say when, open the door," Nicholas said through gritted teeth.

Dusk gave him a look as if to say, 'Are you sure?'

"Ready?" Nicholas replied, ignoring the look of uncertainty from Dusk. Dropping the worry, Dusk nodded.

"And," Nicholas shifted his grip on the stone pillar, so he resembled an Olympian shot-putter. "NOW!"

Dusk pushed off the wall and gripped the door handle. The door flung open. Suddenly, white light spilled into the dark room, and Nicholas had only a glimpse of bodies before he shut his eyes to fight the light. Blind, and with his arms burning from holding up the stone, Nicholas took two steps forward and threw the pillar with everything he had.

He felt it leave his hands, heard the sound of it hitting bodies and crunching bones and then a squish as it mashed whatever ended up underneath it. Nicholas tried to open his eyes, but the light blinded him again.

BANG!

Now, he was deaf as well. The blast was so loud, Nicholas felt the sound wave press against his eardrums. Blind and deaf, Nicholas dropped to his knees. That's when he heard it again. The voice calling him to another world. Nicholas had enough time to think it was fitting to die in a graveyard, and then he decided to give in to the voice. The air grew even denser in the enclosed space, and Nicholas felt darkness close in.

Before he could give in all the way, a hand grabbed him, pulling him to his feet.

"Come on, kid. We're not dead yet."

Nicholas opened his eyes; the light was still bright, but Nicholas began to see things again. The doorway was open. Then, a body stood in the way.

BANG!

The body fell away as Nicholas winced at the sound. Then, they were both moving. The dense air of the mausoleum gave way to the cold air of the day. The light grew brighter, but Nicholas's eyes had already adjusted enough for him to see. His feet had to tiptoe around the mess of bodies that were left below the stone pillar. Once he was passed them, he assessed the situation.

He didn't see a mob of attackers like he thought he would. All around them were bodies, but instead of walking around wanting to feed on their flesh, they lay still on the ground, heads caved in or cut in two. Standing in the middle of them was Will, covered in even more gore than he had been and holding a piece of wood almost broken in half. The two halves held together by mere splinters.

"Will?" Nicholas said, his voice not sounding as strong as he would have liked.

Will turned to them, his eyes wide and breathing heavily. For a moment, Nicholas was afraid that something had happened. Then, Will smiled.

"Hey, where'd you two go? You missed it."

Nicholas was about to say something when a creature appeared behind Will. It was falling on him. There was no stopping it. Nicholas couldn't do anything and.... .

BANG!

The thing's head exploded right behind Will, making him jump and drop his makeshift weapon. The thing that had almost gotten him fell back into the snow, staining it with its green innards.

"Whoa," Will said, turning back to see the thing behind him. "That was close."

Nicholas let out the breath he had been holding in. He smiled at Will, who returned the smile and gave a big thumbs-up. Turning to Dusk, Nicholas was greeted with a shake of a head.

"Kids," Dusk said, holstering his gun while still shaking his head.

The three reconvened in the graveyard, gave each a once-over to make sure everyone was okay, and then looked around.

Will put his hands on his hips and surveyed the bodies. "Now what?"

Dusk turned away and grabbed a body by an ankle, "Now, we clean up."

He started dragging the body across the ground. The ice helped the process, making the body slide with ease.

"Clean up? Where the hell are we gonna put all of them?"

"The only reasonable place to put dead bodies," Dusk said, pointing to a small pile of snow across the way. Nicholas could just make out the shadow of a hole positioned next to the mound.

"In the ground."

Chapter 17

The school bell rang, releasing the kids from school for the day. At the same time, it woke an unconscious Nicholas. He shook awake, feeling the wet mark of saliva across his arm and at the corner of his mouth. Blinking his weighted lids, Nicholas wiped the moisture from his arm onto his pants.

After the three of them had failed to find Father Adrian or any signs of the priest, Nicholas had gone home to rest. He had fallen asleep watching TV and slept the whole night, awaking in his sweat-dirty clothes from the fight. After the rushed morning and sitting through classes, Nicholas found himself unable to keep his eyes open. Somehow, he had become even more tired with more sleep.

Just perfect, he thought, getting up from his desk.

Making his way to the door like a slug, Nicholas couldn't wait to get home. Maybe he'd take a nap after shoveling down a bowl of Cap'n Crunch.

A slap hit his shoulder, making him jump.

"Whoa, buddy. I didn't mean to scare you," Will said, holding his hands up in defense. "What's up? You tired?"

"What was your first clue," Nicholas got out right before a big yawn.

"So, I'm gonna guess you wanna pass on the library today?"

Shit, Nicholas thought, rubbing a hand over his face. He had forgotten he and Will had decided to continue their research after school today. Reaching his locker, he put his forehead against the cool metal.

Will looked him over and spoke before Nicholas could think of what to say, "You know what, man, it's no problem. You get home and get some rest; you look awful."

Nicholas chuckled, "Thanks, Will. You really know how to make a guy feel good about himself."

"It's what I do," Will said, leaning on the locker beside Nicholas's. "Seriously, though, don't worry about it. I'll go down to the library and get some research done. I know we got to be close."

"Research about what?"

The voice came from a few paces behind Nicholas. He rolled over, still using the locker for support, to see Emily standing there. She was looking at the two of them, curious.

It was a moment before either of them spoke.

"Ah, for a paper. For school," Will mumbled out.

"Yeah," Nicholas agreed without really thinking about it.

Emily's face scrunched up as curiousity turned to confusion. "You guys got assigned a paper? Which class?"

"Math," Will said, and then it was overshadowed by Nicholas saying, "English."

Emily looked at the two of them as if they had told her aliens had landed in Pointe's Hollow.

God, we have enough to deal with. Please don't make that true.

"An English paper? I don't have anything due. We just turned in a five-page paper on Monday."

"Well, I don't know what to tell you, Em," Will said, pushing off from the locker. "Me and Nicholas here got a ten-page paper to do, and it looks like I'll be doing all the research for it on my own."

"Wait, you guys are working on a paper together? Like a group project paper?"

Will started to say something but then realized he had nothing to say. Nicholas felt at a loss, too. Will's mouth opened and then closed like a dead fish until Emily spoke up again. "You know what, if you guys are cheating, I don't even wanna know about it."

Will sighed with relief, "Perfect, because we didn't want to tell you about it. And with that, I'll be off."

He spun on a heel and walked away, trying to be nonchalant but failing.

Once he was gone, Emily turned to Nicholas, "You two better not get into trouble."

We probably will, but it's not the trouble you're thinking of. Detention is the least of our worries.

"We won't," he said, with a smile.

"Uh, huh. Sure." She did not attempt to hide her complete lack of faith in the two boys. "Walk me home?"

Nicholas wanted to walk straight home and collapse as soon as he made it into the door, but a power beyond him, deep in some genetic code, told him he was going to walk the pretty girl home.

"Yeah, of course."

The two walked hand in hand down The Hollow's main line of buildings. This was the spine of the town, and everything broke off in paths away from this place. When the two of them walked like this down here, Nicholas imagined them being able to turn and walk off into anywhere. They'd turn a corner, and before they knew it, they'd be in Paris or New York. When, in actuality, they'd hit trees. Always trees. The trees holding them all here like bars in a jail cell.

Nicholas adjusted his hand within Emily's gloved one. She was always colder than he was, so as he walked with his coat unzipped, she was bundled up tight with hat, gloves, and scarf. Her nose was a little red from the wind, making it match her hair. Nicholas thought it was amazing how beautiful a girl could look when most of her was covered up by winter garb. Emily made it all look so good.

"So," Emily said, shocking Nicholas out of his admiration for her. "What did you guys end up doing yesterday?"

Nicholas heard the question and flashes of the green-gore fueled, putrid, undead came into view. Dodging spilling the beans, he gave her the lie he always did. "Not much. Dusk just wanted some things done around the house and the grounds. Pretty boring, but he pays good, and I could use the money."

Emily looked confused, "I thought you and Will were hanging out yesterday. Guy time, remember?"

Nicholas looked confused and then realized he *had* told her that. He hadn't mentioned being with Dusk at all. Past Nicholas had thought it would sound more natural to be hanging out with Will instead of Dusk all the time, so he had switched his usual story. Present Nicholas had forgotten all about that. Present Nicholas also wanted to kick past Nicholas's ass.

"Right, yeah," Nicholas said, thinking fast. "He came with me up to Winter's Hall."

"He did?"

"Yeah," Nicholas said, trying to roll the lie out as it came to him. "Dusk needed some big things in the house moved, and I told Will if he gave me a hand, I could talk Dusk into sliding a few bucks his way. He's got enough money and obviously doesn't know what to do with it. I knew he wouldn't mind to get the job done."

"Oh, I see," Emily said, growing quiet.

Nicholas should have felt good; his lie had seemed to work. But all he felt was guilt. He hated lying to Emily, but he couldn't tell her the truth. There was no way. She would think he was mad, leave him, and maybe even turn him into her dad or worse - an institution. He couldn't have that.

"My father has some notion that Mr. Dusk is a bad guy."

Emily rarely brought up her father when they were hanging out. Nicholas wasn't sure if she knew that her father thought Nicholas was involved in some questionable things or that he was just suspicious of him because of the usual reasons dads of young girls are suspicious of young boys. Either way, they had both seemed to agree not to bring up her dad without having to say a word about it.

"Really? Dusk? He's not a bad guy, just a little," pausing, Nicholas tried thinking of the perfect word to describe Dusk. Not finding the perfect word to describe a gun-toting, monster hunting, but all things considered, hero, he settled for, "eccentric."

Emily nodded, but Nicholas could feel that she wasn't buying into everything. She was holding something back, and Nicholas knew if he wasn't careful, he'd step on the trigger and be caught in a trap.

"He also says you're dangerous, too," she said, looking at Nicholas out of the corner of her eye. It was strange how lovely she could be while she gave him such a threatening look. It said, 'your move.'

"Me? Dangerous? Come on," Nicholas said, scoffing as he thought some cool guy character would in a movie. "He's just saying that 'cause I'm your boyfriend. Dad's don't like the guys their daughters date. No matter who it is."

"That's true," Emily said, looking away again. "But he's already done all that. I know how to handle my dad and the guys I see. But when he tells me to stay away from a guy, it means something else."

"What do you mean?" Nicholas felt like he was getting close to the point of no return, but he didn't know where else to go. Like a deer stuck in the headlights of an oncoming car. He could have run fifteen different directions, but all he did was stand and stare.

"Most of the time, he just says the dad things, but when he says I should stay away from someone, and he says it in his sheriff voice, that means something completely different."

She turned to eye Nicholas again. Nicholas felt his face grow a little warm.

"And he's said that about only two people recently, Mr. Dusk and you."

Warning bells rang off in Nicholas's head. Red flashing lights and sirens blared. 'Run! Run! Get out while you still can!' But did he listen? Of course not.

"Really? That's weird."

Worst thing you could have done, he thought.

"Yeah, really weird. But then I realized you two do spend a lot of time together, and you tell me you help him with stuff around the house," the word 'stuff' was accented by a derisive tone. "But you never say what stuff exactly."

Nicholas didn't say anything. He just stared ahead.

"Now, you say Will helped with stuff, and you two have been acting weird lately, and now I don't know what to think."

That's when Nicholas felt the trap close, and he found himself caught. If he said nothing, she'd just ask the question. If he lied, she'd see right through it. If he told the truth, either she would think it was a lie or she would think he was insane. Trapped, he didn't know what to do.

"I don't know what to say," Nicholas said, knowing it was the wrong thing but not knowing what the right thing was.

"How about you tell me the truth?" Emily said as she stopped walking, making Nicholas do the same. "That sounds like a pretty good start to me."

Nicholas thought for a moment. Really thought about it all. He thought about how he had been pulled into all of this. About how many times he had almost died to monsters no one believed existed. Shifting on his feet, he thought about Emily. How wonderful she was and how much he cared for her. He could tell her the truth; she would believe him. She wouldn't turn him in or run away scared. Something deep down told Nicholas she would stand with him against anything, no matter how much danger that put her in. That fact and that fact alone was why he said, "I am telling you the truth."

She looked into his eyes and saw that he was lying. She let go of his hand and turned to walk home.

"Wait up," Nicholas called after her.

"No, I can make it home from here. Alone," she said without turning around.

A black knot twisted in Nicholas's stomach, and he felt a soft burning in his eyes. He watched her walk away while someone else watched from across the street.

What do I do? I wasn't prepared for this.

Sherri thought this as she stood in the kitchen chewing on her fingernails. A tick she thought she had nipped in the bud many years ago, but somehow had found its way back into her life. She didn't break the nails off; she just chewed on them as if threatening to break them off but unwilling to go through with it.

I mean, I knew teenage years were tough, but this is something else.

She was thinking of her nephew or her surrogate son if she was being honest with herself. Never really feeling the need or the desire to have kids, Sherri wasn't prepared to be in the situation she found herself in. She could tell Nicholas was hiding something. Even with her being a hands-off guardian, she could tell something wasn't right. It had been going on for awhile, and at first, she pushed it aside, thinking it was just her imagination. Then, it turned into suspicion, and now it was a fact she couldn't shake.

It all started with that storm, she thought.

But that wasn't quite right, either. It may have even started before that, but she couldn't be sure. She had been so thankful to see him alive after the night of the storm, even if he had looked like death as he stumbled into the house. She had asked him again and again what had happened, but she never really got a complete answer out of him. Something had happened that night, and either he didn't want to tell her or felt like he couldn't.

So, let's go through the usual suspects.

Running through what could be things Nicholas would hide from her, she first stopped on what parents always jump to: drugs. Sherri had been in her twenties during the sixties and knew all too well what drugs kids could get into, but it didn't fit with Nicholas. For starters, this was The Hollow. Besides a few joints discarded below the high school bleachers every now and again, there was nothing to get into. For another thing, Nicholas never showed any signs of being high.

The only strange behavior that had befallen him was a lack of energy. He was tired all the time, except for at night it seemed. She had heard him up all hours of the night, but she just thought it was what teenagers did; now, she wasn't so sure.

Next option was sex, but again Sherri didn't think that was it. She wasn't going to say hormones were something her nephew or anyone could control, but she had seen him and Emily together. They never seemed to be on top of each other or sneaking in touches when she left the room. Sherri knew what to look for, just as she guessed every parental figure does.

As a teenager herself, she thought she was so sneaky with everything she did, she assumed all teenagers thought that. But now, in her late thirties, Sherri Wake knew that parents missed nothing.

So, why can't I figure out what's wrong with him?

Her chewing had grown almost furious, but she stopped dead when the darkest part of her mind spoke up. The part that would be brutally honest even when it felt like it was kicking you when you were down.

Maybe, 'cause you're not his parent. You're not his mom, no matter how hard you try.

The hand she had been chewing on clenched into a fist and pounded onto her thigh as if she could stamp the thought out of existence. Realizing that wasn't going to work, she stopped and recomposed herself. Fretting over all of this was helping no one. Concluding that it was time she made the next move, she told herself she would confront Nicholas the next chance she had. They would just put all the cards out on the table and talk. She wouldn't scold, and, hopefully, he wouldn't fight. They would talk like two adults, and then everything would be set right. She wasn't sure how it was all going to pan out, but she was ready to try to make it work.

The one thing she did know was that standing around in the house was getting nothing done, and she was not going to let a whole day go to waste. Sherri moved through the house, collected her keys and coat, got into her car, and drove into town. Parking along Harbor Street, she got out and started making her rounds to pick up a few things from the store.

She loved living in The Hollow. The small-town atmosphere where everyone knew everyone was what she had always wanted and all she ever needed. Once she had found it here, she had done everything she could to become a staple in this town. After years here, she could talk to anyone she bumped into on the street and have a full conversation with them. On top of that, she also knew the people to avoid having conversations with. So, when she walked downtown, it was a big affair. She intended to step into the shops and, also, stop to chat with people on the street to hear the gossip of the town. Even during the colder months, there were always people around and things to talk about.

Today, however, her town had fallen short of her expectations. Harbor Street appeared to be abandoned. It was so dead the shops appeared to be closed. Even though Sherri knew full well and good every door would be open if she were to approach them, the buildings still looked deserted. Ever since the bodies had washed up on shore, conversations didn't start with words of greeting, but words of concern and assurance that everything would be okay.

A few months ago, the town had jumped up in defiance of the evil that was falling upon them. Now, however, the town felt deflated. The folk who lived here and loved this town were tired. They all knew this town had its dark times, but like people are known to do, they thought all those times were behind them. They thought it was time to fall back into the small-town lifestyle. However, it would appear this town was not done with everyone.

Sherri walked down the cold sidewalk, peeking in shop windows as she passed. Waving at the faces that looked up at her as she passed, she was pleased to see some genuine smiles on the people's faces. Others, however, looked defeated, and even more just didn't look up from what they were doing.

A cold wind rolled in from the lake, and Sherri had to pull down her hat and fluff her scarf to stop herself from shivering. After it subsided, she shoved her hands in her pockets and went into the general store to pick up a few things she needed to make dinner.

The store's glass door hit the bell dangling above it. The ring cut through the store as if it was a scream. A radio station played softly from the P.A. system, but other than that, the store was as quiet as the grave. Dean, the stock boy, had stopped placing boxes of mac and cheese on the shelf to see who had entered. Sherri waved at him, putting on her best smile as she fought the eerie stillness of the store. Dean managed a soft smile himself and went back to stocking the shelf.

That's how the whole town feels right now, hon.

She left the store with a bag in each hand. She probably could have fit everything she bought into a single bag, but she didn't want it ripping halfway to the car. As she looked down to readjust her grip on one of the bags, she ran right into Emily.

"Oh, I am so sorry, honey. Are you okay? I must have not been watching where I was going."

In fact, it was Emily who wasn't watching where she was going. Her head was down, and she seemed to be moving a little faster than normal.

"I'm okay," she mumbled.

Sherri, having survived her own teenage years, immediately picked up on the fact that something was troubling the girl.

"You sure? You look upset."

Emily looked up at her and tried to put on a brave smile, and bless her heart, she did. "Yeah, I'm just fine."

Fine? Uh, huh, sure.

"What's going on? Did Nicholas say something? 'Cause you give the word Em, and I'll have a good talk with that boy."

"Yeah, I mean no, no. He's great. Just…," she trailed off, and Sherri knew she would never finish. It just wasn't Emily's way. So, Sherri let her off the hook.

"Okay, as long as you're sure. Us girls we have to stick together." Throwing an arm around Emily, she gave the girl a half hug, the bags making it impossible to embrace fully.

"Thanks, Miss Wake."

"Please, Sherri or even Aunt Sherri if you'd like. None of that 'miss' stuff."

This time Emily did smile, for real. "Okay, I'll see you later. I gotta get home to my dad."

"Alright, honey. Have a good one."

Emily gave a short wave and then continued on her way. She made it six steps away and then dropped her head again. Her pace also quickened to the feverish pace it was when the collision had occurred, and before Sherri knew it, she turned and was out of sight.

Sherri watched her go and then shook her head slowly.

Nicholas, what is going on with you?

Chapter 18

The night was confining with darkness. The ground itself was restricted with all the snow that covered it. Dusk padded along unperturbed, however. He liked the dark. It reminded him of how things were before the kid. When his life was darkness. In that darkness, he had become the hunter. There are things that lived in that darkness. These things were the things of nightmares, but they had fears all their own. And their worst fear was him.

In recent times, however, he felt his body giving in to the laze of his new-found life. Besides the few exciting engagements they had had in the past week, things had been slow. Dusk had spent his days drinking soda and eating pizza. A pretty good deal all things considered, but it was during moments like this when he fell back into his old life that he really noticed the effects.

Although thicker than he had been, Dusk was still thinner than most and light-footed. He put these old skills to the test as he slipped into the building without a sound. Even if there had been anyone around to notice, which there wasn't, he had made sure they would have needed the ears of a wolf to hear him.

He moved through the building, almost gliding through space as if he wasn't touching the floor. The stairs came and went in a flash, and he was in the basement, still no one the wiser. The door pushed with a slight whine, but Dusk had anticipated that. He had been here before. He made sure he slowed the door's descent as it shut behind him once he was in the room. Standing in front of him was the person he had come to see. The person had no idea Dusk stood mere paces behind him. At least, that's what Dusk thought.

"Hey, Dusk," Steely said, spinning around on his metal stool, not taken aback by the monster killers presence.

I must be worse off than I thought. No more soda before noon... well, only one before noon.

"Steely, how's business?"

"Booming," Steely said with a smile. Then, face dropping, he said, "Unfortunately."

Dusk moved into the room, nodding as he did so. On the table in front of Steely laid a young girl whose chest had been ripped apart. Her face was pale, but still pretty, and Dusk's thoughts fluttered to another beautiful lady.

"Where's your shorter, younger shadow?"

"Huh?" Dusk said, half there.

"The kid? Nicholas? Where's he at?"

"Oh," Dusk said, coming back. "I left him home tonight. He needed some sleep."

"Past his bedtime. I get it," Steely said, laughing.

Dusk nodded, but he didn't join in on the laughter. He had left the kid home because he had complained about being tired multiple times, but there was something else. Dusk trusted the kid, but something about the way he had been acting worried Dusk. He wasn't sure what it was exactly, but he thought he'd proceed with caution.

"Who's this?" Dusk said, pointing toward the girl on the table.

"Patricia Calvert, twenty-six, from Ohio, and recently married to a Grant Calvert, currently missing. Oh, and recently deceased."

"Thanks, I wasn't sure." Dusk walked closer and leaned in. "Same wound on the chest as the sailor?"

"Yup. A little," Steely motioned the act of reaching, twisting, and yanking. Then, he flexed his fingers as if there was a beating heart in it.

Use to his absurdity, Dusk nodded and inspected the wound further. As far as he could tell, it looked exactly like the sailor's wound, so he moved on. He looked down the girl's body, seeing small, minor scratches and bruises but nothing that jumped out. Going back up, he made it to her neck where he found two small puncture wounds.

"When did she die?"

"A day or two ago. The cold weather makes it hard to narrow anymore."

"I see."

"Notice the wounds on the neck?" Steely asked as Dusk stared at them.

"Yeah, I noticed them," Dusk said, feeding Steely his lead-in line.

"Looks like a vampire to me."

"You don't say?"

"Oh, I most certainly do. Hey, don't you know a vampire?"

"It wasn't her."

"And you know that how? You know where she's been for the past twenty-four to forty-eight hours?"

"Yes."

Steely looked confused, "And where is that?"

"My bed."

"Oh," Steely said, growing quiet. He looked at the floor and thought for a beat. "What's that like?"

"Steely," Dusk said, with a tone that screamed 'don't go there'.

"Okay, okay. The blood bags you asked for make a lot more sense now."

Dusk had requested help from Steely when he had taken in Clara. According to their arrangement, Clara was allowed to feed only on the animals that called the woods around The Hollow home. Usually, Dusk would have fought the notion of giving her human blood after being on a wild game diet for years, but desperate times.

"Tell me about the husband. No sign of him?"

"Nothing so far. There was blood at the scene, but not a lot. Could have been from anything."

"Think he could be our guy?"

Steely shook his head, "I mean, he could have done Alice here, but these two got married at a courthouse in Ohio three days ago. He wasn't anywhere near here during the boat crash."

Dusk nodded, assuming that was going to be the case, but he felt like he needed to ask. The punctures were wounds consistent with a vampire's bite, but Dusk also knew it wasn't Clara. They had an arrangement, and she had been unable to move for days.

So, we do have another vampire in town.

It made sense. Dusk had heard the news from Clara's own mouth. Being a vampire herself, made Dusk take her word on the subject as gospel. But she had also said this one wasn't like her. It was rabid, mad with hunger. And it wasn't alone.

"You gonna try to get her to talk?" Steely said, his voice getting high with excitement.

Dusk thought about it for a moment. "No, I don't think so. Probably been dead for too long and with the cold, hard to say if that helps or hurts us here. I only have so much of the stuff left and with…," he paused for a moment and then pushed on, "Father Christopher gone, I won't be getting any more soon."

"Oh, okay," Steely said, doing his best to hide his disappointment.

Dusk could tell he had gotten everything he could from his visit. It wasn't much, but every little bit helped.

"Well, thanks for the info, Steely. Nice to see you, as always."

"Ah, before you go," Steely said, his voice wavering.

Dusk stood up, hands on his hips, intrigued. Steely usually requested things from Dusk as he was going to leave. More secrets about his life, The Other, or the monsters he hunted. But something in Steely's voice told him this was something else.

"I feel like I should warn you," Steely continued.

Dusk didn't say anything; he just waited.

"The sheriff's asking about you," Steely said, rushing the words out.

"So?" Dusk said. "Isn't that his job?"

"Yeah, but… ."

"He's been asking questions for months now. The kid won't shut up about it."

Steely chewed on his lip for a moment, "It's different, though."

Dusk took that in for a moment.

"All I'm saying," Steely said, trying to stop Dusk from asking questions he couldn't answer. "Is just, be careful."

That shocked Dusk. Steely always seemed to be on the fringe. Death and monsters never seemed to concern him, because he was here in his morgue, protected. Now that the danger was visible to him, he became worried.

Dusk wasn't, though. He smiled, "Steely, I'm going to chase after something that rips the hearts out of people. I think a small-town sheriff is something I can handle."

Steely smiled, too, but not his usual smile. This one was forced out through his thin lips.

"Yeah, I'm sure you're right. What are you gonna do now?"

Dusk paused for a moment, "Well first, I've got a vampire in my bed I have to take care of." He let the sentence hang there, seeing if Steely would take the bait. He didn't, so Dusk continued, "We'll be taking her out to the edge of town tomorrow night, and after she's clear, we'll go hunting."

Steely nodded. Dusk couldn't believe he missed the quirky, strange, and inappropriate joke-delivering Steely, but right then, he did.

"I'll be seeing you, Steely," Dusk said as he turned to leave.

Steely perked up, "See ya' Dusk, be sure to call me if you need anything else. More blood or a hand with something dead."

Dusk nodded as he left the morgue. As he walked through the police station, he took a moment and looked at the labeled door across the room. The words were enough to make Dusk feel like he was looking at the man himself.

One day it'll all make sense, Sheriff.

He turned and made his way toward the back entrance. *Hopefully.*

He was right here... at least I thought he was.

Deputy Donald had his cruiser going at a snail's pace at the outskirts of town. He could hear the tires crunch snow under them as he rolled along, radio off and eyes scanning the tree line. The trees stared back as if to dare him to confront them. The deputy, however, did not fear the trees. He had spent his entire life in The Hollow, and trees didn't scare him.

In fact, he had been running through those trees not an hour ago chasing Richard Dusk. He had been appointed by the sheriff to keep an eye on him, and so far, every time the deputy had had the man in his sight, he had slipped away. By the look of things, he had done it once again.

But he had to come this way.

After losing Dusk within the trees, Deputy Donald had deduced that if he ran back to his car, he could cut the man off on the other side. He was now on the other side of the patch of woods Dusk had been walking through, but there was nothing out here. The town border gave way to trees until the highway. Deputy Donald couldn't figure out what Dusk had been walking out this way to do; he just knew he had to find him. The sheriff had entrusted him, after all.

After a few more minutes of seeing nothing, Deputy Donald was ready to call it a night. He leaned back in his seat, giving up on scouring the tree line. Just as he began to turn the car around and head home, he saw a silhouette in the distance on the road.

Got ya!

The only downside of the car was there was no way to follow Dusk without being seen. His headlights were an obvious giveaway out here in the dark. Dusk had probably even noticed Deputy Donald before Donald had seen him. With some quick thinking, Donald decided he would drive on past out of sight, park, and then double back to follow on foot.

Picking up speed, the silhouette became more defined, and after a minute, it was clear this wasn't Dusk at all. It was a man, from the looks of it, but he carried himself differently from Deputy Donald's man. He also seemed to be bulkier than

Dusk. This was made evident by the fact that the man's top half appeared to be bare to the night air.

Crazy bastard's gonna freeze to death.

A moment's hesitation when Deputy Donald was deciding to forget he saw the man and continue his search for Dusk passed. That moment came and went with his noble notion of duty winning out. That moment could have changed everything if he hadn't been as noble as he was.

His car crunched to a stop on the side of the road. Throwing it into park and grabbing his flashlight from his belt, Deputy Donald left the cop car.

"Hello?" he called out to the man in front of him.

The man stopped moving at the sound of the deputy's voice. Now that the man was completely lit in the car's headlights, Donald noticed how white the man appeared. Blue veins were visible under the ivory skin straining at the protruding muscle.

God damn. How long have you been out here?

"You alright?"

The man began to turn. It appeared he was a little uneasy on his feet. His shoulders seemed to move faster than his lower half, causing a serious wobble effect.

"Have a few drinks tonight, buddy?" Deputy Donald said, trying to sound less like a cop and more like a friend looking to help. He took a few steps forward, one hand raised with the flashlight scanning around, making sure they were alone, as the other hand reached out offering help.

The man made the full rotation just as Deputy Donald could reach out and touch him. But Donald didn't dare. He blocked the light from the headlights now, but the flashlight in his hand revealed the man in his entirety. The sight stopped him dead. It wasn't a man at all, not really.

The thing's entire front half was caked in dark, red maroon. It had been there awhile, looking dry and flaky in spots, but thicker parts still had a sticky sheen like jelly. A warm burst of air puffed from the man's mouth, and Deputy Donald smelled the stench of death and rot.

"What the hell?" Donald said under his breath.

Reflexes sent his hand down to the gun on his hip. His fingers closed on the grip, and then his body was sent flying. The man, or whatever it was, struck a single blow across the deputy's chest. The blow was so fierce, Donald felt his feet leave the ground in an instant. He was soaring through the air until his back smacked the hood of his car.

"Son of a bitch," he moaned as he slid forward.

He was able to break his fall and keep his feet. Trying to catch his breath, Donald raised the flashlight back up to the thing in front of him. It stood there breathing, its whole body heaving. It heaved with such force, it almost appeared to grow.

This time, Deputy Donald wasted no time; he pried the gun free from his holster and raised it.

"Don't move," he said, voice wheezing. He had never fired his weapon before, and he didn't want to jump the gun.

The thing still stood there, breaths happening faster and faster. Deputy Donald felt his gun arm begin to quiver. The thing took a step forward. Before he knew he had done it, Deputy Donald fired his service revolver.

BANG!

A tiny explosion happened on the creature's chest, center mass. The hole disappeared in the gore already painted there. They stood there for a moment breathing, both surprised at what had just happened.

Oh, my God. Oh, my God.

The moment passed, and Deputy Donald was ready for the thing to fall back, dead or dying. But it just stood there, breathing.

"Oh, my God."

The thing screeched and then ran forward, its arms outstretched. Deputy Donald pulled the trigger again and again.

BANG!

BANG!

BANG!

The thing hit him, unfazed by the bullets that pierced its skin. It tucked low and then pushed up, picking up the deputy and causing them both to fall back on the car hood. This time, the impact dented the hood, and Donald felt something snap inside him. The pain was immense, causing his hand to lose its grip, and he dropped the gun. He heard it clatter across the hood and down to the ground.

In survival mode, Deputy Donald began to bat at his attacker. He smacked with his bare hand and with the flashlight he still held, its beam waving around in the darkness. If anyone had been around them, they would have seen the light like an S.O.S. call, but they were all alone.

The thing grabbed the deputy's neck and pushed his head upward. Fight as he might, he couldn't overpower the creature. Without even noticing the deputy's attempts to stop it, the thing dropped its head and bit into the exposed throat. Piercing pain racked Donald, and he wanted to scream out, but only gargling came out. The faint taste of blood fell upon him as he realized the thing's teeth had punctured straight through his throat. Thick globs of blood flowed down his esophagus, landing in his lungs, choking him.

Then, it began to suck. Drinking up every drop of blood that pumped from Donald's heart. Pain like nothing he ever felt cascaded through Deputy Donald, but soon it began to fade. Everything began to fade. His grip loosened, and he dropped the flashlight. The sounds of it bouncing on the car hood echoed like audio ripples in a pool of silence. His vision began to grow dark, and he found it harder and harder to stay awake.

The thing released the deputy's neck. It was time to fight again, to try to escape. But Donald was too weak. His arms and legs felt like they weighed as much as boulders. He wasn't moving anything. He wasn't fighting anything.

The thing gripped the deputy's coat and shirt in the closed fists of both his hands. It yanked and ripped the clothes to pieces. In the distance from where he was now, Deputy Donald felt the cold air lick his skin. Then, he felt the warmth of his own blood that had covered the thing's hand touch him. Pressure on his chest increased to the point where pain once again returned to him. It was so far away, though, that Donald merely groaned at the discomfort. The thing's sharp fingers, or were they claws, pierced the skin there and pushed even deeper.

Pain was there, but Donald was fading faster now. He felt the pressure of the hand digging through him as if he was a box of cereal and it was looking for the prize inside. Pops and snaps emanated as the thing snapped ribs and pulled them free. Deputy Donald was on the fringe of this world and the next. He thought he was beyond all feeling until the thing's fingers wrapped around his heart. The pulse of his blood was paused as he felt the thing squeeze, stopping it mid-beat.

Deputy Donald was being lifted. In his mental state of obscurity, he thought he was going up above. He would be in heaven soon, and all this would be behind him. There was ripping, and then Donald slammed back into the car hood. His killer was the thing that had lifted him, by pulling at his heart. The same heart it now held in its hand.

It was then Donald lost all feeling. As his vision blacked out for the last time, he saw the thing lean down and sink its long teeth into his heart. It was the final thing Deputy Donald saw, but the final thought was far off, back at the station with his adopted police family and Sheriff Gordon.

I tried, I really did.

Chapter 19

Nicholas jumped awake in a sweat and with heaving breaths. Before he even saw what was in the room, he knew something was wrong. He could just feel it.

Had it been a dream?

Nicholas wasn't sure. Everything was masked in a dark, black fog. There was something there. Nicholas could make that out, but he wasn't sure what it was. A dream, a premonition, or whatever it was, didn't matter if he couldn't decipher what it was telling him. All he knew for sure was something was wrong, and someone had died.

Nicholas wiped his face, his hand catching wetness and shaking it off. He let his head drop back to his pillow. Laying there, he tried to calm his breathing. After a few moments, he succeeded. He raised his hand and looked at it. It shook as if Nicholas was cold, but he felt warm. Too warm.

He clenched to stop the trembling and then let the hand fall.

What is happening to me?

Pitch

With no answer in sight, he sat up in bed and tossed his legs over the side. His bare feet dangled. He scooted forward until they touched the ground, but instead of the thick carpet encompassing his toes, he felt something else. It crinkled under foot and gave way to his weight. He could feel the solid floor beneath, but he still pulled his feet back in shock.

Holding his feet up, he looked at the ground. He saw it at the edge of his bed, at first confused. He went to pick it up until he realized it wasn't just at the foot of his bed, it was all over the floor. Every inch of carpet was covered with the ivory color. In places, it rose in piles making his flat floor into a mountainous terrain.

What the hell?

All over his floor were sheets of paper. The white material covered the entire room. Some had even curled up next to the wall covering the molding. A pile sat so high Nicholas thought it'd fall at any second due to the immense weight.

He looked back down below his feet. After a moment of hesitation, Nicholas reached down and picked up a sheet of the paper. His fingers gripped it as if they were worried it would be hot like a pot off a stove. It wasn't. The paper felt normal. It was just a blank piece of paper.

Turning the page over, Nicholas saw that it wasn't blank after all. Typed out neatly on the underside of the paper were four words.

it all ends tonight

Nicholas read it twice and then a third time. How could so few words cause his blood to run so cold? Gooseflesh rippled up his arms as if a cold wind had passed over him.

Maybe it isn't the words, Nicholas thought.

Below the ominous sentence sat the thing that truly terrified Nicholas.

-P

The letter sat there, with its shadow copyright behind it. An accusatory finger pointing to one thing. Nicholas looked over to the typewriter. In the rollers sat another sheet of paper. Crossing without a moment's hesitation, Nicholas went to see what it said. Again, he read the same four words followed by the dastardly 'P'.

Ripping the paper from the machine, Nicholas squeezed it, turning it into a ball. He tossed it aside. It hit other sheets of paper that laid on the ground. Nicholas heard it hit and looked down, hoping he was wrong.

He reached down and picked up a piece of paper from the ground.

it all ends tonight
-P

Reaching down again, he grabbed another.

it all ends tonight
-P

Sure now, but still hoping against hope, he grabbed another.

it all ends tonight
-P

Nicholas tossed the sheets he held to the ground. He looked around at all the paper, knowing each one said the same thing, hundreds maybe even thousands of pages saying the same thing. He dropped into the chair beside the desk, physically and mentally exhausted.

But what does it mean?

A lot of options came to mind, but none of them were good. There was only one person this was from: the man in shadows.

But how?

Turning back to his typewriter, Nicholas considered how this could have been done. No matter which way he thought about it, Nicholas came to only one conclusion. The man in shadows had entered his room and typed these pages. Somehow, with Nicholas none the wiser, he had entered and done this. He must have also entered before and written the letter Dusk had found on the door leading them to the burning Clara.

That had not turned out the way the man in shadows had thought, though. He had to have thought that Clara would die out there. Nicholas and Dusk had saved her, however.

So, maybe he would be wrong again.

Nicholas looked around the room and felt that this had been a lot to go through to end up being wrong. Leaning forward on his desk, Nicholas let his face fall into his hands. After a moment, Nicholas spread his fingers. Looking through the spaces in between, he surveyed what was in front of him. His desk used to be one of his safe places. A place he could draw and write, creating worlds and things. Now, it held the typewriter that had become a totem of dread.

Out of the corner of his eye, Nicholas spied something out of place. Still sitting near the left edge of the desk was the pile of writing describing Dusk and his adventures fighting Mr. Fidel's murder spree. The stack stood a solid block. Each sheet stacked straight on top of the sheet below it.

All but one.

At the very bottom of the pile, one page sat askew. The parts sticking out were blank, which didn't surprise Nicholas considering the page held only a few sentences. The wrap-up thoughts he had had after writing it all down.

The paper slid out from under the rest as if they weren't even there. He was meant to check this sheet. After looking at it, Nicholas knew why.

A day ago the page had read:

days went by. The town had grown quiet, but it was a good kind of quiet. The town was safe because of Dusk and his revolver. No matter what may come, they were safe.

The
End

Now the page read:

days went by. The town had grown quiet, but it was a good kind of quiet. The town was safe because of Dusk and his revolver. No matter what may come, they were safe.

The
THIS Ends TONIGHT

Nicholas felt the blood drain from his face. He looked at the page and knew that he had to do something, or this time the man in shadows wouldn't be wrong. He would be right; this all would end, and Nicholas also knew it wouldn't be in their favor.

How did it all come to this?

Sheriff Gordon stood in the basement of his police station, the station that stood to protect his town, his people. Somehow, it had failed them. He had failed them. He had failed him.

I'm so sorry.

Deputy Donald lay on a metal table in front of him. The majority of his body was covered by a white sheet, but his face was visible in the pale lighting of the morgue. Besides the white complexion and the blue of his lips, Donald looked like he was sleeping. As if he had just fallen asleep on the job, something he had done before. Sheriff Gordon could just yell, and he'd startle awake, feeding the sheriff his hokey-sounding, 'Sorry, Sheriff.'

This time, however, no yelling would wake him. Sheriff Gordon had seen him out at the scene. He had seen the mess of blood and clothing that clung to his deputy. He had seen everything, but out there it was a crime scene. It was just a body of evidence to be collected and cataloged. In here, he was Donald Huckle, Deputy of the Pointe's Hollow Police Force, Sheriff Gordon's right-hand man.

"Sheriff?"

The voice made Sheriff Gordon stir, but he didn't look away from the body. After another moment, he lifted his head to see Steely, looking at him from the other side of the steel table.

"Did you hear me?"

"Ah, no," Sheriff Gordon had to admit. "Could you repeat that?"

"I said, that without a full inspection, I can't name cause of death for the paperwork, but it looks like he bled out. If he was lucky, he was gone before this happened." Steely pointed to his chest.

Sheriff Gordon heard everything, but one thing stuck out. One thing Steely said got lodged in his brain like a kernel of corn at the drive-in stuck in one's teeth. It's something that could go by the wayside, but you can't help but suck and pick at it until it's out.

"Lucky?" Sheriff Gordon's voice sounded hollow even to him. "What about this looks lucky to you?"

Steely shrunk back, "I'm sorry, Sheriff. I said the wrong word."

Sheriff Gordon nodded. He was transitioning to a different state, going from sadness to anger, and the boiling was building up inside of him. Usually, he'd control the explosion and keep it wrapped up. This time, though, Sheriff Gordon wasn't sure he wanted to.

"It wasn't the only thing you did wrong, Steely."

"Sheriff?" Steely said, swallowing hard.

Sheriff Gordon walked around the table. Now, he didn't take his eyes off Steely. This was the farthest he had let himself go, and Sheriff Gordon felt like he was going to push it even further.

"I asked you if you knew anything," Sheriff Gordon said as he grew closer.

"Sheriff, I told you everything I know. If you let me get to work, I can... ."

"Not about this," Sheriff Gordon said, not letting Steely finish. Not caring what he said. "About Richard Dusk."

Steely's face went white. His fingers started to fiddle the air as if he was typing on an invisible typewriter.

Yeah, you son of a bitch. I know you got something. Now, you're gonna give it up.

"Dusk? Wh-what about him? I don't know him."

"There, you did it again."

"Did what again?"

"You lied, Steely. You lied before, and you're lying to me now." Sheriff Gordon's voice was calm, but the steel in his tone struck hard.

"Sheriff, I'm not."

Sheriff Gordon had reached Steely. As Steely began to speak, or lie, again, Sheriff Gordon grabbed him by the front of his shirt and picked the small man up, slamming him against the cabinet. Steely's words were cut off as the breath was forced from his chest.

For a while now, something had been holding the sheriff at bay. A force he couldn't explain was keeping him away from Dusk and all of this. It was as if there was a line he couldn't cross. But now that force broke, and he sprinted across the line. He was done messing around.

This ends now.

"You are, Steely, and Donald is laying on that table because of you and your lies!" It wasn't true, but it was easier for Sheriff Gordon to swallow than the real truth, and it felt good to say it. His voice bounced around the tiled walls, making him sound more like a god than a man. The words boomed, making Steely shrink even more. "Richard Dusk did this, and you know it! You could have stopped it!"

"No!" Steely shrieked, shaking his head. "Dusk could never do that."

"Oh?" Sheriff Gordon said, mocked surprise thickening his word. "I thought you didn't even know the man."

"I do, I do know him. He's a good man. He's only trying to help."

Sheriff Gordon slammed his fist against the cabinet beside Steely's head. The small amount of strength Steely had summoned vanished.

"He's doing a real bang up job, let me tell you," Sheriff Gordon yelled with such ferocity that spit flew from his lips. "What has he done to protect this town, huh? What exactly does he do?"

"He kills monsters!" Steely screamed back.

There were only a handful of words that could have shocked Sheriff Gordon in that moment. Only a few that would throw Sheriff Gordon off his stride and only one to stop him. Steely had used that one word.

Monsters.

Flashes of a suppressed memory of a fur-covered body falling from a window came through the static of anger like a bad TV station. Sheriff Gordon stood in the pre-rain night air looking up into a dark, clouded sky seeing a large body falling to the ground. Falling and changing. A man hit the ground, but a thing had fallen out of the window. A monster.

Sheriff Gordon gritted his teeth. "The only monster here is Richard Dusk."

Steely swallowed, and on his face, Sheriff Gordon saw the desire to argue. Sheriff Gordon didn't give him the chance. He lifted the coroner even higher and looked him right in the eye.

"Now, tell me. What do you know?"

Chapter 20

Nicholas had to spin on his heel when he reached the stairs at the end of the hall. In his haste, he had forgotten to raise the ladder to his room. When he had first moved to the attic, he used to leave the stairs down a lot. After a few times of his aunt not paying attention and running into them, he finally learned to make sure they were kept out of the way. Bending the bottom few feet of the ladder, Nicholas retracted the ladder and let the contraption pull itself back up.

The second stairs Nicholas had to take to get to the ground floor came and went, and with them, the living room followed. Nicholas had his coat thrown around his shoulders, and he was making his way out the back door when he was stopped.

"Nicholas, can I talk to you?"

He turned and saw his aunt leaning against one of the kitchen counters. He had moved through the room so fast he hadn't even noticed her. Usually, if she was in the kitchen, it was a loud and excited atmosphere. This time, however, she was still leaning against the counter with her arms crossed over herself.

"Ah, yeah. But I have to get to Mr. Dusk's. I'm helping him with a lot of stuff tonight. How about we talk later?"

"How about we talk right now?"

"I'm already late. I really need to get going. Mr. Dusk is kind of strict about tardiness."

"I'll call him and let him know you're gonna be late."

Nicholas was already shaking his head before she got all the words out, "No, I'll just go now, and we can talk tomorrow, alright?"

Nicholas started to move to the door again.

"Nicholas, we are going to talk right now!"

Everything stopped for a moment. For years, Nicholas had been living under this roof. As a kid, he had done stupid things as all kids do, but not once had he ever heard his aunt raise her voice like that.

Aunt Sherri opened her mouth to speak and then stopped abruptly, biting her lip. When she spoke, her voice trembled.

"I don't know what's going on with you. I don't."

Nicholas opened his mouth to speak, but nothing came out. He closed it again and looked at his feet.

"There, right there!" she said, fighting through her wavering tone. "You don't tell me anything."

He raised his head again, and he was greeted by his aunt crying.

"I mean, you're out all night with Mr. Dusk, who is great for taking you in, I know, but it's just such strange hours." She sniffled, an arm coming up and wiping at her nose. "And the nights you are here, you're just up all night. And I remember being a kid, I get it, but I just need to know you are alright. People are being murdered, Nicholas. Murdered. Can't you understand why I'd be a little concerned?"

Up all night? Nicholas hadn't been able to fall asleep fast enough whenever he was able to be home. However, someone had tossed paper all around his room last night without him knowing. Maybe that hadn't been the first time.

"Nicholas? Are you listening to me?"

"What? No, I mean, yeah, I'm listening."

"Are you? 'Cause you seem far away. Like you have seemed for months. And now you and Emily are fighting?"

"Who told you that?" Nicholas became defensive. He didn't know why, not exactly.

"I ran into her downtown, and... ."

"And what? And she just told you we were fighting?"

"No, but I know when something's wrong. I'm not stupid, Nicholas."

She pushed off from the counter and moved toward him. Her position shifted forward, leaning on the small island between them.

"I'm just trying to help you."

"I don't need any help, Aunt Sherri," Nicholas said, trying to keep his voice as normal as possible. "I'm fine. Just late." He took a step back toward the door.

"Nicholas, please I'm trying here. I have held back a long time. I have let you come and go whenever you want even with everything that is happening. I think I deserve five minutes of your time. Am I wrong?"

Nicholas felt his jaw clench. It was a strange feeling being in this conversation. It was a place Nicholas had never been.

"No, you're not."

"Okay, then how about we talk. What is it with you and Emily?"

Nicholas shifted on his feet, "It's nothing."

"Nothing?"

"Yeah," Nicholas said, and then repeated, "nothing."

"Well, it's not nothing to her."

Nicholas looked up at her. For a moment, they just looked at each other, and then Aunt Sherri said, "Well?"

Sighing, Nicholas said, "She thinks I'm hiding stuff from her."

"Wonder where she got that idea?"

Nicholas shot his aunt a look. His aunt took it as a challenge.

"When the two women in your life are saying the same thing, kid, it's a sign."

Nicholas rolled his eyes.

"So, what is it?" Aunt Sherri pushed further.

Nicholas looked at her. He couldn't tell her. How would she ever let him out of the house again if she knew what was really out there?

Easy answer, he thought, *she wouldn't.*

"Is it drugs?"

Nicholas gave a short laugh.

"Is it sex?"

"No!" Nicholas said, almost shouting.

"You can tell me, Nicholas. I went through all the same things you are when I was your age."

Nicholas scoffed at that, "Not everything."

"Well, no not everything. I'm not a man, and I wish your father were here to talk to you about all of this, but I need you to know I'm here for you."

Bringing up his dad hurt worse than it should have. Somehow, it took the calm right out of Nicholas. He felt himself grow angry. All he wanted to do was get out of the house and get to Winter's Hall.

"Nicholas, please say something. I'm not your parents, but I can still... ."

"Then, stop trying to be!"

The words shot out of him before he could stop them. The moment stopped them both, because, just like Aunt Sherri hadn't raised her voice toward Nicholas before tonight,

Nicholas had never done the same, until now. He also had never thrown not being a parent in her face. Something he wasn't even aware would hurt her so much.

"I need to go."

He turned and pushed right out the door. He didn't say anything else, and he didn't give her time to say anything, either.

"Then, stop trying to be!"

The words fired across the small kitchen like bullets blasting from a gun. They were thrown out without a second thought, without the consideration of what they would mean if they hit, and hit they did.

Sherri Wake had not wanted to be a mother. When she was younger, she had played with dolls as all little girls do, but as she grew up, the thought of children became less and less frequent until it just became undesirable. Somehow, though, that didn't matter. Nine years ago, she had to take over for a true mother, her sister. She had received an unwanted but satisfying present in the form of a small boy who was scared and alone.

But this couldn't be the same boy, not my Nicholas.

"I need to go."

The young man who had grown from the small boy she was thinking about turned away from her. The movement gave her some reprieve, for when he had shouted at her, there had been a fire in his eyes. An anger she had never seen before; a hatred that didn't belong.

The sound of the door slamming behind him made her jump. It wasn't fear that made her so jumpy. It was just the emotion of the entire situation. She had walked into all of this barely hanging on. The last few days had all gotten so overwhelming with dead bodies of people showing up all over town. To top it all off, Nicholas, her Nicholas, was going out into that world every day with her none the wiser of where he was or what he was doing.

How could I be so bad at this?

You always heard stories about how the teenage years are the worst, but she never had reason to believe those or worry about them. Now, she found herself smack dab in the middle of the climax of her very own parenting horror story.

That's when the burn became too much, and she felt a tear roll down her cheek. She crossed her arms, trying to comfort herself. When the second tear fell, she reached up and brushed both wet trails away. She felt defeated, hurt, and most of all, like she had failed at the only important thing she had been given her entire life. She thought of her sister and how disappointed she would be.

I am so sorry.

He should have been feeling guilty about the whole ordeal. But as he peddled, warm air chugging out like the dark clouds from a ship's smokestack, Nicholas felt only anger. He knew he shouldn't, his aunt was just trying to look out for him, but for some reason, he couldn't shake it.

If she knew what I had been through, what I had done, she wouldn't be worried. I'm not just some kid.

You know if she knew what you had been through, she would be even more worried.

Still, doesn't mean I'm some kid who can't do anything on his own. I've fought real monsters out here. Far worse things than she can imagine.

You don't think she imagines the absolute worst every time you don't come home until morning, if you come home at all?

Oh, give it a rest already. Who asked you anyway?

Nicholas shook his head. If he started taking out his anger on himself, then he'd really be in for it. For awhile now, he had felt like there were two Nicholas's inside his head fighting for control. One day everything would be fine, and then the next, it'd be darker than the day before. He couldn't explain why. But here he was, peddling away from a fight with the one person who had been there for him when he needed someone.

The back tire of the Schwinn skidded on a pile of cold slush. Nicholas fumbled for a second but steadied the ride and got it back up to pace. The rest of the ride went without incident. Before he knew it, he was pulling into Winter's Hall. The majority of his anger had subsided, and now he just felt tired. For the first time, he wasn't interested in going out with Dusk. He just wanted to go home and sleep.

Going home will be fun now that you ran your mouth like you did.

The front door of Winter's Hall swung open, and Argyle greeted Nicholas with his usual nonchalant but polite tone.

"Good evening, Mr. Wake. Mr. Dusk will be down in a moment."

"I'm coming down now, Argyle," Dusk said from the top of the stairs.

He took the steps slower than usual. One arm was wrapped around a small woman's frame. It took but a moment for Nicholas to remember why he came tonight. He and Dusk planned to escort Clara to the town border and let her go from there to wherever she went when she wasn't here.

The two walked down the stairs at a hesitant pace, but even from this distance, Nicholas could see that Clara had improved. When he had last seen her, he could barely look at her. Now, her haunting beauty was back to full volume, and Nicholas remembered he liked the song.

They made it to the foyer landing, and Dusk let his arm fall. He thought she was more than capable of carrying herself now that they were on even ground.

"Hello there, young blood. It's been awhile." Clara's voice fell upon him like warm syrup spilling over flapjacks. It had been awhile, but Nicholas still knew that this was just how it felt to be around a vampire.

"Hey," he said, giving a short wave.

"Alright, let's get this over with."

"Aw, Dusk. The special care you show me is just too much."

Dusk just smirked at Clara and moved toward Nicholas. When the man looked toward him, Nicholas tried to pass off his own confident smirk.

"You alright?" Dusk said, not missing a beat.

"Yeah," Nicholas said, still trying to make it sound confident and laid back.

"Tsk, tsk. Tell me he doesn't lie that poorly all the time."

"Sadly, I can't say that."

Nicholas tried to look at both of them like they were crazy, but they weren't buying it. Eventually, he rolled his eyes, and said, "I just got into a fight with my aunt, that's all."

"Ah," Dusk said, nodding. "What did you do?"

"What? Why did I have to be the one who did something?"

"Take it from me, kid, when it comes to women, whether it is an aunt or a girlfriend, you always did something."

"Mmmm, that is a wise man talking," said Clara. "You best listen, young blood. Do you some good to be more like our Dusk here. You may learn a thing or two."

Pitch

Nicholas rolled his eyes again. "Let's get this over with," he finally said and walked out the door.

From behind him, he overheard Clara and Dusk exchange a few words at his expense.

"I guess he learns rather quick."

"That he does."

Nicholas smiled for the first time that night.

Chapter 21

They waited until darkness fell. Then, Nicholas, Dusk, and Clara left the safety of Winter's Hall behind. The plan was to have Dusk and Nicholas escort Clara to the outskirts of Pointe's Hollow through the woods. They were pretty sure they weren't going to run headfirst into an army of the undead like the other night, but they decided it was best to be cautious with everything that could be out there.

"Where's your friend?" Dusk had asked as he and Nicholas packed up for the trek. On his hip, Nicholas had his knife, and he carried a flashlight in hand. At the same time, Dusk loaded up with heavy iron and a blade of his own. Nicholas knew it probably would have been better to have more people, safety in numbers after all, but after the other night, Nicholas didn't want to endanger Will again.

"He's sitting this one out."

Dusk raised his eyebrows and nodded. "Probably for the best." Nicholas looked up at him. "Besides," he continued, "Nothing is going to happen anyway. We'll be fine."

"You think?"

"Yeah, I mean it's not really like us to constantly be running into danger. The other night was a once-in-a-lifetime fluke."

Nicholas rolled his eyes at Dusk's grin. "Yeah, sure."

The three of them walked through the woods as the last bit of daylight was disappearing below the horizon. Clara removed the dark, hooded cloak she had been wearing to shield herself. Most would need it to keep them warm, but no matter the temperature or clothing she wore, Clara was cold to the very blood in her veins.

The snow between the trees was thicker because of the limited traffic. Not many people walked through the woods around The Hollow, especially while people were showing up dead. It slowed their progress, but that was okay with them. Even though they joked, Nicholas could tell Dusk was on high alert. Nicholas tried his best to be as well, but between the three of them trudging through snow and the chattering of his teeth, he could barely hear his own thoughts.

No matter how much Nicholas and Dusk had prepared and no matter how ready they were, they would have never imagined what happened next to be the way it was to go wrong.

Dusk noticed it first, but he wasn't quick enough. Not because he wasn't good, but because it wasn't what he was ready for.

"Freeze!"

The trio stopped in ankle deep snow. They all turned to look up the tracks they had just made. Standing over the path about ten paces back, wielding a cocked firearm and the devil in his eyes was Sheriff Gordon.

"Nobody move. This ends now."

Cool air rushed against the small hairs about the sheriff's pressed collar. The steel of his gun had an icy feel, and his fingers almost stung. But in his gut, there was a fire burning. It licked and bounced, boiling his blood.

There he stood, gun in hand. Across a small patch of land, his land, the land he was supposed to protect and serve, stood this man, this monster. Sheriff Gordon blinked the cold from his eyes, so he was ready to act.

"Hands up. All of you."

The three hesitated for a moment. "Now!" Sheriff Gordon barked.

They raised their arms. He looked over the three of them. A woman Sheriff Gordon had never seen before, the Wake boy, and Him.

"You." Sheriff Gordon had a bite to his words he couldn't ever remember having before. The anger was beginning to take over, and for once Sheriff Gordon wasn't sure if he cared if it won or not.

"Sheriff, I don't... ."

"Quiet!"

The man's words died. He didn't seem to be someone who got intimidated, but he did seem to know what battles to fight and what ones he could win.

"I listened to you once," Sheriff Gordon snarled. "But no more. I'm finishing this."

Sheriff Gordon straightened as if he was going to fire.

"Sheriff," the Wake boy said as he shifted in the man's direction. It appeared to the sheriff that the boy was preparing to take the bullet for the man.

Sheriff Gordon stayed his eager trigger finger but still kept his gun trained.

"I don't know what you think Dusk has done, but it wasn't him. He's here to help."

Sheriff Gordon heard the truth in the statement. He had gotten good at telling if and when people were lying. The boy wasn't lying. But Sheriff Gordon was beyond caring. He had to do something. It was his job. This was his town. The boy began talking again.

"If you knew what we have done, what he's done for The Holl... ."

"What's he's done?!"

Sheriff Gordon's voice had been sparked red hot again. A red cloud had accumulated in Sheriff Gordon's mind. Moments of clarity came through where he knew what he was doing was irrational. But then there were the other moments when the fog clotted his mind. In this whirlwind, anger and pain combined in a storm. That mind is what fueled him now.

"I know what he's done." Sheriff Gordon raised his gun, which had slipped in the conversation. "He's killed people. He killed Donald!"

"That wasn't me, Sheriff."

"I said I was done listening to you."

"Sheriff Gordon, it wasn't him."

Sheriff Gordon was looking between the two of them. He had to do something. He was done waiting, done trying to figure it all out.

"This ends now," he said, almost under his breath.

Sheriff Gordon took aim, and the four of them sucked in a breath in unison.

A scream split the night air.

They turned and looked further into the woods. Darkness filled the blank spaces between the trees. Somewhere within that darkness, something terrible was happening.

"Oh, no. Not again."

The woman's voice was somehow musical and at the same time haunting to Sheriff Gordon's ears. He felt as if the voice was pulling him toward her and warning him to stay away all at the same time. It was a moment, and the feeling was already leaving, but for that fleeting second, he wanted to go.

As suddenly as she spoke, the woman took off running into the woods in the opposite direction of the scream. Sheriff Gordon blinked and regained himself from the shock of it all.

"Don't move!"

The woman continued to run as if she didn't hear the sheriff. Or maybe she just didn't care. Something had scared her so much, it was as if the devil himself was on her heels.

Then, Dusk moved. He took off in the direction of the scream. Sheriff Gordon didn't think. He reacted. He spun, turning with the man. Gun leading arms, arms leading shoulders, and shoulders leading hips. Before there was a moment to consider what was right, or what was wrong, Sheriff Gordon pulled the trigger.

The bullet flew but missed its mark. The man had disappeared behind one of the trees. Splinters exploded from the trunk. Wood dust and snow popped off in a small cloud.

"Sheriff, no!"

He turned and pointed the gun at the advancing boy. In a flash, hatred melted off the sheriff's face as he realized what he was doing. The gun dropped to his side.

"God damn it. Stay out of the way, boy."

Sheriff Gordon spat the last word. Then, without a second thought, he, too, turned and followed the man into the dark forest toward whatever made that scream.

Snow kicked up behind Dusk's booted feet like waves that crashed against The Hollow's shore. He bounded toward the scream they had heard, weaving between trees and pushing through the snow.

Pitch

Dusk was good at finding trouble, but suddenly, he was unsure of which way to go. He skidded to a stop, snow piling up around his feet.

Silence.

The trees, the snow, and the cool night air had secrets. But they weren't talking. At least not yet.

Dusk waited. Most wouldn't have heard it. Most would have thought it was just the wind or thought it was their ears playing tricks on them. Dusk heard it, however, and he knew it wasn't the wind because his ears were keen, sharpened after years of hunting. On the night wind, a gasp sailed to Dusk's ears.

Now that he had his new heading, his feet were throwing up snow once again. The gasp had not been far away. After a few moments of heated running, Dusk burst through a thicket of trees onto a haunting sight.

Clumps of snow had been piled up in a chaotic pattern like a small child's failed sandcastle attempts at the beach. The piles surrounded a couple standing close together. They looked as if they were in a lover's embrace. This embrace, however, was not warm and fueled by passion. It was cold and infected by torment.

"Hey!" Dusk said, pulling his revolver from its holster.

The couple parted, and scarlet pebbles rained forth in an arc. The pebbles hit the snow, popping like bubbles and sinking deep in the cold with the internal heat.

The macabre sight stared back at the gun-wielding hunter, unafraid. A face of marble with lips of crimson snarled at Dusk. Although the night was cold, the thing wore only pants while its chest sat bare. Suspended in the air by its ivory arms was the lifeless body of a woman. Her arms drifted at her sides as weak as leaves on a tree in November.

The scene hung there heavy in the air for a moment as Dusk took in everything, weighing the options. Then, angry and impatient, the creature screamed at him.

"Ah, shut up." Dusk fired his old revolver.

The bullet struck the thing on the right side of the chest. Gore burst from the expanding wound. However, the creature remained standing. It looked down at the blood spilling from itself, annoyed. A thin tendril of steam poured from the wound.

Dusk lowered his gun a little to see what exactly was happening. Flesh bubbled, and the thing hissed as Dusk's silver bullet popped free. Once it was rid of the disturbance, the thing's wound began to close itself in front of Dusk, skin and sinew stretched across the dark hole, stitching itself together.

"Well, this isn't good."

The woman's body fell into the snow with a puff, as the creature turned, lowering itself, ready to attack. Its claws rolled and cracked as it readied.

Dusk holstered his gun in a slow, methodical movement. Continuing his cautious pace, he began to pull out his tomahawk. His fingers grazed the hardwood handle, worn by use. As soon as skin met wood, it all started.

Bounding forth, the beast came at Dusk, arms and claws first. The thing moved even faster than Dusk had anticipated. Even with his heightened response time after years of practice, he had only enough time to jump to one side, missing the onslaught by inches. The snow softened his fall, but the cold bit at his extremities. Dusk grunted and clenched, trying to get his blood flowing and halt the numbing. With the cold dropping away, Dusk gained his feet. The creature was already on him, slashing and snarling.

Razors in the guise of claws ripped through the air around Dusk. To keep away from the blows, Dusk had to duck and weave like a boxer trying to keep his distance during a late round in a title match. As he maneuvered around the blows, his top half began to move faster than his lower half. Fearing he would lose his footing at any moment, Dusk attempted to counter the fall. Taking a wide step to the left was supposed to create space and time for Dusk to correct himself. That's what it was supposed to do; what ended up happening was that he overestimated his jump and felt the ground slip out from under him. He went down shoulder first, followed by his hip and face. The snow slapped him with its wet cold as if to mock his failure.

God damn snow, Dusk thought. If he continued like this, he was going to spend more time in the snow than in the fight.

He didn't have time to get back on his feet. The monster had been right on him when he fell. Dusk rolled, so he was facing upward at his attacker. As expected, the thing was right there, already making his descent to crush Dusk.

Wanting to raise his arm in defense but knowing it wouldn't stop the beast in time, Dusk tucked his knees to his chest.

It worked. The monster fell onto Dusk, its chest connecting with his feet. Not only did this keep Dusk safe from the gnashing teeth and menacing claws, but it also allowed him to use the thing's momentum against it. Dusk rolled back onto his shoulders, kicked over his head, and sent the beast to its turn in the snow.

The two combatants both took the chance to regroup. Dusk stood, shaking his hands free from clinging snow. The monster seemed to not even notice the snow. Its body felt like dead weight, almost like stone, when Dusk had kicked it. It possibly couldn't even feel the cold. No matter if it felt the cold, it did take a moment to reassess Dusk as an opponent. Dusk assumed it rarely, if ever, ran into a human who gave the thing this much fight. Its shoulders heaved, and fingers twitched as it tried to figure out what to do next.

Dusk didn't want to let this thing get smart. It was a beast, and right now it was thinking like one, which gave him the upper hand. If the human part, no matter how small that part was, started to think, then Dusk could be in serious trouble.

He wiped his nose on his sleeve, "Well? Come on with it then, you ugly bastard!"

The thing's face retracted and then cracked into a fit of rage.

That seemed to work, one half of Dusk's brain said. *Oh, goody*, the other half retorted.

The thing made a noise that combined a scream, a howl, and a bark. It sent ice straight into Dusk's veins, but it melted in a moment due to the fire burning inside him. A duel of ice and fire. Vampire and human. Dusk made his own battle cry as the thing attacked once more.

The distance between the two closed. Dusk's limbs tingled with anticipation. His fingers flexed, he bounced on his toes, and his face contorted into a fiendish grin of anger and desire. A few more breaths, and the fight would begin again.

"Bring it on," Dusk said under a heavy breath.

BANG.

The thing was thrown off stride, mere feet in front of Dusk. A hip exploded from the creature, causing it to stumble. It whipped its head around, snarling.

About twenty yards away, Sheriff Gordon stood, still aiming as heat waved off the gun's barrel. He looked just as angry as he had before, but now he also looked crazed. His eyes were wide, but the pupils were tiny, dark pin holes. They darted around as if unsure what was real and what wasn't.

"Sheriff!"

The beast's pointed ears twitched at Dusk's words, but it didn't take its eyes off Sheriff Gordon. Then, it took a step toward what it saw as the easier target.

"Freeze!" Sheriff Gordon said, trying to make it a yell. If he hadn't had years of experience behind the badge, it would have failed, but even with that, it didn't one hundred percent succeed. Dusk, even from his distance, could see the fear creeping into the sheriff's eyes.

Again, the beast pushed forward. Its steps were direct and deliberate. It was sizing up this new opponent and liked what it saw.

BANG. BANG. BANG.

Sheriff Gordon fired back to back to back, pulling the trigger without hesitation. He hit every shot center mass. Blood and flesh blew out from the creature like party poppers at a New Year's party. The shots would have brought down any person, and any animal for that matter. But monsters were different. They thrived when other things would die. It kept moving, and as it did, its flesh mended itself just like it did when Dusk had shot it.

Sheriff Gordon was a good distance away, but his eyes were keen enough to hit the shots, so he saw what was happening.

"What the hell?"

Dusk couldn't hear the words that were whispered under the sheriff's breath, but he read it on his lips. If he hadn't been able to see the sheriff's lips, he would have known anyway. It was written all over the officer's face.

"Sheriff, run!"

Sheriff Gordon broke out of his stupor. He didn't run as most would at Dusk's word. He was too strong-willed for that. That would have to break before he would run. Unfortunately, the vampire was the perfect thing to break it.

The wraith of a beast thrashed at Sheriff Gordon, head low, arms out, and legs pumping. Sheriff Gordon raised his gun and fired two more shots. Ever the marksman, both shots hit, but still the beast came. It dove, claws reaching.

Sheriff Gordon ducked and stepped to the side. But he was too slow, held his ground too long. Years of being a sheriff of a small town was not good preparation to fight monsters. The beast hit his right shoulder. The blow slammed the sheriff with the force of linebacker. It tossed him through the air as if he wasn't the large man that he was, but a child. His progress stopped only when he came into contact with a tree.

Crunching and popping echoed through the night. Dusk grimaced as he thought the sheriff would hit the ground, out cold, if not dead. This, however, was a grave underestimate of the sheriff's strength. He was back on his feet in moments, shaken, and broken but standing.

The beast was also at it again, running toward the sheriff. Sheriff Gordon moved away, but his weakened legs were not making it easy.

Dusk moved to help. He pulled the tomahawk back, took aim, and then let it fly. The distance was great, situation dire, but Dusk was a true monster hunter.

As the beast dove again, the blade bit into its side. The force put the fiend to the ground. It hit and began to thrash and yelp. Limbs kicked and beat as the monster tried to fend off the burning from the silver sunk in its flesh.

"Sheriff, get out of here!"

Dusk was wasting no time. He knew the sheriff was in bad shape, holding on only by his outstanding strength of will. There was no way to know exactly how bad, but he knew that if the sheriff didn't leave, it was going to get a lot worse.

Sheriff Gordon looked flustered, but he also realized Dusk was speaking sense. Clenching from the pain of his wounds and, Dusk suspected, his hurt pride by receiving help from a man he thought was to blame for many terrible things, Sheriff Gordon began moving in the direction of town. His progress was slow, so Dusk was going to have to buy him some time.

Before Dusk could formulate a plan, the creature was on its feet. The tomahawk was still stuck into the thing's side. It stuck outward like a lame tree branch on a sapling. The thing looked at it in disgust. It gripped it with one clawed hand.

Pulling outward, the thing ripped the weapon from its side with a vicious sound.

The wound sizzled, and tendrils of smoke drifted upward as if the blade had been red hot when it struck the beast. This wound did eventually act exactly like the others. Skin stretched across the chasm like fingers intertwining together to join in a firm union. As the wound finished its self-healing, the beast inspected the tomahawk, smelling the now gore-stained blade. It recoiled from the metal. Then, it looked back at Dusk. Dusk stared back, daring the monster to make a move.

"Come on, then," he said, waving his hands toward himself.

The creature seemed to smile at that. Then, it hissed at him, tossing the tomahawk aside. That's when the beast did make its move; it was just a different move from what Dusk expected. It turned and chased after Sheriff Gordon heading toward town.

"Shit," Dusk said.

He moved to give chase when a hand grabbed his arm. Dusk turned, ready to fight once again, but it was just the kid.

"What's going on? Did you kill it?"

"No. It's gone after the sheriff."

"Well then, what are we waiting for? Let's go!"

Dusk shook his head, "I'm going, you're staying."

"What?" Dusk thought the boy would be hurt and offended by being considered useless or not wanted. Instead, Nicholas looked angry. "Why?"

"She needs you more than I do," Dusk said, pointing at the woman the creature had left on the ground.

"But... ."

"No buts, and no time. Now go!"

Then, Dusk was off. Scooping up his tomahawk from where the vampire discarded it, he turned toward the direction of town. With a heavy exhale, Dusk kicked off to chase after the monster.

Chapter 22

Now that Nicholas was alone, he realized how quiet it was. The snow seemed to mute the noise of the world. He knew everything was happening around him, but it seemed like he stood all alone, as if he was standing on the moon or at the bottom of the ocean. It was nice to be alone.

A cold breeze whipped Nicholas in the face, and he remembered what he was there to do. He turned to the body lying there in the snow. In a few strides, Nicholas was by its side. It was a woman's body without a doubt, but the hair obscured the face. He turned her over by placing a hand on each shoulder.

"Oh, no."

The body was Michelle, Mr. Lloyd's assistant from the library. Her skin had paled to a startling white. There was a wound on her neck, gushing blood.

Nicholas was about to get up and chase after Dusk, believing all hope was lost, when a warm puff of air came out from between Michelle's lips.

"Oh, God," Nicholas said. Nicholas's hand shot out of its own accord and grabbed at her wound, trying to staunch the bleeding. "Hold on, Michelle. Hold on."

Nicholas's hand had to sink into the snow to cover the whole wound. The cold sensation of the snow contrasted the heat from the blood coating his hand from the two punctures in Michelle's neck. Pressing harder, Nicholas tried all he could to get the flow to stop. He couldn't tell if his efforts were worth it, but he had to try.

Michelle's breath was slow and ragged. Pressing as hard as he was, Nicholas could feel her pulse in his fingers. It pumped the blood through the spaces in and around his hand. The blood pumped slower and slower as the heart gave up the fight.

"No, no, no."

A waving fog of breath slipped through Michelle's lips. It slithered out like an eel, swimming up into the winter air. Then, after a few weaker hums, Nicholas lost the pulse. He waited and then removed his hand. Blood still flowed from Michelle's neck, but it was sluggish now that her heart no longer pushed it.

Pins poked at Nicholas's eyes. Fighting back tears and ignoring the twisting pain growing in his stomach, Nicholas brushed a few strands of Michelle's hair off her face. He had seen people die, usually bad people, but people nonetheless. But this was different. She was innocent. She had no idea what was going on in this damned town. Mr. Lloyd had assured him and Will of this as they did their research. She just saw The Hollow as a picturesque town where she could work and enjoy her life. She had no concept of the dark world that was thriving here. Like a cancer, it haunted this place in secret until it reared its twisted face, causing pain and death.

It wasn't only her innocence that hit Nicholas hard. He had not only seen her die, but he had also felt it. He had felt the life leave her body, and it was terrible.

Another breeze wormed through the trees. Michelle was dead, but the world was still alive. Nicholas was still alive. It made the situation even more melancholy.

As sudden as the wind had picked up, it stopped, and the world stilled. All sound came to a dead stop, and Nicholas heard only his own heartbeat in his ears. Everything stopped. Even the blood that had been flowing from Michelle's neck stopped.

Nicholas went through a maddening sequence of hope, confusion, and, finally, realization. Then, everything came back to life, even Michelle.

Michelle's eyes burst open. They had no color. Large, black circles sat on a field of white that was marked by rivers of red veins. They rolled to Nicholas. Her nostrils flared, and her lips parted.

Nicholas could hear his heart beat, but now he could also feel his blood pulse through his body. He almost seemed to sense his veins bulging at his skin.

Her lips continued to part and slide into a smile as Michelle revealed that her teeth were no longer the off-white cubes they had been mere moments before. They now were bone white and jagged in a bear trap-like connection. The connections were locked tight by two enlarged fangs from the top row of her teeth.

Nicholas wanted to say something, but his mouth felt like it was coated in sand. It didn't matter, however, because Michelle didn't want to talk. She grabbed Nicholas, but her arm moved faster than she anticipated, and she smacked him in the chest. The blow sent Nicholas reeling. He rolled end-over-end until he hit just right to stop him dead in the snow.

Laying on his back, Nicholas looked up into the night sky, dazed. Nicholas got to his feet teetering back and forth.

"Michelle," Nicholas said, hand raising in a 'hold on' gesture. "It's okay. Something bad has happened, something very bad. But you're going to be okay."

Michelle snarled at Nicholas. Her pale face tilted to one side like a dog.

"We can help," Nicholas continued. "You're going to be okay, I promise."

After a moment, Michelle settled and looked as if she was pleading for help. It hurt Nicholas in the bottom of his stomach.

Just as Nicholas started to believe that everything was going to be alright, Michelle's face cracked. It was as if her skin was a mask, and now her true face was breaking through. Her hair whipped around as she shook her head in madness. Then, with a snap, she was back looking at him. But instead of Michelle's face, Nicholas saw a demon. Skin wrinkled, brow scowled, and skin beyond white. It was so light it turned translucent.

With a ferocious roar, Michelle or whatever she was now, rushed Nicholas. Still uneasy on his feet, Nicholas had just enough time to get out of the way. He was down on his hands and knees in the snow and then back up in moments. He backed up from Michelle.

No longer Michelle, Nicholas thought. *That's not Michelle. That's a monster.*

The beast circled, angling itself at Nicholas. Not wasting time, Nicholas began to move away. Before he had taken five steps, his back hit a tree. He turned, startled, and that gave the creature the chance to attack again.

Arms swinging, the thing came at Nicholas. Nicholas rolled around the tree. His progress was stopped by a branch. It hit him in the chest, knocking the wind from him. The beast's attack hit the tree but still caught Nicholas in the back. The force snapped the branch Nicholas was pinned against.

For what felt like the hundredth time, Nicholas was in the snow again. He rolled from his stomach to his back. The monster was already descending. It straddled Nicholas and howled. Nicholas grasped the branch that fell with him and swung, catching the thing on the side of the head. Its howl fell quiet, but it was quick to return its attention to Nicholas.

Realizing his first attack wasn't as effective as he hoped, Nicholas raised his hands above his head, brandishing the branch. Without thinking, he thrust it forward. The broken end pierced the beast's chest.

The thing screamed a high pitched, wretched wail that sent gooseflesh rippling across Nicholas's skin. Though he wanted to let go and cover his ears, Nicholas held on.

Around the protruding wooden stake, the thing's skin and, in turn, clothes began to burn. Then, everything turned black and fell apart into thin pieces of ash.

"Nicholas?"

The voice was quiet, confused and pained. Nicholas looked up to see Michelle again. Tears hung at the corners of her eyes. One got too heavy and spilled over, dripping down Michelle's cheek. Nicholas tried to respond but couldn't.

The burning spread faster than before. Michelle screamed. No longer was there an undertone of monster. It was all her. A pure, human scream of fear and pain. Then, she was gone. Small flecks of ash rained around Nicholas as the world grew quiet again.

I killed her.

Screams echoed through the night. Dusk heard it, but he had his own job to do. The kid was going to be fine. He was stronger now. He could handle himself on his own. Dusk didn't always have to be there to save him.

Even though he had left just after the creature did, he had lost the trail. The creature's footprints were recognizable at first. Then, the stride became longer, harder to follow. Dusk looked up to search his surroundings, and then they were gone. He couldn't turn back to retrace what had happened. There was no time.

He had slowed his pace as he scoured the ground for clues. Then, he saw them. Not the creature's footprints but the sheriff's. They were long drags, an obvious sign that someone dealing with a great deal of pain had caused them. Apparently, the sheriff had made good time even though he was fighting stacking odds.

BANG!

Dusk's head shot up. He looked toward the blast. "Son of a bitch." He had fallen too far behind. The creature had found Sheriff Gordon.

"What are you?" Sheriff Gordon said.

The thing snarled in response. Sheriff Gordon had to take in that sunken face. Its skin pulled taught and plastered with gore.

BANG!

He fired and missed. Even though he wouldn't admit it, even to himself, his fear was getting to him. That, mixed with the pain racking his body, had thrown off his aim.

The creature advanced.

Sheriff Gordon thought about firing again. Seeing the gun shake in his hand, he decided it would be useless. He looked around him.

There was nothing.

The creature advanced again.

Realizing he had no choice, Sheriff Gordon flipped the gun around so he held the barrel, and the butt became the weapon. He could feel the heat of the gun through his glove.

The movement jostled his insides. A sharp pain shocked his chest.

At least two ribs, maybe more, he thought. It was going to be a rough time, but he had fought through worse.

"Come on then. I ain't got all night, you son of a bitch!"

The thing screeched in acknowledgment.

It attacked. In two strides, it had cut the distance between them in half. The rest was covered with a leap. The two collided and rolled to the ground. Sheriff Gordon felt his broken ribs scream in pain and another one snap, along with a pop of something in his left shoulder. Coming to a stop, Sheriff Gordon found himself below the beast. It dove its head down. He thrust the gun up at it. Its jaws were snapping, trying to bite the sheriff. In one of the jerking movements, Sheriff Gordon got the gun between its teeth. It clamped down and tried to pull back, but Sheriff Gordon pushed, driving it deeper.

"Choke on it, you bastard!"

It pushed forward as if to comply, but it shook its head as it did, making it hard for the sheriff to keep ahold of the gun. They continued their sadistic tug-of-war, fighting for an upper hand.

Frustrated, the beast began to swing its arms, swiping the sheriff. The flailing threw it off balance, and Sheriff Gordon took the opportunity to push the creature off. It fell back into the snow, freeing him.

The effort took a lot out of him. He tried to get up and strike as the thing was down, but his ribs fought against him. Pain burned through his body, racking his muscles to the point that he thought he was going to be sick. He fell back into the snow.

Before his pain subsided, a hand grasped his thigh above the knee. It pushed, putting its weight on Sheriff Gordon as it picked itself up, making him grit his teeth in agony.

As the beast rose, it looked into the sheriff's eyes. The sheriff's eyes blinked as the pain in his leg intensified, and then he met the creature's gaze. It began to squeeze, but Sheriff Gordon wouldn't look away from the terror in front of him. The pressure increased, and then his skin popped as the thing's claws dug into the flesh. Sheriff Gordon ground his teeth harder, pleading in his mind for it to stop as he felt the warmth of his blood spill down his leg. But if he knew how it would end, maybe he wouldn't have pleaded so hard.

The thing ripped its hand free from Sheriff Gordon's leg. He felt and heard his leg shred. Flesh tore away in ragged ribbons as the blood showered the snow around him. There was a warm iron smell that cut through the cold pine air. With all the pain, the sounds, and the smells, Sheriff Gordon wasn't sure if he even had a leg left.

That's when Sheriff Gordon did something he never thought he'd do. He screamed for his life.

Dusk came on the scene just as the sheriff's scream fell silent. He saw the two. Sheriff Gordon lying in the snow, and the monster lapping up a mess of red that he tried to hold onto as most of it spilled into the snow below.

Knowing there was no time to assess or plan, Dusk rushed them. Lowering his shoulder, Dusk hit the monster, throwing his full weight behind the blow. The thing was so concentrated on its macabre meal, it didn't even notice Dusk until they collided. It went sprawling into the snow, the mess it was holding spilling around it.

The blow didn't leave Dusk unharmed. He regained his feet, putting a hand on his knee and pushing himself to straighten. He looked toward the thing. It was spinning in a circle, looking for what it had lost. It scooped up handfuls trying to regain anything it could, but the blood had disappeared into the snow.

It stopped its frantic search and turned to Dusk. They stared each other down once again. Dusk heard footsteps behind him and knew the kid had come onto the scene. Sparing a glance, Dusk saw he was wielding a broken tree branch. The kid was holding it in front of him with both hands in a death grip.

After a momentary eye shift toward the kid, Dusk looked back to the beast. The creature had shifted its attention to Nicholas. Then, it did something Dusk didn't expect. It took a step back. Then, it turned to Dusk, back to Nicholas, and once again back to Dusk. It was trying to figure something out. Maybe trying to decipher if the two were working together or trying to size up if it could take them both at the same time. Dusk couldn't quite tell.

No matter what it was trying to figure out, it made a decision. The thing straightened and clenched both its fists. This was followed by what appeared to be a distortion in the thing's appearance. It looked like a ripple. As if the thing was made of water instead of flesh. With a violent tearing sound, two huge appendages extended themselves out of the thing's back. They looked like overlong arms with too many joints. Each ended in a single, pointed bone. They seemed to evolve in front of their eyes, and there was no mistaking them for what they really were: wings.

The thing screamed a short wail. Thin membranes spanned the space between bone fingers extending the length of the thing's back. The skin scooped air as the wings began to flap. After a few initial pumps, the thing's feet lifted off the ground.

Dusk lowered himself, thinking the thing would use its new tools to attack. The thing being airborne would leave Dusk and the kid at a huge disadvantage, but they had been through worse. Just as Dusk was formulating a plan to counter this new threat, the surprises continued. The thing gave each of them one last look and then turned and flew off into the night sky.

After a few moments, Dusk believed the thing did leave and let his body relax. The kid ran up to him, still looking up into the sky.

"It flew away?" the kid said.

Dusk didn't respond; he turned and dropped to the sheriff. His legs were almost beyond recognition, and he had lost a lot of blood. They would have to act fast if they were going to save him.

A sound of shifting snow made Dusk turn. The kid was running off into the woods.

"Hey! Where are you off to?"

The kid skidded to a stop, and turned. "We have to go after it."

"We have to help him," Dusk said, pointing at the broken body next to him. "Let it go."

"No. We have to go after it. We have to stop it. We have to kill it!" The kid took off running again.

"Nicholas!"

This stopped him in his tracks. He turned and looked at Dusk. Dusk looked right back, and after a moment, he said, "He'll die if we don't get him to help, right now."

Nicholas looked down at the sheriff, and his face dropped as if he had just now noticed the man. "Okay," he said, jogging back to Dusk's side. "We'll have to keep his leg as straight as possible. Here, we can use this to make a splint." He offered up his broken branch.

Dusk nodded.

As the two got to work, Dusk thought about what he had seen when the kid had turned back after hearing his name. It was something Dusk had never seen in him. Something he didn't think existed in the kid.

Pitch

It was darkness.

Chapter 23

The spinning door at the front of the hospital seemed heavier than any door should be. Its weight seemed to push back on Emily as she tried to get through it as fast as possible. The red and blue spinning lights from the squad car that had picked her up reflected from the glass. It flashed back and forth and added a surreal feeling to the moment and the whole ride here. As if everything had slowed down, and Emily was left at normal speed.

"Something has happened."

Emily had feared these words for her entire life. The only worse fear she had was the pause between these words and what came after them. That pause seemed to be a black hole. Losing yourself and everything you hold dear. Heartbeat after heartbeat would tick by, and you'd still be there, drifting.

The only reprieve she had had from the whole ordeal was the words that followed weren't Chris telling her that her dad was dead, but it wasn't comforting, either. Apparently, her dad was hurt, and by the way, everything was being handled, he was hurt bad. Chris had given her vague details. He had been found in the woods.

Dad? In the woods? This late? In the snow?

It didn't make sense. It wasn't the only thing that didn't make sense. Dusk and Nicholas had been the ones to find him. The person in The Hollow her dad hated the most and her boyfriend. Emily was trying to make sense of all of it. Trying to pull the necessary pieces out of the box to build the puzzle, but then she realized her hands were shaking too badly to do that. She needed to get to the hospital and make sure her dad was okay.

Her fingers were snow white as she grasped the front counter asking to see her father. The nurse asked who she was and who she was there to see. Emily was too lost, though. She just kept asking to see her father. She thought it was absurd to explain who her father was. Everyone knew the sheriff. Later on, she realized that everyone knew her father in The Hollow, but the sheriff's injuries were too bad to be treated by Dr. Ballwin. He had been taken to the nearest hospital, but that was far enough outside of The Hollow for no one to know who her father was, or who Emily was.

The nurse and Emily tried to get the information they needed from each other until Chris came in. He was concerned but still level-headed. He explained the situation, and Emily finally got her answer.

It wasn't good.

Emily sat next to the bed with her arm extended, holding her father's hand. Her eyes were wet, but she had been able to stop crying. Her whole world had been shaken tonight. Things she had feared for years came true, and there was nothing she could do. The only reason she was able to stop crying, the small bit of comfort she had, was the slow rising and falling of her father's chest.

When she had first arrived, he had been in surgery. The nurse had very little information about his condition, but she was able to get the point across. The sheriff was in a very dire situation. He had lost a lot of blood, but the doctor seemed confident that he would pull through.

Emily sat in the waiting room barely holding back her torrent of emotions. She didn't want to break down here in the hospital. Especially with Chris sitting a few seats away from her. She liked Chris, thought he was a good cop, but they weren't close.

Time was hard to keep track of as Emily sat there. It could have been minutes, hours, or even days. She couldn't tell. People came and went. They seemed to move around Emily as if they were on a different plane of existence. Doctors, nurses, and even friends of her dad's like Dr. Ballwin. He came in, put a hand on Emily's shoulder, and then moved to talk with a doctor.

After an indiscernible amount of time, Sheila showed up, and Emily was very glad to see her. Not being as much as a motherly figure as a much older confidant, Sheila had been there for Emily as the woman in her life ever since she lost her mother.

The two greeted each other with a large hug. Emily fell into Sheila's arms. Sheila gracefully held her up and rubbed her back, whispering consoling words into Emily's ear. They conversed for a few moments, but Sheila could tell Emily was too emotionally exhausted to talk for long. They sat in silence until the doctor came and told them the sheriff had sustained substantial injuries. He further explained it had been touch and go for quite awhile, but in the end, they had been able to stabilize him.

The weight of the world cracked and fell away from Emily in an instant. Tears fell, but now they were tears of joy instead of loss. Sheila continued to talk to the doctor, getting the details of everything. Emily heard words like "recovery time" and "long-term reactions," but she wasn't worried about that right now. She just knew her dad was alive, and that was all that mattered.

Now, sitting next to him, she squeezed his hand. Sheila and Chris had come in with her at the start but eventually left, leaving the two of them alone. Emily was told it was likely he wouldn't wake up for a day or two. He had lost a lot of blood, and he was going to need to rest. Emily didn't care. She had to be there.

Something caught her attention from the corner of her eye. Emily turned and saw Nicholas through the small window in the door to her father's room. When she first saw him, her chest warmed, and a smile broke across her face. It was an instant reaction she had when she saw him. Then, remembering he had been the one who had found her father under strange circumstances, circumstances that had to be related to the secrets he had been keeping from her, she became wary.

"I'll be right back, okay, Dad?" Emily said, squeezing his hand again. He continued his slow breathing and steady pulse.

Emily stood up and went to the door. Instead of letting Nicholas in, she shut the door behind herself, moving out into the hall.

"Hey," Nicholas said.

"Hey."

"How is he?"

Emily sighed, "Good, good. Still resting, but the doctor says he should be awake late tomorrow sometime."

Nicholas looked relieved, "That's good."

"Yeah, yeah." Emily chewed on her lower lip for a moment. She was so tired from everything that had happened, but she had to say something. "So, the doctor said you told them that it was a bear attack."

Nicholas didn't say anything.

"They said you… said that you, him, and Richard Dusk had gone hunting, and the bear came out of nowhere."

Nicholas kept quiet.

"So, I guess I was wondering, what story are you gonna tell me?"

This hurt Nicholas. She could read it on his face, but he also couldn't meet her eyes, so she knew she was right.

"What happened?"

Nicholas looked back at Emily. He looked so pained, but Emily was holding strong.

Finally, Nicholas spoke, "Em."

That was it. One word didn't say much, but his tone said everything. It was a tone she had heard her father use with her time and time again.

"What happened, Nicholas?"

Emily was beginning to lose her patience.

"I can't tell you."

"You can't tell me?" Emily was surprised by this, but at the same time had she expected anything else? "My dad is in that bed in there, Nicholas. He could have died tonight, and all you're giving me is a hunting accident. As if that wasn't the most ridiculous thing I've ever heard."

Nicholas lost the ability to look her in the eye. When he spoke, he was quiet, "I'm sorry Em, but I can't tell you. It's for your own good, I swear. I'm sorry."

"Jesus!" Emily finally broke. The situation was just so absurd. "For two people who couldn't stand to spend any time together, you and my father couldn't be more alike. With the way you two act around me, you'd think I was made out of glass."

Nicholas shrunk where he was standing. Emily wanted to scream.

"I'm not stupid, Nicholas. I know something is going on. I don't know why you guys think keeping me in the dark is the best thing."

"Nobody is saying you're stupid," Nicholas finally said.

Well, you could have fooled me, Emily thought but didn't want to stop him from talking now that he finally was.

"There is something going on. But," Nicholas exhaled.

Emily's patience was already frail, so she couldn't hold back anymore. "But what? Why won't you tell me anything? Any of you guys? What is the big secret?"

Nicholas just shook his head. "We are just trying to protect you, Em. Your dad and I are just worried about you. We don't want you to get hurt."

"Well, maybe you shouldn't worry about that anymore."

His head turned back to her, and Emily could see Nicholas's pain. She might as well have stabbed him. Now, however, Emily didn't care.

"I think you should go," she said, reaching up and wiping a tear out of her eye.

"Em, please don't… ."

Emily cut him off, "I have to go back and check on my dad."

Thinking she couldn't take looking at him anymore, she turned, opening the door and then closing it behind her.

She took a moment and then moved into the room, dropping into her chair beside the bed. At first, she didn't grab her father's hand again. She was furious at Nicholas and also at her father. It was very hard to be mad at the man in the bed in front of her, but she was. Everyone seemed to be against her. She felt like an outsider, and she hated it.

Even though she was angry with him, she wished Nicholas was there with her, holding her. She felt so alone. It would have been wonderful to have him near. She looked back to the window in the door, half hoping to see him there looking in through the window.

The window was empty.

She turned back to her father. "Hey, Dad. I'm back now," Emily said, leaning forward, grabbing his hand, the whole while, containing a raging conflict of emotional warfare and fighting back tears.

The thud of the mug shook Nicholas from his mental captivity. Warm tendrils of sweet-smelling fog wafted toward his nose. He tilted his head, so he could look inside the cup. The dark, milky liquid of hot chocolate met his gaze.

"I believe there is nothing hot chocolate cannot fix."

Nicholas looked up and found Argyle looking back at him. It was strange. Argyle was never unfriendly toward Nicholas, but his attitude always leaned more toward dismissive. The act of kindness was out of character but appreciated.

"Thank you," Nicholas said with a weak smile.

Argyle nodded and left the boy to sit and sip the warm comfort. He crossed the room, falling back into his usual demeanor.

"Where's mine?" Dusk said, his feet propped up on a chair and arms behind his head.

"I'm sorry, sir, did you want some? I completely forgot to read your mind when you entered the home."

"Alright, alright. Point taken. Be gone with ya' already."

"Of course, sir, right away, sir."

No matter how deep his sour mood ran, Nicholas couldn't help but smile at the two. It had become a constant over the past few months. It made him feel at home, even though he wasn't.

Pitch

He sat with his chin resting on one of the large wooden tables in the Winter's Hall library. Books lay around him, spines open and sprinkled with pages of notes. Nicholas thought coming back here and getting back to work on their research would help him get over the dangerous events of the night along with everything with Emily. It didn't. It felt exactly like what it was, him hitting his head up against a wall.

Nicholas sighed and put his forehead on the table.

"Must be going well over there," Dusk said.

"Shut up," Nicholas said, not raising his head, so it came out muffled, bouncing off the wood of the table.

He heard Dusk's feet hit the ground behind him and felt him approach.

"Look, kid, it's been a rough night. How about we call it, huh?"

Nicholas didn't move right away. He wanted to stay and figure this out. They'd spent days reading everything they could get their hands on about The Hollow, and all they had to show for their trouble were more questions. Nicholas wanted answers.

Nicholas shook his head, rolling it on the wood, still not wanting to look up. Dusk sighed behind him and went back to his two-chair combo in the corner. When he had first arrived, Nicholas offered to let Dusk help. Dusk had been quick to decline, saying he was more of a man of action and to let him know if one of those books attacked, because he'd be there at a moment's notice to shoot it.

Still, Nicholas didn't stop with or without his help. Nicholas wasn't going to admit the real reason he didn't want to stop. He couldn't admit it to himself. He was afraid to be alone. Not because he thought he was in danger, but because he didn't want to think about everything that had happened. He didn't want to think about Sheriff Gordon lying in the hospital bed. He didn't want to think about Michelle, about killing the thing Michelle had become and her becoming

Michelle once again at the end. And he didn't want to think about Emily.

Emily, the girl of his dreams. The girl who had agreed to be his girlfriend. The girl who had also decided not to be a little over an hour ago. Or at least he thought that's what had happened. She wanted to know what had happened to her father. Not the story he had given the doctors and not one of the half-truths he had shared with her in the past. She wanted the truth.

How could I tell her the truth?

This was a perplexing conundrum. Nicholas thought as more people found out about the truth, it would be easier to tell people, especially ones close to him. It turned out to be the complete opposite. The more people who were on the inside, the more people seemed to get hurt. Will had found out, and how close had he come to meeting his end on his first night out with Dusk and Nicholas. Sheriff Gordon knew little and wouldn't accept what was going on, and he was currently in the hospital. Finally, there was Michelle. She had known nothing. Not one thing about this town and its darkness.

And now she's dead.

With everything that had happened, how could Emily expect him to tell her what was going on? He had been honest when he said he felt like he shouldn't tell her anything in order to keep her safe. Even with what had happened with Michelle, the less Emily knew, the better. The less she knew, the less she would want to help, and the less danger she was in. Thinking it all through, maybe it was better she had dumped him. He had been bad luck and, hopefully, she had gotten out just in time.

Telling himself this did make him feel a little better about things, but he still was heartbroken. Once she went back to see the sheriff, Nicholas had stared at her through the door's window. He looked, hoping she would turn, hoping she wanted him to be there as bad as he wanted to be there. But she hadn't looked up. So, Nicholas left.

He lifted his head, taking a sip of his hot chocolate. He looked at the books in front of him. As he surveyed the table, he tried to see something he hadn't already seen or read a hundred times. He picked up a book from the far side of the table that didn't seem too familiar. After reading a few lines, he remembered he had already been through this part. Deciding to give it one more try, he ruffled around twenty pages and tried again. For a second, he thought he had something fresh, and then he was once again disappointed.

Closing the book, Nicholas tossed it aside. As one hand removed his glasses, the other reached up, pinching the bridge of his nose.

"That can't be good," Dusk said.

Nicholas scoffed, "Don't you have anything better to do than sit here and give me a hard time?"

For a moment, Dusk didn't respond. Nicholas turned to look at him. Without his glasses, it was tough to see him, but it looked as if Dusk wasn't even looking at him. He replaced his glasses to check.

Dusk was standing, his chair forgotten. His eyes were looking past Nicholas. Nicholas was going to ask him what he was looking at when he noticed Dusk's gun was in his hand. Fearing the worst, he turned to see what had grabbed Dusk's attention.

At first, Nicholas saw only the rest of the library. Then, a flicker caught his eye. Outside the big, ornate window, there was a flash of darkness. On the night's velvet sky, sun still down, was a black mass. It resembled a man. A man who appeared to be floating in mid-air.

No, not floating. Flying!

Giant wings flapped behind the body, and Nicholas knew it could be only one thing. He stood, putting distance between him and the window. There was a click as Dusk checked the bullets in his revolver, each one holding a slug of pure silver prepared to hinder the creature as much as possible.

The creature in the sky shifted side to side and then dove straight toward the window. Nicholas took another step back, followed by another. Dusk and he were now shoulder to shoulder.

"Ah, I don't think it's gonna stop."

"Such a shame. I just replaced that window," Dusk said, spinning the chamber and flicking the gun closed.

The thing became more distinguishable from the night. Its muscular body was stark white. Its wings beating the air so hard, Nicholas could hear it through the window. As its wings beat outside, Nicholas's heart beat inside.

It was now so close to the window that the light from inside the library fell upon the thing, and somehow it looked even more terrifying in the light than it did in the dark. There was a moment right before it hit when Nicholas thought maybe the window would stop it. It would hit the glass like a sparrow running into a sliding glass door and bounce off, skull crushed or at least sporting a broken wing.

The window shattered in a shower of tinkling glass. The thing came through the explosion knocking into the desk, the weight of the desk keeping it upright but the force sliding it across the wood floor. It landed on top of the desk. Its wings bent down, almost enveloping it.

Cold, night air buffeted Nicholas and Dusk as the bouncing glass settled around the room. The beast stood and expanded its wings. Once it reached its full height atop the desk, it roared at them like a lion above a fresh kill.

Dusk raised his gun and pulled back the hammer.

"You know, you could have just knocked," he said as he fired.

Chapter 24

The bullet zipped through the air and hit the monster right where Dusk intended. A dark hole popped on the inner end of the monster's left eyebrow. Its head flew back as its legs gave out from under it, and the thing's body crumpled to the floor.

Dusk nodded and dropped his gun back to the holster on his hip. He was proud of himself. He almost brought his hands up and wiped them as if they were dirty to solidify a job well done, but he decided it was a step too far. He turned to the kid and gave him a half smirk instead.

A growl rolled across the room's floor. There was a crackling noise, like that of sizzling bacon. The thing that had been turned into a bundle on the floor shot to a kneeling position. It was looking away from Dusk and Nicholas. The wings that sat large and demonic on its back crinkled and popped as they folded back in on themselves, almost disappearing into the thing's back.

The thing was snarling and snapping as it seemed to tear at its own face. Dark, black blood sprinkled onto the wood floor. It shook its head back and forth, sending the droplets raining around itself. The sizzling sounds intensified, and Dusk caught a rancid, sulfuric smell polluting the winter night air. With a final grasp, the thing tore the bullet it had been digging for from its face. Dusk saw a glint of light as the beast tossed it to the side of the room.

With the popping sound falling silent and the air going back to its fresh snow mixed with pine scent, the creature regained its feet, turning back to the two of them. Dark gore ran down its face as it snarled and spat the stuff free of its mouth. The bleak hole shrank due to the crawling skin around its edges. The flesh moved with spider-like legs as it stitched itself whole.

"Well, there goes that idea," Dusk said.

The kid looked up at him, "That was your whole plan?"

"Well, to be fair, if it had worked, then I wouldn't have needed another."

"It didn't work last time! What made you think this time…"

The thing roared. Dusk reached down and had his revolver in hand again before the wail ended. He aimed and fired. The bullet missed as the thing ducked and ran forward. As it advanced, Dusk fired again. This one hit the monster, but it was a grazing shot. Undead flesh was flung skyward from the thing's shoulder, which threw it off stride for a moment, but it regained its footing in stride. It swung a claw at Dusk, throwing its full momentum behind it. Sliding to the left, Dusk dodged the blow and fired into the thing's side from point-blank range.

The bullet ripped through the thing like an explosion. A segment the size of a softball detached itself from the thing's side and disassembled into oblivion. Like shrapnel from a grenade, the bits soared around the room, painting the floor and books on the near shelf in dark maroon.

A scream of pain and anger emanated from the thing. It tried to turn and attack, but it slipped on its own blood. It was Dusk's turn to try to attack, but he, too, was foiled by the blood, slipping but still standing.

Taking a moment, Dusk looked for the kid. When the beast attacked, the kid had jumped to the opposite side of the room. He was grabbing his knife from his belt and getting to his feet as the beast came to the forefront of Dusk's attention.

Its side was starting to mend, so Dusk took aim again. As he raised his arm, however, the thing's arm also raised. It grabbed the revolver and twisted. Pain wrenched up Dusk's arm while he tried to hold on. His hand clenched, and his finger pulled the trigger. The hammer clicked back to fire, but the thing was holding the chambers, so the gun was unable to roll to a live round. A human would find this nearly impossible as Dusk was tugging on it; unfortunately, this didn't seem to apply to vampires.

After a moment of a standstill, the beast gave some slack and then tugged hard. Dusk felt the gun slip. He tried to regain his grip, but just as he did, that's when he lost it. The gun was ripped away so fast, it was almost as if it wanted to be away from Dusk.

The beast and Dusk separated. For a moment, Dusk thought the thing would shoot him, but if he had a moment to think about it, it was obvious the thing had no need for the weapon. It sniffed the barrel. The smell offended the creature, so he tossed the gun aside. After tumbling end-over-end, the gun came to a skidding stop by the library door, which hung ajar. Argyle had left it propped open when he left. Freedom, just a room away, felt so far out of reach.

Weaponless, Dusk tried to rearm himself. The creature was too close, however, for Dusk to grab the tomahawk out of his jacket, so he backed up as the thing swung on the left and then followed with a right-side swing. Sliding and ducking from side to side, Dusk made it to a bookcase. Still sidestepping, Dusk spun and grabbed two novels from the ancient shelves. They were heavier volumes but still flew just as well. They hit the monster and slowed it down but did little else.

The short advantage was all Dusk needed. He retrieved the tomahawk from his coat. Instead of holding it in the usual fashion with the blade up, he flipped the orientation. The bottom end of the tomahawk was sharpened to a point as the exact thing they needed. A stake.

The beast saw the weapon and, for the first time, showed he understood more than he had shown before. It looked at the point of the wood with wariness. It knew it was its undoing. Snarling, it took a step back. Dusk smirked, feeling the tides of the fight changing. The thing took another step back and ran into an armchair. Growling, it grabbed the chair. Picking it up like it weighed nothing, it tossed the furniture at Dusk. The chair flipped through the air, making Dusk duck to dodge the flying mass.

After watching the thing crash behind him, Dusk turned just in time to see the second chair flying at him. The weight of the chair hit him, and this time he was sent end-over-end.

Hitting the wall, Dusk coughed to catch his breath. Cold air ran over him as he now sat next to the broken window. Small fragments of glass had caught him during his tumble. The small cuts stung, but the pain in his chest was worse. As he tried to catch his breath, Dusk looked up, hoping the beast wasn't after him.

It was approaching, savoring its victory, but Dusk saw the kid make his move to enter the fight. The kid, brandishing his knife, raced toward the vampire, unafraid. There was a fire in the kid's eye. All the recent activity had built up, and now it looked like the kid was ready to let some of it out.

Pitch

The cool steel sliced through the air as Nicholas slashed with the knife. It caught the beast, biting into its ivory skin and causing a crevasse to split across the whole of the thing's back. Contrasting the thing's flesh, ebony gore spilled from the wound, splashing across Nicholas's arm as he struck.

The thing howled in raw pain. It stumbled forward, one arm reaching back as if it could stop the pain by grabbing the gash. More blood spilled onto the floor, and the thing left black sliding footprints as it stumbled.

Nicholas hunkered down, getting ready for the retaliation. The beast spun around, arm swinging. The blow connected with the right side of Nicholas's head, and he felt his feet leave the ground. There was a flash of black. For a moment, Nicholas was in a world all his own. There was darkness, and he didn't feel the pain of the hit. Suddenly, he was brought back to the real world with a crack as he hit the bookshelf.

Nicholas grumbled under his breath as he hit the floor. A few books tumbled with him and hit him as he lay on the ground. Shaking his head, he got to his hands and knees. Pressure racked his chest as the creature kicked him up into the air. His arms flailed back, which sent the knife twirling from his grasp. It skittered across the floor, leaving Nicholas behind, clueless to its resting place.

Nicholas himself skidded to a stop on the ground. This time, he landed on his back, and his whole body was tight as his muscles contracted. He wanted to move, but his body needed a minute to respond. A minute was too long, however.

A hand pressed on Nicholas's chest. The pressure squeezed the wind from his lungs. Coughing, trying to catch his breath as it ran away, Nicholas looked through tear-filled eyes up into the creature's face. Its mouth hung agape, as strands of saliva dangled between teeth. The strands of spit shivered in the warm breath of the monster. It smelt like dirt, sulfur, and blood.

The hand pinning Nicholas to the ground began to rise, readying itself to strike the final blow. Eyes still plagued by tears, Nicholas could only make out the shape. He blinked rapidly as if seeing everything more clearly would help him get out of the situation. As his vision normalized, Nicholas saw not only the creature but Dusk. He stood behind the thing, rushing downward with the tomahawk.

The thing may have noticed because Nicholas noticed, or maybe he sensed it on his own, but just as Dusk's attack was going to connect, the creature shifted. The point of the handle still caught flesh, but instead of striking center mass, piercing vital internals and killing the beast, it struck straight through the thing's hand. It hissed and closed its fist, gaining an odd but effective grip on the weapon.

Dusk, not missing a beat, pulled back on the thing, so the creature's top half had to spin due to the limitations of its arm. This lifted it off Nicholas just enough for him to buck and roll his hips into a full tumble. The whole scene was awkward, giving no one an upper hand. It did result in Nicholas rolling to freedom and Dusk in a vicious tug-of-war match with the devil, fighting over the weapon lodged in its hand.

Coming to a stop, Nicholas made his way back to his feet. His whole body hurt, and his breath was still working on returning. Heaving gasps were trying to get everything back under control. He turned back to Dusk and the monster.

Their battle had taken them across the library. Dusk was holding onto the weapon with two hands now, one above and the other below the vampire's hand. The one below was grabbing wood drenched in the thing's blood. As they fought, some of that mess would begin burning away, causing Dusk's hand to sting.

Pitch

The wooden tomahawk handle hurt the monster worse than anything else. Much like the branch had affected Michelle, this creature was burning away from the stab. The difference being that Michelle's wound had killed her, where this creature found its wound only a mere annoyance. The blood from the wound would flow out, burn, and then flake away.

The thing was infuriated. It tugged, whipped, pushed, and flailed. The idea of kids fighting over a treasured toy came to mind. Dusk being the child trying to take the toy, as the monster was the child beginning to pitch a fit. The effort became so great that Dusk's feet would leave the ground at the start of each thrust.

Dusk began to lose ground. The thing's attempts compounded on each other leaving Dusk very little time and chance to regain the footing he had lost. Finally, two quick jerks back-to-back snapped Dusk's grip apart. As if the children who had been fighting over the toy had decided to play crack the whip, it resulted in Dusk losing hold and tumbling across the room.

With a menacing howl of triumph, the thing celebrated its victory. It turned its attention to the menace still protruding from its hand. With the free hand, it grabbed the tomahawk, and with a wrenching groan and squelching noise, the handle came free. Without waiting for the guck to burn and flutter away, it tossed the tomahawk to the ground.

Nicholas suddenly feared the thing would come for him now. He stood there with nothing left to defend himself, still trying to catch his breath. His fears were unfounded, because the thing had eyes only for Dusk.

They stood about fifteen paces apart. The two stared at each other. Just then, Nicholas realized Dusk, too, was defenseless, weaponless. He didn't know what Dusk was going to do, what he could do.

Both hands came up in balled fists; then, they opened and waved the beast forward. If it had been anyone else, Nicholas would have been dumbfounded. Anyone else would have backed up or run or maybe even cowered and begged for mercy. Dusk wasn't just anyone, though, and so there he stood, ready to go toe-to-toe with a full-fledged monster.

The monster was ready, too. It sprang forward. The weight of the situation seemed to be felt by all three of them in the room. Battles had been fought and won on both sides. But this wasn't just another battle. This was the one that would determine who won the war. For better or for worse, this was where it all ended.

Taking a step back, Dusk dodged the beast's first blow. To Nicholas's astonishment, Dusk punched out with his fist. The jab hit the monster in the ribs. It recoiled and then swung for itself. Dusk was able to dodge, somehow avoiding the lightning-quick attacks of the vampire. Firing two shots this time, Dusk connected with a left, followed by a right. The beast took the hits, not unaffected but still holding strong.

It made another swipe of its arm. Dusk wasn't fast enough, but he did throw up his arm to deflect the attack. Unlike fighting another human, the vampire hit like a concrete block. The arm up saved Dusk, but it still knocked him back a few steps. Shaking his head to clear the blows, Dusk moved to hit again.

Across the room, Nicholas watched as the two connected in the battle. It was like something from legend. The mighty hero taking on the embodiment of evil. A thing of lore and fantasy playing out in front of Nicholas, and it froze him to the spot.

Crouching down, the creature tried to hide from Dusk's blows. Dusk didn't let up. He swung down without hesitation. Unfortunately, the thing's distress was nothing but a farce. It brought its arm up from its bent position, and it caught Dusk under the chin. Dusk was sent flying through the air as if he weighed nothing more than a paper doll. The next second, he was a ton of bricks as he fell back down to earth, crushing a chair on his way down.

The chair was made of simple wood. It was a skeleton in comparison to the ornate chairs the thing had tossed around earlier. That skeleton was brittle, and it snapped like straw, exploding underneath Dusk.

Nicholas saw Dusk lay in the mess of wood. His head rolled side to side as he tried to stay conscious. The thing walked forward, looking down upon the spoils of the war he was ending. One arm reached down grabbing Dusk by the neck as it crouched on one knee above him. The squeezing that followed shocked Dusk to full awareness. Grabbing at the thing's arm, and kicking, he fought to keep the fight going.

It was no use.

Raising its free arm, just as it had on Nicholas, the monster moved to end it. Nicholas realized the only way he had gotten out of the same situation was that Dusk had saved him. Now, it was Nicholas's turn. He had to save Dusk.

But I'm too far away. I waited too long.

He was right. They were all the way across the library. The thing would have Dusk dead and buried three times over by the time Nicholas reached them.

Throw something.

But there was nothing to throw. He looked around him. There were no chairs, no fragments of spent wood. There weren't even any discarded books within reach. He had nothing, so he could do nothing. Because he could do nothing, he couldn't save Dusk.

Oh God, Nicholas thought.

He looked on as the thing raised its hand all the way up. Dusk's retaliation was growing weak. Everyone had made their moves and played all their cards, and the creature had come out on top.

The monster's arm raked downward. Nicholas's mouth opened to scream, but nothing came out.

BANG!

Bits of skin and rivulets of blood rained outward. An eruption of gore blasted away, covering the monster and Dusk. There was a screech of pain.

Everything happened so fast and all at once, Nicholas needed a moment to process.

The thing's hand, the exact hand that was set to extinguish Dusk's life, had exploded. Popping like a water balloon, the hand had been stopped. It seemed that a miracle had come down from the heavens and saved Dusk.

That fact became very fitting when Nicholas turned around to see Father Adrian standing in the library doorway, Dusk's revolver in hand and smoke swimming from the hot barrel.

The thing roared again, and Nicholas turned to see it thrash in pain, a pain so intense, it loosened its grip on Dusk, who seemed to be strong again. His hand released the arm of the creature and grabbed something from beside him. A shattered piece of the old chair came up with his arm. The splintered chair piece stabbed upward guided by one of Dusk's hands as the other hand pushed on the end.

It struck the vampire in the chest, separating the thing's ribs and digging itself deep into the cavity. The screech it had made before was nothing compared to the sound that emanated from it now. It was a prehistoric roar of pain and defeat.

As if in slow motion, the ivory skin of the monster darkened. Its white features greyed and then burned to complete blackness. A moment of stillness halted the room. Then, the thing fell apart. Dust that used to be a ferocious beast of the damned began falling off in chunks. Varied sized flakes floated skyward from the small patches around Dusk.

The fight was over, and Dusk had won.

Pitch

Nicholas fell to his knees. Breath was hard to find again. In the final moments, when he thought Dusk was going to die, he hadn't been able to breathe. Now, he decided it was time to start back up again.

A hand fell on his shoulder, and Nicholas jumped. When he looked up, it could be only one person.

"You okay?" Father Adrian said, concern creasing his face.

Nodding, Nicholas said, "Yeah, I'm okay. Thought it was all over there for a second. Then, you showed up."

"Looks like it's a good thing I did."

You can say that again, Nicholas thought, but he was still too stunned to say it out loud.

"Look, Nicholas," Father Adrian said, growing serious. "I'd like to tell you we were done for the night, but sadly that's just not true."

Nicholas wanted to ask what he was talking about. In fact, he had a lot of questions for Father Adrian. So many, he couldn't decide how to start. Father Adrian didn't need any prompting.

"Yes, I know what's going on here. I know what that thing was, and I know you are at the center of all of it."

So, it was true. Father Adrian was like Father Christopher. Nicholas couldn't be sure the father shared the other's special sight, but it was obvious that Father Adrian knew more than most of the people did in The Hollow.

"And I know something else," Father Adrian said, lowering his head, so he looked at Nicholas over the top of his dark-framed glasses.

"What?" Nicholas asked, still trying to catch up.

"I know who the man in shadows is."

A shock like that in this situation should have sent Nicholas reeling. It was curve ball after curve ball, and every one was a strike right over home plate. Somehow, Nicholas kept his wits about him and stayed calm. Well, relatively calm.

"You do?" he asked. He needed to be sure he had heard him right.

"Yes," Father Adrian said, keeping his words slow, so Nicholas understood. "That's why I'm here. It's time, Nicholas. But we have to do it right now."

Nicholas just knelt there and blinked for a moment. Was he ready to face the man in shadows? He and Dusk had just barely survived this ordeal. How could they possibly be expected to face that right now?

Because we have to. Because no one else can.

Nicholas nodded, "Okay, let's go."

Father Adrian smiled, "Good. Glad to hear it. I'm going to go check on Dusk over there. Take a minute and get yourself together, then we'll worry about what comes next."

With two pats on his shoulder, Father Adrian left his side to see to Dusk. Nicholas took a deep breath in. Finally, everything they had worked so hard to figure out was going to be revealed. The mystery, the questions, the fear: it would all be gone. Nicholas felt like a weight was being lifted off his shoulders. For awhile now, Nicholas had been carrying around this feeling of uselessness, a sense he should be able to do more in all of this. Now, everything he had worked toward was here, ready and waiting for him.

He stood up and turned around to look out the door of the library. Once he walked out that door, he would be on his way to put an end to all of this. It was a great feeling, and now that the weight was gone, he felt his pulse rise in excitement.

THIS Ends TONIGHT

Maybe he was right.

A figment of a thought tickled at the back of Nicholas's mind. A fleeting suspicion of something he could not quite pin down. Something didn't fit. Something just felt wrong. Nicholas wouldn't have been able to explain it if he had been asked to. The best thing he could manage was the word disturbance. There was a disturbance. In the room, with the whole situation. Something bad was going to happen, and Nicholas had to…

BANG!

The world slowed as Nicholas spun back around. He saw but didn't comprehend. Dusk was falling forward. It looked like he had been on his knees, but now he was falling forward. Blood was still misting in front of him as a maroon stain was growing on his shirt. As he fell, his mouth coughed, sending small strings of pink spittle free from his lips. A cascade of gore spattered the hardwood floor of the library. Dusk fell face first into that mess. His arms made no move to catch his fall, leaving his face to bounce off the floor, splashing in blood.

Above Dusk smoke wafted around the barrel of his revolver, its last slug's heat still singeing his insides. Holding the revolver now, standing above a dying Dusk was their assumed savior, Father Adrian.

"Oh, by the way," Father Adrian said, a grin cracking his holy face, "it's me."

Chapter 25

The cold air came in through the broken window, sprinkled with fluffy snowflakes that touched the wood floor of the library and began to melt in small puddles. Papers that had been tossed about in the fight fluttered in the breeze. One was light enough to double over on itself, rolling through the air until coming to a stop a few feet away. All the while, Dusk, the monster hunter, lay in a growing pool of his blood.

"A violent thing, isn't it?" the man who was known as Father Adrian said, looking at the gun in his hand. He tossed it aside and wiped his hand on his pants as if the pistol was the vile thing in the room and not him.

His knees began to feel weak as Nicholas stood open mouthed, shocked at the scene in front of him. The man who had faced countless monsters and personal demons somehow laid dying in the room. A man he had thought was an ally had shot him with his own gun in front of Nicholas. He stood there unable to move or talk or even blink.

How did we get here?

"Aw, come now, Nicholas. Don't look so ghastly."

Nicholas's eyes shifted from Dusk on the floor to the man standing above him. That's what he was, a man, but in this room, he stood as terrifying as any monster Nicholas had ever seen in fiction or reality.

"Go ahead then," the man said, gesturing to Dusk as he stepped away. "He's still alive, you know. Best you get to him soon; who knows how long he has."

Nicholas looked to Dusk. His hero seemed dead already, but then there was a shift. Dusk's body lifted and fell as he took in breath. The sight of him breathing brought blood back to Nicholas's legs, and he moved to Dusk's side.

There was no dodging the blood, but Nicholas didn't even try. The dark red soaked into his jeans as he knelt by Dusk. When they had first met, Dusk had been barely larger than a skeleton. In recent months, he had put on some weight, reaching the size of a slim man, but even that didn't account for the weight Nicholas had to lift and roll as he hefted Dusk out of the blood on the floor.

Grunts and moans came from Dusk as Nicholas raised him up to lay on his legs. When Nicholas finally got him on his back, he was so relieved to see Dusk's eyes open. They were darting around, glassy and distant, but they were open; he was alive.

"Kid, I need you to stop the bleeding," Dusk said. He was talking to Nicholas, but he had yet to settle his eyes on him.

Nicholas nodded, "Yeah, yeah."

Thinking faster than he thought possible, Nicholas ripped the lower two inches of his shirt into two strips. Balling up the cloth, he reached into Dusk's coat and pressed the wads on both the entrance and exit wounds. Nicholas pressed down on the exit wound in Dusk's chest, but for the wound on his back, Nicholas resorted to pinning the cloth between Dusk's body and his thigh as he knelt behind him. The pressure shocked Dusk out of his stupor. His mouth opened in a silent yell and then closed into gritted teeth. A hand shot up, grabbing Nicholas's shoulder. After a moment, Dusk's grasp loosened, and his eyes became sharp. He looked at Nicholas and then to the man who had shot him. His teeth gritted once again, not in pain this time, but in anger.

Father Adrian wasn't even paying attention to the two of them. He was walking around the library inspecting the books on the shelves. It was as if shooting Dusk was nothing more than a regular introduction.

"Who are you?" Dusk spat out.

He leaned up, trying to be more formidable. The effort was in vain, however, when another wave of agony rocked his shoulder, and he slid back down. Nicholas checked and readjusted the bandages, being sure to limit the bleeding.

The man stopped, took a volume from the shelf, and thumbed through it. "Me? I am who you both have been looking for." He closed the book and placed it back on the shelf.

"The man in shadows," Nicholas whispered to himself.

"In the flesh," the man in shadows said, turning to face the two of them. "Well, at least that's what you called me. If I had to be honest, can't say I am a fan of it myself."

"If that's true," Dusk said through gritted teeth, "then why save me?"

"Ah, I believe I shot you, Dusk."

"I meant before. With that thing," Dusk nodded his head to the side, but pain racked him, and he had to give a harsh hiss of pain.

The nod worked well enough, however, as Nicholas and Father Adrian turned to look at the dark ash stain on the floor. Most had been covered by Dusk's blood, but it could still be seen.

"Oh, I see. Yes, that was unfortunate. Simply, he had served his purpose. Less simply, he wanted to kill you, and I wouldn't allow it. Apparently, you two really got under his skin in the woods. He wouldn't listen to any sense. He just kept vowing to rip you limb from limb, and I couldn't have that."

"Why not?" Dusk said.

"Because if he had killed you," the man in shadows said, "then I wouldn't get to." He smiled. For a moment, Nicholas thought he saw razor teeth fill the space between his lips, but they were gone, if they had ever been there to begin with.

"And you're the man behind all this," Dusk said and then spit to the side. Nicholas caught a glimpse of the glob on the floor and could make out specks of red in its murky coloring.

"In a way, yes. But in others, no. It's all very complicated, but for now, and for what comes next, we'll go with yes. I am behind everything that has happened in this sad excuse for a settlement and to you two. More than you even know." He sucked in a harsh breath. "I am the man in shadows, the nightmare of nightmares, the antithesis of everything you've been worried about and preparing for."

He paused, stood up straight, and cleared his throat in a flourish. "My name is Adrian Pitch. You two will call me Pitch."

The floor shifted under Nicholas. Pieces to a puzzle that sat unfinished for too long somehow started falling into place. Things began to take form in his head, but somehow they still made little to no sense. He had been right all along. The man from the book and the man in shadows were one in the same.

"Nicholas, it is exactly what you think," Pitch said, putting his hands behind his back.

That's impossible, Nicholas thought.

"No, it's not," Pitch said, shocking Nicholas even further. Then, he laughed, a true and honest laugh. "I'm sorry, it's just you should have seen your face. No, I can't read your mind, Nicholas. I have just been thinking about this meeting a long time and have a pretty good idea how this is going to go. Actually, exactly how it's going to go." Pitch smiled as if he was in on a joke just between the two of them.

"How can that be?" Dusk said.

"That will be explained in time. You will think a lot of this is impossible, but I promise it is very possible and very real."

Nicholas looked up at Pitch, still not wanting to believe everything he was hearing. Not wanting to believe everything he was thinking. Yet, somehow it was all undeniable.

"But you can't be," Nicholas said, not much louder than his previous whisper.

"And yet, I am."

Dusk shifted again. He was getting impatient listening to this nonsense, but he could do nothing but listen.

"How?" Nicholas asked.

Pitch smiled, "That is a question I believe no one really has the answer to, but I am all the same." Pitch tilted his head toward Dusk. "He seems lost, and I don't think it's due to the blood loss, although I'm sure that has a hand in his pale complexion. How about we clue him in. What do you say, Nicholas?"

Still fighting internally about whether this was all true, he told Dusk what this seemed to be. "Pitch was the man in the book, remember? The witch trials one."

Dusk took a moment but only a moment. "And you're claiming to be that Pitch?"

"Yes, I am."

"So, you wrote it, I assume," Dusk began to sit up, strength seeming to come back. When he took a sitting position, the bundle of Nicholas's shirt came loose, and a large gob of blood fell free until Nicholas pressed the bandage again. Dusk's hand took Nicholas's spot, having a better idea of where to apply pressure to his wound. Nicholas backed away slightly to give him space but stayed close enough to help if Dusk needed it.

"Actually, no. I didn't write it. Couldn't write it, in fact. It was what created me you could say. Of course, I've had a hand in making the man you see today, but that book is what started it all."

Created him? Nicholas felt lost again.

"What do you mean?"

Pitch looked at Nicholas with a pitying glance. "Nicholas, I'm disappointed that you haven't figured it out yet. Of course, I'm not surprised." He smiled then, a wicked smile that said very clearly, he had a secret. "The world I am from, The Other, I believe you call it. I tell you, you people love your strange little nicknames," he chuckled as he brought his hand around and began waving it as he spoke. "That world is made of awful things. The worst things people could imagine. Exactly the worst things people can imagine, in fact."

Nicholas all of the sudden felt like he knew exactly what Pitch would say. He knew the three would be right here having this conversation without a doubt in his mind. Knew it so clearly, it was as if he had already been here. He just didn't know how he knew.

"Monsters, ghouls, ghosts, murders, and all the things you thought were under your bed or in your closet when you were young are there. Because this world created them. My world, your Other, is where everything ends up. So, you see," Pitch laced his fingers in front of him and his face cracked in a violent grin. "We are literally the very nightmares of this world."

Nicholas swallowed hard, feeling his face trying to go as white as the snow that still fell in through the broken window.

This is madness. This is crazy, Nicholas thought. He also knew it was true.

"And you're saying this book," Dusk said, panting at the effort of just sitting up. "Is what created you in The Other."

"That is correct," Pitch said, nodding.

"But how could you still be alive?" Nicholas said, putting aside the absurdity of what Pitch was saying and going at a different problem altogether. "The book took place over a hundred years ago. Even if what you say is true, Pitch, that Pitch would be dead."

Again, Pitch smiled. "Clever boy," he said. "You see, that story is what created me, but when I gave it to you, I couldn't spill all the beans, now could I? So, I made slight edits to the story."

It was him, Nicholas thought. *Not only did he kill all those women, but it was him all along.*

"The witchcraft whispered about in the town, this town, in fact - you did have that bit right after all, Nicholas - was never caused by any of those women. Nor any of the men in the town in fact, but one." He paused, savoring the intrigue, but Nicholas and even Dusk at this point knew what he was going to say next. "Me. You ask why I am still alive, Nicholas, when other men would be dead? It's because I am not just a man. No man could do what I have done. No, no man indeed. I am so much more than a man. I am a warlock."

As he said the word, dark tendrils of grey smoke rolled over his fingers as the skin underneath turned black as night, black as pitch.

"Not that impressive I grant you, but you'll just have to take my word for the fact that," he began walking along the wall of books again, "this is but a small example of my full power." He raised his right hand and began running his fingers along the spines. Every book he touched grew sick with rot and fell as a putrid mess in the matter of a moment.

The sight was haunting, but the notion that somehow Nicholas knew all of this already made his blood run cold. He'd had this feeling before. With clues in their past investigations, he had had notions of where to look and seemed to be in the right place at the right time for answers. This was on a different level, though. It was as if he was living a rerun of a TV show he could only half remember watching.

"So, you're a fake magician, very good for you," Dusk said, venom tipping his words.

"Oh, no Dusk. I assure you I am very real. As real as you, in fact."

The words held no sting but hit the two heroes' breath hard with the weight of implication. Nicholas looked at Dusk, but Dusk wouldn't meet his eyes. He wasn't looking at Pitch, either. His eyes were distant, not foggy, but thoughtful.

"No," Nicholas said, knowing he had nothing to argue with.

"Yes," Pitch said, smiling, his finger back to the pale peach color of skin. They didn't hold the usual red tones most hands held but a green undertone instead. It reminded Nicholas of undead things, but he was much more and much worse. The worst of all the monsters they had faced.

"Dusk, tell me, before you became the proud, quiet monster hunter you are today, what did you do. What was your job?"

The vile voice speaking his name brought Dusk back to the room and away from his thoughts. He said nothing, however; he just looked at Pitch, hatred in his eyes.

He was a businessman, Nicholas thought. *A successful one. He managed to buy this place and take care of Angela.*

"I was a successful businessman," Dusk said, remembering his past life. A life he had shared with Angela. "But that was a long time ago."

"Yes, yes, of course it was. But I assume you still remember what type of business you did right?"

"Yeah, it was…," Dusk's words cut short, however. His brow furrowed as if his entire train of thought had become derailed and crashed into wreckage. Nicholas looked down at him, shocked. He had never seen Dusk look so lost.

"That's what I thought," Pitch said, dropping his shoulders in mock sympathy. "It is to be expected," he looked to Nicholas. "What is a sixteen-year-old from a piss ant town such as this one supposed to know about big city business anyway?"

Most would think after everything that had shocked Nicholas tonight, he would have become numb to the sensation. Most would also be wrong. He had yet to have confirmation of his fears, but he already knew what Pitch meant.

"What the hell are you talking about? Stop talking in riddles," Dusk said and then coughed. Nicholas could hear what he hoped was phlegm and not blood weighing down each explosion. "Make sense, damn you!"

"Take it easy, Dusk. This stress isn't good for your health." Pitch smiled the same wicked smile that was becoming a nefarious signature. "Now, this may be tough to hear Dusk, but you, too, are from another world."

Dusk laughed. It was a series of harsh barking with no joy. "You're insane."

"I told you it'd be hard, Dusk," Pitch said, speaking to him as if he was a child who was just told Santa Claus isn't real.

"You're wrong," Dusk said. His laughing had died in the flames of anger.

Pitch smiled, "No, I'm not. And he knows it." Pitch shifted his eyes to Nicholas.

Nicholas had gone away from the conversation, the room, and The Hollow. He was in his own head. Mere hours ago, Nicholas had held his entire world in a glass ball, as if everything he knew to be true was enclosed inside a snow globe. Even the existence of monsters had only shaken the fake, white flakes of snow in the globe, creating a maddening flurry. However, after time, they settled, and once again Nicholas had become accustomed to the world he knew now, only different, the small structures in the glass covered up or just obscured by the flakes.

This was not just a shake of the globe. This time, the globe slipped from his grasp. The smooth surface struck the ground. With a shuttering crack, the globe had exploded, spilling everything onto the floor. Nicholas was now looking at everything he had known in a new perspective. Without the protective glass between him and the small internals, Nicholas couldn't ignore the obvious any longer.

"I did it," he said, not aware he was going to say it out loud until he heard his own voice. He had somehow made all this happen, not Pitch. Nicholas had been the one who had done all of this.

Does that make me... the monster?

"Yes," Pitch said, and it took Nicholas a moment to realize he wasn't answering his thought but commenting on his words. "Go on," he cooed, with the hint of madness Nicholas knew the man for but had yet to see in full force. "Go on, my boy."

Nicholas swallowed, and it hurt worse than it should have. His throat was dry, leaving his tongue like sandpaper. "It was me," he said again, a little louder now. "I did all of this."

Nicholas felt himself begin to speak, not sure how to say what he now knew to be true. "I somehow...," Nicholas paused thinking of the right word, "created all of this."

Nicholas looked at Dusk. Dusk's eyes were there to meet him. For a moment, it was just the two of them in the room. Pitch was forgotten; The Hollow was forgotten; the world was forgotten.

"I created you."

Dusk just kept looking at Nicholas. His face didn't change in the slightest, leaving Nicholas not knowing what to say next.

The laughter saved him, but he didn't feel any relief in its rotten mirth. Pitch was laughing in response to their terror. It was something Nicholas had seen countless times in his films, but not until he was in the room with it did he feel the intensity of the laughter of the insane.

"Isn't it wonderful?" Pitch said, in the middle of his laughter.

The two on the ground looked away from each other to stare at the laughing madman. Dusk's eyes flared with daggers, and Nicholas looked on, angry but knowing.

"Oh, come now," Pitch said, calming down. "You have to see the poetic comedy in all of this. You both have been trying to figure this out for months. Trying to figure out who's behind it all, and it was Nicholas all along." This time he laughed so hard that his eyes closed as he dropped his head back, cackling at the ceiling. "It's really quite obvious if you think about it. A monster-hunting, rich man living in an extravagant house in the middle of nowhere with a butler. Seems to jump right out of a comic book or, in this case, right out of the mind of an adolescent boy who liked to make up stuff just a little too much."

"How can this be?" Nicholas said. He knew how it had happened, didn't he? Then, why was he asking?

Because I need him to say it. I don't know why, but I need him to say it to make it real.

Pitch's laughter subsided, and then he said, "It is not uncommon for children to create imaginary friends when they experience a loss. In this case, imaginary is just a matter of perspective."

"Loss? What loss?" Nicholas felt the answer behind a door in his mind. It was a door he said he wouldn't open. So, there it remained, closed to the world.

"Well, the loss of your parents, of course," Pitch said as if it was obvious.

Nicholas supposed it was.

"My parents," Nicholas said. Flashes of memory stung the space behind his eyes. First, his mother's face, soft, beautiful, laughing; then, his father's, strong, thoughtful, and sincere. Then, he was back in the room staring at Pitch.

"Yes, your parents. After their deaths, you created Dusk. A fearless monster hunter designed to perfectly combat anything that could make you suffer loss again. Of course, no one is perfect, and that same pain of loss was embedded into your fantasy, causing Dusk to have a past of the same loss you felt. Heartbreaking really."

Nicholas stood up and moved toward Pitch with clenched fists, but then he stopped dead. He wanted to argue. He wouldn't be to blame, not for this, not for Angela, not for anything. But he couldn't, because he was just that. He was to blame for everything.

"It's not all your fault, however," Pitch began, and for the first time that night, he took a step toward Nicholas. "You see, this is partially my fault, but I swear it was completely unintentional. It worked out for me in the end, but believe me I didn't think it was going to for the longest time."

He took another step toward Nicholas. Somehow, the room seemed to be shrinking as he advanced, making him feel even closer than he looked.

"Kid," Dusk said, caution infecting his voice.

Nicholas didn't move, however, nor did he shrink away. He stood there, and said, "What are you saying?'

"You see, I'm the one who gave you reason to create Dusk in the first place."

The words hung there for a moment, and then he finished.

"Because I'm the one who killed your parents."

Nicholas felt his knees give out on him. He had not seen this coming. Somehow, the place he had been pulling answers from all night had run out, and now here he was, hurt more than he had thought possible.

"No," Nicholas fought. "No, they died in… they died in a… in a car…," but the words just wouldn't come.

"What? In a car crash? I suppose that's true, but it was no accident."

He took another step forward, and now they were less than a foot away from each other. Nicholas could smell Pitch. His stench was a mixture of old wood and dirt, like a tomb.

"I pushed their car off the road with no more effort than it took me to shoot your hero over there." The smile was worse up close. Whatever feeling he had in his legs before now slipped away. Nicholas didn't know what was holding him up, but he prayed it would stay.

"Why?" Dusk's voice cut through the room.

Pitch turned to him and a moment later, so did Nicholas. Although broken, Dusk was holding on better than most. He was sitting up the best he could, trying to hold on to any form of control he could.

"What?" Pitch said, his voice falling from his cordial tone into a ferocity that was buried beneath.

"Why are you telling us all this? Why don't you kill us and be done with it?"

Pitch straightened up. At some point, he had leaned into Nicholas without Nicholas even realizing. Dusk's question didn't seem so crazy now. Pitch had them in the palm of his hand, and he could close it, squeezing the life out of them with his very fingers at any time.

"Because it's what I'm supposed to do."

Dusk scoffed, "Says who?"

Pitch smiled with faux warmth, "Says Nicholas."

Nicholas looked at the two of them. Again, he was lost. It appeared Pitch still hadn't shared his entire hand.

"Believe me, if I had it my way, I wouldn't have told you a thing, but all in all this has been a lot of fun."

Pitch looked at Nicholas for a moment and then sighed. He seemed disappointed but not surprised. He turned and walked away from Dusk and Nicholas. As he walked, he reached into his coat and pulled something from the inside pocket.

Nicholas tensed for a moment, not knowing what he had to fear but fearing all the same.

When Pitch turned around to face them again, he held not a gun, not a knife, but paper. About thirty sheets of off-white, crinkled pages were rolled into a tight roll, held in form with a single rubber band. Pitch slipped the rubber band off, letting it fall to the ground. He then unrolled the sheets and cleared his throat.

"The gun was deafening in the room. Even with the shattered window, the blast reverberated amongst the walls, causing a cacophony of noise. The bullet ripped through Dusk's chest with satisfying ease. Dirty gore burst forth, covering the library's floor, stunning the boy into shocked silence. Dusk fell to the same floor, still alive but defeated."

Pitch looked up from the page and smiled.

"No... no...," Nicholas said, not wanting to believe that he had written that. "I didn't... I couldn't write that."

"You're right," Pitch said, smug and in control. "Not without a little help at least, which reminds me."

Nicholas didn't feel anything at first, but then there was cold. It started with the tips of his fingers and toes and then moved through his legs and arms. It felt like someone was peeling a cold layer of skin from his body straight through his back. He backed up to the desk. Once it hit his torso, the cold was so harsh it burned. Nicholas gritted his teeth, hands gripping the edge of the desk. The two, cold edges met in the center of his gut with a pop that he felt in every bone, and then the cold was gone.

As Nicholas caught his breath, he saw something he had seen only one time before. His shadow began moving on its own. It rippled and warped like pavement on a hot summer day and then solidified. Once solid, as solid as a shadow could be, the figure appeared to take a deep breath in and then let it out. It looked one way and then the other, and seeing Pitch, it slithered across all the surfaces between Nicholas and him, contouring to the world around it. When it reached Pitch, it paused for a moment and then popped into its position behind him.

Pitch took a big breath of his own, and then said, "Ah, that's better."

Flashes of a dark room lit by a single desk lamp flowed in front of Nicholas's eyes. He was there. He could see himself sitting at his desk, but he couldn't remember this happening. As if he was watching a movie of his own life, the vision spun around to reveal his face staring with blind eyes. Below the face, hands typed away on a typewriter. Thin lines of darkness connected his arms to a pair of shadow arms that floated above. These arms had their own hands, which mimicked the act of typing on open air. Whatever they typed ended up on the page below, however, because Nicholas's fingers followed in tandem with every keystroke.

Nicholas suddenly felt all the anger and hostility he had been dealing with for the past few weeks disappear. Regret and sorrow fell upon him like a wave. How had he treated everyone so poorly? Aunt Sherri? Dusk? Emily? If he ever made it out of here, which it seemed like he wouldn't, would he have anyone to go home to?

My God, what have I done?

"Now, where was I?" Pitch looked back at the pages in front of him. "Oh, yes." He began reading and walking around the room.

"Dusk lay on the floor, bleeding and dying. The boy could only look on and do nothing, blah, blah, blah." Pitch skimmed the rest of the page and then tossed it aside. It fluttered down to the ground. As soon as it touched the wood of the library floor, the paper burst into flames, curling around the edges as it darkened to a diseased black.

"The boy listened to Pitch with eager ears. He wanted the answers to the situation he had found himself in but was afraid what they would mean, blah, blah, blah." Another page was cast aside, and it followed the same steps as the first.

Flutter, touch, burn.

"Knowing it was true but not wanting to believe, the boy stood there, reeling from the fact that he was the cause of everything. All the horror, all the monsters, and all the death. Blah, blah, blah."

The page took its trip.

Cast, flutter, touch, burn.

No reading this time, and another page falls.

Cast, flutter, touch, burn.

And another.

Cast, flutter, touch, burn.

"As the final resistance gave way, it all fell... oh, wait. Actually, I'm going to keep that to myself. Don't want to spoil the fun."

In his reading, Pitch had made it to the door of the library. He stood there, holding the pages in his hand.

"I guess you'll just have to wait and see," Pitch said as the pages burst into flames in his hand. He tossed the papers, and instead of falling to the ground like burning paper would, they flew across the room, piercing the bookshelves on both walls. As they struck, the old volumes caught fire with little resistance. The room began to crackle with the life of flames as it devoured the world of kindling it found itself in.

Dusk pushed off the ground. He went sprawling across the library, arms outstretched. Falling with an ungraceful plop, he landed next to his revolver. With the speed of lightning, he rolled, aimed, and fired at Pitch.

Click.

Silence.

Click. Click.

Dusk looked at the gun in his hands, betrayed and heartbroken.

"Looks like you're out of ammo," Pitch said.

Dusk scowled like an animal and reached for the extra rounds in his coat. Pitch, however, thought otherwise. His hands rotated, which sent a book flying from a shelf across the room. It flew from its spot and toward the open hand. As it flew, Pitch shifted his hand across his torso, and the movement caused the book to curve on its trajectory. It struck Dusk's hand holding the gun with a decisive thud. Nicholas also thought he might have heard a series of snaps as bones broke. Teeth ground together, stifling the shout that begged to escape. The gun and the book flew past him, sliding across the ground into the far corner.

Pitch had chosen a book that wasn't engulfed in flames, so Dusk didn't have to fight the sizzle of burning skin along with broken bones, but even then, Nicholas didn't know how much more he could take.

"Dusk, I expected nothing less from you. However, you should have known it was worthless. I told you, I know exactly how this is going to go."

Nicholas looked from Dusk, even more broken than he had been, to Pitch. It was crazy, all of it.

How did we get here? How is it all my fault?

"Well, unfortunately, our time is up. I must be going."

Pitch reached in front of himself and buttoned his overcoat in preparation for the world outside. The notion of a world outside this room made Nicholas dizzy. Would he ever see that world again? The smell of thick smoke clogged his nostrils, making him think the chances were not good.

Pitch turned to leave, but Dusk spoke up before he could leave the door.

Pitch

"Pitch!" the shout was hoarse but strong.

Adrian Pitch, the man in shadows, turned back to the dying monster hunter with an eyebrow raised.

"I am going to kill you," Dusk said, voice still rough but sure. "I promise you. I am going to kill you."

Pitch smiled. Without turning all the way around, he said, "I remember you promising to save a loved one years ago."

The room went quiet. Even the fire seemed to fall silent in the room.

Pitch walked out the door, waving and without looking back, and said, "Maybe you shouldn't make promises you can't keep."

Then, he was gone.

Chapter 26

The room roared with life but stunk of death. Flames were climbing over the walls, crawling across the floor, and Nicholas just stood there in the middle of all of it.

How had this… .

"Kid!"

Dusk's yell made Nicholas jump. He turned to the broken man on the floor and realized it wasn't the first time Dusk had called for him. Another quick moment for him to remember where he was and what was going on, and then he was off across the room.

He knelt down next to Dusk, throwing the hunter's good arm around his shoulder and lifting the man off the ground. The arm held the hand that the book had struck, and Nicholas noted that it already looked swollen and showed no signs of stopping.

"Dusk, I'm sorry… I… I…," Nicholas said, still trying to get a hold on the situation.

"No time. Move!"

The two shambled toward the door. As they started, Nicholas dropped down and picked up Dusk's revolver from the floor where he had dropped it. The movement left Dusk groaning and uneasy on his feet, but Nicholas was back up, and they were moving again.

The library behind them began to turn into a furnace. Walls became blackened husks of their former selves, and books rolled in on themselves degrading away as if time had sped up for them. Hungry flames licked up the furniture legs, which supported the tables that held their books for research. As the two strode passed, Nicholas saw all the books and the answers they may hold catch, and he was forced to leave them to burn.

They made it to the open door, hoping to find refuge from the smoke that started caking their lungs. Their reprieve, however, was not in the hall. A thin, orange line of heat was drawn across the wall. Nicholas imagined Pitch running his finger along it as he walked past, maybe even whistling a jolly tune.

Small flames had already begun to spring to life along the length of the line. Further down a portrait was raging with fire, its old canvas catching with ease. Above that picture, Nicholas noticed the ceiling had even begun to catch. This was no average fire. It ate with a ravenous hunger that would not relent until the entire place was devoured.

A flash of a safety video he had watched in the first grade, or maybe it had even been kindergarten, came to him. He assumed it was something every kid watched in some form or another and one they all thought they'd never have to use.

"Take off your coat!" Nicholas shouted at Dusk.

To Dusk's credit, he didn't argue even when the jacket had to be yanked from his bullet-ridden shoulder. He yelled out in pain, but by this point, he deserved a good scream. Nicholas took the coat and, in one toss, covered them both with the thick garment. In the video, the family had each taken a blanket to cover them from falling debris. In the current circumstance, Nicholas was working with what he had.

"We have to move!" Dusk shouted.

Nicholas didn't need to look to know the flames from the library were right behind them. He felt the heat licking his back even through the coat. Tucking the revolver in the large pocket of the coat, they pushed on, fighting the heat, the pain, and the end they both felt coming.

They reached the top of the stairs, and Nicholas could see clearer air down below. From where they were now, the world was covered in a layer of thick smoke that made their eyes burn and lungs scream. The stairs, however, led to lower ground, which would lead to cleaner air. If Dusk had been able, they would have been crawling on the floor to stay within the fresh air in the upper hall. It was another tidbit Nicholas had learned from his safety video. But as things were, he just set his eyes on moving to the lower stairs.

Was that six, eight, maybe ten steps away?

They could make it. Then, it was just a straight shot out the door. Again, the flames were on their back, however.

No, definitely not normal fire, he thought, not believing any fire could move so quickly without the help of magic. In his mind's eye, he pictured a demon made of red fire chasing after them. Large, clawed hands plunged deep into the walls of the hall, and it was pulling itself forward. Horns whipped with wicked embers, and a tongue licked the air, tasting its meal of flesh.

Nicholas pushed to begin the descent down the stairs. Dusk reached out with his injured hand to grab the railing to help, but Nicholas pulled him away.

"No! Look!" The words sent him into a fit of coughing.

The railing had another thin line traced down it. A continuation of the one that had ripped the wall, the line sat glowing, ready for them to grab the rail.

Dusk nodded, and they took it step by step, swaying side to side. At first, Nicholas thought he had imagined the clean air on the stairs. Every step seemed to grow warmer, not cooler. Around the seventh step down, Nicholas found it easier to breathe. He knew Dusk was struggling, but he tried to push him even faster. He would not let them die in this house. That wasn't going to be his fault, too.

Without realizing it, they reached the bottom. The ground floor felt more solid underfoot than the upper hallway and staircase. The air was much easier to breathe down here as well. Now, all they had to do was make it across the foyer.

Twenty steps? Maybe only fifteen.

They could do it. They would do it. They were going to make it out. That's when the world above them broke apart, and everything came crashing down.

It was as if he was outside the lighthouse again. Instead of cold from the rain, he was hot from the fire, but the noise and the feeling were the same. With an enormous crack, the monster had broken through the brick tower, which had turned out to be its own demise. This time, the fire broke through the ceiling of the first floor spilling the second floor down upon them. It rained, and Nicholas could only close his eyes and hope.

There was a push on his lower back, and he was flung forward. Nicholas lost hold of Dusk, but the coat was tucked around his head, and it came with him. A few stuttering steps were followed by a flailing fall, and then Nicholas was on the ground. A moment after he hit, the house hit behind him. The world rumbled as if the earth itself had decided to open up and eat them, the house, and every single spark of fire.

Once the world settled, Nicholas jumped to his feet. His vision swam, and for a moment he thought he'd fall back down. Then, things began to clear. He turned to help Dusk up, but Dusk was no longer beside him. His head whipped back, hopeful.

The floor above them had collapsed. Large, wood beams lay crisscrossed on top of the splintered floor and a mess of other things the fire had made unrecognizable. The worst part was that Nicholas saw no signs of Dusk.

"Dusk!" Nicholas shouted.

No answer.

"DUSK!"

A small bit of the debris shifted. Nicholas hoped beyond hope it was more than wood giving way. Suddenly, a spot to the left from the original movement opened up as Dusk pushed a part of the floor off of him.

Thank God, Nicholas thought and ran toward him.

If Dusk had looked bad before, he was horrible now. A gash had sliced his right eyebrow and the bridge of his nose. The fiendish wound ended at a point below his left eye. Blood cascaded down in torrents over his cheek and into his mouth. He spat at the liquid, sending small dots flying through the air. Without the thick coat to protect his clothes, small fires were catching all over his torso, eating away his shirt. Nicholas patted them out as softly as he could, but the hits still made Dusk groan.

"How many lives you got?" Nicholas said.

Dusk spat more blood, "I'm pretty sure I'm all out."

The remaining wood above them cried out in protest at the strain, and Nicholas decided there was no time for small talk. He offered Dusk a hand, but when Dusk moved to take it, he froze in anguish.

"My leg. It's caught."

Nicholas looked over Dusk. It wasn't just one leg; it was both of them and one hip. Half of him lay under the rubble of the ceiling. Nicholas gritted his teeth but didn't give up.

"Give me your hands," he said, standing up.

Dusk reached up with one good hand and one the size of a grapefruit. Giving up on being tender now, Nicholas gripped both wrists and pulled. Dusk slid forward a fraction of an inch and screamed louder than Nicholas had ever heard anyone scream. Clara had screamed higher when the sun landed on her skin, but Dusk was louder.

Nicholas stopped pulling. Before he could formulate the next plan, a hand fell upon his shoulder.

It's him, Nicholas thought with sudden surety. *It's him. He's come back to watch us die. He will pick me up and toss me into the fire without a second thought.*

When Nicholas turned, he actually saw Pitch standing there in the foyer. His hair shining in the flame light as his eyes burned with fire all their own. But the moment passed, and Nicholas saw the man for who he really was.

"Argyle!"

The elderly butler stood with his head down using his coat as a cover just like Dusk and Nicholas had done. Nicholas felt such a relief at the sight of him that it was as if the fire stopped burning. Then, the ceiling gave another moan, a short pop, and then settled.

"Argyle, Dusk is stuck. Grab his hands. I'm gonna lift the beam."

Nicholas didn't wait to see him confirm the order. He knew he would. Nicholas stepped over Dusk, lowered himself, and assessed the beam. It was larger than he had expected, still solid, but the outer layer sizzled with heat and embers. Without thinking too long, Nicholas plunged his hands under the beam. The heat was like nothing he had ever felt. Every small hair on each finger curled back and burnt away to nothing, leaving Nicholas with only skin to fight the unrelenting hunger of flames.

"Now!" Nicholas shouted, unable to give Argyle a three count.

They both gave it all they had. Nicholas lifting, Argyle pulling, and Dusk screaming.

After a moment, Nicholas's body gave up, and he had to let go. His hands came away from the beam black, and he wouldn't be sure for hours how badly he had burned them. By then, though, he didn't care.

"Argyle! Get Nicholas out of here!"

Dusk's shout was like the cracks of gunfire in the madness of the flames. They cut through with ease, and Argyle looked at him.

Nicholas looked at him, too. *He can't be serious.*

"NOW!" Dusk shouted again, and that came across as cannon fire.

Argyle gave one curt nod and grabbed Nicholas. Still dumbfounded, unbelieving Dusk would say such a thing, Nicholas allowed himself to be grabbed and pulled away from him.

"NOOOOO!" he heard himself scream. "NO! You can't! We have to save him! Let me go!"

He began kicking and elbowing at the old butler. Somehow, the old man was stronger than Nicholas realized. Whether it was adrenaline or something Nicholas had just overlooked, he didn't know, but he cursed the strength anyway.

"I said, let me go!"

As they moved toward the door, Nicholas reached for purchase on anything to help him get back to Dusk. There was nothing for the first few swipes; then, he felt something. It was soft and warm, and Nicholas imagined it was a curtain from one of the front windows. He grabbed the material and pulled at it to bring him back in. It came with him without protest. He looked down and saw that it wasn't a curtain; it was Dusk's coat. He had grabbed it from the floor where he had dropped it.

He looked from the coat in his hands back to Dusk, still trapped. Dusk was staring at him, too, eyes shining with tears amongst the flames. Nicholas's eyes had been burning from heat, but now it worsened with the pain of loss.

"NO! I have to save you! I have to save you!"

Pitch

He passed through the front door, cold air kissing his face.

"I HAVE TO SAVE YOU!"

Everything hurt. Dusk spit blood for what felt like the hundredth time. His head pounded, and his shoulder burned worse than all the places he had been touched by fire. The lump he used to call a hand beat in time with his heart.

Thump, thump.

"NO! I have to save you! I have to save you!"

The kid was screaming, giving Argyle one hell of a fight. A fight he would lose, however. Dusk knew Argyle was a good butler, a good man. He wouldn't let the kid come back to Dusk.

Dusk would have to wait alone for death to come. Lying there, he waited for him to come in whatever form he came. When he did finally come, Dusk knew him and called him by name as he was taken from this world forever.

"I HAVE TO SAVE YOU!"

Dusk felt the tears fall down the left side of his face. He relished the soft sting the salt in them sent through the gash they found there.

"You already have," he said.

Nicholas and Argyle fell in the snow with a soft plop. The cold was a violent shock to Nicholas who had been so warm for so long. It was so cold, it burned him. He had a moment to think, *burned by fire, burned by ice, damned if you do, damned if you don't.* Then, he was up, running back toward Winter's Hall.

"Nicholas!" Argyle yelled, but Nicholas ignored him. He had taken him away. He had left Dusk in there. He didn't deserve to be listened to.

Nicholas took three steps when the rest of the second floor collapsed onto the first. When the mass hit, warm air flashed outward and caught him mid-step. The blast pushed him off balance, and he fell in the snow again. He rolled and jumped back up to see the house.

There was no way in, and that meant there was no way out.

The entire house had caught now, and it burned so high up in the air, Nicholas assumed it could be seen from distant worlds. Cold wind from the lake made the flames dance in the night sky.

Nicholas couldn't look away from the house. His eyes went back to the front door. It once had led to the entryway he had been through so many times, but now it led nowhere. Beams and flooring blocked the frame, creating a burning wall that no one but the devil himself could get through.

All at once, Nicholas felt his legs give out underneath him as his whole body became too tired to hold him. The snow cushioned his fall, and, in his sorrow, he didn't notice the cold.

He's dead. Dusk is dead. And it's all my fault.

That's when the tears came. He didn't stop them, couldn't even if he wanted to. They flowed down his dirty cheeks causing clean streaks to scar the layer of soot painting his face.

The night hung heavy with the weight of death as Nicholas knelt in the snow, crying alone.

Alone and hollow.

Chapter 27

Black coats and scarves whipped in the wind like gothic pennants the day they buried Richard Dusk. Due to the condition of the remains it was a closed casket ceremony. The magic fire had destroyed everything. Even the body of a great monster hunter was turned to nothing but black ash in its devastating wake. For a man few truly knew, he had many mourners. Almost all the people of the small town came out to see him off into the next life. If you had asked them why they had come or if they had known the deceased well, most wouldn't be able to give a clear answer. They came all the same.

Aunt Sherri stood next to Nicholas, touching his back off and on, making sure he knew she was still there. Argyle had come sporting a somber, all black suit. It was different from his usual butler attire but just as regal. Will had come with his grandparents, Betty and Howard, and they whispered soft words of comfort in Nicholas's ears when they had first seen each other and embraced as you do when loss is what brought you together. Emily had come too, her red hair blowing in the wind and looking beautiful yet melancholy against her black dress. She had hugged Nicholas, but he could still feel the distance between them. It hurt at a moment he didn't think he could hurt any worse. Behind her, Sheriff Gordon stood tall and hard as a statue. He was dressed in a black suit that was a touch too small around the neck and had been altered to accommodate the thick cast encasing his leg.

Nicholas stood next to the dark, wood coffin in an almost catatonic state as it was lowered into the ground. His outer wounds were healing, the worst of which were his burned hands, which hung wrapped at either side of him. Internally, however, his wounds festered and threatened never to heal.

After he had come home from the hospital on the night of the fire, he cried in his Aunt Sherri's arms all night until he fell asleep. The next morning, she tried to talk to him, to find out what had happened, but Nicholas wouldn't talk. Not about that night or about anything. Aunt Sherri went about making arrangements for the funeral with Argyle. She knew everyone in town, and it made it easier on Argyle to get the affairs in order. It also made it easier for her to have something to distract her.

The day after the funeral, Will came over to check on Nicholas. They talked, Will more than Nicholas, but it was better than Nicholas sitting alone staring at things only he could see. After an hour or so, they seemed to be getting into a normal rhythm. It was somber and slow, but it was heading in the right direction. Then, Will ruined it.

"So, I've been doing some research, and I think I'm making real progress. Some of the books I took out of the library at Winter's Hall have turned out to be really great. I have this one book that has got some interesting things about urban legends that I think will lead to some good stuff."

Nicholas looked at him, confused. "Progress on what?"

Now, Will was the one confused. "On finding," he looked around to make sure Aunt Sherri wasn't within earshot. Then, he finished, voice lowering just to be safe, "The Other."

Nicholas's face went slack. Any happiness that had been there washed away to nothing with a single swell.

"We're done with that," he said.

"What?"

"We're done. I'm done."

Will's eyes widened, shocked. He scooted on the couch and turned toward Nicholas. "What do you mean you're done? I know you're hurting right now, man. But we have to get that bastard."

A dagger stab of pain rocked Nicholas as he thought of Pitch. His wicked smile, his fiendish eyes.

"We have to get him for what he did, for Dusk. We…"

"IT'S OVER!" Nicholas shouted, making Will jump. "Dusk is dead!" From the kitchen came the clatter of dishes as Aunt Sherri dropped a dish because of the sudden commotion.

Nicholas stared at Will with the fury of a wild animal. "It's over. He won. We lost. End of story."

Will's mouth hung agape as he stared back at his friend. Then, he started shaking his head, and he shut his mouth in a tight line. "No. No, you can't mean that."

Nicholas took a deep breath in. "I can, and I do."

Will shook his head harder, looking deep into Nicholas's eyes, looking for any weakness in his resolve. After a moment, he realized Nicholas wasn't going to budge on this, and Will grew angry.

"Fine. You can be out if you want, but I'm not done. It's not over, and I'll prove it." He jumped up and went to the door, grabbing his coat on the way. Turning back for one final look, Will said, "He wouldn't want this."

This time the pain felt like an explosion going off inside Nicholas; a burning so primal flared up in him that it took all he had not to cry. Without a response, Will left, the heavy front door slamming shut behind him.

Nicholas stared after him. He wasn't mad at Will. Will was reacting to the information he had, but he didn't have all of it. He didn't know everything. He didn't know this was Nicholas's fault. He didn't know what Pitch had said and what Nicholas knew in his heart. Nicholas himself had been the one who had killed Dusk. With just words, he had shot, broke, burned, and finally killed him.

That night Nicholas lay in his bed staring up at the ceiling. He felt tired but didn't want to sleep. Every time he slept, he dreamt of fire. He was tired of the burning, so he laid there awake, staring at nothing.

Not knowing why, Nicholas turned his head and looked at the typewriter that still sat on his desk. The very tool of destruction that had killed his best friend. Thinking of it in that light gave Nicholas an idea.

Moving across the small room, he sat in front of the typewriter. Cold air came in through the open window at the other end of the room. It chilled his skin, sending gooseflesh rippling over his arms. He picked up a piece of paper and rolled it into the typewriter. Without thinking about it too much, because it wouldn't work if he thought about it too much, he typed:

`Richard Dusk thought that he was going to die, but at the last moment, he was able to break free and escape the fire. He crawled to freedom and took a deep breath of cold winter air.`

Nicholas stopped and looked around. Nothing different. He didn't know exactly how this all worked, but he was pretty sure he would feel it when it did. Right now, he felt nothing besides the cool wind from the window.

He tried again, typing:

`Dusk survived.`

Again, he paused and waited. Nothing.

He stretched his fingers, gritted his teeth, and pressed every key down firmly.

`Dusk lived.`

Nothing.

`Dusk is alive. Dusk is alive. Dusk is alive. Dusk is alive. DUSK IS ALIVE!`

There was nothing. No matter what he tried, nothing felt different.

Anger raged through him like a swarm of angry hornets. He gripped the sides of the typewriter and lifted it off the desk. He strode over to the open window, the mass of the typewriter making the walk more effort than it should be. With a violent toss and ferocious scream, he sent the typewriter flying through the air. It tumbled straight down because of its weight and crunched hard against the pavement of the driveway below. Little pieces broke apart and scattered across the surface while heavy parts scraped and bent.

Nicholas looked down upon the typewriter, broken and rendered useless on the driveway and thought, *I know how it feels.*

Will sat in the old, wood chairs of the library surrounded by books. He had been through almost all of the books in front of him at least once. In the past six months, he had been reading and searching for answers alone. The school year had ended and had started back up again in that time, and he still found nothing.

If there had been other people searching with him, he would have found the positivity. He would have pulled out an old favorite of his grandfather and quoted Thomas Edison.

"I have not failed. I've just found ten thousand ways that won't work."

But he had no one. He was the only person still fighting for answers, and he couldn't lie to himself as well as he could to others. Hope was all but lost.

He tossed aside the book he was rereading and exhaled. The piles around him were examples of his failure. He had separated the books into two, large piles at first. Books from the Pointe's Hollow Library and then books from Winter's Hall.

The only things remaining from that house, Will thought.

It was a silly thing to do considering they all belonged to the public library now. But he had to stay organized, so that's how they sat. Inside those two, large piles, they were sorted into subject matter and then from largest to smallest, so the piles didn't tumble.

Even with all this prep work, his effort had been for not. He had not found anything that had pointed to The Other or this Adrian Pitch. Both seemed to exist only in all their minds, not on paper.

Besides this book, Will thought, picking up *The Hollow Trials*.

Pitch

Will had read this book twice since the fire and wasn't able to draw anything from it that Nicholas hadn't already pulled out. It felt like it should hold more answers, but so far it was reluctant to share any of them.

He placed the book aside and looked through the volumes in front of him. On the pile of books from Winter's Hall sat a smaller volume on urban legends of the Great Lakes. Will remembered the book, because it had been the one he had told Nicholas about the last time they had talked six months ago.

Time flies when you're having fun.

He picked it up, not sure why but feeling like he should. If he was being honest, he couldn't remember what it was about. He had read it that night after talking with Nicholas, and all he could see was red. He had been so angry at his friend he barely took in any of the information he tried to read. So concerned with proving Nicholas wrong, he flipped through the pages with little attention to the small details, looking only for the big thing he needed.

He flipped through the book until a page made him stop. Catching the page, he opened the book wide, so he could read what was written there. Once finishing the page, he blinked and reread the entire page, this time with greater concentration.

Oh, my God, he thought.

A moment later, he was out of the chair and running out of the library. He ran, book in hand, toward someone who didn't want to see him.

Nicholas laid in bed staring at the ceiling. He found himself doing this a lot over the past few months. He'd go downstairs and spend time with Aunt Sherri watching TV or eating dinner, even sticking around afterward to help her with the dishes. She didn't think he was involved in the process enough to do the cleaning, but she let him dry and put away, which was fine with him.

Any time he spent alone, he could be found up in his room. Sometimes he'd be sitting at his desk doing homework, sporadically looking up at the blank wall in front of him, remembering the pictures that had been there half a year ago. They sat in a shoe box in the bottom drawer of his desk, out of place, out of mind. If he wasn't at his desk, he was in bed staring at the ceiling, just like he was now.

For months, he laid there content with letting the days roll by. Pages were torn off calendars, and seasons changed from winter to spring to summer, and now they were approaching fall. He was fine with all of that for six months, but today something was different. He just wasn't sure what it was.

Nicholas shifted on his bed, and the TV popped to life. It startled Nicholas until his hand found that he had rolled over onto the remote. The old tube warmed up until the picture came through along with the crackling audio that was so familiar that the hair on the back of Nicholas's neck stood on end.

"Hello, boys and ghouls, boos and gals. It's me, Graveyard Jerry. The undertaker with the movies that'll make yer scream!" Jerry howled with laughter. He had forced the words 'make yer' out in a poor attempt to make them rhyme with 'undertaker'.

This wasn't right. Nicholas hadn't watched *Darkness Falls* or anything on this channel for a long time. If the television ever did get clicked on, it was a sitcom or a sporting event. Something to put noise in the room but easily ignored.

Nicholas moved to switch the channel but then paused as Graveyard Jerry started up again.

"Now, I know you all are dying to see what happens next." He laughed again at the lame pun. "What will happen? Oh, my!" Jerry waved his fingers around mystically. "I know, but I'm not telling you. You all will just have to watch and find out if you dare." Another laugh.

Nicholas was ready to see the soft transition of the camera as the next movie would start up, but Graveyard Jerry wasn't finished quite yet.

"But I will tell you this," he held up one finger, and the camera began to push in to get a closer look at Jerry's teeth, which were as crooked as the gravestones in the set behind him. "This is a story that won't end with a fizzle. These two titans of terror are gonna go out with a bang!" He motioned the cloud of an explosion with his hands as he made the sound effects through his make-up covered lips. "You're not gonna wanna miss this, I assure you."

Nicholas turned off the television then. He was going to go back to staring at the ceiling until he heard something faint coming from outside. At first, he thought it was some kids outside enjoying the warm days before they began to fall cold again. Then, he heard his name.

"Nicholas!"

Wanting with every bone in his body to ignore the call, Nicholas sat still on the bed. Then, the notion that something was different today came back over him, stronger than it was before. He felt pulled to the window. Before he realized it, he was up and moving across the room.

The window looked out over the houses in the small subdivision whose streets were all named for trees. Nicholas could see the coast from his small room, but nothing out there held his interest today. What had pulled him to the window was jumping up and down on his front lawn.

It was Will, and he seemed to be holding a book in one hand and pointing at it with the other.

"Nicholas! Open up! I found it! I found it!"

For a moment, Nicholas considered falling back into his bed. He wasn't being pulled as he had been to the window, but something was trying to coax him back there. A darkness he had found solitude in over the past six months. A darkness he thought had won. Then, he was moving downstairs, away from that darkness.

Will almost burst into the house when Nicholas reached the living room and opened the door. He was out of breath, and sweat caked his forehead.

"Nicholas!" Will shouted between huffs. Clouds of air shot out of his mouth like the exhaust out of an old car. "I found it! I found how to get there! We're gonna make that bastard pay, man. Oh, yeah, he'll pay alright, 'cause I found it!"

Nicholas heard everything, but it all was happening too fast. He had been out of this for too long, and he couldn't understand what Will was saying. Suddenly, for the first time since the fire, Nicholas didn't feel alone. He was here, with Will, who was trying to do something real. It felt good.

"What? What do you mean you found it? Gonna make who pay? What are you talking about?"

"The Other!" Will said, shoving a book in Nicholas's face. "I found how we're going to get into the Other, and then, we're gonna kill the man in shadows."

End of Book Two

Find out how it all ends in...

The Hollow Trilogy: Book Three

Wake

Kickstarter Supporters

Spike
Dakota Hoch
Tyler Bradshaw
Benjamin J Crockett
Nana & Papa Kruscke
Alex, Stephanie, Grant and Zander
Jack & Evon Lintern
Bill Herman
Jeff and Molly Wurzler
Betsy Romankewiz
Devin O'Rourke
Edward Dean II
Josiah Wood
John and Sherri Kruscke (Mom & Dad)
Alec and Stormyi Kruscke
Michael Porter
Dan Chisholm
Josh, Caila, and Elaina Jacobs
Linda & Mike Kruscke
Rowen Skyi Kruscke
Andrew G
Stephanie Galbraith and Carolynn Rozelle and Lily🐈
Empress of Tarot
Lynn DeGrande

Jonnie McVaugh
Anonymous
Alichia Crandall
Telvia Laurel
Todd "Lord Skyrim" Grunow
Dalton Butts
Kiki Diehl
Stephanie Eisenhauer
Paula Mulnix
John Wurzler
Emily Voelzke
Bonnie Jacobs

About the Author

Brent Kruscke is a homegrown cinephile from Leslie, Michigan. He graduated from Lansing Community College with a degree in Digital Media and Film and has had a passion for the mysterious his entire life. He currently resides in Mason, Michigan with his cat Ashley and lifelong turtle friend, Franklin. *Pitch* is his second novel.